The Urbana Free Library

To renew materials call
217-367-4057

DISCARDED BY THE
URBANA FREE LIBRARY

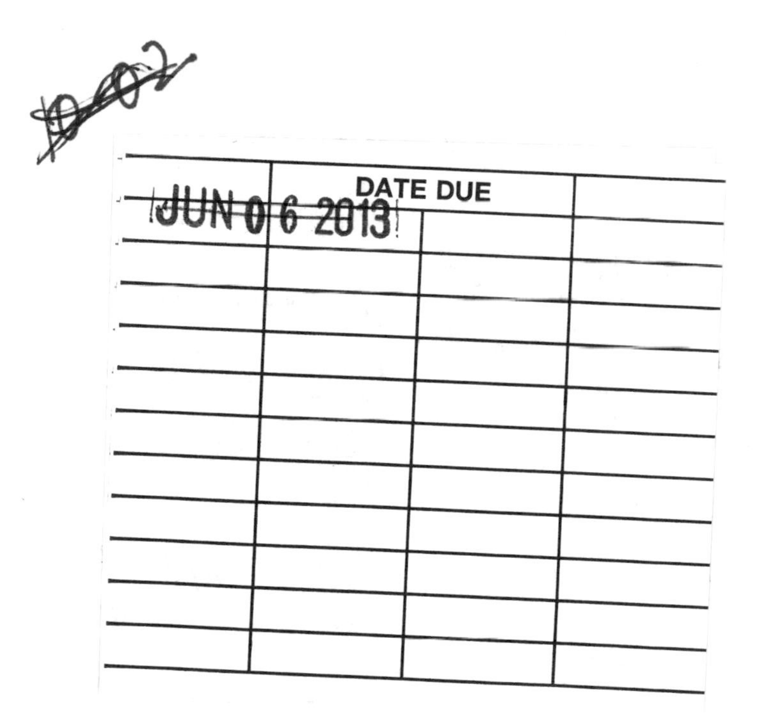

Generations of the Heart

Books by Viqui Litman

THE LADIES FARM

GENERATIONS OF THE HEART

Published by Kensington Publishing Corporation

Generations of the Heart

Viqui Litman

URBANA FREE LIBRARY

KENSINGTON BOOKS
http://www.kensingtonbooks.com

KENSINGTON BOOKS are published by

Kensington Publishing Corp.
850 Third Avenue
New York, NY 10022

Copyright © 2002 by Viqui Litman

All rights reserved. No part of this book may be reproduced in any form or by any means without the prior written consent of the Publisher, excepting brief quotes used in reviews.

All Kensington titles, imprints and distributed lines are available at special quantity discounts for bulk purchases for sales promotion, premiums, fund-raising, education or institutional use.

Special book excerpts or customized printings can also be created to fit specific needs. For details, write or phone the office of the Kensington Special Sales Manager: Kensington Publishing Corp., 850 Third Avenue, New York, NY 10022, Attn: Special Sales Department. Phone: 1-800-221-2647.

Kensington and the K logo Reg. U.S. Pat. & TM Off.

Library of Congress Card Catalogue Number: 2001095358
ISBN 0-7582-0157-5

First Printing: June 2002
10 9 8 7 6 5 4 3 2 1

Printed in the United States of America

Chapter One

When Ryan Plummer asked Darlene Kindalia to have his baby, Darlene didn't remind him that they already had done the horizontal hokie-pokie and that procreation had never been the object of their endeavors. She settled for a tart, "In your dreams!" accompanied by a withering glance.

Ryan was, after all, her client, and the one who had plucked her from the hospital transcription pool and set her up as a freelancer. He was also the one she had straddled in the very same high-backed, reclining, leather office chair from which he tendered his present offer, and Darlene figured that gave her some privilege in speaking her mind.

She had stuck her head in the door only to say *hi* before she dropped the transcripts off, and her right hand still grasped the envelope with the sheaf of printed pages and the cassette tape. She hadn't meant to crush him, yet now he looked so despondent that Darlene regretted even her mild retort. "Don't you think you have enough kids?" she asked as she stepped into his office.

"Jill doesn't," he replied glumly. He motioned her toward one of the upholstered chairs that faced his desk, but Darlene chose to stand.

"You and Jill ought to work that one out yourselves," said Darlene, though she sympathized with Jill. Jill's little boy was probably overwhelmed by the three kids from Ryan's first marriage. Even so, Jill had married him with that baggage. And Darlene knew Ryan: with four kids to put through college, his yearning for more children was only to prevent Jill from leaving and taking what little community property had been left by her predecessor.

Ryan raised his eyes and gazed up at her. "We are working on it," he said. Darlene hadn't seen him up close in a while, and it was unsettling to learn that his wide eyes and long lashes still moved her. Not as much, she assured herself. Not so much that she held his gaze too long, or sat down. She wasn't buying into any more of that *my-wife-doesn't-understand-me* crap. Even with Jimmy missing since Sunday with her Camaro, she'd do better cruising for a replacement at the Sydonia Farm Bureau than here in the Fort Worth office of Ryan Plummer, M.D.

"Jill and I just need a little help, that's all," Ryan said with the air of a man coming clean. "We need . . . I wish you'd at least sit down, Darlene. Come on," he coaxed, standing up himself and moving around to the two upholstered chairs that faced his desk. He motioned toward one as he seated himself in the other. "This is hard enough without you glowering down at me."

I have an hour before I head back, Darlene thought as she sat next to him, facing him at an angle. This was how he sat when the mass was malignant or the blockage required surgery. This was the configuration that enabled him to put his warm, nurturing hand atop the one that grasped the arm of the other chair, to personally hand over the card of the oncologist he recommended, to locate the exact location of the problem on the pull-apart models clustered on his desktop.

Darlene awaited his pronouncement much as his patients would and, she supposed, with the same wariness about his accuracy in assessing the situation.

"Jill can't conceive," Ryan told her.

"Who conceived Tyler?"

"Taylor," he corrected. "Jill, of course. I mean, she can't conceive anymore."

"Anymore," Darlene repeated. She blinked and looked at the color rising in his neck. "You mean you . . ." He shook his head. "She? She can't . . . she had her tubes tied?"

Ryan nodded.

Darlene had never met Jill, but she knew whose idea this must have been. "You made her have her tubes tied?" Darlene demanded. "After one child?"

"Hey, that was the deal," Ryan protested. "She knew it when we got married." He took a breath and spoke more slowly. "Taylor's my fourth child, Darlene."

She knew that, of course. Jill's pregnancy and Taylor's infancy had defined the temporal perimeters of her relationship with Ryan. Once Taylor started sleeping through the night, Ryan had been far less insistent on seeing her, and they had fallen into this friendly patronage. It had been a relief, really. Guys her own age didn't have as much money, but they liked going out and having a good time. She didn't think Ryan had ever taken her out to a club, and rarely to lunch or dinner.

"So she agreed and you agreed and now you want another baby?" Darlene wiggled back into the chair to get comfortable. "Has anyone ever explained to you that you can't always get what you want?"

"Don't you think I know that?" He waved a hand at his office in a derisive gesture. "Don't you think I learn that again every day?" He shook his head, obviously struggling to control his emotions. "But I . . . this would be something we could get, Darlene. With your help."

"Oh, I'm all ready to help you and Jill."

He ignored her sarcasm. "Darlene, Jill and I are together on this. We really want this baby. We're hoping you'll care enough to help us."

"Care enough!" Darlene rolled her eyes. "What happened? She catch you with someone else?"

"No. C'mon, Darlene, it's nothing like that!" His eyes had grown even larger and he bit his lip a little before he spoke again. "Darlene, Jill and I want another child. We want it so much."

"I want another child, too," Darlene opined. "A little brother or sister for Tiffany. That doesn't mean I'm getting it."

"But you will!" Ryan offered. "You and Jerry—"

"Jimmy."

"Jimmy. You and Jimmy, you'll figure out a way—"

"Jimmy's been unemployed for most of the time I've known him and now he's disappeared with my Camaro!"

"Oh, Darlene, why didn't you say something? Here I am rattling on about my problems—mine and Jill's—and you're . . . you've been—"

"Screwed. Screwed over by a car thief."

"What are you going to do?"

Even knowing he had an agenda, Darlene drew comfort from his interest in her problems. He's not a total jerk, she thought. She hadn't been totally stupid to score this guy.

Darlene exhaled hard, then shrugged. "I've already moved back in with Rita."

"God, Darlene, I know how much you hate the Ladies Ranch."

"Farm," she corrected automatically. "It's not that so much—though Sydonia's pretty hard to take after Fort Worth—it's having Rita say 'I told you so' every other minute." She thought about her upstairs room at the Ladies Farm and she felt a pang of guilt. Della and Kat, the women who ran the bed and breakfast with her mother, had never hesitated in welcoming her. And they let her drive the Accord as long as she worked it out with Kat, who was some sort of consultant in Fort Worth. "They do look after Tiffany for me, though. And they did take me right in."

He looked ready to say something but he stayed silent, gazing at her sympathetically. It felt good to relate the Jimmy fiasco to someone who didn't remind her how stupid she'd been. "I guess," she said finally, "I should never have let that asshole move in with Tiffany and me. I don't know what we'll do now."

"You've been in tighter spots," Ryan told her. "Your transcription service is coming along, your kid's okay, you're getting child support, aren't you?"

"Only when Jason manages to stay employed for a whole week." Darlene considered her ex-husband and the parade of boyfriends who had preceded Jimmy. "God! I've slept with a bunch of losers!"

"Hey!" Even his laugh sounded good. "I resemble that remark!"

"Oh, not you. You're a shit for cheating on your wife," Darlene explained, "but you were always nice to me." Her eyes burned, but she didn't care.

"Look," Ryan said gently. "There's something you need to know."

She braced herself for the worst: he was HIV positive, he'd helped Jimmy steal her car, he was hiring a full-time transcriptionist and wouldn't need her services anymore.

"Jill and I . . . we really want this baby." He held up his hand to stop her response. "Just listen," he pleaded. "It means so much to us, and you're the perfect candidate. You've had one healthy child, you're young and strong and healthy—"

"I don't want—"

"Just listen, damn it! Jill and I will pay you . . . Darlene, we'll pay you to have this baby for us."

"Pay?" Darlene hated the squeak in her voice. "You want me to—"

"We want you to be a gestational carrier. A surrogate. Have a child from an *in vitro* embryo. You know: bear a child conceived in a laboratory from Jill's egg and my sperm."

"And you'll pay me for that?"

"Yes."

Darlene closed her eyes and breathed deeply. Her curiosity about Jill and Ryan had vanished, but her fears about living the rest of her life in Sydonia stayed perched on her shoulder. She had been the fastest typist in her high school, but it would take thousands of pages to dig her out of her financial mess. She pictured her shoulders rounding as her fingers grew knobby and her butt grew huge while she hunched over the keyboard. When she opened her eyes again, he was still sitting next to her, still watching her. Darlene leaned toward him so that she could hear him clearly. "How much?" she asked. "How much would you pay me?"

Chapter Two

Even though Kat knew the kid couldn't see her through the storefront, she checked her watch as Darlene pulled the Accord up to the Starbucks. Then she draped her trench coat over her arm, shouldered her purse, grasped her briefcase, and pushed the door open with her hip.

As Kat headed for the driver's seat, Darlene popped out of the car. "All yours," she murmured, scurrying around to the passenger side as Kat deposited purse, briefcase, and coat in the backseat and slid behind the wheel.

Darlene was still buckling herself in when Kat put the car into first and headed for Sydonia. "We have to stop at the grocery," she advised Darlene. "And you need to call your mother. Phone's in my purse."

Darlene scowled, then reached into the back and fished out the phone. Kat already knew the news: they'd found Darlene's abandoned Camaro in Louisiana and Rita's husband, Dave, was towing it back to Sydonia.

From Darlene's monosyllabic responses into the phone, Kat gleaned that she was not overjoyed.

The girl sighed. "Well, of course I appreciate Dave!" she said into the cell. "If it wasn't for Dave, we wouldn't have had a pot to piss in, growing up." Kat could hear Darlene warming to the subject. "I'm the one who always appreciated him. I'm not the one who divorced him to marry someone else!"

Angry children always upset Kat, particularly grown ones. She had lost track of the conversations that Darlene had derailed since her arrival at the Ladies Farm. Della, Kat's other partner in the bed and breakfast, shrugged off the venomous exchanges between Darlene and Rita, but Kat felt compelled to insist that Darlene respect her mother, even though the girl's accusations usually jibed with Kat's own assessment of Rita's history. "She's just angry," Della would dismiss the outbursts with a shrug. "She'll outgrow it."

"I don't care," Kat would retort. "Every time Darlene takes one of these tantrums down Memory Lane, Rita can't focus for a week." Rita's salon was a big attraction for guests at the Ladies Farm. Even when she did not personally provide the service, Rita's prescription for a mud pack or full-body massage, aerobics or pedicure, convinced guests to spring for the added services that gave the Ladies Farm a chance at solvency.

Listening to Darlene now, Kat felt a stab of pity. As tough as the multiply pierced, dramatically made-up kid appeared, the defiance never convinced. Kat knew that the poorly concealed vulnerability was yet another defense, one that worked particularly well on male protective impulses. Even so, Kat always wondered what a decent education and a wider horizon might do for Darlene.

Darlene's voice grew calmer. Kat turned into the Albertsons, and fished around behind the driver's seat with her free hand as she pulled into a parking space and yanked the emergency brake. The list was in the side pocket of her briefcase, where she had tucked it after checking in at home. There seemed to be a shortage there of fresh greens, which Kat could remedy with enough spinach for both their dinner tonight and the lasagna for weekend guests.

Darlene shook her head as she ended her phone conversation. Her honey-colored hair was shaved close on one side and angled across her forehead on the other side. With her eyebrows plucked to nothing on her tawny skin, only her aquamarine eyes gave any hint of softness and warmth, and they were not welcoming now. "She's so stupid!" Darlene hissed. "Ever since she married Dave again, it's like they were never divorced, like there never was a Wendell, like we never packed up in the middle of the night, all those times!"

Kat found the list with her fingers, slipped it from the briefcase, and waved it in the air as explanation of her errand. "No matter what she did then," Kat reminded Darlene, "she means well now. Dave's getting the car, isn't he?" Kat pulled open the door and slid out before Darlene could recount more history of Dave and Rita.

Darlene sat holding the phone. Damn it! she fumed. Only Rita could distract her from what she needed to think about. Quickly, she dialed again.

It rang three times before Carla picked up. "Alvarez Cleaners."

"You busy?"

"It's six-thirty, Darlene, what do you think?"

Darlene shook her head. "Sorry," she told her sister. "Call me back tonight?"

"I heard they found the Camaro," Carla said.

"Yeah." Then, struggling to keep her voice even, "I've got a doctor's appointment tomorrow, think you could drive me?"

"You sick?"

"No."

"Oh, Jesus, you're not—"

"No! I just need a ride, Carla." She could hear customers in the background, imagined Carla with the phone wedged between shoulder and ear, counting change and nodding thanks, just like Rita. "Call me tonight, okay?" Darlene requested. "After the kids are down?"

"I don't know, Darlene. I'd have to bring the kids."

"Rita can watch them," Darlene assured her.

"I don't know."

"Just call me tonight, okay?"

Eventually, Kat returned, and Darlene was careful to explain that she had called her sister and to thank Kat for the use of the phone.

"Do me a favor?" Kat said. "Can you put it back in my purse for me? Thanks."

Darlene loved Kat's purses. They were always Etienne Aigner or Gucci or Coach, of rich, thick leather with heavy brass accents. Everything of Kat's smelled like Norrell, her only fragrance, and everything was made of great stuff: leather and silk and linen and wool. Her jewelry was real gold. Even the silvery stuff was actually white gold. Darlene inhaled deeply as she unzipped the bag to catch all the Norrell and leather smells she could before she placed the phone inside and zipped it shut.

They rode without speaking for a while. Kat was one of those people who liked to drive, and Darlene tried not to interrupt when she could tell Kat was thinking. Instead, Darlene looked out the window at the dribs and drabs of the Fort Worth suburbs: little bursts of apartments, clusters of houses and duplexes, a strip mall with a video store, dry cleaner, and gas station, then a family clinic, an insurance agent, and a storage center. Darlene didn't especially care for this edge of the city, but she might be able to afford it if she passed the physical tomorrow and agreed to do what Ryan had asked.

Not just an apartment, Darlene told herself now. Maybe I could get a duplex, at least to rent. Of course, it would take almost a year to do that, and she doubted she could stand the Ladies Farm, or at least living with Rita, till then. But maybe Ryan, if she explained it to him, could figure out something. He had always been generous, Darlene thought, and right now, he needed her.

"How's Ryan?" Kat asked.

Darlene drew a quick breath. Had she said something? "Ryan's great!" she answered, terrified.

"Oh, God!" Kat said. "You're not sleeping with him again!"

"Who said I slept with him ever? Why are you asking about Ryan, anyway?"

Kat chose the first question. "Well, Ryan told me all about it, when it happened and when it was over. You forget who recommended you to him as a transcriptionist. Don't you think we keep in touch?"

"If you keep in touch so much, why don't you just ask him who he's sleeping with?"

"You know," Kat advised, "I was just trying to make a little conversation. We don't have to talk about Ryan." She shook her head a little. "You seemed pretty happy when you picked me up."

Darlene was sorry she had jumped all over Kat, who at least treated her like an adult most of the time. "I was happy," Darlene recalled. "Then I had the privilege of talking to Rita."

"It sounds to me as if your mom—your mom and Dave—are bailing you out. Isn't Dave towing your car back for you?"

"Charlie Ondine," Darlene replied, sinking into the car seat. Charlie was one of several traders in parts and used cars who drifted through Dave's station with stories about titles and repos, rollovers and head-ons. In her mind they were like a flock of transplant surgeons, all laboring over the same body till it was emptied of usable organs and the stripped carcass could be sent to the graveyard. Darlene hadn't asked what favor Dave had done, or promised to do, for Charlie Ondine.

She roused herself for an explanation. "It's just, you know, depressing for my boyfriend to steal my car and all my money."

"I know," Kat said. Then, more sharply, "What do you mean, your money?"

"You can't tell Rita," Darlene insisted. "Promise?"

"I won't tell if you don't want me to," Kat pledged.

The saddest part, in Kat's view, was the predictability. The seven hundred dollars hidden in the tampon box, the checks Darlene had written for his lawyer, the forty dollars she had handed him to get a money order for the electric company. No one has to tell Rita, Kat thought as Darlene detailed the investment in Tiffany's Little Miss Bayou costumes. Rita's probably guessed it all by now.

"Darlene," Kat said as she pulled onto the farm-to-market road toward Sydonia, "did it ever occur to you to just go back to school and get a degree in something useful so you can make a life for Tiffany and yourself?" Kat was working hard to avoid criticism of staking financial goals on the success of a four-year-old in a local beauty contest, particularly one that required Jimmy to deliver them to his hometown of Shreveport in the Camaro he had stolen.

"What's a life?" Darlene's voice dripped resignation. Then, for some reason, her face brightened and her tone grew cheerier. "Anyway, I don't need to go back to school. I just need a good set of wheels, a new computer, and a place to live."

"That's my point," Kat countered. "How do you think you'll get those things?"

"Not by going back to school," Darlene replied. Then, "Oh, give it up! I'm already married and divorced, with one kid. The latest boyfriend stole my car and all my money. I can't just park Tiffany somewhere so I can relive my childhood. I got my GED. You see how much good that did me!"

Kat knew sales. She knew you didn't convince someone you were right by proving that person wrong. So she clamped her lips together in a way she knew made her look like a disapproving schoolmarm and tried not to calculate Darlene's young age.

You should give it up, Kat conceded silently. She's Rita's daughter, not yours. Kat was trying to formulate a more acceptable conversational gambit when Darlene spoke again.

"Do you know anything about *in vitro*?"

Kat jumped to the extent that the seat belt allowed and forced herself to watch the road. "*In vitro* fertilization?"

"It's when they take an egg—"

"And a sperm," Kat instructed, "they take sperm."

"No, an egg," Darlene insisted. "A fertilized egg, and they put it—"

Light dawned. "Surrogacy. You mean surrogacy: implanting a fertilized egg into another female—"

"Surrogacy." Darlene pronounced it *sirgacy*. "What do you know about surrogacy?"

"You know, in *my* youth, we just put on our push-up bras and our perkiest smiles and waited tables when we needed money."

"But this would be helping someone else," Darlene said. "And my body's already wrecked."

Kat cast a quick, sideways glance and shook her head. She didn't know how anyone who lived solely on Dr Pepper and corn chips could look as good as Darlene. Life was unfair, Kat reflected. She had never seen Darlene work out, even at the Ladies Farm, which boasted a mirrored workout room with treadmill and stair climber and resistance circuit. Kat doubted the kid did anything for that burnished complexion except splash water on it. But even after one child, Darlene possessed sylph-like proportions and a pouty-lipped, wide-eyed beauty that overcame the prickly hair and black nail polish. It will catch up with her, Kat reflected, speeding up a little because she, herself, needed to work the stair climber before dinner. I didn't work out either at her age.

"They tell you anything about the hormones?"

"What hormones?"

Now Kat had her attention. "They shoot you full of hormones so they can get more eggs out at one time."

Darlene sighed a huffy, exasperated whoosh of a sigh. "They're not taking 'em. They're putting one in. Implanting it."

She obviously had learned a new word.

"Implanting an egg?"

"Uh huh. A fertilized egg."

"I think there are still hormones," Kat said, though she wasn't sure.

"And then," Darlene concluded, ignoring the hormones, "all I have to do is be pregnant for nine months and my job's over."

"You just hand over the baby, huh?"

"Yup."

"And how much is this worth?"

"You can't tell Rita."

"*I* won't. But *you* should." Kat laughed. "And I think she'll notice, don't you?"

"Well, about being pregnant. But I meant about the money."

"How much?"

"Twenty-five thousand," Darlene said. "I'm getting twenty-five thousand dollars just to be pregnant!"

Again, Kat took a breath before she responded. "How much do you make a year?"

"I'll still make it," Darlene countered. "I'll work till the due date, induce labor, and collect it all at one time!"

"Who . . ." Kat started, then stopped. "Ryan? Ryan and Jill Plummer are hiring you as a surrogate mother?"

"A carrier," Darlene said. "A gestational carrier. It's their embryo, her egg and his sperm. And why not?" she demanded, warming to the argument. "I'm strong and healthy and I take care of myself when I'm pregnant. Look at Tiffany. She would have been Little Miss Bayou Queen in her age group if Jimmy hadn't stolen the car and all my money."

"Tiffany is extraordinary," Kat assured Darlene.

"And smart."

"And smart," Kat concurred. "But Ryan Plummer?"

"What's wrong with Ryan Plummer?" Darlene asked, then shrugged. "Anyway, I might not do it. I'm just thinking about it. And I have to go to a specialist. In Dallas."

Kat downshifted as they rounded the back side of Castleburg Dairy and ascended the hill into the Sydonia city limits. "Why Dallas?"

"Some specialist. Lantern, Lantin—"

"Lantinatta? Nicholas Lantinatta?"

"Yeah. You know him?"

Kat concentrated on the road and tried to shrug. "I called on him a few times, when he had a little office in Fort Worth one day a week. He used to be Dr. Fertility. And Genetics," she added, to be absolutely truthful.

"I have to have a physical first," Darlene continued. "Tomorrow, with this OB-GYN Ryan knows. Dr. Kaplan. Know him?"

"Her," Kat corrected. Her consulting business involved practice management, so she knew most of the doctors in Dallas and Fort Worth. "Good OB." Ryan was smart that way. "Is this legal?"

Darlene shrugged. "Ryan says it is."

"Ryan's a doctor, not a lawyer."

"I haven't said yes, yet." Kat could hear the struggle for nonchalance. Then, as they tooled into Sydonia proper, past the darkened law offices and the silent courthouse illuminated by spotlights through which the live oaks cast eerie shadows, "You're not going to tell Rita behind my back, are you?"

Chapter Three

Earl Westerman thought Darlene Kindalia was the prettiest girl he had ever known. He had believed that in high school, when he was a blocker for the Sydonia Sabers by virtue of his immense, albeit flabby, girth; and he believed it now, while he was looking after his aunt and uncle's old place until Darlene's mother and her friends got around to remodeling it and renting it out.

Darlene's beauty hadn't prevented him from marrying Patty after he heard Darlene had run off with Jason Kindalia. He had been young, and Patty had been pretty, too. More importantly, she had been willing to sleep with him. She just hadn't been willing to live in Sydonia. Eventually she divorced him, moved to Dallas, and then to Houston. He missed Earl, Jr., whom he now saw briefly during the summer and on holidays, but most of the time he didn't think much about the boy. Earl didn't blame Patty for divorcing him any more than he considered the marriage inconsistent with his dreams of Darlene. Man's a man, he thought. No crime in that.

Now, though, sitting in the kitchen of the Ladies Farm with Della, the only one who seemed to have no real work schedule, he thought that maybe his time had come. "You think she'd go out with me?" he asked in a low voice.

"I don't know, Earl. Why don't you ask her?"

"I have," he said. "She said no." Della shot him a look to tell him he had his answer, but he ignored that and surveyed the roomy kitchen.

Della set two mugs of coffee on the oak table. The mugs were red and had been made by Pauline, the woman who had died the previous year of a heart attack. She and her husband had started the bed and breakfast as Sydon House, after Sydonia's founder. Earl wasn't sure how Sydon House had become the Ladies Farm, since that had happened while he was figuring out how to make a living and keep Patty home, but the next thing he knew, his aunt and uncle, Gladys and Ray Hutto, had sold their place on the other side of the Nolan to all these women and left for the Big Bend.

"Earl, just because Dave wore Rita down doesn't mean that will work on her daughter."

Della seated herself and pushed a plate of cookies toward him.

"No thanks," he shook his head and put up his hands. "I'm really working on my weight."

"It shows," Della said. "Rita said you've been working out."

"I hope that's okay," Earl said. "Using the workout room. I don't go in there if there's ladies there."

She smiled and Earl guessed she must have been pretty when she was young. "It's fine, Earl. Look," she leaned forward, her green eyes opened wide, "I barely know Darlene. Maybe hanging around will work. I sure don't know." She shook her head a little and picked up one of the cookies. "I'll say this about her: she's a hard worker." She bit into the cookie.

"She is," Earl agreed. He lifted the coffee and sipped a little. Women seemed to love flavored coffees. This one was pecan and probably decaffeinated. "I am too, you know. No matter what Aunt Gladys and Uncle Ray tell you." He sipped again. "I worked McDonalds when I had to. Dairy Queen when I was fifteen. Construction. Baled hay. Sold cars. What I'm good at though . . . I'm good at putting people together."

"You're a matchmaker?" Her humor was a lot gentler than Rita's, who thought anyone who cared about Darlene was a fool.

"Not so far." Earl grinned. His mother had told him his smile was his best feature, because he had such straight, even teeth. He thought his teeth were too big, but women saw things differently. "No, I match people who are selling things with folks who want to buy them."

"What sort of things?"

Earl could tell that Della was being polite, that she probably knew he was just killing time so he could be there when Darlene got home. If Darlene parked under the carport, she had to walk right through the kitchen to get to Rita's salon, where Tiffany was. Certainly Della already knew he bought and sold things. Nonetheless, he plunged into a description of his trading business. "Old furniture, plumbing fixtures, real estate—you name it—I can move it over the Net!" Earl bragged.

Della listened without much comment, so Earl threw himself into automatic and rattled on, meanwhile taking inventory of the collection of glass refrigerator boxes displayed on the shelf above the outside wall, and the variety of Calphalon pots and pans suspended from two ceiling racks over the island in the center of the kitchen. Everyone wondered how these women made a go of it; if they folded, there would be assets to liquidate.

He was describing the market for blue ware—the blue-glass dishes Californians and others seemed to prefer for summer—and the supplier he had tracked down in Mexico, when he heard the Accord out front. "Fifty percent less what they charge in those catalogs," he promised Della as he listened to the motor die and heard two car doors closing.

Damn! he thought as the front door opened and low voices murmured in the living room. Why did they park out front? Why couldn't he be sipping coffee in the living room?

Earl rattled on a little more about crockery and flatware, relaxing only when he was certain the footsteps were headed toward the kitchen and not upstairs.

Darlene entered through the service hall, her oversized purse slung over her shoulder and her open jacket revealing the deep vee in the neck of her clingy sweater.

"Hi, Darlene," he greeted her, rising as he spoke and embarrassing himself with the scraping of the chair against the tile floor. "Whoops," he mumbled, then reminded himself to smile at her. He stepped toward her to reach for the grocery bag she carried by the handles. "Here, let me take that."

"Hi," she said in that preoccupied way she had, ducking her head a little as she lifted the sack filled with some kind of greens and deposited it on the counter. He caught a whiff of musky perfume as she headed straight past him, close enough for him to count the four tiny earrings that sparkled in her perfectly shaped ear and to see her scalp through her spiky blond hair.

"Still cold out?" he ventured.

She frowned as if dragging herself out of some deep thought as she stopped her forward motion to turn toward him and fixed her blue-green eyes on him. This was the part Earl liked best. Her eyes were very round and very pale and when she drew in her lower lip for a second before she spoke, he knew he had every bit of her concentration. "Freezing," she replied. Then, to his joy, she smiled enough to show the dimple in her left cheek and reveal her prominent eyeteeth. "I'm gonna get one of those parkas all lined in fur. That'd be perfect on a day like this!"

Earl started to tell her he could get her one of those from a Korean he'd met on the Net, but the idea of finding her bargains conflicted with his vision of providing the parka himself and instead he just stood there grinning for a second, then told her, "Well, you know Texas. Stick around a minute and the weather'll change." It was lame, but it got him an accepting shrug and another smile before she headed through to the dining room and on to the salon.

"What's up?" he heard Della quizzing Kat as Kat poured her own cup of coffee and headed toward the table.

Kat's shrug was different than Darlene's. Darlene looked playful when she shrugged; Kat looked dismissive. "Well, I'll leave you ladies to mind the farm," Earl excused himself. He looked back at his almost full cup of coffee, reached over and took it to the sink. *That Earl*, he could just hear them remarking in Darlene's presence. *Now there's a thoughtful boy*.

Ryan Plummer set down his recorder and checked his watch, then called Jill. "What's going on?" he asked, holding the receiver with one hand and removing the tape from the handheld recorder with the other. He tossed the tape atop the stack of files in his *Out* basket while he listened to Jill's report.

"He's sleeping," she said. "I think the Tylenol helps. Where are you?"

"At the office. How's his energy? Was he alert?"

"A little better. Maybe it's working."

"Maybe," he said, trying not to discourage her. "I wish I could get home earlier."

"Was it a zoo today?"

He eyed the files in his *Out* tray and the larger stack that awaited him. "What you'd expect after two days away."

"Away at the hospital." Her voice was bitter in his defense.

"Did you get dinner?" he asked, fumbling in the drawer for another tape.

"I was waiting for you," she said.

"It'll be a few more hours," he advised, snapping the tape into the recorder.

"Did you talk with your friend . . . the one at NIH?"

He set the recorder down. "Just for a few minutes," Ryan said.

"What did he say?"

"You have to know Josh," Ryan said. "Pure research, a real plodder."

"Ryan, what did he say?"

"It's remote, Jill. Experimental and risky, based primarily on success in leukemia treatment."

"But he's doing something."

"Yes. And he's sending me a packet. Jill, we have to keep treating him the way we have been. Our best shot is still remission."

"I understand," Jill said.

He could hear her anxiety, her rush to assure him that she wasn't allowing herself any false hope. "We have to do whatever we can to build his strength, in any case," he said.

"Well, we can do that."

"We have been doing that," he concurred. Jill didn't say anything, and Ryan pictured her in the kitchen, cradling the phone in both hands, furrowing her smooth forehead as she stared at the silly bronze figurines she kept on the glass shelves that separated the work area from the kitchen table. Give her something, he thought. "Especially you, with the diet and vitamins."

"Then what?" she asked.

Ryan twirled around in his office chair to study the photo of his son. He checked the whites of the eyes, the robust skin tone, even searched for bruises on the chubby arms and legs at uncharacteristic rest by order of the studio photographer. For the thousandth time, Ryan assured himself that there had been no sign, nothing he had missed.

"I'm not exactly . . . he's not exactly sure," Ryan said finally. "Josh is still working out the protocol. It's very, very preliminary. That's why I didn't bring it up. Until I see the packet, until Ballangee takes a look, there's no telling."

"Well, then," she chirped, "let's just keep on keeping on. Is it coming to the office?"

"I wanted to see it as soon as it gets here," Ryan confirmed. "And it'll be a few days, anyway, before he gets everything together. I mean, this is a favor, Jill. He's really not ready, yet."

"But you'll let me know as soon as it comes?" she said.

"Yes, of course. I'm just trying not to get too excited," he said. "No matter what, this could be a long haul."

"But shouldn't we," she paused, groping a little for words, "don't we need to be tested? All of us?"

"There's no rush, no need to panic," Ryan counseled. "We don't even know right now if a donor could help." Or what kind, he thought.

There was no sense in upsetting her. She didn't need to know right now that none of the family and friends who had given blood would be the right kind of match for Josh. All she needed to know was that if a donor—if some sort of transplant—could help, then they would find a donor. Or make one.

He assured her once more that they would do whatever they needed to for Taylor. And he promised he wouldn't stay too late at the office.

"Come home soon," she implored.

"As soon as I can."

He picked up the recorder and opened the next file. It was a middle-aged woman with gallstones. Ryan had advised her to have her gallbladder removed, but she didn't want surgery if she could avoid it. Ryan knew that when the stones caused enough pain, she would want the surgery immediately, but she didn't believe him when he told her that. Not enough pain, he thought, clicking on the recorder.

"Watch me!" Tiffany demanded from the hall. Darlene and Tiffany shared the Janis Joplin room, which opened off an octagonal, oak-floored hall that Tiffany found the perfect venue for performing her Little Miss Bayou Queen routine. During the winter, there were rarely guests during the week and they had the hall to themselves. "Come here and watch!"

"In a minute, Tiff." Darlene was rummaging through her top drawer for her sex books, but she wasn't having much luck. They were mostly pamphlets anyway, given to her by the obstetrician who delivered Tiffany and by the clinic where she got her pills. But there might be something about surrogacy, or at least infertility, in them.

"Wa-ah-ah-ah-ah-ah-ah-ch mmmm eeeeee," sang Tiffany at her most operatic. "Watch me, watch me, watch me," she called out, hip-hop style, then talked her way through, "Watch, watch, watch, watch me, baby, baby, watchme, watchme."

Darlene shook her head and kept rummaging. All that stuff about the JonBenet Ramsey murder gave Darlene the creeps, but Tiffany loved the costumes and makeup and singing and dancing. It would have been cruel just to stop it. Besides, what if she won a really big pageant? Those big ones paid off, no matter what anyone thought.

Of course, Jimmy's disappearance with all her money and the trunk full of costumes in the Camaro had stopped it anyway. Tiffany, however, believed Jimmy was coming back and then they'd leave for the competition, so she practiced every day, particularly when she had an audience.

Darlene sighed and turned toward the door. "Okay, I'm watching."

"Out here," the child insisted. "You have to see my entrance."

Darlene stepped to the doorway. Tiffany posed ballerina style in the entrance to the room across the hall, with arms above her head and her lead foot at right angles to her back one. Before Darlene could warn her that she must remember to roll the rug back into place when she was done, Tiffany leapt into the center of the hall, sliding like an ice-skater along the polished floor into a half-kneeling position from which, arms opened wide, she launched into *I Am Your Angel*. Her arms described obstacles—no mountain too high, no river too wide—while her face contorted with the effort of belting out the song. As she reached the refrain, Tiffany struggled to her feet and began a series of twirls. "I'll be your cloud up in the sky, I'll be your shoulder when you cry," she warbled, all the while turning with her arms out and her head tilted at what she must have assumed was an angelic angle.

Darlene hoped no one downstairs was bothered by her daughter's thumping. Her singing had lost considerable volume as the necessity of breathing during the strenuous twirls interfered with her phrasing. Even so, Darlene didn't dare begin her applause. That must wait until the very end.

Darlene knew it was Rita climbing the stairs behind her by the enthusiastic hum-along that accompanied her tread. When she felt Rita's hand on her shoulder, Darlene ordered herself to relax, but she knew Rita felt her tense.

"Oh, baby, can you belt out a song!"

This did not please Tiffany, who stopped and glared at her grandmother. "Mamaw!" She stomped her foot. "You interrupted me!"

Oh, damn! thought Darlene.

"Now I have to start over!"

"Tiffany Jewel, I'm shocked at your lack of professionalism," Rita scolded. "What kind of singer interrupts her song to answer a comment from the audience?"

Tiffany started an adamant retort, then stopped as she considered Rita's criticism.

Darlene wasted no time; one second more and Tiffany would be howling. "Mama," Darlene proclaimed, "Tiffany's a real trouper and you know it. She just paused to take a breath; she's not stopping." Darlene watched her daughter's eyes narrow. "Are you Tiff? *I'll be your cloud . . .*" Darlene encouraged in her own reedy alto.

"I'll be your cloud up in the sky," Tiffany started, gaining certainty as Rita and Darlene held their breath. *"Your mountain when you cry,"* she sang as she launched a new series of pirouettes.

"Carla called," Rita whispered to Darlene as Tiffany's voice rose. "Said she'll be over tomorrow, let her know what time. You two up to something?"

Darlene shrugged, though even that did not dislodge her mother's hand on her shoulder. "Nothing much. I can't do much; I don't have any money." She wondered how her sister got three kids down while she was still waiting on Tiffany.

"Well, if you're going shopping," Rita admonished, "you remember you've got a daughter who needs school clothes a lot more than her mother needs another push-up bra."

It was a typical, feet-in-the-stirrups exam. By the time she climbed on the table, Darlene had peed in the bottle, given blood samples, and answered three pages of questions asked by a soft-voiced girl her own age in teddy-bear print scrubs. Only the sonogram surprised her, with everything so tiny and still. In Darlene's last sonogram, the whole picture had been throbbing away with Tiffany. Darlene knew there was no one there now, but the lackluster appearance of her internal organs disappointed her.

The doctor, Marta Kaplan, seemed happy though. Dr. Kaplan was nice. When Ryan had stepped into the examining room, she had asked Darlene if his presence during the examination was okay before she drew back the sheet and asked Darlene to scoot down to the edge of the table.

"This all looks good," she said now, more to Ryan than to Darlene. Darlene didn't mind. He was paying for the exam. Let him examine all he wanted.

"How was your last delivery?" Dr. Kaplan asked. Darlene, lying on her back with her head turned so she could see the screen, gave a small start.

"My delivery?" she asked, aiming her conversation down between her bent knees to where the doctor was. "With Tiffany? Fine, I guess."

"And I think we're just fine here," Dr. Kaplan said. "Who's doing the AI?"

"TFS," Ryan responded. He stood behind Dr. Kaplan, who was seated on a stool, and he had been stooping to peer over her shoulder and get a better look. Now he straightened up and winked at Darlene, as if this was some sort of shared experience. "Lantinatta himself."

"The master." Then, in a louder voice, Dr. Kaplan said, "Just relax, now, Darlene. Let me get this Pap smear and I'll let you out of here."

Darlene heard the crinkle of cellophane as the nurse, who had remained silent during the entire exam, unwrapped the Pap kit. Darlene felt the swab up against her cervix. "Easy," the doctor said; then, after a moment, "There you go."

Ryan had turned from her to watch the nurse. Darlene felt that they must be exchanging knowing glances down at the business end of the table. Just a raised eyebrow from Ryan to the nurse or Dr. Kaplan. This is how it looks when you start fucking at sixteen, they were thinking. Healthy and ready for more, but halfway down the invisible road to ruin. White-trash pussy.

Chapter Four

"Don't you want to go home?" Carla asked her when Darlene suggested they stop at Whataburger. "I just can't wait to take a shower after one of those things."

Darlene would have guessed that after three children you'd hardly notice a routine examination, but Carla had assured her otherwise. "The shower can wait," Darlene said now. "How often do we get to have a soda together without the kids?"

"So: Good to go?" They were sitting in a booth, sharing fries and eating cheeseburgers, even though it was too early.

Darlene nodded, took a gulp of Diet Pepsi. "I don't know why they don't have Diet Dr Pepper," she complained, holding the cup up to Carla. "They always have regular, but not diet."

Carla reached for a fry. "What's next?"

Darlene looked at her sister, who had let her hair go brown and kept her nails clipped short and unpolished. "They have to get the blood tests back. Then I go see the guy in Dallas. And a shrink, too."

"A shrink! How come?"

Darlene shook her head. "They want to make sure I don't go psycho, run off with the baby."

"I'd go psycho if I had to *keep* another baby," Carla said. She had had three children in five years, plus an abortion that only her husband and Darlene knew about. "What do they do, ask you stuff?"

"Ryan says they'll just ask a bunch of questions about why I'm doing it, how I'll feel handing it over, that stuff."

"You think they'll ask about Mama, about our childhood?"

Darlene snorted. "You mean: Rita fucks Wendell, Rita fucks

Dave?" She turned her head from left to right. "Wendell? Dave? Wendell? Dave? Tom? Dick? Harry?" she mocked.

Carla took up the theme. "Trailer? Apartment?"

"Red hair? Green hair?"

"No hair!" Carla exulted.

It wasn't that funny, but they both laughed. The last time Wendell had trashed the trailer, Rita called the police and followed through on her threat to file assault charges. The memory of Rita, bald-headed and eyes brimming as she sought corroboration from her daughters, still shook Darlene. Her stomach churned as her childhood fears of being torn from her mother and sister vied with her dreams—and fear of their discovery—that her real parents would appear any day to rectify what was obviously some switched-at-birth tragedy. *Come get me*, she used to pray. *She's shaved her head and screams at us so the whole place can hear*.

Carla surveyed their surroundings the way she did any time they talked about Rita. Darlene didn't care anymore who knew about her mother, the hair slut. She told people about Rita the first moment she met them. It explained why she'd run off with Jason when she was sixteen. Why Carla married Carlos that same year. Who could live with Rita back then?

"I don't care what they ask me," Darlene vowed. "I'm a grown-up now. I'm fine. I'm just helping a friend—friends—have a baby they want more than anything else."

"So what are you going to tell her?"

"Just what I—oh, you mean Rita?"

Carla nodded.

"That I'm pregnant. That I'm giving up . . . placing the baby for adoption." She shrugged, then grinned. "If it gets too bad, I'll move in with you."

Carla rolled her eyes, which were the same cobalt as Rita's, but rounder and softer. "I'll just fit you in with Mama A and Maria."

Carla's mother-in-law lived with them, sharing a room with the only girl, Maria. Darlene didn't know how different that was than living at the Ladies Farm, but Carla never complained about the crowd. Carlos and his mother acted like it was normal, almost an extension of their family business, a dry cleaners started by Carlos's grandfather.

Carla got serious again. "Really. You're not going to tell her? About the money?"

"Not a word," Darlene vowed. "And you can't, either." She

sipped her soda, fiddled with a fry, took a deep breath of the burger-and-fries aroma. "It's just . . . I'm worried about the shots."

"The hormones?"

Darlene nodded. "Someone else has to do them, the doctor said. And it has to be the same time every day."

Carla saw where they were heading. "Not me, baby! You know how I am around needles!" Then, "Why can't you do them yourself? Mama A does her insulin."

"I told you: it's a long needle, it has to go in your butt."

"Not my butt!" Carla held up her hand.

"I'm thinking I'll ask Kat," Darlene confessed.

"Kat?"

"She's really nice," Darlene offered.

"She's a bitch." Once more, Carla looked around the deserted Whataburger to see who might have heard her language.

"You don't know her. She's just got a smart mouth, like Rita, but she's really smart."

"If she's so smart," Carla countered, "how come she's alone, with no husband, no children?"

"Because she's so smart," Darlene shot back. "Because she doesn't need them. She makes as much money as any man."

Carla shook her head. "So what? What good does money do you, if you don't have a family?" Her eyes narrowed. "You think she's gay?"

Darlene shook her head. "I don't think so. She was married. And sometimes she dates." Darlene grinned. "And she's never made a pass at me!"

"And you think she wouldn't tell Rita?"

"I don't think so. She doesn't like Rita that much, if you notice. It's just business with them."

"That's just it," Carla pointed out. "It is business, and she's a businesswoman. That's what she does. So why's she want to get crosswise with Rita?"

Darlene shrugged. The same thing was bothering her, but she couldn't deal with that right now.

"Ryan said I could do it at his office, so I might just drive in every day."

"I think doing it in his office is how you got into all this. Does his wife know who you are?"

"If screwing Ryan got me enough money to get out of debt and get my business off the ground, then that's a good thing." Darlene sat up straight. "Besides, you keep forgetting that I'm doing this for Ryan and his wife. That's a pretty big thing: having a baby for someone else."

By this time Carla had finished her burger and wadded the yellow wrapping into a ball, which she now fired across the table at her sister. "That's the point, asshole: it is a big thing. You're not thinking about it at all! You're thinking about the money, but what if something goes wrong? What if they change their minds, or the baby's retarded, or you end up in a wheelchair? What if Ryan's wife figures out who you are and decides she's not paying one dime to you no matter how pregnant you are?"

"None of that'll happen. You don't have to be so down on everything I do!" Darlene retrieved the wadded wrapper, which she had batted onto the floor, and held it in her open palm. "This will fix things for Tiffany and me!"

"You don't know a thing about her, do you? His wife?"

"I know everything I have to know: she wants a baby and she wants me to have it for her!"

"You know what Ryan's told you. You don't even know if she's agreed to pay you."

The greasy-wrapper ball slipped onto the table. Darlene looked at her sister. "You think I ought to meet her? Before I do it?"

Kat reminded herself that she could change her mind at any time. She pictured a flowchart with the possibility of interruption at each juncture. Just like a space launch, she thought. Mission aborted.

"Ms. Naylor," the receptionist said, "the doctor will see you now."

Kat felt certain that her tone conveyed disapproval. She knows I'm the last person Lantinatta wants to see, Kat thought.

Disapproval might have mattered, long ago, the first time Kat met him. But then there had been a motherly nurse in a starched uniform and cap who had smiled warmly and approved of everything. Every patient deserved solicitude then. That time, Kat remembered as she seated herself in an upholstered chair at a round walnut table, there had been a metal desk and straight-backed chairs. She and Hal had sat in them while Dr. Lantinatta, young and robust, explained their options.

The current office was teal and plum, with accents of yellow and tangerine, sort of Miami-on-the-prairie, Kat thought. In the corner stood a striking, life-sized sculpture of entwined bodies assembled from spare auto parts. It conflicted with the soothing tones of the room, as if the sculptor didn't accept the decorator-imposed tranquility.

Tearing her gaze from the metal couple, Kat eyed the pamphlets displayed on the wall nearest to her: *What Couples Should Know About Infertility, AI, Surrogacy for Parents, A Guide to Becoming a Gestational Carrier*. She started to reach for the guide, but stopped when she heard steps at the office door.

Dr. Lantinatta was still handsome in a reassuring, fatherly way. His hair had turned completely silver and he was heavyset, with a broad, open, well-lined face and eyes that looked vulnerable because of their pale lashes. Kat thought it odd that someone perhaps a decade older than she would not wear glasses, and was reassured, as he turned to shut the door behind him, to catch the silhouette of his contacts.

He stretched out both hands to her and she took them. "It's good to see you looking so well," he said, and she could not tell if he recognized her or if he would have remembered her at all except for her name on his appointment sheet. He sat at the table. "What brings you here?"

"I want," she took a breath. "I want to know," she said clearly, but then she could feel her lips tremble and she stopped until she could continue to the end, even though she knew, now, that he understood why she had come. "I want to know," she said again, "what happened to my daughter."

He nodded and looked thoughtful but said nothing for a moment. Then he said, "When was that?"

"Twenty-four years ago. In October."

"And the baby's father?"

"Hal and I divorced two years later. That's why I took my maiden name back."

He nodded. Then he reached around to a stack of file folders on his desk and pulled one off the top. It wasn't hers, Kat could see. It was marked "Philadelphia."

Dr. Lantinatta drew a printed form from the file. "At that time, we placed through the Family Adoption Center, in Philadelphia. They later became Delaware House, and that is who would have your records." He placed the form flat on the table. "This is a consent form, allowing Delaware House to contact your daughter on your behalf. Then, if she agrees to be contacted, they'll put you in touch."

Obviously, he remembered nothing. "According to you at the time, my daughter has an IQ of thirty and, if she's lucky, can sit up."

He stared at her and Kat felt the fire in her face. In a second, his eyes widened. "Kircher," he said quietly. "Your married name was Kircher."

Kat nodded. "You told me it was a group of nuns. In the Appalachians."

He nodded back at her. "I'm sorry," he said. "I just assumed it was . . . even when you indicated you were married at the time, I thought it must have been a routine placement." He looked directly at her and pressed his lips together. "I owe you an apology. Those records are all in storage and I didn't think we needed to pull your file. I didn't realize who you were. I'm sorry."

"Don't be sorry," Kat advised. "Just tell me what happened to my daughter."

Dr. Lantinatta shook his head, studied his hands. "It was a group of nuns, somewhere in the Blue Ridge. They had to close the facility—there seems to be a shortage of nuns—and they consolidated somewhere else, maybe Richmond or Washington. I guess," he glanced around, gesturing with his hands, "we can make a few calls, find out who's got . . . where the residents are now."

His gaze settled on her. "If that's what you want."

Kat drew a breath, but he continued. "Ms. Naylor," he said, "is there some reason you would do this now? You know," and he leaned forward, across the table, shaking his head, "are you prepared to deal with this? To know, for instance, that she may not have survived past a year?"

Kat shook her head. "I don't know what I'm prepared for," she said. "I don't know if I'm prepared for anything: that she died, that she's a vegetable chained to a bed, that some miracle occurred and she's in law school or a rocket scientist." Now the tears came, but she didn't bother to wait or conceal them. "Maybe some loving family adopted her, nurtured her until all that kindness made her flower into a fully formed human." She bit her lip and held up a hand to stop him as he started to speak. "What I know," she said, "is that I want to know."

* * *

"Who's Darlene Kindalia," Jill demanded, "and why does she want to meet me?"

"It's not what you think," Ryan replied, then cursed his automatic response. But then he relaxed. Of course that was what she thought first. Best to reassure her. "Darlene's a transcriptionist. She's the one who does my tapes."

Jill hadn't moved from the center of the room. In one hand she held her turtleneck sweater, the other hand clutched protectively at her breast.

Ryan, in shirt and tie, had only come back upstairs to check on Taylor and bid goodbye to Jill. He stifled the urge to check his watch; whatever this set him back, he'd have to take the time. "Honey, I . . ." he took a step forward, anchored her upper arms in his hands. "I asked Darlene to do something for us . . . for Taylor."

"What do you mean?"

"Here," he offered, motioning toward a corner of the freshly made bed. Jill stood where she was.

"Ryan?"

"Honey, Taylor . . ." he thought for a second, then started again. "Honey, Josh . . . Josh's protocol: it's not what we were thinking." He ignored her shocked look and slid an arm around her, guiding her to the side of the bed. "It's not really a marrow transplant."

Jill sat rigid, staring down at the sweater still in her hands. "What do you mean?" she asked.

"It's a transplant," Ryan said. "But not marrow." She looked up and he hurried on. "I mean, you know, when they do a marrow transplant, what they're doing is transplanting the fluid in the center of the bone—"

"I know what marrow is!"

He forced himself to keep the edge out of his voice and he massaged her back with one hand as he spoke. "I know you know. I'm just trying to say that the marrow is rich in stem cells, and that's really what they're transplanting."

She continued to stare at him and he saw her eyes narrow. "Do you mean stem cells like—"

"Embryonic stem cells? No. These are similar, but not nearly as controversial."

Jill gave a short laugh. "That's good to hear."

"But they are difficult to come by," Ryan warned. "These stem cells are the cells that make other blood cells. Some circulate in the blood system. But mostly they reside in the marrow. When they're transplanted, after we've killed off the patient's own stem cells, they start manufacturing new, healthy blood cells." She said nothing, but Ryan could tell she was following. "The thing is, Josh says that the best way, the best kind, he thinks, would be umbilical stem cells."

"Cord blood?"

"Exactly."

"They gave us a pamphlet about banking cord blood when we had Taylor."

"Yeah, well," he said, "good thing we didn't. His blood couldn't help anyone." He said it as gently as he could. "But the right cord blood, from a healthy donor who was the right match—"

"You mean, from another baby?"

"Not just another baby." He smiled. "Our baby."

He pulled her a little closer, buried his face in her hair and drew comfort from the herbal scent of her shampoo. This was Jill, he told himself. Still the same Jill. "We have the embryos," he reminded her. "The ones we stored."

She backed off a little to look at him. "What are you saying?"

Too many emotions worked across her face. He couldn't read it. "We froze the embryos in case we changed our minds," he said.

"In case you changed your mind," Jill said. "I've always wanted another baby." Then, her voice strained, "What does she want, Ryan? Darlene Kindalia?"

"She wants to help," he said. "I asked her."

Now the alarm was unmistakable. "Help how?"

He stroked her hair, which spilled over her shoulders and onto the silk of her camisole. "The embryos. She can be our carrier. Our gestational carrier."

"Our gestational carrier." She repeated the words slowly.

Easy, he counseled himself silently. "You want her to have our baby."

He had thought about this one. "It's the best way, Jill." She stared at him. "And I know you want another baby."

"And do you?"

"Come here," he mumbled, pulling her toward him. She leaned in, but he could feel her resistance. "Jill, I want this baby."

She remained still.

"I do, Jill. No matter what I said before. Honey, look." He pulled back a little to make eye contact. "What do you want me to say? I didn't want another baby. I'm not trying to tell you different. But Taylor . . . Taylor's situation . . . don't you think that's made me re-evaluate what's important? Don't you think I've had to question my own values? Haven't you?"

Finally her eyes brimmed over. "Oh, Ryan."

"Shhhhh." He held her tight and waited.

Finally, she said, "But why do we need her? Why should someone else carry my . . . our baby?" Suddenly she pushed away from him. "It's me, isn't it? Taylor . . ." Horror suffused her face. "It's me and I shouldn't have . . . shouldn't ever have babies!"

The worst thing in the world was watching Jill turn away from him, twisting around to throw herself facedown on the bed, dissolving into tears. Damn! Ryan consulted his watch, blew off his early hospital visits. It would take at least another half hour now, but with luck he could still make the first office appointment.

Usually Jill just needed comforting, which Ryan had mastered. Hugging and stroking her without coming onto her was tough, but it did the trick most of the time and she was always willing later. When she despaired like this, though, Ryan never knew what to do. Thank God he managed to keep her happy most of the time.

Tentatively, Ryan stretched across the bed next to her and touched her shoulder, which was shaking with sobs. "Jill," he said softly. "It's not you. It's not anything you did."

She turned, and her tear-drenched face twisted in fury. "Don't lie to me."

"I'm not lying!" Her ferocity shook him. "Don't cry," he whispered. "Don't cry. It's . . . I thought you'd be happy. It's what you wanted!"

She sat straight up. "You didn't want another child, I begged for it and you didn't want it. But now, now that you need those stem cells, you think you can just inject some little bimbo and get what you want . . . and throw me a bone in the bargain!"

He wanted to grab her and shake her. You don't know a thing about what I want, he yelled silently, but there were the things you say and the things you want to say, the way you feel and the things you do to make yourself feel better. Tears welled up in his own eyes at how bitterly she had misread him. "I just know that we will both welcome another child. And I know that we—you and I both—will do anything if it helps Taylor."

She swiped at her wet face with her open palm. "It's not that easy."

Ryan breathed deep and held her gaze. "I know. It's not easy for me either." He ducked his head a little. "Look, I should never have talked to Darlene without talking to you." He took another breath. "I'm sorry."

"You should be," she retorted. "How do you think I feel, your arranging to have a baby with another woman. Like you're ordering flowers from the damn florist!"

"You're right," he said. "It's just that she popped into the office the other day and we started talking and I thought: she's perfect. She's healthy, and she's had one pregnancy. Jill, you can't be pregnant with Taylor going through this now, but this way, this way—" he stopped himself.

"I could be pregnant. You just said—"

He was ready for this one. "I said you didn't cause Taylor's illness. But Jill," he leaned toward her, "Taylor needs you full time."

"I'd just be pregnant, Ryan. I'd still be Taylor's mother."

He had thought about this one. The trick was to stay logical. "Of course you would." Don't think about what could happen, he ordered himself. Don't go there. "But he'll need transfusions. You can't give blood if you're pregnant."

"I forgot about the transfusions."

She looked so contrite, Ryan wanted to wrap his arms all around her, feel that smooth skin under his hands.

"And it—the transplant—could be a long haul," he warned. Whenever we start, he thought. "We'll have to kill off his own marrow, wipe it out completely." Be cruel now, he told himself. Preventive cruelty. "We'll be at the hospital all day, every day. He'll be in isolation. Do you really want to be pregnant—or just recovering—then? When he needs us most?"

Watching her chest rise and fall, he wanted to reach under the camisole and tease her nipples to full attention. That, he knew, would lead to disaster. Finish this first, he told himself.

"It's still no excuse," he assured her, raising his eyes to her face. "You're right, I had no business talking to her before I talked with you. And now, the only thing I can think of," a deep breath, silently urging himself to go for it, roll the dice, "is, I'll just tell her to hold off awhile." He took another breath. "Nothing would change, really. We could wait a little, see how Taylor does. Maybe we can look around for another carrier. Someone we both trust." He shook his head, reached out for her hand. "I'll call Darlene," he said.

Jill looked at him with alarm. "We can't wait. You know that."

I do, he thought. Awkwardly, he scooted over and drew her again into his arms, but she pulled away enough to face him.

"Let me meet with her," said Jill. "I have to . . . we have to . . . do this now."

Chapter Five

Rita didn't know what Darlene was up to, but she doubted it was anything good. "She barely noticed when you said Charlie wouldn't be back till Monday," Rita said to Dave. "She squawked all last week about needing a car right away, and now, nothing."

"Well, maybe she's just letting Earl drive her around."

Rita eyed her husband warily but said nothing. Instead, she settled into the little boudoir chair tucked in the corner of the cavernous bathroom and studied him. Rita always enjoyed watching him shave after his morning shower. Most people didn't know he was so fastidious. Careful grooming was one of the reasons she had married him the second time; most men let themselves get sloppy, but Dave was meticulous, showering here in the morning before he put on fresh coveralls, then again at the shop, before he came home to her. That kind of fussiness had exasperated her the first time, but she had come to appreciate it.

When he finished, she stood and reached up from behind to ruffle his hair as he was rinsing his razor. "You want me to trim this before you go?"

He shook his head. "I'll get by this afternoon," he promised, "you can take care of it then." He was all business, there at the bathroom mirror. She reached a hand around to the front of his briefs. He'd never worn boxers, another point in his favor.

"Anything else you want me to take care of?"

He turned, kissed her lightly, and turned away to slip his work clothes off the hook on the door. "You save that for this evening, darling. When I can give it the time it deserves." He grinned, then stepped into his pants.

"You're getting too much!" Rita said. "If you're not interested in being late for work, I'm giving you way too much." She shook her head, then cinched her robe and followed him back across the hall to the bedroom to resume their earlier conversation. "Poor Earl. That boy's not going to get a thing for his troubles."

Dave chuckled. "I imagine he's getting something, or he thinks he's going to get something."

"That's just what I'm saying," Rita rejoined. "Darlene won't care one bit, what he thinks he's going to get!"

"You know," Dave's voice came from down low, because he was bent over, tying his work boots, "most mothers'd be happy to know their daughters weren't giving it away for a lift."

"I'm not saying she should be giving it away for lifts," Rita said. "I'm just saying she shouldn't be encouraging poor Earl."

Dave snorted. "Poor Earl! That boy's got a free ride. He's living for nothing up at Huttos, he's spending his day e-trading, and the rest of his time's spent cooking up schemes to get in Darlene's pants." He slapped his cap on his head, walked over to where she stood. "You ask me, they're made for each other."

Rita shook her head. "That's one thing about Darlene, she doesn't want to be living with her family. Not with Carla and not with me. Especially not with me."

He kissed her cheek, pulling her close and rubbing his hands over her back. "You're a good mother and she's going to be fine," he recited.

She ignored the automatic response. "You like this robe?" she asked him, looking down at the flowered nylon.

"I like what's in it," he teased, then pulled a little on the ruffle that adorned the neckline. "Yeah, the robe's nice, too."

She knew he didn't care, but another nice thing about Dave was that even when he didn't care, he always tried to say what she wanted and pretend interest anyway.

Earl couldn't believe it was this easy to get Darlene alone. All he had done was invite her to surf on his system and she was there, in his living room, at his keyboard. He thanked Jesus he had bought the case of Diet Dr Pepper the first time he had heard her mention it, and that he had both a clean glass and fresh ice courtesy of Aunt Gladys and Uncle Ray's super-deluxe refrigerator.

"What are they going to do with this place?" Darlene asked, eyeing the saggy furniture and scorched fireplace.

Earl shrugged. "Beats me. So far, all they've done is come over and argue over what goes where. I think they're wanting some kind of classes, workshops or something."

Darlene shook her head, held her hand out for the Diet Dr Pepper. "Thanks." Then, "I don't know why they'd do that. With that fireplace and the window wall over the river, it'd be a perfect honeymoon cottage." She looked exasperated, as if it were obvious. "That's what I'd do."

It didn't take her a second to figure out how to move around Netscape, Earl noted, even though she used Explorer at the Ladies Farm. He was glad he had checked his mail earlier, so she wouldn't know his password was *darlene*. She did not need his help at all to launch a search, but she didn't seem to mind that he pulled up a chair from the kitchen and sat close enough to enjoy her perfume.

"This doctor I transcribe for's going to pay me to have a baby for him," she related as she zipped the mouse around and jumped in and out of her search results. "This one looks good."

Haveababy.com featured a variety of options, none of which interested Earl, since he was trying to wrap his mind around what Darlene had just told him. While she dove into something that looked like personals from people trying to sell their eggs and sperm, Earl focused on her little shell of an ear, adorned this morning only by a single gold loop so threadlike it trembled as she breathed.

Pay me to have a baby! Did that mean the usual way? Earl was pretty sure not, though he had heard Rita talk so often about her daughter's willingness to couple with men who treated her badly that he wasn't certain. Anyway, the method didn't matter, though Earl did prefer that this project have more to do with a laboratory than a motel room. What mattered most right now, thought Earl, was that Darlene didn't see his alarm, didn't register his shock, until he got her to tell him a lot more about what was going on.

"So what's the going price these days for a healthy baby?"

"That's what I'm trying to find out," Darlene said, studying the screen. "These are all college girls bragging about their eggs. They think someone's going to pay them fifty thousand just because they scored a high SAT."

Earl himself had scored an SAT that had guaranteed automatic admission to the University of Texas, surprising most people who knew him at the time, including his parents. He didn't mention it now, though; he doubted Darlene had even taken the SAT, since she'd been so wrapped up in Jason Kindalia she rarely appeared at school at all.

"So, you're just selling your eggs?" That didn't sound too bad.

Earl didn't know if Darlene's disgust was directed at him or the college girls, but her little snort was not a good sign.

"I guess it's kind of a personal thing," he offered.

With that she turned from the screen and fixed him with a neutral, totally uninvolved gaze. "It's a business thing is what it is," Darlene corrected. "Pure business."

"What I meant is just you might not want to talk about it with me."

"I'll talk about it," she said, turning right back to the computer. "As long as you're not running to Rita about it."

"Why would I run to Rita?" he asked. Then, to get back on track, "So you're not selling your eggs."

"They've already got eggs. And sperm. They had them fertilized in a laboratory and froze them, just in case."

"Just in case what?"

"In case they wanted more children." All this time she had been scrolling through text in a different part of the site, but now she slowed down and studied it. Earl figured it was all right to look at it with her, and he leaned forward to read along. It was a letter from a girl who had had a baby for someone else. She was talking about her husband giving her shots, and how he didn't want her carrying anything more than twins, so they hadn't implanted more than two embryos.

"And sure enough," burbled Janet, "we got twins."

"Huh," Earl grunted despite himself. A husband! It would take a lot of money for him to let his wife make babies for someone else.

"So how much did she get for this?" he asked.

"Hush! I'm reading."

"Sorry," he mumbled, then resumed his own reading. But he couldn't find anything about the money, just how happy Eddie and Grace were when Janet delivered their bundles of joy.

Darlene shook her head, started scrolling through similar postings. "Damn!" she said. "Every one of these is married!"

"You'd think it'd be the opposite," Earl said.

She squinted at the screen, backed up to the search, tried another site. "What do you mean?" she asked in time to the clicking and scrolling.

Emboldened by her acceptance, Earl took his stand. "I wouldn't let a wife of mine sell her body as an incubator. I'd make sure she had what she needed, so she didn't have to do that."

"I'll bet you would," Darlene murmured to the scrolling and clicking. She didn't even incline her head. "I wonder if any of them post their . . . oh! here's one." She turned to him. "Is that printer hooked up? I need to print this contract."

He checked the green light on the laser printer, nodded without comment, and in a second it was churning out pages.

"Here's a different . . . no, I think it's just the same. Here's a different one," she chirped. Glumly, he watched her hit the *Print* icon again.

"Well," she said, returning to the search, "at least I'm seeing the contracts." She clicked on *gcarrier.com*. "Look at this: Fifteen thousand, twelve thousand, eighteen." Darlene sat back in the chair, a fabric-covered executive recliner that Earl had scouted off a liquidation site. She was facing the screen, but she looked as if she were thinking, not reading. Even as she rocked back, she wiggled the mouse right and left, making the on-screen pointer jump side to side, but there was no clicking, and no pursuit of additional information.

"Twelve thousand to carry someone else's baby for nine months and then give it up?"

She nodded, bit her lower lip.

Earl was indignant. "Eighteen thousand? That's the highest? How much are you getting?"

"Twenty-five," Darlene said.

"Well, that's better than eighteen, but it still sounds low to me!"

Darlene turned and looked at him. "See, I think so too. But look at these numbers! I don't want Ryan thinking he can just go online and pull a cheaper—" she fumbled for the right word, "you know, carrier, off some Web site and the hell with Tiffany and me!"

He had forgotten Tiffany. Even though he had taken her to preschool with Darlene this morning, he had not given her a thought in relationship to Darlene's intentions as a gestational carrier. "Here," he instructed gently as he slid the mouse out from under her hand. "Let's try another site."

Four sites later, they were cautiously optimistic, having found carriers asking as much as thirty. "And you've got value-added," Earl enthused, completely forgetting her inexperience. "It would cost him thousands more if he goes through one of those agencies. And you're here! If he gets someone out of town, there's travel expenses. They won't be there for the sonograms . . . even the delivery will be somewhere else. I don't think they'll like that."

He couldn't remember her looking shocked before, though he had certainly noticed her sadness when she moved into the Ladies Farm after Jimmy stole her car. Now, though, she seemed confused, bewildered, even a little frightened, as if he had exposed dangers she hadn't seen before. "How . . . how would you tell him that?" she asked.

He grinned. "Oh, that part's easy, you don't tell him anything, you show him." The furrow in her brow grew deeper and he thought he would do anything to smooth that high, pale forehead back to perfection. "Look," said Earl, clicking open his spreadsheet. "We'll lay it out for him, them, I guess, in dollars and cents. Why you're worth more. We'll let them draw the conclusion. You're someone they know, right?"

She nodded.

"They can trust you; when you say you don't smoke, they know that's true. And they've seen Tiffany—" she shook her head, "no? well you can take her over there, so they know you've had a healthy kid. There's no travel expenses, no negative history . . . and the beauty of it is, you put it all on the charts, in color if you want. Dot points for every advantage. They'll be begging to pay you more!"

He knew he was overselling, but just the softening of her gaze made it worthwhile. "So," she asked, "you think I should meet her . . . Jill?"

"Is that the wife?"

Darlene nodded.

"Hell—I mean, excuse me—of course you should!" The *excuse me* just popped out, he knew it sounded dorky, apologizing for his language, like she hadn't heard everything in the book, right from her own mother if you thought about it, but sometimes he couldn't help it.

"Because I didn't ask him." Her eyes grew lively, and a smile played around her mouth. "I just figured, fuck it, I should meet someone before I get her egg put in me! So," she took a breath, remembering, "I called her. This morning!"

"And are you meeting her?"

Darlene nodded. "That is," she looked down at the keyboard, "if I can get a ride into Fort Worth." She tilted her head to one side.

"Maybe I'll ask Kat," she said, but even Earl knew she was hinting for him to drive her.

Shoot! He wasn't that thick!

Kat was sitting at the desk that used to be Pauline's and was keying expenditures into the computer when Darlene called. "I called his wife," she said.

"Whose wife?" Kat asked; then, knowing who had driven Tiffany to preschool, asked, "Earl's? I thought he was divorced."

"Earl? No! Jill Plummer! Ryan's wife!"

"You called Jill Plummer?" Kat tried to remember Della, in the next room, but her voice still rose. "Jill Plummer?"

"She doesn't know anything about me and Ryan," Darlene whispered. "That's not why I was calling. But I want to look at her. I want to know whose egg's going in my body."

"Well," Kat advised, "you'd better let her think you're as worried about whose sperm's going in. She might wonder otherwise. And why are you whispering?"

"Oh, I'm at Earl's. He's just making a pit stop, so I thought I'd check in. Rita needs to pick Tiffany up at preschool while I'm at this meeting."

"Well, let me just transfer your call to Rita so you can explain what she needs," Kat retorted, then grinned at the image of Earl, hitching up his pants and excusing himself: *Gotta make a pit stop.*

"Well, you don't need to get huffy." Darlene was still whispering. "I just thought you'd want to know I called Ryan's wife."

"Well, that is mighty interesting," Kat conceded.

"She didn't know who I was."

"That's a good thing, considering." Kat worked at keeping her own voice low.

"I don't mean about me and Ryan. I mean she didn't know I'm her carrier. Ryan hasn't told her."

"She said that?"

"No, but I could tell. When I said my name, she just said 'yes?' you know, like I was selling long distance, or portrait photography."

"So she didn't know your name," Kat summarized. "But she probably does know what you'll be doing for her. Right?"

"Sure. I guess so."

"You're sure? Or you guess so?"

"Are you a detective or what? I don't know. I'm meeting her at three, I'll find out then. Can I please speak to Rita?"

"I was only asking," Kat said. "Anyway, be careful with this." Something else occurred to her. "Does Ryan know you're meeting?"

"I guess . . ." Darlene's voice grew firm. "I don't know. But I'd bet yes from the way my beeper's gone off twice with 911 calls from him."

"Are you going to call him back?" Kat looked up to see Della leaning against the doorway.

"Sure. But not too soon. Earl says it's good not to let him get too sure of me before we settle on the price."

Kat shook her head and frowned at Della, but made no direct reply. "Let me ring back to the salon," Kat said.

"Who's she calling?" Della asked laconically.

"Who is *who* calling?"

"*Whom* is who calling. Darlene. Don't be coy."

Kat ignored her friend's irritated look. Della often looked irritated, often was irritated; you couldn't run your life by it. Besides, Kat wanted her take on this.

"Ryan Plummer, M.D., the slime our baby Darlene was humping a few years back before she took up with Jimmy the wonder boy."

Della frowned. "That's eons in Darlene-years. Why's she calling him? Are we having a shoot-out? Do we need to warn Rita and Dave?"

"Absolutely not! And don't let Darlene know I told you, either. It's just that you overheard."

"Overheard *what*?"

"Ryan asked our baby girl to be a gestational carrier for himself and his wife, Jill."

Opening such a huge topic required a seated conversation for Della, who flopped herself down on the saggy sofa that occupied the wall below the front window. "What do they need a carrier for? God! It sounds like a disease." Della lowered her voice to newscaster pitch. "A gestational carrier was apprehended today just outside the Sydonia city limits. She is accused of spiriting away zygotes valued at half a million dollars."

"Obviously, this is a chore they can't do themselves," Kat said. She glanced around, but she knew that Rita was booked all morning and wouldn't be appearing till lunchtime. "From what she told me, they've already got the embryos frozen, they just need her to actually carry the pregnancy."

Della considered this. "She's probably a good choice. Healthy as a horse." She twisted her hair around her finger. "Pregnancy didn't slow her down at all, according to Rita. How much is she getting for this adventure?"

"Now you really can't tell Rita," Kat warned, but Della just shook her head.

"Like Rita won't know," she shot back.

"Twenty-five thousand." Kat said no more, anxious for Della's assessment.

"That sounds so puny, for nine months of your life. Not to mention the stretch marks and hemorrhoids."

Kat nodded. Della never tried to spare her feelings as the only childless one among them. As far as Della was concerned, it was up to you to speak up if a conversation hurt your feelings or presumed an experience you didn't have. Kat preferred that treatment to the whispers and quick hushings that had greeted her for years after the supposed death of her premature infant. Della's behavior showed respect.

"I suppose it's a fortune to Darlene," Della speculated. Kat nodded. "You know," and now Della stretched out, her head resting on the rolled sofa arm so that her hair fell off the other side in an uneven fringe of high-tech auburn against the sofa's faded blue pinstripe, "it'll be fun to see Darlene with Alana and her gang."

Della had insisted on booking the Hutto house for a group of Orthodox Jewish women in the spring and took particular delight in trying to picture the Ladies Farm and environs through their eyes.

"Well, it's a study retreat," Kat pointed out. "Maybe they'll study Darlene."

"Not to mention Earl. Are we going to get him out of there?" Della asked.

Kat shrugged. "Not till we go to settlement. And that's hanging on Gladys and Ray. They don't have to do anything till June according to our agreement."

"And that would be fine," Della said, "if they hadn't left the house vacant till then. It's driving me nuts."

Kat sighed. It was an old argument, and one that had not changed. Gladys and Ray Hutto hadn't expected to move so quickly, and they were reluctant to deed the property until they were sure they were really settled and wanted to move their household things. Meanwhile, Earl was house-sitting, and the plans for turning the place into a retreat were on hold. Which would have been okay, Kat pointed out every time they had this discussion, if Della hadn't taken Alana's deposit for a retreat in May.

Now, though, she waved a hand in the air. "The place is clean, Earl's a good caretaker, all we have to do is move out the furniture, put Earl up here for a few days, stock the place with fruits and vegetables and let them say their mumbo-jumbo over the kitchen."

"They're going to make our kitchen kosher," Della replied primly.

"Whatever." Kat had little use for religious ritual, though she had no objection to accommodating Alana and her friends, who were bringing in their own pots and pans, as well as meats and cheeses shipped over from Dallas. The young women from New York primarily wanted a place to be left alone in between women-only sessions of hiking, massages, and crafts classes, all of which the Ladies Farm was happy to provide. Evidently, they thought it would be exciting to tour Texas, and were proceeding on from the Ladies Farm to San Antonio and then the Big Bend.

Kat turned back to posting invoices, flipping on the *Num Lock* and keying in dates and amounts. "Is this discussion over?" Della asked from the sofa. Kat could tell from her voice that she was still prone.

"I thought so," Kat replied, not turning. "We agree twenty-five thousand's way too low for breeding baby Plummers; I don't know what else we've got to do except fret over the kid."

"That's Rita's job," Della observed. "She'll do plenty of it when the time comes."

Chapter Six

Darlene stood outside the Starbucks and looked in. The weather had warmed up, and she had left her coat in Earl's car, opting for a leggy look in a lime mini. It was a little spring-colored, she knew, but it was together, especially with the black turtleneck and black tights. She wished the suit jacket were lined, but no one would see that it wasn't if she kept it zipped.

The woman sitting by herself at the table without even a cup of coffee in front of her had to be Ryan's wife. She was just sitting, watching the door, not even pretending to be interested in a magazine or a date book. Darlene straightened up, tugged a little on her bolero jacket, and pushed the door open.

She walked straight to the table. "Mrs. Plummer?"

The woman stood, towering over Darlene. "Yes. Jill, please." She stuck a hand out as if they were businessmen, and Darlene shook it.

"Jill," Darlene echoed. "Hi."

Jill waited for her to sit down before she seated herself. Too late, Darlene thought about getting coffee, but decided to let it go for a few minutes. She didn't like coffee that much anyway.

"Do I look the way you thought?" Darlene asked.

"Pretty much," Jill said. "Ryan said you had real short blond hair, so I knew to look for that." Jill's voice was agreeable, but not that friendly, and Darlene noticed that Jill didn't ask her what she had been looking for, as if everyone in the world was supposed to recognize Jill Plummer and already knew how she looked.

"Ryan beeped me this morning," Darlene offered in the way

Earl had instructed. "But by the time I could call him, he was at the hospital."

"Yes," Jill said. "He missed his morning visits, so he ran over at lunch."

Earl had insisted Darlene bring this up so that Ryan didn't think she was avoiding him. "You want him to think everything's going along until you sit down to talk about more money," Earl had told her in the car. Darlene agreed, but she didn't like making these explanations to Jill. She could just tell Ryan when she talked to him. "Anyway, he can call me tomorrow—" Darlene caught herself, "or tonight from home, of course."

Jill nodded, and looked at her expectantly. Other than getting this look at Jill, Darlene wasn't sure why she had set this up. Except, or course, that she wanted to know how much Jill knew about her. "You know," Darlene said, "I already have one child, Tiffany."

Jill nodded. "Ryan told me. He said she's healthy and that you had a trouble-free pregnancy."

Darlene brushed at her hair with her fingers. "Oh yeah. Real healthy." She thought about taking out her pictures, but decided to wait. "I take real good care of myself when I'm pregnant. I cut out coffee and alcohol—not that I drink much anyway—and I've never smoked. Have you?"

Jill shook her head no, smiling slightly as if the thought amused her.

Darlene looked around at the bistro tables and wondered if she was overdressed. Jill wore a sweater and jeans, with half boots and a Fendi bag. The jeans annoyed Darlene a little, as if Jill didn't think the occasion important enough to dress a bit. Actually, Jill was annoying Darlene a lot.

"Look," she said, "I'd like to know why you're doing this and—" she thought back to Earl's advice, "I'd really appreciate it if you could share your expectations with me."

Jill looked a little startled but she didn't speak immediately, as if she was thinking really hard before she answered. "I—Ryan and I—just want another baby. It's not very complicated." Jill looked straight at Darlene, who was thinking that if she hadn't been raised in a salon, she wouldn't have known that the honey-toned highlights in Jill's shimmering mane had been added, probably by someone as skilled as Rita.

Darlene shrugged, feigned innocence. "So why don't you just get pregnant?"

Jill studied her hands. "Sometimes it's not that simple. I—we—had a lot of trouble the last time, we needed, um, help from a fertility specialist."

This was new. Darlene tried to make eye contact, but Jill was still looking down. "Was that Dr. Lantana?"

"Lantinatta."

"Lantinatta," Darlene repeated. "So he helped you before?" Jill nodded. "You know, I've got an appointment with him next week. After I see the psychologist. What's he like?"

"Oh! Nick?" Jill looked unprepared. "He's really sweet, he was friends with my dad, golfing buddies." She smiled at Darlene. "And he loves Ryan. Ryan refers cases to him all the time, even though Ryan doesn't really do, you know, obstetrics or anything. You'll like him."

"Good," said Darlene. "I like Dr. Kaplan, too."

"Oh, yeah," Jill said. "I've met her. She's nice, too."

Now that she held Jill's gaze, Darlene watched her closely. "So these eggs, embryos, you've got in the deep freeze, they're from last time?"

It was hard to judge color in someone so tawny, but something changed as Jill shook her head. "No, they . . . well, maybe in a way." She smiled in a sad way at Darlene, almost apologetically. "We, I had a lot of trouble conceiving and then I got real sick." Darlene thought she saw the lower lip tremble, but maybe not. "I miscarried once, and then, with Taylor, they just put me to bed and I stayed there." She took a deep breath. "So then, Ryan thought—Ryan and I—it would be better if I just had my tubes tied. I mean, he was just thinking about my health and everything, but, just in case, we had these eggs extracted and fertilized in the lab, Nick's lab, and now," she shrugged again, "I want another baby so much, and Ryan doesn't think I should be pregnant, and that's why he asked you."

It confirmed Darlene's belief that these rich bitches—with necks so long they didn't even have to roll down their turtlenecks—were too high-strung to be healthy mothers. Their Caribbean tans and sculpted arms masked some inner decay that prevented the easy stride through pregnancy Darlene herself had enjoyed. It's why there's so much trailer trash, Darlene told herself now. We know how to fuck and have babies.

"Did he tell you he was asking me?" Darlene asked.

"I think he was afraid you'd say no. I don't think he wanted to tell me until he knew you were going to do it."

"Well, I haven't exactly said yes," Darlene cautioned, mostly because it was what Earl would term an opportunity. Personally, Darlene thought putting your feet in the stirrups was a pretty big sign of commitment.

"I know," Jill said. "And I guess I'm just getting used to it, too."

"Getting used to what?"

"The idea. You know: a carrier. Ryan and I had a long talk this morning about it," now there definitely was color coming up in her face and Darlene pictured a discussion that did not feature much clothing, "and I know when I went through all that to have the eggs removed—you have to have shots and then the procedure itself is very painful—I was basically saying it's okay. Even so, it's one thing to pay to have all this stuff done, and to go through it all, and it's another to say, okay, now, I really want another woman to have my baby for me. I mean," and here her eyes widened and Darlene saw gray and brown and green that gave a different meaning to the term *hazel*, "I guess I'm jealous in a way." Jill smiled. "Even though it takes place in a laboratory, it's so personal, so intimate, it's something I shared with Ryan, and now you're doing it." Suddenly the smile disappeared and tears filled the hazel eyes. "And everything right now . . . it's so hard, and I want to have our baby myself. Just Ryan and me!"

Darlene pictured a U-Haul. First went the clothes—hers and Tiffany's—and then the furniture: glass shelves and sectional sofa, triple dresser and king-size bed. Somehow the new car, a Mustang or a Celica, was upended into the trailer, and then, in a feat of unearthly powers of compression, the apartment—no, her duplex!—ripped whole from its foundation, deposited into the flatbed as it rolled away, farther and farther away from Sydonia and the room she and her daughter would share forever at the Ladies Farm.

Darlene put her hand over Jill's and scrunched down a little so she could look up into Jill's downcast eyes. "It will be just you and Ryan. I'm just a carrier, like a . . . a . . . baby-sitter."

Jill stared at her.

"Really!" Darlene enthused, impressed with her own inventiveness. "Your baby now, Taylor? You leave him with baby-sitters sometimes, don't you, when you and Ryan go out, or if you go on vacation?" She took a guess. "Maybe even just to go to aerobics, right? Where is he now?" Darlene read Jill's silent stare as agreement.

"This is the same thing. It's your baby. Yours and Ryan's. Just like Taylor. You're just asking me, hiring me, really, to take care of him for a while."

Darlene resisted the urge to sit back and bask in the glow of good feeling. Instead, she concentrated on Jill, who was still staring at her. Darlene smiled sympathetically. "Jill," she said, "let me show you pictures of Tiffany." She dug into her one good tote and fished out the album. "See," she started, "that's her first sonogram. See . . . here!" She slipped the print from its plastic protector. "See what we wrote on the back: everything perfect!"

Jill smiled politely, but didn't reach for a closer look at the print.

"And here's me," Darlene continued smoothly, laying the print flat and turning the page to show herself at nine months. "Fresh air," she noted of the profile shot next to her Camaro. She pointed to her hand down near the corner. "And bottled water, too!" This brought a smile from Jill.

When Darlene turned the page, Jill leaned forward a little to study Tiffany as a newborn. "Let me get you a cup of coffee," Darlene offered, sliding the album over to Jill. And with that, Darlene headed for the counter, where she treated both Jill and herself to two grandes, even bringing the milk and sugar to the table so Jill wouldn't have to get up and fix it herself.

"I got decaf," Darlene assured her, settling back in.

"These are wonderful!" Jill said. "Tiffany's adorable. You must have done something right."

"Thanks," Darlene said, glad she had removed the beauty pageant shots. You never knew what someone would think of that.

The two of them doctored their coffee in silence, Jill still smiling at the closed album. "How old is Taylor?" Darlene asked her.

"Twenty-eight months," Jill answered automatically.

"Oh, the terrible twos," Darlene said, but Jill just nodded and kept quiet.

"Is he in preschool? Since we moved back to Sydonia, I've been taking Tiffany to preschool where my friend, Lakeesha, used to work. Lakeesha's real smart, she's my partner now, in the transcription business. She grew up all over the world because her dad was in the army, and she says preschool's about the best thing you can do for your kid—preschool and nursing. She's the one who told me to stop drinking—I mean any alcohol at all—when I was pregnant," Darlene rattled on, trying to get away from the nursing part, which might upset Jill because she would never do it for this new baby, even if she had for Taylor, which Darlene doubted because she suspected Jill would have trouble with that too if she had so much trouble being pregnant.

"Lakeesha's black, African American, and neither one of her babies could drink milk, they had lactose intolerance, so she had to get this very expensive soy formula, which is a real pain to mix." Darlene paused for a moment, remembering those days, when she and Lakeesha had both been pregnant together, and they used to spend hours flipping through the baby magazines at the Mini-Mart picking out clothes for their babies. Then she realized she'd gone right back to milk as a subject and hurried on.

"So, anyway, Tiffany loves preschool, especially since she loves to entertain—sing and dance—and they always pick her to do solos in the little skits and things they do."

Jill sat warming her hands on the cup of coffee, but she hadn't drunk any yet. Darlene switched gears. "My sister, Carla, has three kids, so at least Tiff has lots of cousins. I didn't mean for her to be an only child, but she'll have to wait for brothers and sisters till I find a husband who'll stick around for a while!"

This brought a little smile to Jill, and even a tiny chuckle. "I figure, 'best I can do for Tiffany right now is let her see her cousins all the time, and play with Lakeesha's kids—she's got two now—till I get out on my own again and things are a little more stable."

Jill nodded. "I thought Taylor would have his brothers and sisters from Ryan's first marriage, but they're so much older."

"I know," Darlene said, then thought that maybe she *shouldn't* know. "I know what you mean. It's good if they're a little closer in age." She tilted her head and smiled. "How many children are there, from Ryan's first marriage?"

"Great save!" Earl congratulated her when she related the conversation on the ride home. He insisted that she tell him everything, line by line, and if she tried to summarize, he interrupted her, saying things like, "Tell me exactly what she said," or "How'd she look then?"

"And you left it that you'll go to the counselor and then get back to Ryan?"

"Yes. I already told you!" Darlene didn't know why Earl was so elated. She felt kind of a letdown, but when she tried to explain it to

Earl, he informed her that it was only because she had set no clear goals for the meeting so she had no sense of accomplishment.

"Look," he explained, glancing at her from behind the impossibly huge wheel of his Expedition, "you wanted to see what she looked like, and you did. You wanted to know if Ryan had told her, and you made sure he did. You wanted to know if she'll go through with it, and that's yes. It's Ryan who's calling the shots here, so now you go back to him to talk about the money."

"She didn't actually say yes," Darlene corrected, but she didn't want to go into it with him. She also didn't want to go through the rest of the agenda: what Jill knew about her, what Jill might do if she found out. Darlene trusted Earl, but he was simple and there was no point getting into all this with him. "She said she's getting used to the idea. She didn't know anything about it till this morning."

"And now she thinks it's the same as hiring a sitter," Earl countered. "I'm telling you, she's in. And he's in. The only thing left is the money. So you need to prepare for that."

"And the counselor," Darlene reminded him.

"Oh, that's just a bunch of mumbo-jumbo. They're just looking to see that you won't go psycho on them."

"I know that," Darlene said.

"And that you'll let them decide about reduction and termination."

"What do you mean, reduction?"

"You know: if they implant two embryos and decide they only want one."

"You mean like an abortion?"

He stole a glance at her. "Well, yes. Didn't you read those contracts you printed out?"

Darlene wanted to point out that she hadn't had all afternoon to study the subject, the way he had, but she stayed quiet.

"They don't terminate the whole pregnancy, like if something was wrong. Just, say, they decide one is better than two, like one could be healthy, but maybe with the two there, they won't both thrive, they'd have low birth weight and maybe serious problems. So they pick the healthier one and take out the other one."

"That'd be a funny feeling," Darlene said, thinking about it. "Knowing you were a twin but only one of you made it."

"Well, it's up to Ryan and Jill. That's the deal on all these things."

"I guess you're an expert on this, too." Probably he'd been on the Web the whole time since he dropped her off. She bet Earl knew a dozen places he could go to log on.

"It pays to be thorough." His voice was genial.

Give it up, she told herself. "You're right," she said gently. Then she settled in for the rest of the ride. The hills were bare and brown, and the few cars they passed already had their lights on. He's just trying to help, she told herself, but she didn't want any more conversation. She wanted to think.

Earl made it sound as if the only question was how much Ryan and Jill would pay. But what if they didn't want to pay more? What if they decided to find someone else?

There was something about a big, warm car in a cold dusk. Warm and safe, the way you would be if you had a big house and could close the curtains and switch on a lamp, the way they did in the commercials for the electric company. Darlene snuggled down in her seat and sighed.

Why had Ryan made it sound as if Jill was pushing him? And what if Jill decided she couldn't go through with it at all?

Then you're no worse off than you were, Darlene told herself. You and Tiffany can stay at the Ladies Farm until you get some money together. Dave will fix the Camaro. Earl will keep trying to help you . . . maybe he can put together a new system for you. Kat will find you more clients if you ask. It'll just take longer.

Chapter Seven

When he told her he'd meet her in the mid-cities, Kat knew it had to be bad. But she didn't insist that he tell her over the phone, or via fax or e-mail. She found the appointed restaurant in Grapevine, just north of the airport, and she waited at a table, nursing a Perrier and lime.

He was out of uniform, in jeans and a knit shirt covered by a red down-filled vest, and it took her a second to recognize him till she realized that this time he was wearing glasses. "I appreciate your meeting me here," he said. "We're scouting a new office out this way, close to the airport, and I didn't want to make you wait."

"Well, thank you for that." She watched him slide into the booth. He unzipped the vest, but left it on. When the waitress appeared, he ordered coffee and pie; then, when they were alone again, he put a large envelope on the table. "There's a picture." He nodded at the envelope. "A letter."

Kat reached for the envelope.

"She's living with a family in Virginia."

Kat fumbled at the metal clasp and pulled out the photo. It was a close-up of a girl with a misshapen face. She wore glasses and her head tilted to one side and seemed stuck directly onto her shoulders, one of which was higher than the other. She was wearing a white ruffled blouse and she was smiling.

"They call her Laurie," he said. "I didn't read the letter, but they told me they'd be okay with a visit."

"Dr. Lan—"

"Why don't you call me Nick," he suggested.

* * *

Charlie Ondine had backed the Camaro around the side of the station so that Dave's customers would not be greeted by the scavenged reminder of the brutality possible on their highways. The car's body still sparkled from the paint job applied by one of Jimmy's friends two years previously, but the wheels, with their custom covers, were gone, and the right front fender was crumpled in a way that spoke volumes about a drunk driver sliding off a highway and into a ditch.

The trunk still held the sack of Tiffany's outgrown clothes that Darlene had been saving to give to Carla for Maria, but the pageant costumes were gone, probably sold to a resale shop for a fraction of their worth. In the front, from the rearview mirror, dangled the scarlet tassel Jimmy had presented to her the day after she confessed to him how cheated she felt that she had dropped out of high school to marry Jason.

Of course, that had occurred in the days he had been trying to court her a little, and he had tied the tassel around his dick and invited her to a private graduation ceremony all their own. Jerk, Darlene thought now, looking at the crumpled fender and smashed headlamp. The passenger door wouldn't even open. The turf crammed up in the wheel well could re-sod someone's front yard.

"Well that boy didn't do anything halfway," Rita chirped. She stood there with her hands on her hips and leaned a little into Dave.

"It's not that bad," Dave said, but Darlene knew he was just trying to be nice. He stepped forward and ran his fingers along the fender, as if there were just a little dent he could coax out. "Here," he motioned to Earl. "Let's crack the hood."

Dave was an engine man. Darlene knew that if he thought the thing would run, he didn't care about the body around it. He'd put a green fender on her midnight blue Camaro and smile while he listened to the engine hum.

And Earl! She watched him trying to help Dave pry the hood open. What did Earl know about cars?

"Come on, baby," Rita said suddenly, wrapping her arms around her own midsection. "Let's go inside while they fiddle with that thing."

Darlene started to tell her Tiffany was still at school, but, of course, Rita was addressing her, not Tiff. "It's cold out here," Darlene agreed, turning and walking to the front of the Quick Stop.

Inside, she wandered over to the nacho cheese dispenser, where you could scoop as many jalapenos as you wanted over your chips and then, with a press of the lever, drown them in hot yellow cheese. Lakeesha's daughter, Sarita, had a fondness for jalapenos, which Darlene attributed to the fact that Lakeesha's husband, Eddie, was Mexican. But Lakeesha swore it was because she ate so many hot things when she was pregnant with Sarita.

"What're you smiling at?" Rita asked her, coming over to stare at the cheese dispenser.

"Nothing," Darlene said. Then, "When you were pregnant with me, did you eat anything special? You know, like cravings?"

"I couldn't eat anything when I was pregnant with you," Rita said. "Most of the time I was so sick poor Carla had to take care of herself and pour Wendell his whiskey."

"Did you drink?"

"No," snapped Rita. "I didn't smoke either." She tilted her head to one side, thinking back. "I think by then I had stopped smoking anyway. Didn't do drugs. Didn't smoke. Didn't drink." She grinned. "You'll have to blame it on something else."

Darlene's face grew warm. "I'm not blaming anything! I just wondered."

"Good God, Darlene!" Rita's grin faded. "You're not pregnant again? With that car thief?"

"What if I was?" Darlene retorted. "What difference would that make? Carla has three kids; why can't I?"

"Carla has a husband and a house, even if it is a little one! Carla can feed three children."

"And I can't feed one! Is that what you're saying?"

"I'm saying, even if you could, why would you want to have a baby with that lowlife, Darlene?"

"It wouldn't be with him, exactly," Darlene said. "He's gone. He wouldn't have anything to do with it."

Rita looked around the empty store, picked up a drink cup, and jammed it under the ice machine. "You really are, then?"

Darlene shook her head, looked down. "I don't know, I don't think so. Well," she calculated furiously, "if I am . . . if I am, I'm not so sure—"

Jabbing the cup against the lever, Rita filled her cup with ice, then jerked it over to the Mountain Dew dispenser and filled the cup. Finally, she turned. "What are you saying?" she asked. "Are you saying it might not be Jimmy's?" She squinted at her daughter and Darlene concentrated on keeping her eyes wide and unblinking. "Who the . . . oh, my God! . . . Earl? *Earl*?"

Darlene lowered her eyes, stared at her shoes a second to gather her composure. "It's too early to even know I'm pregnant yet!" she protested, shaking her head. She tried to look fierce. "And I certainly don't need you playing guessing games about who the father might be."

Rita studied her daughter for a moment. "Darlene Marie, you'd better think long and hard about this one."

Darlene rolled her eyes, but said nothing.

"I mean it, Darlene. You might think it's funny, playing with a boy like that, but he's not going to shake loose the way those others do. You have that baby, he's yours for life whether you want him or not."

"I don't see him playing daddy to the son he's got already," Darlene said.

"This won't be the same," Rita predicted. "Trust me."

Jill dressed him carefully, choosing the red corduroy over the blue because it seemed to give him better color. "Let's go see Kathy!" she encouraged, fastening the snaps along the pants legs, careful to avoid the bruises. "Let's go see Kathy and Tammy!"

Taylor gazed up at her but made no sound. Even when she tickled his tummy before sitting him up and holding him in her lap to put on his shoes and socks, his gaze remained steady, appraising.

"What should we take with us?" she asked him. "Huh? Should we take Boynton?"

"Neevil!" Taylor replied. "Neevil!"

"You want to take Evil Knievel for a car ride?" She smoothed on the socks, pulled on the athletic shoes with the flashing lights at the heels. The plush toy modeled like a man on a motorcycle had been a joke, but once Ryan named it Evil Knievel, Taylor had refused to part with it. "Let's find Neevil, then," she told the boy. "And let's take a book, too, just in case we want to read."

He was already sliding off her lap, lurching toward the shelves piled high with toys. She had put the thing there during his nap, and it gladdened her that Taylor could stagger to a toy on the other side of the room. She brushed off his torpor; he was still waking up. She knew he was getting better.

At the clinic, Kathy drew samples through the central line and confirmed Jill's expectations. Taylor's red cell count was higher, but only a little.

"I knew it," Jill told Ryan, who had met them there. They watched Kathy suspend the bag of red cells on the stand in preparation for Taylor's transfusion. "I could tell he was getting better."

She hated the look Ryan gave her, as if he pitied her ignorance. She knew that the transfusions always raised his red cell count. But this time it had held for three days! That meant something, no matter what the doctors—even Ryan—thought. But she kept her thoughts to herself and let Ryan give her a quick squeeze before she sat next to the bed and began reading to Taylor as the first of the transfusions made its way into her son.

"Moo! Moo!" she read. "Can you say that, Taylor? Moo, moo?"

He sat back against the pillows, still because Kathy, the love of his two-year-old life, had told him he needed to stay still, and he whispered, "Moo, moo." The sheets were sprigged with dancing hippopotami, and the pillowcase looked ridiculously gay behind his pale hair. He moved only his mouth when he spoke, and even while he answered his mother, his eyes followed Kathy, who studied his face and stroked his hand as she searched for the first signs of adverse reaction.

At least there are no more needles, Jill thought as they all watched her son. The port in his chest might be cumbersome, but Taylor hardly noticed, and it meant he rarely got stuck with needles.

Ryan stood at the foot of the bed the way she had seen him stand dozens of times when the patient was a friend and they stopped in together to pay a nonprofessional visit. Even then, she could see Ryan taking it all in: the flutter in the eye, the sallow color, the drab hair. Jill was so proud of her husband; he was so smart. Even her father had been impressed with him. But she wondered, watching him standing at the end of his son's bed, what reached him. Surely he loved Taylor. She knew he did as surely as she knew he shared her late-night tears. But the detached part, the medical Ryan, she called it to herself, was always watching and measuring. One of us has to, she told herself. He's looking out for us all.

Taylor stirred a little. She hadn't believed it the first time, when they told her it would happen, but now she looked for it: the new blood revived him, almost as if he were waking from a deep sleep. He would begin to stir a little, and his eye movements grew rapid. His breathing deepened and his face gained color. Jill looked quickly to Ryan for confirmation, and the slight flicker, the pressing together of his lips told her it was going as hoped. Leaning forward, she took Taylor's hand in both of hers. "That feels better now, doesn't it, honey?"

"Yes." He took a deep breath, then reached with his other hand to grab Evil Knievel and hold it up for her to see.

"Evil Knievel's feeling better too, isn't he?" she said.

He nodded, holding the stuffed toy aloft and turning it for her to see where they had glued a tube to the cyclist's chest to mimic his own line.

"Oh!" Jill said. "He's feeling much better!"

Ryan slipped around to her side of the bed, leaned over to touch his son's head, and gave a little shake to Evil Knievel. "He's getting that good, slimy green color back," Ryan told Taylor. "Even the chrome in his bike's starting to sparkle."

Taylor giggled. "It's slimy! Slimy!"

There was a cocktail of drugs, including a pain reliever and a marrow stimulant. "We're not doing that one today," Tammy said, flicking her fingers against the filter on the line that ran to Taylor. She wriggled her nose and smiled at Taylor. "You get a vacation, buddy."

Taylor smiled. If Taylor could have two women, Jill knew Tammy would be the second. Tammy and Kathy obviously filled his dreams, and Jill wondered how he would ever return to the immature flirts of his preschool.

"What's up?" Ryan asked.

Tammy shook her head. "No cocktail on the menu today. Dr. Ballangee."

Ryan nodded, looked at Jill. "Let me see if he's around."

When Dr. Ballangee finally responded to his page, Jill and Ryan were entertaining Taylor in the large playroom attached to the outpatient clinic. The hematologist, somber and deliberate, stepped easily among the toys and children covering the carpet and occupying the kid-size chairs and tables. Jill and Ryan had staked out a corner lined with a sort of beanbag sectional from which Taylor threw foam missiles—footballs, basketballs, baseballs—at his father.

Dr. Ballangee nodded at Jill and Ryan, then held his arms out to Taylor, who leapt up to him. Taylor babbled a little at the older doc about throwing and catching while the physician examined his eyes and ruffled his hair. Quickly, the toddler slid down to the floor to chase the balls that Ryan rolled across the corner. Jill looked up at the specialist, and he sat next to her on the sofa.

"I wish I had better news," he began. "But the rest of the tests came back and they confirm what we thought: it's not viral; it's pernicious."

"But his blood count is up," Jill said. "He is responding."

Dr. Ballangee nodded. "The transfusions definitely help. But we've got to stop stimulating the marrow."

"You don't think it was an infection at all? Bacterial or viral?" Ryan asked.

The older man shook his head. "With viral hemoporosis, you see a much swifter response, and stimulating the marrow produces healthy cells. What we're seeing here is the opposite: the more cells he makes, the more porous."

"Well what else is there?" Jill asked. "Isn't there some other medication?" Ryan had told her that the metallic taste rising in her mouth was the taste of bile, but that knowledge did not assuage the bitterness.

Dr. Ballangee shook his head. "We have medications to help preserve the life of the cells he receives through transfusion. But this is so rare, there's so little research . . . you understand: the body, Taylor's marrow, will continue to produce the porous red cells; what we've seen happen is that the porous cells crowd out the transfused cells, that they circulate, but fail to pick up or deliver any oxygen."

"Well, there must be something, someone else . . ."

Dr. Ballangee rubbed at his forehead, looked down at his shoes. "There is some chance, you know, that . . . we see about a thirty percent spontaneous remission in hemoporosis; of those, over half seem to recover fully at five years." Dr. Ballangee looked at Ryan. "And there's Josh Wittstein, at NIH."

"I've spoken with him," Ryan said. He took Jill's hand. "And Jill and I have talked about it."

"Is he even ready?" Dr. Ballangee asked. "Approvals, funding?"

Jill turned toward Ryan. He hadn't said anything about that.

"He will be," Ryan said. "Probably before we're ready."

"Well," Ballangee said, "let's hold off as long as we can. Build Taylor up. And pray he goes into full remission so we don't even need transplant."

Before the first transfusion, Kathy had explained that the blood transfused to Taylor would be cold; that even though they warmed it prior to transfusion, it was less than normal body temperature and that while there was no long-term effect, it could cause discomfort. And Jill, even though Taylor hadn't complained, had imagined cold circulating through his little heart, fingers of frost clutching at his insides to the point of pain. She thought, listening to Dr. Ballangee, that she must have drawn the cold into herself, to spare her son, and that what she felt now, as this respected specialist told her that there was no defense except prayer and experimentation against the malformation of her son's red blood cells, was the cold stored from all Taylor's transfusions, unleashed throughout her body and freezing everything.

Chapter Eight

Ryan closed the door before he returned Wittstein's page. They had been playing phone tag all week and he had to respond, even from home, with Jill and Taylor in the kitchen. Thankfully, he had always returned pages from his den—how else could he have dallied with Darlene except to let Jill think he wanted to avoid any compromise of patient confidentiality—and she barely noticed when he carried his tumbler from the kitchen counter to his desktop.

He sipped his drink before he slid a coaster over the leather inset of his desktop and set the drink down. His father-in-law had introduced him to single-malt scotch, and this particular bottle had been payoff of a bet. Jill knew nothing about Ryan hustling her father on the golf course, and he doubted she'd mind the source of the bottle, but the secrecy increased the pleasure.

Wittstein answered on the first ring, and the scientist wasted no time on pleasantries. "These trials were just approved, we haven't even decided on number of subjects, or locations."

"I imagine finding patients will be a challenge; with a disease this rare, anyone living past three or four has to be in full remission, so you'd have to cull from the ones who fall out of that, or the two-year-olds." While he talked, Ryan reached into the file drawer to his right and pulled out the folder with Taylor's history.

"Finding suitable subjects is an obvious challenge. Though that's one of the advantages of the Web: we can reach every clinic in the world that diagnoses hemoporosis. Even if we get no further than identifying patients, we'll be adding significantly to existing knowledge."

"Not much help for the patients," Ryan said. He drummed his fingers on Taylor's file.

"Practitioners always say that, but they're the first to scream if experimental treatment produces unintended results. A population study might yield clues about the etiology that will save lives later in the process."

Ryan smiled. Wittstein was still the same mild-mannered geek with whom he had shared a lab station through four semesters of chemistry. He imagined Josh, in a wrinkled shirt and a rayon tie, sitting upright behind his government-issue desk, working late in pursuit of obscure diseases in underfunded studies. Poor guy! He didn't even realize that his subjects were obscure, or that his haircut was a disaster.

Ryan knew that plodding trial-and-error by the Josh Wittsteins of the world had been responsible for most of the advances in medical treatment in the past hundred years. And he appreciated Josh's dedication when, Ryan knew, the guy could double or triple his income if he worked for a pharmaceutical firm. Besides, Josh, after all, had coached him through chemistry.

"So, if I have a patient, you want us just to hold on while you get your paperwork in order?" Ryan asked.

"Do you have a patient?"

Ryan smiled at the file, opened it. "Yes."

"And the diagnosis was confirmed?"

"Harry Ballangee."

"Really? Didn't he retire?"

"He cut back on his teaching when he moved to the med school in Fort Worth, but he's still practicing. He's tight with Jill's dad."

"How old?"

Ryan knew he was not asking about Harry Ballangee, and he filled Josh in on Taylor's history, flipping through pages of reports as he spoke. When he finished, there was silence, and Ryan pictured Wittstein scribbling his notes. Ryan filled the pause by reaching for his drink.

"Would the parents consent?" Josh asked finally.

"Yes," Ryan said. "I believe so."

"Do they understand the odds against finding a donor?"

"That's one of the reasons they're so anxious to get qualified, Josh. They're growing their own: *in vitro*."

There was a second or two of silence, and Ryan imagined Josh considering this. "With PGD?"

Ryan smiled, fingered the preimplantation genetic diagnosis report. "They've already done that—they had five embryos, two perfect matches."

"So they'll implant both?"

"Both. Better chance for the pregnancy."

"That would be ideal," Josh finally broke the silence. "An exact match from a full sibling. Perfect. Provided the patient survives until the donor's birth."

"Or until we harvest."

"I can't imagine terminating to get cord blood." Josh's voice had lost all its detachment. "Not that late."

"Well, let's hope we don't have to go down that road," Ryan replied.

"It will be September," Ryan told Jill. "At the earliest. If it's even possible."

"And what do we do until then?"

He had waited until they got Taylor to bed. There had been only wine with dinner, and then one more scotch, which he held in his hand now. Even so, he spoke carefully, not wanting her to move too fast, to see farther than she should. "Well, the medication will help," he said. "And the transfusions."

"I know all that," she said. "It's just so puny."

Ryan set his drink down atop the lingerie chest. They were in Jill's dressing room, an enlarged, carpeted closet with a three-part mirror and two tufted, rose velvet chairs with heart-shaped backs. She had been like a child, clapping her hands and hopping with excitement when she had first seen this room, with its skylight and gilt-edged dressing table. And he had thought, then, that everything would always be good as long as he could give her what she wanted.

"He's used so much blood," he told her. "We ought to get the church to put it in the bulletin, get a few more people to donate." Maybe she'd take the bait and organize a blood drive. "It's not like you can just get more at the store."

"I want him to have my blood," Jill insisted. "It helped him before." She was sitting on the little bench before the dressing table; her earrings, the big gold hoops that flashed against her tawny hair and skin, lay on the tabletop, next to a silver-backed brush and a carafe of filtered water.

"And you'll be able to give again," Ryan assured her. He maintained his post in the doorway, watching her. "But you're not allowed to give more frequently, so we'll still need other donors. And we need to replace what he's used."

"I know. It's only right. I'll send in something for the bulletin. Do you think he'll be okay till September?"

"No promises, Jill. Right now, though, he seems to be getting stronger. If he goes into some sort of crisis, we'll do another exchange."

Jill remained impassive, but he knew she was thinking back to the days surrounding the diagnosis, when they had finally replaced all of Taylor's blood with new blood, then waited in agony to see if his vital organs, or his brain, had been oxygen-starved for too long. It had taken so long to distinguish the disease from anemia, and it had seemed so unlikely that Taylor would not improve with ordinary care, that Taylor had been in danger of stroke or system shutdown by the time they exchanged his blood. Ryan kicked himself, now, for dismissing Jill's fears as the hysterics of a first-time mother.

Ultimately, none of it mattered. Once Taylor stabilized, all they could hope was that the red cells they transfused would counter the cells Taylor produced, cells so porous they delivered no oxygen; that they could keep his blood supply and fluid volume in balance; that he would not have a severe transfusion reaction; and, that his body, the stem cells in his marrow, would stop producing porous cells. At least, thought Ryan now, until we can give him new stem cells.

Jill shook her head and smiled wanly. "Isn't it funny? Two months ago we were evaluating preschools and now we hope he's alert enough to watch cartoons."

"There's something else we have to think about," said Ryan.

"I already have. I don't want Darlene. I know she's perfect, but I want to do this."

"Jill, listen—"

"No, you listen! I don't want someone else pregnant with my child. I want to carry my own child. I called Lantinatta again and he told me that if he implants, he can do a lot more things this time to make the pregnancy easier. He says there's a lot of progress."

"Did he tell you that you can't give blood if you're pregnant? Even for your own child?"

"We've already talked about that! But you've said yourself the blood supply's perfectly safe. And just because you don't match, it doesn't mean someone else won't. Maybe the kids—"

The velvet bench at the dressing table had a low, carved rail along its back. Jill was turned so that her shoulders and her long hair filled the mirror. Facing him, her luminous eyes and upturned face were a plea for him to give her his way.

He rushed forward, knelt next to the bench. "Honey, it is safe, and we'll get whatever transfusions we can. But your mom's the only one who matches, and she's had hepatitis. I even had Ryan Junior tested, since he's seventeen—"

Her arm, braced on the gilt rail, tensed. "You told Kim?"

Shit! There was no end to the ways she could resent Kim for being his first wife! At least this time he had the right answer. "All I did was tell her I'd cover the out-of-pocket for the kids' physicals if I could run their lab work through my office. I don't want the kids to know any more than they have to right now. They're scared enough as it is without telling them about medical experiments and marrow matches."

Jill's breathing grew more regular. "Yeah." Her gaze softened. "Doctor Dad can fix everything." She looked down at his hand still on her arm. "What now?"

"Here," he said, rising to a half-squat to gather her in his arms and help her stand. "Come here." They sank to the rose-colored carpet. "Comfy?" he asked when she nestled against him.

"Not comfy enough to give up," she replied.

"Jill, two out of our five embryos are a perfect match."

"So we could have twins."

"We could. Or we could implant both embryos and get no pregnancy at all. *In vitro's* no sure thing, Jill. Even under optimal conditions."

Jill wriggled out of his embrace. "And my uterus isn't optimal?"

"Jill! We've been through this. Look," he said, "you almost miscarried last time. How are you going to feel if you're two or three months, or six months, and you lose the baby?" Or worse, he thought.

"We could try again." But her voice had lost certainty.

Ryan exhaled slowly, pulled her back to him. "We're going to do everything possible for Taylor. You and I. And Darlene. Because she's perfect. She's young—"

"You think I'm too old?"

"I think you're perfect." He nuzzled her neck. "But you're thirty. She's twenty-three. Every year makes a difference. She's healthy. Actually," he smiled at the memory without her seeing, "I knew her when she was pregnant, she was just bursting with good health."

"You really think this is right?"

"I not only think this is right, I think you think this is right. I think you're just afraid not to insist on getting pregnant yourself."

"She—Darlene—does seem ideal," Jill said. "I mean, what you told me about her is right: she's totally naive, and full of attitude. But she's feisty. And optimistic. I like her."

They half-sat, half-lay on the deep carpet for a few moments, considering. Finally, Jill spoke again. "It's just, you're right: I want to be the one that does this. I mean, I gave birth to Taylor. I want to give birth to the baby who saves him."

"Think of yourself—think of us—as the parents who are bringing this new baby into the world."

"I know what Ballangee says," Jill said as if he hadn't spoken, "but I always think back to that time I was supposed to be on full bed rest and I spent the morning with the decorator trying to get the furniture ordered for Taylor's room. Riding over to those showrooms in Dallas. It was so stupid!"

Ryan thought about the scotch perched atop the lingerie chest at the door, but he dared not turn his head even to look. "Jill, it's nothing you did. Nobody knows what causes this. Taylor was perfectly healthy when he was born."

"You don't know that." The agitation resurfaced in her voice. "It could very well have been something I did, something we don't even think about, like chlorine in the pool or carpet glue, or flavored coffees."

Now he really wanted the scotch. "Jill, it could have been anything, but we'll never know. Millions of women do all the things you did—and far worse—and produce perfectly healthy babies."

"But I didn't."

Ryan sighed. It always came back to this. And none of it mattered. Except that it mattered to Jill. It doesn't matter what else I have to do, he thought. Or what we have to pay Darlene.

"It's probably better this way."

"What?" He shook his head to bring himself back.

"Darlene. I believe what she told me, that she takes care of herself when she's pregnant." She paused. "And it's obvious she wants the money. And her baby is perfectly healthy, isn't she?"

"Tiffany? Oh yeah."

Jill giggled. "What a name!"

"Well, her daughter is a perfect jewel!"

"Is that what she told you?"

"Sort of. Anyway, she's a good mother. She's healthy. Her baby's healthy. We want a paragon of gestational virtue, not an arbiter of good taste."

"We . . . we have to schedule the exam with Lantinatta. As soon as possible."

He nodded. His back was starting to hurt, and he leaned on her a little to straighten himself. But he remained still, determined not to interrupt her.

Jill turned toward him to kiss him. Then she said, "We have to get Darlene's signature on the contract." She spoke rapidly, but in even, thoughtful tones. She was strategizing now, engaged in the campaign, and Ryan knew he was safe.

"Lantinatta requires a psych profile," he reminded her. "For Darlene. I went ahead and scheduled it." He held his breath.

"Good," she said.

Ryan breathed out.

"And we can't tell her," Jill declared. "Not one word," she warned her husband. "Who knows how much she'd hold us up for if she knew," Jill said.

"Not one word," Ryan agreed with his wife.

Like Dr. Kaplan, Elizabeth McCutcheon, Ph.D., was nice to Darlene and very positive about her plans. "You're very focused on your goals for yourself and your daughter," she said.

The two of them sat together on upholstered chairs set before an oak coffee table. Behind them, the floor-to-ceiling windows overlooked a small stand of Bradford pears whose leafless silhouettes mimicked pear shapes. No doubt in a month or two the bare branches would issue clouds of blossoms. An ornate, table-like desk occupied one corner of the office, facing out toward the chairs and the large windows. Darlene could imagine this pleasant, middle-aged woman, with her upswept auburn hair and her silver-rimmed glasses dangling from a chain on her neat bosom, sitting serenely in the high-backed chair, gazing out at the blossoming pears and penning notes in longhand on colored papers, making judgments about people like Darlene who visited her here.

"Well, I kind of have to be focused," Darlene said. "Who else is going to look out for us? Not Jimmy!" She had told the counselor all about Jimmy stealing her car and how she had had to move back in with her mother. Darlene figured Ryan already would have shared that much, so there was no sense trying to keep that part secret.

"And your mother?" asked Dr. McCutcheon. "Will she be helping you?"

Darlene smiled. "Yes and no. I don't think she'll be too thrilled about this—you know, having a baby for someone else—but I moved in with her when I was pregnant with Tiffany, and she supported me the whole time . . . I don't mean money, because I worked right up to my due date. I mean, you know, helping me find work and everything. Even when Jason disappeared and I didn't have insurance because he quit his job and they sent the insurance papers to the wrong place, even then she figured out a way for me to have Tiffany with the same doctor I started with." She tilted her head to one side, looked at the psychologist. "Rita and I don't always get along, but she's smart and she does a lot with what she has. She's a hustler."

"How about you?"

"Oh, I hustle all right!" Darlene tossed her hair a little. "That's when I got into medical transcription, when I was pregnant with Tiff. One of Rita's customers got me the job."

"And if your mother doesn't accept this arrangement . . . if, for instance, she asks you to leave, how will you handle that?"

Darlene knew this was a trick question. She wanted to say that she could manage on her own, that she didn't need Rita, but counselors didn't like that. They wanted you to admit that you needed others and then they wanted you to show how healthy and well-adjusted you were by telling them who in your life you were comfortable asking for help. It shouldn't be a lot of people, Darlene knew; that would show a crippling dependency on others; but she had to demonstrate the existence of a support system. Counselors liked support systems.

"Well, my two closest friends are my sister, Carla, and my friend, Lakeesha. Both of them are married and have children, and they could always squeeze in Tiffany and me." Darlene looked down at her hands and smiled a little half-smile, to look secretive. "And my friend Earl; he lives right across from the Ladies Farm, and I know he'd help me out any way he could because he's been on his own too; he was pretty much raised by his aunt and uncle."

Dr. McCutcheon nodded. "So you've got a strong support system." She leaned forward a little in her chair next to Darlene. "What about Ryan and Jill?"

"Of course I know they'll help me any way they can. But you know, I want to be a partner in this, not a dependent. It's important that the three of us all behave like adults, so we can all do what's best for the child we're creating." Darlene knew she was playing this one just right. "So, yes, I know I can turn to them for extra help if I need it, but I don't expect them to rescue me. I want to fulfill my terms of our agreement, and I know they'll fulfill theirs." She opened her eyes wide. "Hopefully, I won't have to ask for a thing more than that!"

"How long have you known Ryan and Jill?"

"Oh, I've known Ryan a long time!" Darlene said. "He was one of my first customers when I started freelancing. I just met Jill the other day. She seems real nice, too!"

"So you don't know Jill well?"

"Not so far," Darlene said. "But I'm sure we'll get to know each other a lot better. I mean, a thing like this is bound to bring people closer, don't you think?"

Dr. McCutcheon nodded, pursed her lips. She reached for the file on the coffee table and opened it to study its contents. "Have they told you why they need your help?"

"Not in so many words. But she had a tubal ligation. And she had a real bad time, her first pregnancy. I think that's what it is."

Frowning, Dr. McCutcheon turned a little so that she could look out at the bare branches, then turned back to Darlene. "You know, of course, that a tubal ligation would not prevent a woman from having an embryo implanted in her uterus and carrying it to term?"

"Oh, of course." Darlene worked at keeping her voice steady.

Now they got into a contest of silence. She knew that Dr. McCutcheon wanted her to elaborate, but Darlene knew better than to rush in to fill an inquisitive silence. Darlene wasn't going to be lured into chattering on about why Jill and Ryan were hiring her to have a baby when she didn't know why. Damn, Ryan! Why hadn't he told her this about the tubal? Did he think she knew everything medical just because she typed his precious transcripts?

Finally, Dr. McCutcheon yielded. "Well, that might be something you want to discuss with them. Two other issues that are very important in these situations are reduction and termination. Have you had any conversations about these issues?"

At least Ryan, in their long phone conversation the previous evening, had prepped her for this one. Darlene assured the psychologist that she would honor whatever the Plummers' decision would be concerning terminating the pregnancy and that she, herself, had had an abortion in high school and then gone on to have a healthy pregnancy. "We won't implant more than two embryos," Darlene assured Dr. McCutcheon. "And Ryan says they're pretty comfortable with the idea of twins, so that probably won't be a problem, but they'll be the ones to say."

"What does Jill say? About a reduction?"

"Well, I've talked mostly to Ryan." Darlene paused to look thoughtful. "And I guess I just assume he's talked with her. But you know, it's up to them anyway, so whatever they work out between them, I'll accept."

"It's unusual for the husband to take the lead in this. Usually it's the wife."

"Is it?" Darlene didn't want to sound too guarded. "I suppose I've spoken more with Ryan because I've known him for so long. My mother's friend, Katherine Naylor, referred him to me as a client."

If this woman knew Kat, she gave no indication. "Well, we've had a good talk. What I'd like you to do for me now is complete a personality assessment—a standard multiple-choice inventory—that will help me complete your profile. It's something we ask everyone to do." Dr. McCutcheon stepped out for a moment and returned with the receptionist. "Kelly will get you started on the assessment." The psychologist held out her hand. "It's been a pleasure talking with you, Darlene. I wish you much success down the road."

There was a second door to the office, and it led to a hallway and a small room with a desk, a chair, and a window in the door. "This is pretty self-explanatory," Kelly told her, before leaving her with a number two pencil, a test book, and a scannable answer sheet. The printed instructions directed Darlene to read each statement and then rate how much she agreed or disagreed with the statement on a scale of one to four.

There were a lot of statements about health with which Darlene knew to disagree a lot. She had to chuckle when she came to the one that said, *I've seen a lot of doctors over the years,* but she resisted the urge to "agree a lot" and marked it "disagree a little." Darlene did not waste time agonizing. But there were four hundred statements and it took a long time. Periodically, she stopped to count a page to make sure most of her answers fell into the two middle columns: "disagree a little" and "agree a little." She saw only one obvious lie-catcher: *my favorite writer is Martin Szycinski.* She knew there was probably no such writer and she disagreed a lot.

Darlene agreed a lot with the statement, *I have a lot of interest in sex* and disagreed a lot with most of the statements about drugs and alcohol. The statements fell into three categories: drugs and alcohol, relationship with others, and personal feelings. Darlene figured it was all right to show a little anxiety about money and her future, and she certainly had to agree with, *My relationship with my spouse or partner is not going well.* But overall, she thought as she leaned against the straight-backed office chair and set her pencil on the little desk, this survey reflected an even-tempered, cheerful, well-balanced person.

Darlene stretched her arms straight up in the air and wiggled the cramped fingers of her right hand. She lifted her feet and held her legs straight out, alternately flexing her ankles and pointing her toes. She smiled, her first smile in several hours. She had aced this test. She was an ideal carrier: very healthy, tough in times of trouble, and generous enough to carry a pregnancy to full term for two people who couldn't have a baby on their own.

Dear Birth Mother, the letter read, *we've waited with both joy and dread to hear from you all these years. As you can see from the picture, Laurie is a bright-eyed young woman of twenty-four now. She has a sparkle in her eye and, despite the fact that she faces enormous frustrations every day, she is sweet-tempered and loving.* Kat skipped through the inventory—*muscle atrophy . . . spinal malformation . . . in-dwelling catheter . . . jaw reconstruction*—and studied the weekly routine. There was speech therapy, therapeutic horseback riding and water therapy at a community center. There was a weekday care group for four hours that included classes in language and counting. *The funds you have provided so faithfully over the years have been spent mostly on medical costs not covered by insurance and for special equipment, such as the combination saddle-brace that enables her to sit on a horse led by another rider.*

Through constant stimulation, through the loving warmth of friends and family, and through Laurie's unyielding refusal to be bound by limits set by other people, she has become an inspiration to us, to her sister and to her two brothers. She speaks with difficulty and will probably never read, but she knows her colors and can count to eighteen.

When she moves her fingers along her rosary, and whispers the words that only God can understand, her face lights with a glow that reveals a special kinship with her maker. We may puzzle about what kind of God would make such a human, but it is clear that Laurie feels only gratitude for her life. And it is in that spirit—because you gave her life and entrusted us with her care—that we invite you to visit. We hope that you agree that it would do Laurie little good to know of your relationship. It is doubtful she would understand. To her, we are her parents. But surely, for you to visit and get to know her would enrich your life in the same way it has enriched ours. The letter ended with contact information and a few suggestions about which hours were best for Laurie and what gifts she would like. The laser-printed letter was signed *Pam and Tom Kroszyk* in blue ink, as if they were cordial, casual acquaintances. Kat felt sure that the firm, feminine signature indicated Pam was accustomed to speaking for both of them, at least about Laurie.

When she had first read the letter, sitting across the table from Nicholas Lantinatta, Kat had remarked, "They're very Catholic," then felt embarrassed, but he seemed only amused.

"Well, yes. The nuns who placed her would see to that."

Now, alone in her room, rereading the letter for the hundredth time, Kat was struck more by the letter's composition, how compact and direct it was. They had wasted no words on their own emotions and obviously had thought hard about what she would want to know. They had assumed she expected some sort of accounting for the funds she had sent, but she noticed that they never offered any thanks. Nor had they asked about Hal, and she wondered what they thought about him. Was there a different letter for him? Did they know that she and Hal had divorced shortly after the birth, and that Laurie had brothers and sisters from Hal's second marriage? Did they know that she had sent the money to a relief office in New York and that their letter was the first confirmation that her monthly payments had reached the intended recipients?

When Richard Morrison's widow, Barbara, had shown up last year, the pregnancy had all come back to Kat: the surprise that she was pregnant so soon after her wedding, the shock that her feelings did not mirror Hal's excitement, the fantasy to which she retreated, day after day, that this was Richard's baby, that now Richard would leave his wife and proclaim his love for her.

These days, with Barbara dead, Kat and Della never spoke about Richard. But now Kat wondered if last year's fury at learning about his affair with Della had been linked in some way to her emotions surrounding the deeper secret of her daughter's birth and placement in an institution.

She and Hal had agreed never to discuss it, and she did not know if he had ever revealed the child's existence to his current wife. Hal had moved his new family to California, and they had lost touch. Kat had no idea how to contact him, let alone broach the subject of wanting to reveal all to her best friend. She did not need Hal's permission to tell Della. But it amazed her that this revelation would come with so little ceremony.

She was sitting in her Eames recliner, the last remnant from her house in Fort Worth. It matched nothing in the room, which featured mismatched oak-veneer chests and bedside tables. Pauline had insisted that she take the painted dressing table so that she would have a mirror in the room, and Kat, whose former home had been a proud assemblage of contemporary masterpieces, had shrugged and acquiesced. She had never planned on staying long at the Ladies Farm; just enough to develop a steady stream of revenue for Pauline. Her own things remained in storage. But then Pauline had died, and Barbara had required so much care, and there had been the question of ownership, and so little reason to leave, that Kat had settled in.

She swung her heels off the footrest and brought herself to an upright position. If I stay, she thought, I'll redo the room. Nothing severe, but updated, with cleaner lines, and a merciful retirement of the chintz bedspread and ruffled curtains.

Kat folded the letter but did not slip it back in the envelope. Instead, she took Laurie's picture and the folded letter downstairs. Flops, their retriever, lifted her head from her mid-morning nap to watch as Kat passed through her own office—the one she had shared with Pauline—and stepped into Della's.

"I need you to look at this," Kat said to Della. Through the doorway, she could see Flops with her head raised, monitoring the meeting.

Della read without comment and without moving from her chair. Her worktable faced a window that offered a tiny slice of the Nolan River and a generous portion of the denuded hill from which their neighbors, Castleburg Dairy, had launched a futile search for gravel.

Della turned to face Kat, who had seated herself in the upholstered rocker next to the bookcase.

"You had another child?" she asked. "You and Hal?"

Kat shook her head and, before she could answer, saw Della leap to the wrong conclusion. "*Not* with Hal?" Della said, her voice rising. In the next room, Flops rose to her feet and padded toward them.

"*With* Hal," Kat said. "I was pregnant only once. Right after I married Hal."

"So this was the miscarriage?" Della's luminous gaze regained its serenity and Flops settled on the floor between them.

Kat nodded, glanced at the dog. "I couldn't tell people," she said. "For one thing, it was too painful. And, even more, because I didn't . . . I knew they would say I was horrible. To give her up. To put her away like that."

"It doesn't sound like she was put away," Della said, reaching down to scratch the top of Flops's head. After Pauline's death, Flops had attached herself to Barbara; only lately had she relinquished her post outside the room Barbara had occupied and returned to warming the floor next to Pauline's old desk.

"No, she wasn't put away, but that's what we intended. Look at what we thought the prospects were. Especially after what they told us about her, her minimal capacity, and all the physical problems. At least in an institution, they could care for her physical needs. When we placed her, that's what we thought we were doing."

"So are you going to go see her?" Della still trailed her fingers over Flops's dozing form.

"Of course," Kat said. "Wouldn't you?"

"I don't know." Della shook her head. "Are you going to tell her, you know, that you're her mother?"

"No," Kat replied. "I'm not anyone's mother."

Chapter Nine

Darlene figured she'd sleep with Earl right after they confirmed her pregnancy, while she was still thin. That wouldn't hurt anything or compromise anyone's paternity, and after a few times, she'd just tell Earl they couldn't do it anymore. But she had to do something to thank him for the way he was helping her get more money from Ryan.

"I love the upholstery in this thing," she said as she slid off the leather seat of the Expedition.

Earl had e-traded a shipment of estate jewelry and a timeshare in Kenya for the car, which was enormous. Now, having zipped around to hold the door for her in Ryan's parking lot, he puffed up a little, then shrugged as if it wasn't any big deal. "Who wants to visit Kenya anyway?" he said, then grinned as her feet touched the ground with a little bounce.

His skin looked raw from razor burn, and Darlene reached over to dust a crumb of tissue from just below his sideburn. "No sense letting Ryan know you shaved for this," Darlene said. A deep flush reddened his neck and crept up the side of his face.

Damn! Maybe she wouldn't have to sleep with him. Maybe a kiss would do it.

"Now, he's going to make us wait," Earl coached. "The trick is for us to look like we're having such a good time out there in his office that we don't even notice."

When he set up his laptop in Ryan's waiting room, Darlene realized Earl had planned everything. In fact, they were so intent on studying the Shopper's Galaxy pages he had stored that morning, the nurse had to call her name twice before they realized Ryan was ready.

When they were ushered into Ryan's unoccupied office, Earl switched gears and entertained her with lightbulb jokes. "How many brunettes . . . ?" he was asking when Ryan appeared.

"One," Ryan answered, walking around the desk. "One brunette to screw in a lightbulb, because she's got all Saturday night to do it." Ryan leaned over Darlene to extend his hand to Earl. "Ryan Plummer."

"Earl Westerman," Earl replied. Of the two hands gripped across Darlene's lap, Ryan's manicured fingers looked almost weather-beaten compared to Earl's pudgy flesh.

Ryan seated himself behind his desk, leaned back, and nodded at them, turning his right palm up on his desk. "Your meeting," he invited.

"We need to discuss the money," Darlene said, hating the nagging tone in her voice. Fortunately, Earl picked up the ball.

"I took a look at the Net," Earl said. "And I know you're the one Darlene wants to help, but, truth is, she can do a little better with one of those matching services in Houston or even out of California."

Earl opened the briefcase on his lap, the snap of the metal clasps exploding into the now silent room. "Here," he said, retrieving a sheaf of papers and handing them to Ryan. "These are comparables, so to speak."

Ryan was silent, his eyes flicking over the charts, the graphs, the profiles of potential gestational carriers. The silence made Darlene uncomfortable, particularly when she noticed that little vein throbbing at Ryan's temple. He had another one, in his neck, that always throbbed below the collar line, and she bet that one was pounding right now. She smiled to herself, remembering the way she used to watch his neck while she climbed onto him on that chair.

She shifted a little and Earl smiled at her, encouraging her, she thought, to be patient while Ryan reviewed Earl's data. She smiled back, conveying a cheeriness she didn't feel. Ryan didn't like meeting Earl this way; he probably didn't like meeting Earl at all.

Finally, Ryan lowered the papers to his desk and looked up at them. He smiled. "How much do you want?"

"Fifty," Earl said. His voice was peppy in that friendly puppy-dog, I-know-I'm-a-flabby-geek-but-I-blocked-for-guys-like-you-in-high-school-and-I-just-want-you-to-like-me voice that always made Darlene want to be nice to him, but she doubted it would gain much ground with Ryan.

Ryan frowned quizzically. "What do you base that on? That's higher than anything here." He seemed genuinely puzzled.

Earl nodded in agreement. "I know." He smiled a little, leaned forward in his chair. "And Darlene probably can't walk out of here and get fifty this instant. But, you know, she doesn't have to be in any hurry." He half-winked at Ryan as if they were sharing some secret. "We both know she wants out of the Ladies Farm, but truth is, she and Tiffany have a home there forever, 'long as they want it. So there's no emergency here, she can wait for the right offer."

Ryan nodded. "And we can be shopping for a cheaper carrier."

Earl waved a hand. "I'd invite you to. The way we look at it, you should feel completely satisfied with Darlene before you make a commitment like this. You should feel you can't do better."

Ryan looked at Darlene. "You feel that way? You want me to start shopping around, maybe call a gyno friend or two, see who they'd recommend?"

Darlene swallowed. "This is a little scary, Ryan. Having a baby for someone else. That's why I wanted to meet Jill."

"She said that went real well, that you all hit it off."

"We did," Darlene said. "Except that neither one of you will say why you really want to do this."

"I told you," Ryan said. "We don't want Jill to be pregnant."

"No, Jill told me that. You told me she couldn't get pregnant because of her tubal ligation." Take a breath, Darlene told herself as Earl studied his boot tops. "But you could implant in her."

Ryan sighed, shook his head. "Look, it's really personal—"

"More personal than getting pregnant with your baby?"

"Look, Darlene, Jill just doesn't like to talk about it, it makes her feel like . . . I don't know . . . like she's deficient."

"What? What makes her feel deficient?" Darlene asked, thinking: you never used to mind telling me Jill's secrets.

"You know. That she shouldn't really . . . Darlene, Jill can't get pregnant again. She almost miscarried last time. If she miscarries this time, she'll . . . she can't take that, Darlene."

"She can't or you can't?" Darlene said. Despite her effort, her voice rose in accusation. "You're the one who's making the rules here."

But he didn't yell back. "You're right," he said. "I couldn't deal with Jill being pregnant again. I nearly went crazy the last time, looking after her. And this time, we'd have to think about Taylor—"

"You mean, you might have to take care of your own son?"

"Oh, give me a break! We're talking about my wife and child here, Darlene. We're asking you to do something to help us."

Earl had warned against this and Darlene saw that it was a mistake to push Ryan. She struggled to regain her composure and keep her tone factual. "So it's not just that she had a tubal ligation; it's that you're worried about a miscarriage?"

"And about her health, Darlene. Jill, right now . . . Jill's very fragile." He looked straight at her and for a second Darlene forgot that Earl was even in the room. "We need your help."

"And I want to help," Darlene conceded. " It's just . . . when we talked before—the first time—about this, I was mostly thinking about the physical part, being pregnant and all. Now, though, I've read a little bit, about the shots and all. And I've had a chance to think about it and I can see it's a lot more commitment than I thought."

"You don't have to raise the kid, Darlene, you just spit it out. We're the parents."

"I know that!"

"I think," Earl interjected, "reading about all this, the letters from the other gestational carriers and so forth, it makes you realize how much emotional energy this takes. They all—all these women—talk about how glad they are they did it, but they talk about a sense of loss, too. And a sense that they've given up a lot of control. And that's necessary, don't get me wrong, it's your baby, you should call the shots, but there's a cost to the carrier for that." He paused to breathe. "And now, telling us how fragile Jill is, how much is riding on this. Imagine how Darlene feels here."

Ryan watched him, waiting.

"Probably you and I can only guess at what that's like." Earl smiled again.

Ryan matched Earl's sincerity with a smile that encompassed them both. "I agree with you. We all need to be totally committed. And it's nice to see Darlene's got someone looking out for her." He returned Earl's wink and raised him a nod. "No sense in her rushing into something brand-new without doing a little research. Us too, for that matter." He nodded again. "I guess I just thought, seeing that we've known each other so long, working together and all, and—I don't know if you know this, but Darlene and I have actually been partners in the sense that I underwrote her startup costs for a computer and all when she left the hospital and went out on her own—I just figured once Darlene and Jill had met, the circle'd be complete. I didn't count on your wanting to double your money."

Earl hadn't known, of course, and there was no way Ryan would miss the red flowing up from his collar until his whole face looked like it was on fire. Even so, Darlene had to give Earl credit: he managed another smile back, with a slight shake of his head. "You got me on that one, partner! I didn't realize you've helped Darlene out before. But that's great! It means that both of you already trust each other! I love to put together deals like this!"

"Is that what you do?" Ryan asked. "Put together deals?"

"More or less," Earl said. Ryan would probably laugh about the way Earl puffed up. "I locate a lot of merchandise on the Net—international goods: you know, Mexico, Honduras, Korea—and I arrange shipping and resale here in the states. Or the other way. There's a lot of market in Central America and even the Pacific Rim for certain kinds of manufacturing equipment, used stuff, parts and all."

"Gotta keep those sweatshops going," Ryan cracked.

"Earl found me a bundle of stuff for Tiffany," Darlene offered. "Clothes and dance costumes and even snacks, like those pudding things, by the case."

Again the man-to-man thing. "That's just a little surfing; most of that stuff's real high markup. If you take a little time, you can always find something: you know, dented and scratched, etc."

Ryan followed with a nod. "So, Darlene, you won't do this unless I come across with fifty thousand dollars?"

"I'm sorry, Ryan. I just can't."

Was that a flicker in his eye? Had she surprised him? Darlene didn't dare turn her head to get Earl's assessment.

"Well." Ryan shook his head. "You've got me. I'm not sure what to do. The thing is, my wife likes you, she wants you. Things in the Plummer household have been much better since you agreed to do this, Darlene, and now, I have to go home and tell my wife you won't do it, we can't afford you. You will break my wife's heart."

She felt herself coloring, but thankfully, Earl had recognized an opportunity. "Well hold on there, Dr. Plummer. Let's not break a lady's heart right this moment. Two ladies, since Darlene wants so much to do this. Maybe Darlene could take, say, forty-five. That would work for you, wouldn't it?"

"Twenty-five works for me."

"Now, Dr. Plummer—"

"Ryan."

"Ryan. Let's don't play this way. You want to do this. Darlene wants to do this. You've all but said it's worth more than twenty-five to you. Let's don't make a game out of—"

"Forty."

"Forty?"

"Forty."

"Darlene?"

She squeezed a tear out of her closed eyelids and exhaled. "Forty."

Darlene had seen lots of sharps disposal containers in doctors' offices, but before she and Earl attended injection class, she had never envisioned one in her room at the Ladies Farm. Sitting in the conference room at Texas Fertility Specialists with five other couples, Darlene studied the red plastic container with the biohazard symbol on the front and thought about where it might be stored so that Rita would not find it.

There were five couples in the injection class, and all of them were facing a worse series of shots than Darlene and Earl. As they sat around the big table in Dr. Lantinatta's conference room, the nurse displayed PowerPoint images on monitors at either side of the room. The nurse was describing injection of the follicle stimulator, to help these women produce more eggs. Darlene sat back in her chair and looked around the room. She'd pay attention again when they started discussing progesterone.

Ryan and Jill already had their embryos. All Darlene had to do was prepare the nest.

These women were older, in their thirties. They dressed like Kat, and their husbands—they were all husbands except for Earl—wore khakis and long-sleeved knit or denim shirts. Jill and Ryan resembled these couples, Darlene thought. And, listening to their descriptions of egg extraction, Darlene concluded that Jill's fragility could be traced directly to that experience. It wasn't only the threat of miscarriage, Darlene thought. It was the fear that she'd have to go through that egg extraction as many times as these women had.

Darlene didn't blame her for playing the odds and going with a carrier. I'd pay someone too, thought Darlene. If I could.

The nurse described how the powdered drug in the tiny vial had to be reconstituted with water from another vial via syringe. Darlene followed the instructions to draw up the liquid and inject it into the vial of powder, then withdrew a measured amount back into the syringe. She used her right hand to stab the needle into her practice orange, and her left to operate the plunger that delivered the mixture into the orange. She withdrew the needle, and smiled, then turned to look at Earl, who was just plunging his own needle. He had been a step behind her all evening, slow and careful. About what you want, Darlene thought, from the person who'll be shoving a needle into your butt every day.

When they finally got to the progesterone shots, the nurse displayed a sketch of a butt, divided into quadrants to show them the upper, outer corner where the injection was to land. Darlene sneaked a look at Earl, whose eyes were glued to the image as though nothing could be more fascinating than this simple line drawing. He was red to the roots of his pale hair, prompting Darlene to wonder, as she often did, how he had managed to father a child.

The nurse explained the difference between the gargantuan needle used to draw up the progesterone from the vial and the merely gigantic needle that delivered the progesterone to the target. Her comments drew chuckles, but no apprehension from the other couples. They were all working on producing their own babies, and it was clear that any pain was worth it to them if they could get pregnant and make it through.

Darlene drew the liquid out of the practice vial, even though she knew this wasn't a shot she could give to herself, and she practiced changing to the smaller needle once the syringe was filled. Progesterone is oil-based, the nurse explained, which makes it more uncomfortable after injection. Just close your ears, Darlene instructed herself, jabbing the orange one more time. With her left hand, she plunged the syringe, then withdrew the needle and looked up in triumph.

Earl was watching her, his loaded syringe held aloft in his left hand. "Your turn," she said lightly, and he smiled just a little, then turned his attention to switching needles and sticking the orange. He was cool, she decided, in his odd way. His hands remained steady and his gaze fixed; if Darlene's presence, or the prospect of her naked butt, distracted him, he gave no indication right now.

She allowed herself a moment to watch his fingers, quite long for someone so broad. Of course, he wasn't pudgy anymore, the way he had been in high school. Now he seemed, somehow, smooth. His hands were very clean and unmarred except by a variety of old scars that decorated his knuckles. Those would be mementos from the Sydonia Sabers, Darlene guessed, nicks and scratches from grinding them into the turf of practice fields and the sharp edges of high school opponents. He sported none of the gnarled veins or roughened skin of manual workers or dedicated outdoorsmen; she supposed he shot a dove or two in the fall, but didn't spend a lot of Sunday dawns in either deer blinds or bass boats.

Once he removed the needle from the orange and dropped it into the sharps container, he noticed her studying him and his face grew red. "I'm going to feel like a pincushion," Darlene said. "No matter how good you are, it's just going to sting."

The woman next to Darlene laughed. "Don't worry," she said. "You'll be so filled with raging hormones, you won't even notice pain from the needle."

"Oh, not me," Darlene sang out. "I've been pregnant before, it never got to me." The woman glowered, her mascaraed eyes narrowing slightly as Darlene realized how annoying it must be for an infertile woman to hear about Darlene's easy pregnancy.

The woman's husband leaned forward and grinned at Darlene. "I just figure if she bitches at me, I'll remind her who's giving the shot!"

Darlene smiled back at him, but she thought his wife probably didn't appreciate the comment. The wife, though, just laughed and glanced back at her husband. "Well, this is the third time we've tried this, so maybe three's the charm!"

"This'll be your third pregnancy?" Darlene kept her voice lower this time.

The woman nodded. "We came close, last time, but I had a second-trimester miscarriage." She smiled. "So it's try, try again."

"Well, three's bound to be the charm," Earl said from over Darlene's shoulder. He held up his orange. "Too bad we can't inject these and you ladies could just eat 'em."

The woman and her husband both nodded glumly and Darlene

turned her attention back to Earl. "It won't be that bad," he assured her. "It's just a shot."

He wanted to pick her up at the Ladies Farm, but Kat suggested that they meet in Fort Worth for dinner.

"Maybe he doesn't want anyone to see you," Rita said, frowning a little as she snipped at Kat's hair.

Kat studied her reflection in the salon mirror and tried not to supervise Rita too closely. "Maybe I don't want anyone to see him," she said. "Anyway, I don't know him that well. I want my own car nearby."

"Well, you can always check into the Worthington if things heat up. He's a doctor; he can afford it."

Kat made a face, but said nothing. Rita delighted in teasing her about her drunken tantrum at the downtown hotel the previous year. During a fit of pique that the bar was not open at six A.M., Kat had pitched a chair over the railing on the mezzanine that overlooked the lobby. Fortunately, though not surprisingly, the chair had missed the chandelier for which she had aimed, and crashed down into a potted ficus. Memory of the episode was still so painful that she had asked Della not ever to tell her what the total damages were. She had simply signed over a certificate of deposit, which Della had cashed to settle with the hotel. There had been a certain satisfaction, though, in hurling the chair. It felt good to throw something heavy from a great height.

"I'll bet they wouldn't even know who you are," Rita said.

Kat agreed, particularly since the hotel itself had been sold, the lobby remodeled, and the manager who had aided Della in spiriting her out of the hotel had transferred to a hotel in Chicago. It didn't matter. Kat associated that lobby with the afternoon she had learned about Della's affair with Richard and, no matter how far behind them, it was still a painful memory.

"It's a first date," Kat said. "We're not going to any hotels. We're going to the Kimbell, we're going to dinner, and then I'm coming home."

Rita picked up the blow dryer and aimed it at the side of Kat's head. "What're you doing at the Kimbell?" she yelled over the noise.

"There's an exhibit of treasures from the Russian royal family," Kat said. "Paintings, icons."

"Any of those eggs?" Rita asked. "I always like those Faberge eggs."

"No. They came later." Kat watched Rita working and wondered if she herself could make a living doing anything that required her to stay on her feet all day. She's so cheerful, thought Kat. It was odd that she had lived with Rita and Della for several years, but only now noticed that Rita had a determinedly sunny nature. Rita was more excited about this date than Kat herself.

Rita switched off the dryer, patted Kat's shoulder, and stepped back to admire her work. "Damn, I'm good!"

"You are," Kat agreed. Rita never seemed to do much, but the effect was always strong. Kat's taffy-colored hair fell in precise swoops from her side part to where it feathered over her ears.

"Of course, you did get it all when they were giving out good hair," Rita conceded. "Even Darlene's hair doesn't fall that well."

"Yeah, but her roots aren't gray."

"No. It's my hair she's turned gray!"

"Oh, she's okay," Kat said. "She's a hard worker." Kat never knew what to say to Rita. Kat had seen dozens of women like her, dragging their kids from one man to another, then crying in shock when their little girls ran off with men themselves. Two and three generations of women who spent the rest of their lives working hard to pay for their early folly. "And she's smart," Kat added. Which was true, too. Kat just hoped Darlene was smart enough to handle what she had gotten herself into with Ryan Plummer.

And that, she thought later, as she pulled her car into a space in front of the Kimbell Art Museum, was another reason to keep Nick Lantinatta away from the Ladies Farm. Darlene would freak if she knew Kat had introduced her mother to the man who was going to implant the embryo she would be carrying for money.

Rita had exhorted her to wear a dress, but all Kat owned were worsted suits with shoulder padding and long sleeves, to be worn with silk blouses and matching pumps. She had no dating wardrobe. So she had opted to masquerade as her leisure self, in jeans and pullover sweater, topped by a plaid blazer. Hopefully, no norther would blow in tonight, and the blazer would be all she needed in the crisp Texas winter.

When she saw that he was also in jeans, she felt better about her outfit; better still when, eyeing the long lines to the special exhibit, Nick asked, "Could I interest you in a nice stroll on a pleasant moonlit night?"

Which is how they wound up walking briskly along the streets of the nearby neighborhood. "I thought we'd get a chance at conversation in that museum," he said, "but I don't think there was much chance." He glanced back over his shoulder at the barrel-vaulted roof line that gleamed white in the darkness.

"No," she agreed. "Those big exhibits . . . I don't know, unless you go during the day or to a special reception, they're always crowded."

"Yeah." They headed to the walk that bordered the west side of the building, an open lawn edged with trees. "I should have asked you back in January, when I got the invitation to the members-only opening."

"You didn't know me in January." She paused. "You didn't even know me when I showed back up in your office after twenty years."

"True. Are you going to hold that against me?"

"I don't know what I'll be holding against you," she said, then laughed to let him know that was a joke. "I didn't really expect you to recognize me, but I did think you'd remember the name."

"Well, I did, after I connected you with that . . . with Laurie."

"It's odd for me that she has a name, after all these years," Kat said.

They stopped at the wide, brick-paved boulevard for a few seconds, then crossed in a hurry, ignoring the *Don't Walk* signal. As they stepped off the curb, he took her hand. The contact startled her, but she had no inclination to let go when they reached the other side of the street in safety.

"When are you going to see Laurie?" he asked. He nodded toward a side street to indicate their direction, and they strolled forward past a few closed offices and a sandwich shop or two.

She started at the question, but the warmth from his hand gave her courage. "You're assuming I've already decided that I will see her." She hazarded a glance up at him, and thought she saw him raise his eyebrows a little, though the darkness made it hard to tell. "Well, I will, but I haven't called them yet." She related some of the scheduling challenges presented both by her consulting practice and activities at the Ladies Farm. "Even in winter," Kat said, "it's hard to get away on a weekend because we almost always have guests."

They picked up their pace as they moved across another small street and climbed along a block of older homes. There were restored bungalows and a number of two-story houses, most of both types painted brick. Most of the homes boasted the deep front porches with arched entries that bespoke Fort Worth building styles of the 1920s and '30s.

Nick was quiet, and Kat became curious. "Is that why you asked me out? To find out about Laurie?"

"No. I asked you out because, when you came to see me, I thought you were brave and, I don't know, interesting. A lot of birth mothers contact us, but they mostly focus on their own need, their need to know. You were more . . . I don't know, more concerned about the child."

"Well, that's flattering," Kat said. "Though maybe too flattering. I mean, I am concerned about Laurie, but it is my curiosity, my need to know that got me to your office."

"True. But these birth mothers—" he sounded cautious, "a lot of them, anyway—seem to be out to reclaim the child in some way. Rebuild themselves. You seem more—I don't know—more confident. Successful. You don't need to be someone else."

"Now that is flattering," Kat responded. Then, feeling reckless, amended, "Though, not as flattering as 'I thought you were really hot and I couldn't resist your beauty.'"

"Well, that too," he said in a mild voice.

Kat laughed. "Shameless fishing for compliments pays off again!" She grew even braver. "You know," she said, "I know almost nothing about you."

He shrugged, then filled her in. Two grown kids, an ex-wife in Dallas, a burgeoning fertility practice soon to relocate to the mid-cities, close to the airport and to his home. A new house with a workshop/garage to do welding. "Metal sculpture."

"That couple in your office? That's yours?"

"Guilty."

"I loved that!" She recalled the two muffler-torsos with their shock-absorber legs intertwined. "I wondered where that had come from. Have you got more?"

"Oh, the moment I love: let me invite you back to my place to see my works of art."

"Hey!" Kat said, pushing a vision of Rita's smirk from her mind. "I'm game! Though maybe not tonight."

"Well, how about Saturday?" he asked.

She shook her head. "Guests, remember? But, you know, once they've checked out Sunday afternoon, I'm pretty footloose."

"Good. Sunday afternoon." They had stopped at a gentle rise on a street that, in the style of most prairie cities, ran straight east and west. When they turned back toward the east, they could see downtown Fort Worth, lights outlining the small collection of office towers rising above the Trinity River.

He chuckled, dropped her hand and took her by the shoulders. "Okay, so far we've exchanged backgrounds, discussed our mutual attraction, and made the next date. I think it's time to kiss. Don't you?"

"Absolutely." Then she held back for a moment. "But we're still going to dinner, right?"

"Oh, certainly. And we can even kiss again, after dinner."

"Oh good," said Kat. She reached up to put her arms around his neck as he leaned down to her. For good measure, she stood on tiptoe and gave herself permission to feel like a schoolgirl.

Ryan thought Ballangee's office looked as academic as its occupant; stacks of journals and books filled the space. Ryan looked at the clutter as he settled himself into a wooden Bank of England chair and thought, he must have a separate conference room for patients. Though he doubted Ballangee saw many patients at his office. By the time a child needed Harry Ballangee, the kid was in the hospital. Even meetings with parents took place there for the most part, Ryan guessed. It was clear from the clutter, though, that Harry used this office. It must be where he churned out his papers and e-mailed his network of colleagues. He could coordinate a research project from this office, Ryan thought.

"How's Taylor?" Harry asked when he entered. He shook Ryan's hand and motioned at him to sit. Then he looked around in a distracted way and, with a smile, moved a stack of papers and books to clear a seat for himself.

"Doing better," Ryan said as Harry positioned his chair facing Ryan's.

"Good. Let's schedule him for a cognitive baseline now, while he's well; that gives us a benchmark to gauge any future episodes."

"I'll tell Jill," Ryan said, but he failed to imagine how he would explain to his wife that they needed a starting point against which to measure their son's diminished intellectual capacity as his porous blood cells failed to deliver sufficient oxygen to his brain. "I talked to Josh."

"Wittstein? What's he got for us?"

Ryan laid out the scenario: the research was funded, he had gained approval for the protocol, Josh originally had planned to perform the procedures in his clinic, but now he wanted to farm them out. Qualifying as a site depended on alliance with a teaching or experimental lab that boasted a qualified authority, an in-place diagnosis and treatment program, and the ability to identify research subjects. "You've got most of the boilerplate in place, don't you? From your marrow studies?"

Ballangee waved a hand as if the bureaucratic procedures would not slow an experienced grant-meister. "This isn't like Josh," the older man observed. "He's usually more interested in population studies, genetic patterns, gross statistics."

"He still is," Ryan said. "It's why he's so open to trying protocol here. It's a low-profile disease, rare occurrence, no discernible population pattern. He's interested in multigenerational tracking, survey work, all that." Ryan smiled. "Same old Josh."

Ballangee nodded and waited.

"But he learned from the master," and now Ryan nodded at Harry. "There's more money attached to clinicals, it's easier to show some progress. And it's possible, isn't it?"

Ballangee nodded more thoughtfully. "It's worked for sickle cell in some cases, particularly if they transplant prior to stroke."

"He hasn't got a lot of money. He needs sites with marrow programs in place, and a good patient or two. Wherever possible, he'd like to use cord blood."

"That's a tough one."

"If you're looking for a match in what's been banked, there's so little of it. But we're growing our own."

"Growing your own?"

"As it happens, Jill and I have embryos stored."

"So Jill—"

"Not Jill," Ryan said. "We've lined up a surrogate, a gestational carrier." He explained about the two embryos that could produce matches for Taylor. It was easier, thought Ryan, for Ballangee to grasp the intricacies of donor matching for a stem cell implant than to accept the concept of hiring someone to carry your biological child.

Ballangee pursed his lips. "And Jill's on board with this?"

"Harry, other than spontaneous remission, this is the one hope we've got." Ryan leaned forward, resting his elbows on his knees and opening his hands to his former teacher. "Look, I asked Josh to send you the protocol, a draft of the application guidelines. If you're not interested, I'll understand. I can always see where the sites will be and take Taylor to them. It doesn't have to be here. But I figured, knowing Josh and all, you'd see an opportunity."

"Oh, it's a great opportunity," Ballangee replied, leaving Ryan to wonder how the man might express boredom if this was how he exhibited interest. "You know what's involved here: the chemo, the antirejection, the infection risks?"

Ryan nodded impatiently. "And I expect we'll go over them in excruciating detail when it comes time for disclosure. That's one of the reasons why I'd like to do it here, if we're going to do it. But you know, Harry, it's the only possibility of a true cure. Even if he goes into remission, we'll be waiting, watching to see—"

Ballangee shook his head. "Not really. It's very rare that a patient converts again. Once the porosity disappears, it's over." He looked thoughtful. "And you and Jill, you're just starting on this. Don't rule out the possibility, Ryan."

Ryan nodded. "You're right, of course. It could happen. But you know Jill. I can't raise that hope, Harry."

"I can see that the idea of a transplant—doing something—is a lot more attractive than trying to wait and see." Ballangee tapped his fingers on the desktop, then smiled at Ryan. "And I suspect another child is welcome in any case."

"Of course!" Ryan enthused. He leaned in. "Though, 'tell the truth, this carrier business is pretty complicated. I mean," he lowered his voice, "there's so much uncertainty just in whether the pregnancy will take." It was a relief to admit all this. "We've leveraged it, with the carrier, who's younger than Jill, so the chances are good. Hormone shots, all that. Even so, when I think what could happen—"

"Don't rule out that remission is one thing that could occur," Ballangee cautioned.

Ryan nodded, but ignored the comment. "In a way, the uncertainty's one more reason I'm glad we're using the carrier. If something does go wrong with the pregnancy, at least it won't be on Jill. Or if we need the cells early—" he looked at the older man "God! I don't even want to think about it."

Ballangee sat still for a second. "You couldn't take them too early, anyway," he said carefully.

"No."

"I imagine there's not much sense worrying about that. Since we're doing everything we can to help Taylor."

"There's not much sense talking about it either. I mean with Jill. No sense worrying her."

"No sense," Harry Ballangee agreed. He stacked the papers Ryan had given him in a neat pile and folded his hands on top. "And I'd like to participate. For the sake of the research, as well as for you and Jill."

"I appreciate that, Harry. It will be better all around. You're close to home. I don't . . . Jill and I don't want to hand our boy over to strangers."

Chapter Ten

The smoothest, roundest butt Earl had ever seen was positioned perfectly across his bed, its most attractive portions defined by their creamy contrast to bikini tan lines. And this perfection would return to him every day, Earl knew, every morning between eight-thirty and nine, as long as its possessor believed that he, Earl Westerman, could maintain a steady hand.

"Come on, Earl," she grumbled. "I don't have all day. I've got to get into Fort Worth to deliver transcripts and pick up tapes, and I've got to get the tapes back to Lakeesha by noon. Otherwise she won't be able to do 'em till tomorrow."

"Just getting the alcohol," Earl mumbled. He had assembled his materials on the metal tray of a TV table abandoned by Gladys and Ray. Last night, he had scrubbed the tray with disinfectant, then covered it with a sterile pad he had ordered from a medical supply site. But at six this morning, when he was setting out the syringe and vial, he thought it looked too clinical—they hadn't talked about any of this in the class—so he tossed the pad and covered the tray with a clean towel that he had washed on the hot cycle with bleach and then tumbled dry. Either he would have to wash the towel every night, or he'd have to scrounge around some more in the trunks in the garage to see if there were more towels.

Of course, his experiences with laundry had taught him that if you threw enough Clorox onto anything, it would turn white, so maybe some of the pink flowered things he'd been using for dish cloths would work. He wished he had someone to talk to about this, but his favorite confidant, Aunt Gladys, was down in the Big

Bend and rarely used the telephone, preferring to dispense her advice face to face on her front porch.

He tore open a gauze square, careful to avoid contaminating the surface with his freshly scrubbed hands. Maybe he could call the nurse who had taught the class. She seemed nice. He just didn't want all this preparation getting back to Darlene.

Balancing the gauze on the tips of his right fingers, he used his left hand to remove the loosened screw top to the bottle of alcohol. With as little superfluous motion as he could muster, Earl folded the gauze twice with one hand, pressed the gauze against the top of the bottle, tipped the bottle to saturate the pad, then leaned down over Darlene and stroked, ever so carefully, the upper, outer right quadrant of that lovely bottom.

"You only have to do a little area," Darlene reminded him. "You don't have to disinfect my whole butt."

"Right," he said, tearing his gaze away and turning back to the tray. Quickly, he flipped the top off the progesterone vial, saturated a Q-tip with alcohol, and swabbed the top of the rubber stopper. He unwrapped the eighteen-gauge needle, attached it to the syringe, drew the plunger back and stabbed the needle into the vial. Then he expelled the air into the vial, turned the vial upside down and drew one centiliter of progesterone into the syringe. He studied for bubbles and saw none, so he withdrew the needle and exchanged it for the smaller needle, which he fastened to the syringe.

Darlene lay diagonally on the bed, her head and shoulders pointed toward the far corner, her legs spread a little to straddle the corner nearest him. Earl stared for a second at the jeans and panties—pink, with lace trim—which she had jerked to her knees without ceremony before throwing herself face down on the bed. Then he drew a sharp breath, leaned directly over his target and stuck the needle into Darlene's smooth flesh. With his left hand, he plunged the syringe and then withdrew the needle.

She lay still just long enough for Earl to envision her rising slowly to a kneeling position on the bed. He would run his hands up under her little knit shirt and then down over that perfect butt to help her tug her panties back in place. With one arm tightly around his neck, she would use her other hand to stay his. "Let's leave them off," she would whisper, and his hand would glide back up her leg.

Suddenly, she erupted in movement, backing her butt into the air and pushing herself off the bed to a standing position. In a flash she had straightened and pulled panties and jeans into place, not bothering to turn away as she fastened the snap on her jeans and the French-cut briefs disappeared until tomorrow. Had he caught a glimpse of feathery hair beneath that tender belly? Earl blinked, but she was already gathering up her purse.

"I have the heating pad warmed up," he offered weakly. "It said . . . the nurse said the sting would go away better with a little heat. I ordered those snap-activated hand warmers, but they haven't come yet."

She waved a hand at him and headed out the bedroom door. "I'm late enough as it is."

"Want a Diet Dr Pepper for the road?" he called after her, nearly running to the refrigerator.

She stopped, turned, and waited for him to bring the cold can. She smiled as he popped the top before holding it out to her.

"Are you sure you're okay?" he asked.

"Fine," she said, starting to turn. Then, as if she had forgotten something, she turned back to him. "You were perfect," she said. "I didn't feel anything."

Jill set the stroller brake and lifted Taylor onto the ground. Without a backward look, he lurched down to the sandpit, where two other toddlers were decorating each other with sand. The Vista Gate Association had been torn apart two years ago by home owners who objected to the sand in the play area that bordered the community duck pond. It was one thing for the climbing bars and swings to be anchored in receptive mulch, but installing an actual sandbox for tykes with shovels and pails took retro to a new low.

Jill herself had attended that meeting. Eight months pregnant, she had insisted that Ryan accompany her and defend the idea. It must have been raging hormones, Jill thought now, placing a protective hand over her sorry abdomen. Flat and toned, it could not possibly be the source of courage for public action these days. Now she had to rely on her heart to spur her to action on behalf of her child.

Taylor had stopped halfway down the short slope and looked back anxiously. "Would you like your truck?" she asked him. "Your truck and your shovel?"

The mother who accompanied the other two children looked up

and smiled benignly from the other side of the sandpit as Jill held out the plastic dump truck and shovel. "Yes," Taylor said softly. "Truck." He toddled back, right hand extended, and took the truck from Jill.

"Oh, look!" said the other mother, whom Jill had seen at the park before, "he's got a dump truck! Would you like your trucks?"

Jill smiled at the other woman, who was sitting on the stone ledge along the far side of the sandpit. She supposed the woman would be glad for Taylor's influence if he could show her children it was more fun to shovel sand into a dump truck than to pour it in each other's hair.

Taylor approached warily, one arm clutching his truck to his chest, the other, grasping his shovel, extended for balance. He stepped off the stone apron into the pit, teetered from the impact, then sat . . . hard. Jill held her breath in anticipation of his sobs, but Taylor continued unperturbed in his mission. He retrieved the shovel, which had fallen during his descent, and stuck it in the sand. The tool was more scoop than shovel, enabling him to fill the truck, lodged protectively between his outstretched knees.

Jill made her way around to the other mother, who was watching her son, a boy a little bigger than Taylor. "Want your shovel, Benny? C'mere and get your shovel, honey."

Benny finished his study of the interloper and jumped to his feet. Taylor had yet to take note of Benny's presence. Jill supposed Taylor had lived so intensely in his own world, surrounded by adults begging for his response, that other children were like dogs and cats to him: something you pet at risk of getting scratched or bitten.

He must be feeling better, Jill thought, seeing that the winter sun made Taylor's dull hair reflect a ray or two, and gave color to his chalky skin. Trusting that the panic in the voice of Benny's mother indicated she would intervene before Benny took too many more steps in Taylor's direction, Jill seated herself next to Benny's mom. As soon as Benny had been safely diverted, she would introduce herself. Meanwhile, Taylor, in his red hooded sweatshirt, continued to shovel sand as Benny's mom lunged forward, plastic shovel in hand, to intercept Benny.

"Here!" the mom exclaimed, leaping and pivoting in one motion so that she herself landed in the center of the sandpit, seated between Taylor and Benny. She placed the shovel in Benny's hand. "Here! Let's scoop up some sand! I know! Let's make a sand castle!

Want to make a sand castle?" Benny struggled, but could not loose himself from her grip.

Meanwhile, Benny's sister, who had continued to sift sand through her fingers, arose and, giving wide berth to her brother's struggles, approached Taylor with hands open in front of her. Taylor looked up for a second, then resumed his shoveling. Sister responded to the gesture of acceptance by seating herself next to the truck. Slowly, carefully, the dark-haired child lifted a fistful of sand and deposited it into Taylor's truck.

This defection enraged Benny. Screaming, he launched himself from his mother's arms, assailing his sister and overturning the truck. "Oh, Taylor!" Jill said, rushing to his side as he raised his shovel. Benny lunged for the shovel, and barreled into Taylor's midsection, knocking him backward. Taylor had just begun to whimper. Jill could hear his mewing below Benny's screaming and the wailing of Benny's sister, who had been knocked aside and now rose and stomped forward. She pushed Benny from behind. Amazingly, Benny yielded, allowing his sister, hands outstretched, to fall directly onto Taylor's belly.

He was vomiting by the time Jill extricated him and held him upright by his armpits. With a helpless, eye-rolling shrug toward Benny's mother, Jill turned Taylor slightly and let him fall to his hands and knees so that he could finish puking. Damn it! thought Jill, a protective hand on her son's back. He didn't get to play two minutes! Behind her, Benny and his sister were still tussling, wailing together as their mother struggled.

Behind her, Jill heard a sharp intake of breath before the girl let out a shriek. One hand on her son, Jill turned to see the child pointing at Taylor and shrieking hysterically. "Blood!" she screamed. "Blood!"

Jill saw the crimson on the sand, tiny rivulets winding their way through Taylor's partially digested breakfast. "Shhh," the other mother was comforting her two children. By their muffled sounds Jill knew the other woman had drawn them to herself.

It's nothing, Jill wanted to tell them. Nothing at all, just a little blood. Tiny tears, probably in his throat or upper digestive track. Nothing at all compared to the hemorrhaging he used to have. She closed her eyes against the revulsion in the little girl's face. These little things are a sign he's getting better, she told them silently. Much better.

* * *

Darlene let the contents of the three big envelopes slide out onto Lakeesha's dining room table. "How'd it go?" Lakeesha asked, pulling up a chair and sorting through the tapes.

"Okay," Darlene said. "I stopped by the family practice on Hulen, it turns out they don't have anyone doing just transcription, they'd love to try it, I can pick up tapes on Wednesday. I left them five tapes, too." She nodded at the two tapes Lakeesha held in her hand. "Waxman needs his tomorrow. Want me to take it?"

"You bitch!" Lakeesha snapped back, laughing and setting the tapes down in front of her. "You know what I'm asking about."

Darlene laughed too. "Okay, I guess. As long as I don't watch Earl nearly creaming his jeans."

"I thought it was supposed to hurt?"

Darlene shrugged. "Not so far. It stung for a second. That's about it. I imagine it'll get a little sore once he hits the same spot a few times."

"I don't know why you didn't let me do it."

"Come on, 'Keesh, you do too. It has to be the same time every day, and we'd never make it on weekends. I'd never make it out here, and you'd never get your old man out of bed on Sunday mornings, not to mention the kids and all."

Lakeesha shook her head. Darlene knew she had hurt her friend's feelings, but Lakeesha and Eddie lived up the highway, toward Fort Worth, and Darlene was sure it never would have worked out. She wasn't sure Eddie liked her much, even though they'd all been friends in high school. There'd been a time or two when he and she had gone out in high school and she hadn't put out. She figured guys pretty much accepted that as part of the game, but she thought maybe Eddie held it against her a little more because she was white, as if she hadn't held out on white guys. Anyway, considering how Eddie had married her best friend, Darlene was relieved.

"It's not just you. I think Kat's a little ticked I didn't ask her to do it, either, but I don't know how she thinks we could have kept it secret from Rita."

"I don't know why you won't tell her. What do you think she'll do?" Lakeesha's eyes were enormous, round, and gold-brown. After baby Mike was born, she'd cut her hair down to almost nothing, a fuzzy crown, making her eyes and classic profile even more pronounced.

Darlene sighed. "I'll tell her when I'm ready. It's just . . . I don't want nine months of her nagging me about this. Taking money for babies. You know!"

Lakeesha shook her head. "Not me, honey. I don't know!"

"Well, but you know Rita!"

Now Lakeesha tilted her head a little, as if thinking back, and Darlene supposed she remembered the times they had crowded into Lakeesha's bed, both of them, so Darlene wouldn't have to go home and face Wendell. Lakeesha didn't think that was Rita's fault, but Darlene knew better. She knew that Rita'd been out running around instead of keeping an eye on that drunk. Once Carla eloped, Darlene had been on her own.

"Anyway, she thinks I'm already pregnant."

"Seriously?"

Darlene grinned. "And she thinks it's Earl!"

Lakeesha shook her head and Darlene could tell she didn't really think it was funny. "That poor boy!"

"He's having the time of his life," Darlene assured her. "And you know what? He's nice." Lakeesha just stared. "Really!"

"Well, I guess he is," Lakeesha said. "That's a pretty nice thing he's doing, putting a needle in your butt every day for nothing more than the joy of seeing it." She stacked five of the tapes in front of her, swept the others off the edge of the table and into a big envelope. "You might give him a heads up about taking heat for being the daddy here."

"Oh, 'Keesh, come on! He's having a good time." Darlene hated it when Lakeesha got this way. Lakeesha'd grown up military and she could pull this judgmental thing.

"Why don't you bring him by here?" Lakeesha asked.

"You want to make sure I'm doing him right?"

"I want to see him. I haven't seen him since high school, and he was pretty much a dork then. Now he's got a modem and a little jingle and you're showing him your ass and pretending he's the father of your baby. I want another look at this boy. We'll smoke a brisket, pop a top, he and Eddie can shoot beer cans off the fence." She smiled, but Darlene couldn't see any humor in her eyes. "You know, you're going to have to tell your mother sometime."

Darlene took the envelope from her friend. "I know. I just want to be pregnant when I do." She thought of something else. "I've got to tell her soon, though. Kat's dating that damn doctor!"

"Ryan?"

"No!" Darlene gave a little laugh. "Not Ryan!" For a while after she and Ryan had stopped seeing each other, she had sent Lakeesha to pick up his transcription. "He's still happily married, remember? No, Kat's dating Lantinatta: the one who owns the fertility practice!"

"It's hard to imagine her dating anyone," Lakeesha said.

"That's what Carla says about her, too. But I think it's that we can't imagine her dating anyone ordinary. No one in Sydonia, for sure."

"Well, no one in Sydonia," Lakeesha conceded. "And I'll say this: anyone who mixes up babies in test tubes, that's not ordinary."

"It's not a test tube baby!" Darlene contended. "I'm giving birth to it. Don't look at me like that—I am. And he—Dr. Lantinatta—probably is extraordinary. Extraordinary enough for me and for Kat!"

Chapter Eleven

Rita set the toast down on a napkin atop the kitchen table and smoothed her hand over her granddaughter's hair. "I'm going to trim those bangs this afternoon, get 'em out of your eyes. How's that?"

Tiffany nodded and reached for the toast. She licked at the jelly, then frowned. "Is this grape?"

"Of course it's grape, honey!" With one hand around the jar's label, Rita screwed on the cap and put the container in the refrigerator. "Would Mamaw give you anything but grape?"

"Yes," said Darlene as she walked into the kitchen.

"We're having our private time," Rita said.

"Well, you're having it with raspberry preserves," Darlene said. She turned to her daughter. "Tiff, come on and eat that toast. Drink some milk, too. We've got to get going."

"I want grape," Tiffany said.

"You want Wonder Bread, too," her mother retorted. "But this place doesn't have normal food. We're in fiber heaven, baby, and we've got to roll with it. You want me to make this into PB and J?"

Tiffany nodded, and Darlene whisked the napkin with the toast from in front of the child.

Rita took a breath. "Honey, I didn't know you wanted PBJ. Here, Darlene, you go finish your makeup, I'll get the sandwich." She reached into the toaster for the slice she had made for herself.

"My makeup is finished," Darlene said through gritted teeth, and Rita frowned.

Carefully setting the second slice of toast on the counter in front of Darlene, Rita said, "Okay." Then, turning to Tiffany, "Honey, you want some more milk?"

"She's got milk!" Darlene said. She jerked the refrigerator open and yanked out a jar of peanut butter.

Rita stared at her daughter and wondered about the timing of this bad mood. "Baby, you're having some kind of bad morning!" she said. "You sure you don't want me to make that sandwich?" She wished Darlene would let her fuss with Tiffany and go find at least one pair of earrings. Much as Rita objected to the line of holes along the shell of her daughter's ear, the sight of Darlene's lobes without a single glint of gold or rhinestone was just depressing.

"I'm not your baby!" Darlene told her. "And neither is my daughter." She stuck a knife into the open jar and grunted a little as the congealed peanut butter resisted her effort.

This has to be PMS, Rita thought. Then, with a lurch, Rita recalled what Darlene had told her and what Rita had firmly put out of her mind. She looked at her daughter, and found all the telltale puffiness she needed. There were hormones involved, that was sure.

Rita guessed that now was not the moment to lean forward and tug the rib-knit shirt down to cover the gap between shirt-bottom and the waistband of her daughter's jeans.

Tiffany had left her chair and wandered into the dining room. Rita heard her singing in a low voice, accompanied by a rhythmic thump that signified a dance step. It was a good way to keep her distance from a hostile parent, Rita thought. They had only two guests, a couple on their way from St. Louis to Houston for a month of baby-sitting while their grown children went to Europe. Della had served them breakfast in their room, so no one would need the dining room till that evening.

Even so, Rita wondered about four-year-old jelly fingers trailing along the rungs of the dining room chairs. She was stepping toward the dining room when Darlene exploded. "Dammit! Isn't there a goddamn thing in this place that normal people eat!" She slammed the knife onto the counter, the peanut butter and torn toast stuck to the blade.

In the dining room, the singing and thumping halted.

"Here." Rita turned and approached. "Go get some earrings. I'll make fresh toast and take Tiffany to school when she's done eating."

"I'll make the toast!"

"You are scaring your daughter to death!" Rita hissed. "Now go and do what I told you and stop terrifying that child!"

Darlene tilted her head back and stared up at the ceiling. "Oh, this is just great!" She gave a little laugh. "Lessons in motherhood from the world's worst mother!"

"You could've done a lot worse than me!" Rita defended herself. "And this isn't about me, anyway. It's about you and Tiffany. And . . . and . . ." she motioned at Darlene's bare midriff.

"You're right about that: It's not about you! Tiffany!" Darlene yelled. "Tiffany Jewel, you get back in this kitchen!" She glowered at her mother.

"Darlene—"

"I mean it, you just back off! I'll get my daughter ready and then we're out of here! I don't need your help!"

"Darlene, I'm just trying to make it a little easier. Honey," Rita fought to keep her voice even, "honey, I can't fix what happened all that time ago. But I'm here now. I've got a nice place for all of us to live." She motioned with her hand to encompass the whole kitchen. "Hell, I've even remarried your favorite stepfather. What do you want, Darlene?"

Darlene had picked up the table knife and now she used it as a pointer. "I'll tell you what I want," she said. "I want to make a peanut butter and jelly sandwich for my daughter. I want Peter Pan smooth and Welch's grape jelly and soft, white bread to spread it on! I want strawberry-flavored milk, the way she likes." Darlene's lip had started to tremble and, in her mind, Rita could see a line on a graph plummeting downward, representing the angry hormone, and another line crossing it, heading straight up. That was the tears and despair hormone.

Again the knife clattered down on the counter. "And I want out of this crazy place!"

Rita looked at the counter and saw a tiny chip, just a sliver of the high-resistant compound that had been the pride and joy of her friend Pauline. This had been her kitchen, the one she had designed and built with her husband Hugh, back when they had first started the B & B. Rita could remember her washing it, wiping it down, and polishing it dry, night after night. The cost of that counter probably exceeded six months' pay for Rita, when her girls were little. It was the nicest counter in the nicest kitchen Rita had ever cooked in. Or even made peanut butter and jelly sandwiches in. "You want out?" she repeated. "Honey, no one's keeping you here. You want out, you go! You just make sure you do right by Tiffany, or I'll come get her. I swear I will."

Darlene was in full sobs now, leaning on the counter, head in both hands.

"Come on," Rita addressed her granddaughter, who had halted her return a few steps into the kitchen, "let's go get breakfast at Papaw's. We'll get ourselves a burrito, and then we'll wash our hands and brush our teeth, and I'll take you to school."

Tiffany stood still and looked toward her mother.

"Give your mama a kiss and tell her you hope her day gets better. Come on. Mama needs a little sugar right now."

Tiffany walked closer to her mother, whose shoulders were still shaking. "Come here, honey," Darlene whispered, straightening up and swiping at her eyes with the back of her hand. She held out her arms and Tiffany sank into them.

"Don't cry," she said, kissing her mother's wet cheek. Rita watched Darlene clutch the child to her, Tiffany's running shoes with the lights on the heels digging into Darlene's back.

"Mama's fine," Darlene said, pulling back a little to look at her daughter. "Don't you worry about Mama. You just go with Mamaw and let her feed you at Papaw's store. You can sit at the counter."

Tiffany nodded, slid down her mother's trunk, and ran over to her grandmother. Rita took the child's hand. "You okay?" she asked Darlene.

"Yeah, fine," Darlene said, calmly, running a finger over the little chip in the counter. "I can fix this," she said, but Rita knew better.

"Dave'll take care of it," Rita said. "Come on, Tiff."

"Are you okay?" Earl asked her when she showed up.

"Yeah, fine," Darlene said, stomping into the bedroom. "This is what I look like without makeup, that's all." She glanced at the paraphernalia on the tray and started unzipping her jeans. "I had a fight with Rita; that's why my eyes are so red. I'll get over it."

"What'd you fight about?" he asked, turning his attention to the gauze and the alcohol. Behind him he heard her flop onto the bed.

"Same old shit," she mumbled into the mattress. He turned and got her swabbed, then moved quickly into the injection, on her left side this morning.

"Ow! Jesus Christ, do you have to wiggle it while it's in there?"

"I didn't wiggle it," he said, dropping the whole assembly into the sharps container. "Do you want to try one of these hand warmers? They came in yesterday."

He heard her sigh. "Sure. Whatever."

When he turned again, having snapped the plastic pouch at its center and felt the grainy filling heating up, she was scrabbling around with her arms until she found the pillow and pulled it under her shorn head. "I can't sleep, either," she grumbled, as he placed the pouch gingerly on the sore spot. Carefully, he folded over a corner of his Aunt Gladys's chenille bedspread and covered Darlene with it.

"Just take a nap," he invited, and, with a quick glance at the TV tray, he backed out of the room.

She wasn't even surprised when she woke up at Earl's. She checked her watch, and then she rolled onto her back and lay still for a moment. She guessed that this room must have been Earl's when he was young and stayed with his aunt and uncle. Gladys and Ray had converted it into a guest room, with maple furniture and plaid curtains, and now they had left all the furniture behind. Darlene heard that all they had now was a foldout sleeper in their double-wide.

From the other room, she heard clicking. That would be Earl on the Net, moving product. Things went from one place to another, things in huge, seagoing containers or railroad tanks, and as they moved, money would be transferred. Earl had taught himself about it, with no one to show him how. He was a lot smarter than people she heard about, the ones Kat and Della discussed, who bought and sold stock, making and losing thousands in a day. At least when Earl got stiffed, he still owned what was in the containers.

There was light through a crack in the curtains, but Darlene studied the ceiling. She had the Suburban, in which she had delivered Kat to the airport the day before, so there was no hurry. She could e-mail her transcripts, then pick up tapes this afternoon, or even tomorrow morning. But she didn't want to get up right now. If she got up, she would have to think how to make it up with Rita while getting Rita to stay out of her business, and she could never figure how to do that.

And she should get Tiffany from school, instead of letting Rita do it. But maybe Rita should, Darlene told herself. I'm just too weepy.

She used the bathroom before she wandered out to see Earl,

splashing water over her face and even onto her head, then toweling dry and fluffing her bristly hair into place with her fingers. For a second, she wondered if she had a spare pair of earrings in her purse, then told herself to forget it.

Without speaking, she found herself a glass and pushed it under the ice dispenser. Then she opened the refrigerator and withdrew a Diet Dr Pepper. She looked around as she poured, opening a drawer and surveying the mismatched flatware. Earl looked up at her and smiled, but he made no comment. To the left of the kitchen window, the cabinet held cereal and spaghetti. Darlene stared for a second. "You like Jif?" she asked. "Jif better than Peter Pan?"

"That's probably from Gladys and Ray," Earl said. "Mostly, I just buy what's on sale. Store brand usually."

"Smooth or crunchy?"

"Smooth. Crunchy tears the bread. You feeling better?" He had turned from his desk to look toward the kitchen. His computer sat on a folding table he had set up in the living room, a few feet away from the window wall, but allowing him to see out when he peered over his monitor.

"Some," she replied. She sat on the sofa. It was leather, with ornately carved wooden arms. Pseudo-Mediterranean. Earl had found it at a yard sale. Two of the cushions were mended with duct tape, and Darlene wondered if he would mind if she turned the cushions over. Instead, she pulled at the cotton blanket, striped in bright colors and fringed with cotton, and spread it over the tape. "I'll be okay, once we get this baby planted."

"Just another week," Earl said.

"Another week and nine months," Darlene replied. The sofa was next to his worktable, so by turning she could see out the window, but only upward because of the angle. There were a few clouds now, in the sky between the trees, but the sun was strong. "Nine months of Rita."

"I didn't know it was that bad," Earl said.

"It's like, everything she did wrong, she's going to make sure she does right with Tiffany. You know, tuck her into bed, make her brush her teeth, feed her regular meals. She even reads her Dr. Seuss. Like Tiffany cares!"

Earl smiled as if he couldn't help himself. "Well, I always was kind of partial to Horton the elephant myself."

"Trust me, if it doesn't sing and dance on Saturday morning,

Tiffany's not interested. Anyway, that's not the point." Suddenly, Darlene felt as if she were suffocating. She slurped at the soda, held the glass up to her forehead. "Is it hot in here or what?"

"Seventy-one point five," Earl said proudly, reading it off the sensor he had affixed to his computer table.

He just doesn't get it, Darlene fumed. No one gets it. What's the fucking use? She was suffocating. She felt her skin drying out and tightening up, ready to split.

"Oh, well, maybe it's warmer where you are, here—" He stood and yanked on the pull chain for the overhead fan, which began to revolve silently.

"I need some cool air!" Darlene jumped to her feet and headed for the sliding glass door that led out to the little deck.

"Careful out there!" Earl warned.

He stood awkwardly in the center of the room, but by then she was through the door. She guessed he was warning her about the railing, which was pretty rickety. Even so she leaned out over it, letting the fiftyish weather cool her. Quickly, she counted, thinking what it would be like to be five or six months pregnant in August and September. Oh God! thought Darlene. How am I going to stand it, waddling around, sweating?

She remembered what it had been like to sit with that belly at the computer. Finally, she had rigged a keyboard holder from a bedside stand at the hospital where she worked, and that had enabled her to stay employed in word processing until Tiffany came.

I could always stop for the last month or two, Darlene reminded herself. Find another freelancer and let her and Lakeesha handle it. It was easier to think out here, in the cool air. For forty thousand, I could just drive around and pick up work, Darlene told herself. Call on people.

Earl jostled the sliding door behind her as he joined her outside. She supposed he didn't want her to think he was sneaking up on her, and however annoying, he meant well. She took another deep breath.

"It's not bad in the sun," he said. "Here's a coat, just in case."

"Oh, Earl, you didn't have to do that! Thank you, though." She gathered the lapels together as he draped the jacket over her shoulders. "What a gentleman!"

"At your service."

"I really do appreciate everything, Earl. I mean it. Not just the shots, but I mean, I was just thinking how, I would have done this for twenty-five, but you got Ryan up to forty."

"Oh, now, you could've done that, Darlene. I mean, I'm glad I could help with the Net search and all that, but, you know, you're real smart, Darlene, and, you know, feisty. You stand up for you and Tiffany."

"No, I couldn't have done that," Darlene insisted, and the admission brought home how truly alone she was in all this. "I couldn't . . . I can't really do anything much. That's what got me into this: I can't earn a living; I can't keep a man; I can't even keep a man from stealing my car. About the only thing I can do is make babies!" She turned her head. Damn these tears!

"Oh, now, Darlene," he began, then she heard him fumbling around. "Oh, um, here!"

She turned slowly, looked. In her experience, this was either where the guy wanted to console you by putting your hand in his pants or he was trying to find the door. "What is that?"

He held the flimsy cloth out to her. "It's a handkerchief. For you." The white cotton flapped a little in the breeze, its blue-striped border the style of some antique curtain.

"A handkerchief?"

He motioned slightly with it, gesturing for her to take it. "Yeah. I . . . my Uncle Ray always carried 'em, and they left a whole stack behind, ironed and everything. Go ahead." He waved the thing again. "It's clean."

Gingerly she accepted the handkerchief and dabbed at her eyes. A man's handkerchief, she thought. She had seen plenty of men in suits, with silk pocket squares. But the closest she had ever come to a man with a handkerchief was Dave, who always had some sort of grease-stained cleaning cloth hanging out of the back pocket of his work pants.

"Hey, listen, Darlene, cheer up. You'll get your forty thousand from Ryan, and that'll make a nice down payment someplace for you and Tiffany. Your business is going good; once you get settled in your own place, things'll be fine. Dave will fix up that Camaro in no time, you own it outright, you'll be living for next to nothing while you sock money away. Then, you deliver the baby and boom! You're ready for a whole new life!"

"Boy, you've really planned it all out for me!"

He didn't even know enough to defend himself. "Nah. I just listened to what you said, Darlene. It's pretty much what you told me you wanted to do. Except about the car, of course. I know you don't like that part."

"You bet I don't," Darlene said. "That first payment from Ryan's going for a new set of wheels. No more used cars, either. I'm getting something with a warranty. And I don't care what Dave and Rita think of that."

"I guess you want something dependable."

"And good-looking."

"I suppose that's important. First impressions and all that."

"You're humoring me, aren't you? Well, fuck you!" Darlene said without any force. "I'm getting what I want, and I want something that looks good and gets me where I want to go."

"Now, don't get mad, Darlene." His voice was annoyingly calm. "All's I'm saying is why don't you put things in the order you want them? And if you want the fancy car more than moving out of the Ladies Farm, then go for the car. But you just sound so miserable over there, and like you want something more substantial for you and Tiffany, I just thought the car might not be as important."

"Why do I have to choose?" It started out as a demand, but it ended in tears, like about half her sentences that morning. That made her angrier. "Damn it! Other people get nice cars and nice houses, why shouldn't I?"

"I think you should get whatever you want in your heart," Earl told her. "You deserve it, Darlene."

Thank God it was Earl. Who else would respond so generously to her shameless fishing? I don't care, thought Darlene. Sometimes you just need encouragement.

"And you will get what you want, Darlene," Earl continued. "As long as you keep at it."

"Yeah," she said finally, wishing she could match his intensity.

The trees along the river were mostly cottonwoods. From the deck, Darlene could look down on the treetops, where they were starting to feather out a little. They blocked the view of the Ladies Farm where the lawn sloped down to the opposite bank. From here it looked wild, a winter forest just coming into spring. She thought about how when Tiffany was a baby and Jason had disappeared she had bundled Tiffany up for a ride in the canoe. Then, looking at the baby, she had thought for a moment of pushing the canoe into the river and letting it float away. Fortunately the stream flowed right over the spillway and the noise of the water rushing over the low stones on its way to Castleburg's had jolted her alert to the possibility that the canoe could capsize.

Instead of Tiffany being plucked from the water by a kindly farmer, her baby could drown, or be bashed on the rocks.

The moment had passed in a second, and Darlene had shoved off with Tiffany, paddling upstream against the mild current, cooing to her baby girl. There had been hundreds of those moments as time went on; her initial horror had faded almost to amusement. She and Lakeesha joked about it, but she knew if things were ever really dismal, she could drop Tiff there. And she'd return the favor for 'Keesha.

Now, though, looking at the trees was like looking at some high school picture of herself, unformed and ignorant about the world.

Earl was talking, but she hadn't been listening. "What?" she said now. "What did you say?"

"That there's always room here. Those ladies own it anyway. You'd have your own room, and I wouldn't bother you, I swear. We could even put up some bookcases, make a separate little place for Tiffany out in the living room, so you'd have a room to yourself."

The second she looked at him, he started turning red. She knew he would, but she had to see if he was serious. It wasn't that she hadn't thought about what he was proposing. Darlene just knew there would be a price. And he had to understand she couldn't do anything that might jeopardize her setup with Ryan.

"Tiffany would miss Rita," she said almost automatically.

"Well, she'll be right across the river. It doesn't take five minutes to drive around through town." He thought for a minute. "One summer, we rigged up a rope across to the Freschatte kids, with pulleys. We used to clip things, notes and stuff, and pass 'em back and forth across the river." He smiled. "I guess they thought they were humoring some little kid, but I was in love with the daughter."

"Melissa?"

"Yeah. She used to baby-sit me. I thought she was the prettiest girl I'd ever seen." He took a deep breath. "Till you, of course."

"Oh, Earl, don't say that. There were plenty of pretty girls. Patty, for one."

"Yeah, but not like you. When you moved here—"

"Back here, you mean. I'll bet you didn't even know I was born here."

"Really?"

"Sydon Memorial," she told him. She wanted to get off the subject of herself. Who knew what kinds of things he might say now, and it would be better if she didn't hear them. "Of course, Carla was born in Fort Worth. But, you know, by the time Rita was ready to have me, Wendell was long gone. No one knew how quick he'd be back." Darlene thought a second. "I guess that's why Mama's so fond of Dave. She didn't marry him till much later, but I think, when she first moved back here, he must have helped her out some. His mother baby-sat us, while Mama was in Fort Worth during the day."

"Then what happened?"

Darlene shrugged. "Then Wendell showed back up and treated us to the Wendell and Rita show."

"I guess I was just safe up here on the hill with Uncle Ray and Aunt Gladys. Sort of like *Father Knows Best*: Uncle Ray driving into the General Dynamics plant in Fort Worth every day, Aunt Gladys taking me to school, working at the library. Anyway, I'll bet Tiffany would like to be sending notes to her mamaw on the rope across the river."

"Have you lost your mind?" Darlene asked him. "You rig up a rope, first thing Tiff'll do is try crossing the thing hand over hand." She shook her head and tried not to look so severe. "Tiffany'll do just fine without any ropes. She'll get used to living over here, long as Rita picks her up from school so she can get her time with Mamaw. It'll work just fine."

They were not what she had imagined. Kat had pictured them as youthful idealists, quick and long-limbed, and perhaps they had been. But when she rang the bell at the modest suburban home, it was answered by a stocky, middle-aged woman whose clipped gray hair and makeup-free face made Kat self-conscious about her carefully coordinated travel wardrobe.

Pam, in jeans and a sweater, ushered her in as two small, dark-skinned boys peeked out from behind her knees. The dog, a yappy black and white terrier, stood posted in the center of the hall, admitting entrance but allowing no forward progress until Pam signaled approval by hugging Kat. The boys, who looked about six, backed up as Pam ushered her inside. "Tom's picking Laurie up from riding. They'll be here in a few minutes."

"We're making bread," the smaller boy volunteered. "With soda."

"Irish soda bread," Pam explained, leading the way through a living room that featured a mantel packed with framed photos, all of children. Laurie was one of many who came here, Kat realized; the only one to stay. She followed Pam back to a large maple and copper kitchen. Everything seemed covered by a layer of flour, and Kat gratefully accepted Pam's offer of an apron. I'll put my jeans on later, she thought.

"I happen to be quite good at sifting and stirring," Kat informed the boys, who hopped around, dragging chairs to the table that served as a work counter. "What can I do?"

So she was wearing an apron the first time she saw her daughter. And she was sifting flour and baking soda while listening to Mark, the older boy's, discourse on why the raisins were soaking in the milk. Suddenly Matt, the younger boy, sprang to life as Flash, the terrier, began to bark and jump. "Clear the path!" Matt screeched. "We didn't clear the path." He disappeared out the side door, where Kat heard a car pulling up.

"House rule," Pam explained, turning from the counter where she was greasing and flouring baking pans. She seemed unperturbed to find herself caring for small children in her middle age. "No toys in Laurie's chair path."

Kat released the sifter, which was anchored to a large bowl, and turned toward the door. It led to a covered driveway in which she could see through the window a large green van pulling into the far side of the drive.

Outside Matt was still shrieking, flashing by the window with the terrier, who was surely his inspiration. Within Kat, the urge to rush outside wrestled with her desire to maintain her composure and quietly work herself into Laurie's routine. Rushing won, encouraged by Pam's smile and Matt's yelling, "She's here! She's here!"

"They're so excited," Pam said. "We told them we were getting a visitor from Texas, and they found Texas on the map site and mapped the whole route."

Kat barely heard. She was pushing open the storm door and then she was standing on the wide concrete carport, watching a man in his fifties waiting as the side door of the modified van slid open. The car was parked up against a homemade ramp that was even with the van's floorboard. "She's here from Texas! Our friend from Texas!" Matt shouted, and the reverberations off the brick house and carport roof were terrifying.

Kat saw movement inside the van and realized that it was someone in a wheelchair, backing up, maneuvering an exit, as Matt danced around on the pavement and his father turned to extend a hand to Kat. "Glad you're here," he said, grasping her hand with both of his. "I'm Tom." He was a tall, craggy-faced man, who had lost most of the hair on top of his head. "Laurie's excited about having a visitor." He lunged for Matt as the boy danced by. "Hey! Slugger! Is the path clear inside?"

"Yes."

"How about a jacket next time you run outside?"

"It's warm! I'm warm!" He squirmed away and looked inside the van. "Come on, Laurie!"

There was creaking, and the hum of an electric motor, then feet in slip-on leather walkers, and jeans, and the arms of the motorized chair, topped by curled hands, the right one operating a control device.

The funny thing was, she looked like Kat. Kat stood there, watching the child maneuver the chair to the top of the ramp. Then the girl stopped and looked up. Matt's shrieking stopped and Tom stood still and Kat looked up at her daughter's face. In the picture, the almond shape of her eyes and her wide, smooth forehead hadn't shown through, Kat thought. And the thick, taffy-colored hair had just looked brown.

Kat ignored the little line of drool, and the bobbing of the head. The girl's jaw was malformed, making her smile grotesque. But Kat had locked in on her gaze, and she stepped forward, face to face, as the girl sat in the chair atop the platform of the ramp. "Hello, Laurie," she said, holding a hand out and then placing it on top of the girl's left one. "I'm Kat. I came all the way from Texas to see you."

"Kat," the girl said softly. It was a mushy sound, the initial consonant almost an *H*. "I go inside," Laurie muttered in explanation, then turned all her concentration to the panel beneath her right hand. The ramp led in a gentle diagonal from the car to the door, so Laurie did not have to negotiate a corner, and Kat gathered from Tom's watchfulness that maneuvering into the house was not a skill Laurie had perfected. Nonetheless, they all stood clear as the chair rolled down the ramp to the door. Even Matt was silent as he tripped over to the door and held it open for his sister.

"How was riding?" Pam asked, giving Laurie a kiss as she wheeled by. "Let's get cleaned up and then we'll get you some lunch." She looked up and smiled at Kat, then turned back to Laurie. "Would you like Kat to help us in the shower?"

Laurie's bedroom adjoined a specially equipped bathroom in which "cleaning up" included emptying the bag into which her catheter drained and sponge bathing her as she sat in a special sling seat over the enlarged tiled shower. Kat followed Pam's lead, removing her shoes and socks before stepping into the enclosure and operating the handheld sprayer. When Pam backed out to find fresh clothes, Kat found herself alone with Laurie.

"Is this water warm enough?"

Laurie nodded.

"Too warm?"

She shook her head no.

Gingerly, Kat took the soapy washcloth and washed Laurie's front, soaping up her neck and shoulders and under and around her small, drooping breasts. "Can you lift your arms?" Kat asked softly, but Laurie just looked confused. With her left hand, Kat took Laurie's wrist and lifted it high to get the soapy cloth over the length of her arm and along her armpit and side. Behind her, Kat heard Pam reenter the bathroom.

"How are you doing?" she called in. "Here," she said, stepping back into the shower. "This is the two-person part. You lift."

Kat continued to hold the arm aloft.

"No, from under her arms. Out of the chair, that's right."

Kat, with both her arms under Laurie's, lifted the girl out of the chair so that her legs dangled as Pam washed between her legs and examined her buttocks. Laurie's arms hung by her sides; even the curled hands could not grasp Kat's arms. This is my daughter, Kat thought, hanging limp in my arms and being examined for pressure sores. She's been horseback riding and now we're showering and then we'll have lunch. Kat clutched Laurie to her.

"All clear," called Pam, and Kat relaxed her grip to lower Laurie to the chair. "Thanks," Pam said. "I can't check her when I do this on my own."

Kat nodded. She still wore the apron, and she was soaked through from sweat and shower.

"Okay, Laurie Lee. Let's see if Kat can wash your toes." She handed the cloth around to Kat.

Kat stooped and balanced on the balls of her feet as she resoaped the cloth. "Here," she said to Laurie. Kat grasped an ankle. "Let's see those toes."

"We'll get washed, and then dried," Pam said, draping a towel around Laurie's shoulders as Kat knelt at her feet. "And then maybe Kat can help us with lunch."

Kat paused in her washing for only a second to consider the task of spooning lunch into the mouth of her twenty-four-year-old daughter. They take the little ones to keep themselves young, Kat thought, soaping the washcloth and lifting the atrophied foot with its tightly curled toes. She ran the soapy cloth along Laurie's sole, then massaged it with her bare hand. They've grown old doing this.

Chapter Twelve

It was still the nicest examining room Darlene had ever seen. She stood in the center of the room where they would implant the embryo and nodded automatically as the nurse instructed her on changing into the examining gown and hopping up on the table. Once she was alone, Darlene peeked at the counter to make sure the little pass-through door was shut, then changed into the gown and hung her clothes on the padded suit hanger, suspending her jeans from the clips and smoothing her blouse over the top. There was really no reason to take off her bra, but she did, and placed it with her panties on the shelf in the curtained and carpeted dressing room.

She stood before the full-length mirror. Darlene pushed the flowered gown open in the front and studied her boobs, which were tender and much fuller, but still disappointing. When she was growing up she had assumed grown women all developed huge breasts, like her mother's. But even when she'd been nursing Tiffany, her size hadn't fulfilled her expectations. Now, though, she wouldn't even be nursing. But it was fun, seeing herself a little chesty without being pregnant yet.

Turning to her side, she studied her profile a little, pushing her belly out and pulling it back in. "Goodbye to that for a while," she said. She shrugged the gown back in place and stepped out to the table.

The neatest touch was the booties. They were floral, in tones of pink and purple to match the drapery and wallpaper, and they were attached to the stirrups.

She sat up on the table, her legs dangling off the side, until she heard the nurse knock. Then came the parade. First the embryologist, with Ryan and Jill in tow. He had thawed the embryos and graded them, and the trio had agreed to implant two. Darlene nodded, shrugged. She had signed a contract agreeing to implant up to three. Then Lantinatta and two nurses prompted her one more time to recite her agreement that if she got pregnant from the implantation that Ryan and Jill would be the ones to decide whether or not to continue the pregnancy, unless it imperiled her health.

The embryologist had retreated to the lab on the other side of the pass-through, and Dr. Lantinatta patted the table next to where she sat and said, "Why don't you swing around and we'll get started. You haven't emptied your bladder, have you?"

"Nope," Darlene answered. The clearest ultrasound for the procedure depended on Darlene's bladder exerting the correct pressure on her uterus.

"I'd forgotten all about that," Jill said. "Are you uncomfortable?" She and Ryan stood uncertainly near the head of the table.

"I'm fine," Darlene said. She didn't know why everyone made such a big deal about not peeing. She never had a problem with that, even when she had been nine months pregnant, and she was really fatigued with reminders from the nurses, who had even called this morning.

"Your friend, uh . . . Earl, is out front," one of the nurses said. "Did you want him to come back?" It was standard for the surrogate's support team to join the intended parents at the implantation.

"No, that's okay." Darlene didn't mind, but she figured Earl would be just as happy not seeing the procedure. Especially with Jill and Ryan in the room. "He can just come in afterwards, when I'm lying down," she instructed.

She was on her back now, scooting down toward the end of the table. The nurse took her bare feet and put them into the warm booties. Lying this way, with the two nurses and Dr. Lantinatta at the end of the table and the paper blanket draped over her lower body, Darlene had a much clearer view of Ryan and Jill than of anything that was going on with her body. She felt someone insert the speculum. Then the nurse leaned over and switched on the monitor for the ultrasound. She smiled at Darlene.

This was the kind of place where even the goop for the ultrasound was a comfortable temperature before the nurse reached under the draping and spread it over her belly. It felt fine going on.

Standing at the side of the table, the nurse positioned the ultrasound low on Darlene's belly, and studied the screen. "You want the lights?" the other nurse asked. The ultrasound nurse nodded, and the lights dimmed.

"There," said the one standing by the table. She nodded at the monitor.

Between her knees, Darlene saw the top of Dr. Lantinatta's head tilt back. "That's good," he said.

The room light came up again. "Okay, Darlene," the doctor said. "We've got a clear shot of your uterus. We've got two embryos graded excellent, ready to be passed through. I've got the trusty turkey baster. How are you feeling?"

"Fine."

"Ready?"

"Ready," Darlene said. She thought about the shots. More than ready.

The lights dimmed, throwing everything except the bright ultrasound screen into shadow.

Oddly, for such a high-tech place, they cued the egg man by opening the little pass-through door and one of the nurses putting her face there to announce, "We're ready."

They had shown her the long, needle-width syringe that would be inserted into her uterus. They had explained that before the syringe was inserted, they would examine the embryo dish under a microscope to make certain that both microscopic embryos were in the syringe and no longer in the dish. Recalling the explanations filled the few moments between the announcement that they were ready and Dr. Lantinatta's saying, "Okay, Darlene, here are the eggs. We need you to stay perfectly still now."

In the semidarkness, Darlene had glanced at Jill before turning to the screen, and she guessed Jill continued to bite her lip while the straight line that was the syringe advanced into the fuzzy background that was Darlene's vagina and entered her cervix.

"Small cramp," Dr. Lantinatta said, and Darlene said, "Uh huh," but the little spill out the end of the needle—light gray splash against medium gray fuzz from the tip of the black line—and the needle's hasty retreat distracted her from the discomfort.

"Good job!" said Dr. Lantinatta. "How are you feeling?"

Darlene blinked. "Fine," she said. The lights came up a little bit, but not bright. Someone pulled the speculum, and the nurses busied themselves with what she guessed was cleanup at the counter.

Dr. Lantinatta stood and walked to the side of the table and took her hand.

"That went perfectly. How are you feeling?"

"Fine," Darlene repeated. She wiggled around a little on the table, flexing and unflexing her toes as she slipped the stirrups and slid up the table.

"Are you comfortable lying here?" He motioned toward the alcove. "Is that your pillow? Would you like it?"

"Yeah," she said.

"I'll get it," said Jill. Until she spoke, Darlene had lulled herself into thinking that just she and the doctor were making these babies. Since the splash, she had forgotten completely about Ryan and Jill.

Darlene lifted her head to let Jill slide the pillow under her, then she closed her eyes. Ryan had been silent through the entire procedure, Darlene realized. He was probably worried he might say something to her in front of Jill that might sound too familiar. Now, though, he spoke to Jill. "We ought to just let her rest," he whispered.

With her eyes still closed, she heard them walking out of the room. Darlene listened to the two nurses shuffling papers and moving things. One of them came to stand by her bed, taking her hand to feel her pulse. "How're you doing, Darlene?" she asked in a cheery voice.

"I'm okay," Darlene said. "It only hurt for a second."

"That's good." As she spoke, she covered Darlene with a blanket. "We need you to lie still about another seven minutes, okay? Then, if you'd like, we'll get you a bedpan and you can empty your bladder." She pulled the blanket up to Darlene's chin. "But we need you to stay down, on your back, for a total of twenty minutes, okay? And then we'll move you to the bench over there. Is that all right?"

"Sure," said Darlene. "I'll just wait till the twenty minutes and use the bathroom when I get up. But, could someone get Earl and tell him it's okay to come in now?"

She opened her eyes when she felt him take her hand. He raised his eyebrows in a question and she smiled. "I don't know why I'm so sleepy," she said, breaking into a yawn as she spoke.

"But you're okay? You feel okay?"

"Yeah. Fine. Haven't I started to glow, yet?"

"Glow? Oh!" He got it, but shook his head. "You're always glowing, to me."

Darlene struggled to keep her eyes open one more second. "I knew I did the right thing, moving over to your place."

Kat looked up at the skylight above Nick Lantinatta's bed and considered what a mess it would be when it leaked. In Kat's experience, all skylights, even skylights in modern suburban bedrooms with sitting rooms and elaborate, sunken-tub bathrooms, leaked. It was only a question of when.

"I've been an innkeeper too long," she lamented, explaining what she had been thinking.

He smiled, tugged at her hair a little, but made no comment. His silence alarmed her, and she considered that he had equally dour professional observations about his own area of expertise. This left her particularly vulnerable, since it was a bright, sunny afternoon, allowing the skylight to expose her without mercy. She smiled at him as she drew the sheet a little higher under her chin.

"I really appreciate your picking me up at the airport," she said.

He shrugged. "My pleasure." Then he grinned and kissed her. "Literally."

Kat laughed. They had gone from the airport to a late lunch on the closed-in patio of a Mexican restaurant, and then to his home. They had, she reflected, behaved in a mature and responsible way, dropping the pretense of examining his metal sculptures and agreeing to take their reunion to the bedroom instead of conducting their debauchery in the living room. A king-size bed in a well-appointed bedroom and bath was far kinder to middle-age romance, Kat thought.

"Well," she laughed now, "I'm glad you don't play golf."

"I'm glad you thought to come back on a Wednesday afternoon," he said.

"That wasn't exactly an accident." She bent her head a little, nuzzled up against his chest.

"You feeling better now?" he asked.

"Uh, yeah."

"I meant about Laurie."

Kat closed her eyes a second, opened them back up. Part of the attraction to Nick was the comfort of lying in the arms of someone who knew her worst secrets. But that comfort conflicted with the notion of jumping into bed with the man to erase the details of a painful visit to her disabled daughter.

"The easiest thing," Kat told this man now, "is to say I don't have a daughter. It's what I've said all along: that Hal and I tried to have children, but our one pregnancy ended with a baby who died in childbirth." She noted his impassive expression, knew it was a professional skill that protected the listener as well as the speaker. "But you know," and here her voice faltered a little before she regained her determination, "that's not so easy once you've seen Laurie. I mean, on the one hand, Pam and Tom are the real parents. Not just real: heroic. But there's something, I don't know . . ."

"A biological urge?" Nick suggested lightly.

"No," Kat said. "Not biological at all. Sort of . . . behavioral. Like, it's just the right thing to do, to acknowledge that I gave birth to her, that I was unable to raise her, that I have been able to help, but that I acknowledge it. Acknowledging it . . . I don't know . . . that seems like something, some little thing, that I should be able to do."

"Because it seems braver than hiding it," he said. He had propped himself up on one elbow and was stroking her shoulder.

"Yes," she agreed. "Does that sound silly?"

"It's not silly," he said. "It's a little bit of what I was referring to when I asked you if you were really ready to know what had happened to your daughter. You just have to think through who else might be affected by your acknowledgment before you go public."

"Well, Della already knows. And my folks are dead; so are Hal's, I think. So it's really not that many people."

"Except Laurie and Tom and Pam and their other kids."

Kat raised her head off the pillow. "Well, I wouldn't tell Laurie," she said emphatically. "Pam and Tom are her parents, there's no doubt about that. And the other kids are certainly aware that Laurie is adopted. All of them are adopted, except their two oldest."

He didn't say anything, but his mild expression had the capacity to alarm. "You think I should tell Laurie?" she asked.

He looked thoughtful, but Kat raced forward before he could speak. "You think Laurie might hear it from someone else? She wouldn't even understand. It wouldn't . . . you think she would understand? Who would tell her?" She felt herself laughing maniacally. "You just jump into the conversation whenever you feel like it, okay?"

"She knows her mother and father, doesn't she?" He rolled away from her, slipped into his shorts and headed for the bathroom. "I'll be back in a second."

"Take your time," she said. She reached for the phone and called the Ladies Farm to alert Della that she wouldn't be home that evening.

"Let me see if I've got this right," Della said after they exchanged greetings. "You just visited your daughter and now you're spending the night with the doctor who placed her for adoption?"

"He placed her in a special home; she's han . . . she has special needs. The home placed her for adoption."

"How'd it go?"

"Better than I would have guessed, but terrible in a lot of ways," Kat told her friend. "She's severely handicapped. I could never have done what they do," Kat said. "Not then. Not now."

"You sell yourself short."

"Maybe." Kat didn't want to discuss it. "Anyway, are you okay if I wait till tomorrow?"

"No problem," Della said. "We have two people coming in tomorrow evening, six on Friday."

"I'll be home by noon," Kat promised. She could tell by Della's voice that Tony would be spending the night.

Later, explaining it to Nick over a bowl of microwaved popcorn, she said, "Della's a lot happier these days, with Tony around. I don't know why they don't remarry, except that she doesn't want to seem too much like Rita."

"Rita's the marketing one?"

"No, that's Della. Rita's the hairdresser. Actually, Della's the manager, these days, since Pauline died."

They had moved downstairs to a cavernous living area with the kitchen at one end and a built-in video screen at the other. He had offered to show a movie, but even selecting one seemed too much of a challenge right now. Instead, she got up and wandered around the room, surveying the metal pieces—sculpted furniture and welded figures—before seating herself on the stainless steel love seat that was all liquid curves and polished surfaces.

Nick had brought her suitcase in from the car, and Kat had changed into sweats. They were navy, with a vee-necked top and white piping along the sleeves and legs, and had proved insubstantial against the cold in the northeast.

"I had to buy a sweat suit," Kat told Nick now. "A really heavy one. You can't believe how cold it is there in the mornings. Especially with no carpet. For Laurie's chair."

Nick sat on a sofa, his feet propped on the large iron and wood coffee table before him, and a huge stack of mail by his side. He had set a shopping bag up next to the sofa and he was chucking mail as they talked. "Sorry," he explained now. "Wednesday's the only time I have to go through this. Is their house heavily modified?"

"I think Tom's a frustrated inventor," Kat said. "He's built these incredible ramps so she doesn't have to back up . . . backing up really confuses her. And a sling seat in the shower. And of course he's modified their table—they have a big, eat-in kitchen, no dining room—to accommodate the chair. And you wouldn't believe her bedroom: all the drawers are perfect height for her, so even if she can't reach and pick out anything, she can look in when Pam opens the drawers and she can choose what to wear. It's really important to her."

"Where'd you stay?" he asked, dropping a magazine into the rack on the side of the coffee table.

"Well, at first I was at a motel, but after the first night, Pam just thought it would be easier—you know, I wanted to know the whole thing, what it's like getting her up in the morning, what it takes to feed her, all that—so I just slept on the sleep sofa in their family room."

"You really wanted to punish yourself, didn't you?" He looked up from the mail. "Bathing, toileting, feeding. Hard penance."

"I wanted . . . I didn't want to be one of those Disneyland Dad types . . . you know, the ones who only see the kids on vacations and holidays. I wanted to know what her real life is like."

Even as she spoke, Kat realized how stupid it sounded. She couldn't be a Disneyland Dad because she wasn't really any kind of parent; her "child" had a mother and a father. "I know I'm just a tourist there," she offered now. "I don't want you to think I'm deluding myself."

"This is an odd date," Nick said. "We eat lunch, we go to bed, we probe the most agonizing corners of your past while I sort mail."

Kat pushed herself up from the metal love seat, which, even through the sweats and a chair pad, had grown hard and unforgiving. From behind the sofa, she put her arms around him, nuzzled his neck. "So, does that mean you want to screw around?"

He reached up over his head and pulled on her arms, turning as he tumbled her onto the sofa. Her back pressed deep into the soft fabric of the upholstery as he slid her knit pants off her legs. Cushions and mail slipped away; his clothes, her clothes were tossed somewhere, Kat didn't know where. At some point they bounced onto the floor themselves, careful to slide away from the sharp points of the coffee table, challenging themselves with stacks of pillows and a fringed, shawl-like blanket Kat had foolishly assumed to be a fashion statement by some decorator.

His mouth tasted of cola and the hair on his chest had a soap-and-sweat scent that prompted her both to rub against it and to bite his shoulder whenever the possibility presented itself. They grew slick in the afternoon light. From the floor, the skylight in this room felt kinder, more golden, and through the patio door the greenery of late Texas winter—live oaks and hollies, punctuated by grayish sage and mounds of purple and gold velvet pansies—gave a greenhouse feel to the warmth and moisture. Even their urgency had a slowed-down, merged-to-their-surroundings feel, as if she were rubbing and stroking and taking into herself some quality of all the natural, neutral fabrics, the burnished metal and polished wood, and above all the art of Nick's creations, the bent and shaped, forged and sculpted solidity of all the things around them.

They ended in a heap, grinding and grunting their way to a mutual collapse, an implosion, Kat thought, on the nubby fabric of a rug whose colors she could not have described. She gave him a moment to catch his breath, but no longer, because she had to ask, "Do you think Martha Stewart does this?"

"Punch line as climax," he answered, rolling backward and pulling sofa pillows up for their heads. "Fear of intimacy. Fear of silence. Fear of scrutiny."

She lay on her back and closed her eyes, feeling around with her hands for the shawl, but having no luck. "That's an odd word, when you think about it: *scrutiny*."

"Fear of conversation."

She thought she was falling in love.

Later, they showered in the master bathroom, promising themselves a long soak in the tub at some later date, and then they ordered in Chinese food, moo shui pork and kung pao chicken, which they ate near the kitchen end of the great room, at a table in front of a wood-burning stove fueled by a gas log. He was explaining the advantages of the gas log, including the timer control, when

Kat thought about Darlene and decided she had better tell Nick that she knew her. She wasn't sure why, except that she didn't want, later, for him to think she had concealed something from him. It was odd; deception was the hallmark of all her relationships with men, and her glimpses of her friends' relationships convinced her that she was not much different in that regard from anyone else.

Nonetheless, his explanation of the gas log was followed by her explanation of how Darlene Kindalia, in whom he was going to implant an embryo, was the daughter of one of her partners in the Ladies Farm.

Nick shrugged. "We implanted this morning; it went fine. I think Marta Kaplan's her regular doc. Once she checks out, she'll go back to Marta."

Oh, Kat thought, spreading plum sauce onto a pancake and spooning shredded pork and vegetables atop the sauce. He thinks I told him because I'm concerned about Darlene.

Even after she moved over to Earl's, Darlene continued to let Rita pick up Tiffany at preschool and keep her till around five. It hadn't taken Earl an hour to set up her computer for her, and Darlene spent most days doing her word processing in the morning and delivering transcripts and picking up tapes in the afternoon. Then she'd swing by the Ladies Farm to get Tiff, take her to Earl's, and the three of them would have dinner.

Her days still began with the shot, which Earl administered after she—or sometimes Earl—returned from taking Tiffany to preschool. Since the implantation, though, the shots bothered her less. Darlene believed her body simply ignored the shots and was moving into pregnancy in its customary way. They wouldn't let her confirm at the doctor's office until the ninth day, but Darlene was sure.

That's why, after she dropped her last transcript, she stopped at the Wal-Mart. She had tried hard not to shop there since high school, when it was the source for all her makeup and most of her wardrobe, but the women in the injection class swore by the Wal-Mart test. Even the nurse, when Darlene asked her, had admitted that most of their patients did their own test even when the instructions told them not to, and that everyone thought the Wal-Mart test was best.

The store on the highway outside Sydonia had closed, but there was a large, twenty-four-hour one in Fort Worth, and Darlene figured the tests there would be fresher anyway.

And of course it would be silly, once she was there, not to stock up on stuff she needed. When she moved out, she had been surprised at how many things—cosmetics, toiletries, vitamins—she needed that had just come with her room at the Ladies Farm. Even her nail polish had been available in Rita's salon.

Earl was pretty good about basics: toilet paper, paper towels, even toothpaste were stored in cartons he had stockpiled from deals on the Net. But Darlene preferred her own brand of mouthwash, and Tiffany had grown fond of bubble baths from the courtesy bottles at the Ladies Farm. So she found a bottle of Scrubbles in a dancer-shaped bottle, which she figured would ease Tiffany's transition, and then she threw in a few multi-packs of socks and panties as long as she was walking through the kid things.

The pregnancy tests were in the family planning aisle, below the condoms. Wal-Mart had replaced their store-brand stuff with the Equate label, but she could tell it was still theirs. Darlene wondered for a moment if she should get the two-pack, but she knew it wasn't necessary. This was Monday, and she could go to the doctor's on Friday. Besides, she was sure. She just wanted to make it official.

The transcription tapes she had picked up today weren't due till Wednesday. Tiffany had an all-day trip to the Museum of Science and History in Fort Worth tomorrow. Darlene smiled. She'd pack a nice lunch for her, maybe get some of those small packs of Fritos while she was here. Then Darlene would have the whole day to herself.

She put the test into the basket. She'd give it one more night, use it right after her shot in the morning. Darlene wavered for a second over the condoms, but, what the hell: he deserved some choice in this. Ignoring the price, she tossed the deluxe sampler pack into the basket and then headed out to look for the Fritos.

Darlene skipped out of Fort Worth before traffic got too bad. Kat had taken the Accord all week, and Della needed the Suburban, but Darlene had Earl's Expedition. She sat up higher than she did in the Suburban, and she looked down at all the other cars, including the other SUVs. She figured she would let things settle down a little with Rita before she asked Dave about the Camaro. It was still sitting at his shop, but she knew he had checked out the engine and was talking to a friend in Odessa who ran an auto graveyard and could get him body parts.

Maybe what Earl said was right. Maybe she should let Dave fix the Camaro and she could make do with that while she used Ryan's money to get herself someplace to live. Her business was going okay. If she moved back to Fort Worth, she could work the doctors in Arlington and the mid-cities, maybe even Dallas. There were lots of women like Lakeesha, who would freelance as long as she paid them cash.

Tiffany was playing in the area reserved for her at Rita's salon. She had her earphones on her head and she was singing along to some country song. Rita had a fascination with the George Jones/Tammy Wynette relationship, and she had passed several CDs of their greatest hits along to Tiffany. "C'mon, Tiff," Darlene encouraged. "Let's get everything put away for Mamaw."

Rita glanced over from her comb-out. "Show Mama what we got her," she called out.

Tiffany broke into smiles. "Here, Mama. We got Herby Wonders."

She fished a cardboard package from her backpack and held it up to her mother. Darlene, who was sitting in the play area, trying to reassemble Barbie's Harley so they could hit the road, looked up blankly at the package. The little box was decorated with green leaves and the logo of the Herbal Wonder organization; through the years, Rita had brought home thousands of dollars' worth of pills, potions, beauty aids and decorative accessories sold by her regular customers. "You have to buy something," was her ground rule, and their lives had been filled with decorative spice bottles and scented candles because of it.

Darlene reached out a hand to let Tiffany give her the package, which contained, according to its box, the miracles of natural goodness in convenient daily doses. Vitamins and minerals nature's way.

"Oh!" Darlene exclaimed. "Herbal Wonders." She held her arms out to Tiffany, who charged her and they tumbled backward together. She buried her nose in her daughter's hair and hugged her tightly. "You are such a sweet girl to give something to Mommy! I can hardly wait to get home to take these." Darlene sat back up, set Tiffany, who still wore the headset, on her feet. "Come on!" Darlene said. "Let's get cleaned up so Mommy can get home and take her Herby Wonders." She turned away before she rolled her eyes.

They almost made a clean getaway, making it as far as the Expedition, but Rita evidently put down her brush to run out after them, brandishing the vitamins. "Darlene! Look what you forgot.

Now, Tiffany, you make sure Mama takes these!" She thrust the package of vitamins through the open door at Tiffany.

Tiffany, buckled tightly down on the seat, took the vitamins eagerly. "Mom!" she said with exasperation.

"Tiffany, what a close call! Now you thank Mamaw for remembering them for us. Go on!" Darlene urged her daughter.

"Thank you, Mamaw," Tiffany intoned.

Darlene forced herself to be gentle as she closed the car door, and she waited until Rita had followed her all the way around to the driver's side before she wheeled on her mother.

"Don't you ever tell my daughter to take care of me again! Do you hear me? I'm the adult, and I'll take care of myself! And my daughter!"

"Now, Darlene, I know you're an adult," Rita said. "But, honey, if you're making me a new grandbaby, I want a healthy one."

Darlene gripped the door handle, but didn't open it. "Did you tell Tiffany about this baby? Did you?"

"Well, now, of course not," Rita said. She put a placating hand on Darlene's arm. "Though I do think she's ready for a baby brother or sister."

Darlene jerked her arm away "What'd you tell her?"

"I told you, Darlene, I didn't tell her anything! But she sees babies at the shop, Darlene. She sees her cousins, and Lakeesha's kids. If she had a baby sister or brother—"

"You just kiss that goodbye," Darlene hissed. "I know you: You're thinking this baby's Earl's and I'll be so grateful he treats me well I'll marry that poor slob and settle down right next door. Well, get this straight. I'm carrying this baby for someone else. For money. This baby's not Earl's. It's not mine. And it's sure as hell not yours!"

Chapter Thirteen

You have to comb out Lou Barkham, Rita told herself as she watched the Expedition churn up a wake of gravel on its way up the driveway and onto the street. You can't leave a customer sit like that, with half a head.

"Sorry," she said as she returned to Lou. "It's just like Darlene to run off without her vitamins."

"She's looking real good," Lou said. "Some girls just let themselves go, when they've got a kid and their husband . . . or whatever . . . runs off. Darlene keeps herself up. Where's she working now?"

"She does freelance transcription," Rita said. She worked the back-combing brush along the left side of Lou's crown, feathering it just a little to give it height. "We've got some serious roots here," she admonished her longtime customer. "You want me to set you down for color next time? We can just do the roots."

"Nah. I'll get it," Lou said, and Rita didn't argue. Another home dye job was going to kill the ends of Lou's oversaturated red hair, but she'd just bring it to Rita to fix, and Rita would.

"Did you have a good weekend?" Rita asked, hoping she hadn't asked that earlier. It didn't matter. Lou was off and running with a description of her daughter's travails as proprietor of the fountain at Sydonia DrugRite. Evidently her duties had conflicted with the regular Saturday get-together by the WaLuKa trio, a group of three clerks from the courthouse who seemed to be joined at the hip. They had made the cake for Rita's wedding when she married Dave, and they were famous for their peach cobbler, which they sold at the peach festival.

Dave always said it was that cake—Oh, God! Dave! Rita gripped the rounded brush and turned away so her face wouldn't show in the mirror. "Let me blow-dry the rest," she mumbled. *What would she tell Dave?*

Earl was his cousin for one thing. And for another, this was just the kind of mess he was always fixing for her. But who could fix this?

She switched on the blow-dryer and watched Lou's gray roots swirl away from her scalp. She wound the hair idly around the cylindrical brush in her right hand and studied the pattern of hair falling into place as she pulled the brush out. It never failed, Rita thought, winding and releasing hair as she aimed and re-aimed the dryer. Once the hair gets the right cut, it doesn't much matter what you do to it, it'll fall right into place.

Tears welled up as she recalled her Uncle Jack, who had trained her in his barber shop and promised to send her to barber school. That was before he ran off with his manicurist and settled in Muskogee. The barber shop had been sold to pay off his debts, and Rita had eventually struggled through the Waverly School of Beauty. At least she got her license before she married Wendell.

She smiled as she switched off the dryer and smoothed Lou's hair. Admiring her own work always comforted her. But it didn't fix things.

They had guests, which meant that after she ushered Lou out and swept up, she washed, and then hurried to the kitchen. Kat had made it back from Fort Worth, and Della was directing her in what went into the walnut and spinach salad besides walnuts and spinach. "I'll get the table," Rita offered, grabbing a chef's apron and slipping it over her head.

"There's three of them," Kat advised. "They brought a friend. Male. Recently widowed."

"Well, whip out the red meat," Rita said.

Kat shook her head, and Della laughed. Rita pulled place mats, flatware, and dishes from the sideboard in the dining room, and set three places at the oak table. Then she returned to the kitchen and pulled a container of jalapeno corn chowder from the refrigerator. "We've got biscuits, right?"

"Fennel," Della confirmed. Since Pauline's death, Della had taken over menus and most of the cooking. Her cooking was less consistent than Pauline's, which had forced them to keep the freezer stocked with emergency meals, but it was also more adventurous than Pauline's. Rita liked the way Della combined things, even if she made biscuits with whole wheat flour. And the guests seemed happy most of the time.

"I'm serious about the meat," Rita said. "Don't you think we ought to at least crack open a few chicken breasts?"

"Which ones?" Kat asked Della. "Soy-beer-ginger, lemon-garlic, herb and spice?"

"Oh, come on!" Della threw up her hands. "This is an intelligent, sensitive guy of the millennium. Guys like that don't need meat at every meal!"

"Well, we didn't say steak," Kat said. "Even Nick thinks dinner means meat of some kind." She turned to Rita. "Did you get a look at this guy? Does he look carnivorous?"

Rita shook her head. "Look at us! Not one of us is sure about what to feed a man for dinner. We're pathetic!"

"Lemon-garlic," Della said. "With skins. Under the broiler."

"We are pathetic," Kat concurred, opening the freezer. "It's a good thing we have each other."

"Amen," muttered Della, who seemed deflated by Rita's pronouncement. She sat down on the stool and looked at the biscuits, which were set to go into the oven whenever the guests showed up.

"Where's Tony?" Rita asked.

"Home. I sent him home." Della lifted a hand, then dropped it again. "He's got a big job at the shop, he has people coming in at six in the morning to do the collating. It's a specialty thing, it all has to be done by hand. What about Dave?"

"He's late at the store tonight, Cynthia quit, and Luis fell off a ladder helping his father unstring the Christmas lights—only because they're moving and he didn't want to leave them—and I forgot to ask Darlene if Lakeesha wants to come in a few nights a week, when Eddie's home to watch the kids."

"How's Darlene?" Kat asked.

Rita studied Kat's expression. "Why?" she asked. "How do you think she is?" She and Kat had few silences and fewer unspoken disputes. But Rita saw the struggle in Kat's eyes and felt her own narrowing. She bit her lip.

Rita felt without seeing that Della started to speak, then stopped.

"I think Darlene's pregnant," Kat said. "That's how I think she is."

"But you didn't think you should discuss this particular pregnancy with me: her mother?"

"She asked me not to."

"She asked you not to?" Rita didn't even try to keep the shrillness from her voice. "She asked you not to?"

"Listen, Rita, I told her to tell you. I'm the one who's always telling her to talk to you. But she didn't feel she could." Kat was still holding the freezer bag with the chicken breasts, and she held it up in resignation. "That's all. I'm sorry. But she wouldn't trust me ever again if I told you. And I knew, sooner or later, she'd have to tell you. And, honestly, think about it"—she set the bag on the counter and gave it an annoyed look—"what difference does it make when you know? It wouldn't have been any less upsetting if you had known two months ago."

"You knew two months ago?"

Della slid off the stool and stepped around to put an arm around Rita. "Rita, let that go. You've got enough—"

"Two months ago?"

"Honey," Della said, "the guests—"

Rita hated *honey the guests*. It was their version of *not in front of the children*, and she wasn't through. She jerked her shoulder out from under Della's arm. "I'm not done." She advanced toward Kat. "And the guests aren't here yet. If I had known two months ago, I could have talked her out of it."

"Face it: If you had tried to talk her out of it, she would have done it for a buck-fifty!"

"Kat!" Now Della strode between them, but Rita pushed past her. She got right up into Kat's face. But that was when she realized she didn't know what to say. That didn't stop her, though. She could sputter.

"She listens to me," Rita insisted.

Kat didn't back up. She didn't blink. She did smile. "She listens to you and does the opposite," Kat said in a reasonable voice.

"You bitch! You think kids are so easy to raise, they just do whatever you tell them? I'm the first one to tell you Darlene's got her own mind, and I'm proud of it." Now Rita smiled back at Kat. "You might not like to admit it, but that independent streak's just like me."

"Oh, I'm the first to admit your daughter's a lot like you," Kat said. "I just see it as my duty to help her overcome it."

Rita tried to get her breath, tried to formulate a response, but Della interrupted.

"Kat, how about getting that chicken into the microwave?" Della said. "And how about both of you just backing off a little?" She turned to Rita. "You know Kat's not what's upsetting you. What's upsetting you is that your daughter is a gestational carrier."

"Is that what they call it?" Rita started off sarcastic, but by the end of the sentence she realized how pathetic it was: Della and Kat knew more than she did about her baby girl.

"Rita, why don't you just go talk with Darlene?" Kat suggested. "Take a long ride, away from Earl—Della and I can watch Tiffany if you want—and talk to Darlene."

Rita shook her head. "Nah. I know Darlene. She'll talk when she's ready. You're right," she told Kat. "If she thinks I want to talk, that's the last thing she'll do. I'll wait her out."

She tried to explain it later to Dave, but he just blinked and continued getting ready for the next day. It was quiet in the store; if anyone stopped at all, it was just to fill up at the pump and pay with a swipe of the credit card. In the green of the fluorescent lights, Dave occupied himself with pulling breakfast burritos and sausage sandwiches from the freezer in the back and putting them in the cases up front.

Rita pulled out another dolly and pushed it over to the stacks of candy bars. She pulled a box of each kind and stacked it in the empty carton on the dolly. Then she wheeled the dolly out to the front and began replenishing the candy display. Once Dave was done with the breakfast case, he worked on the bread, moving the old bread to the half-price rack. "Well, whose baby is it?" Dave asked.

Rita shrugged. "Some doctor and his wife. One of her clients." She reached down for a box of Milky Ways, and started opening it. Then she looked sideways at Dave, who was putting the old bread into a red plastic bin at the end of the next aisle. "Well, not just any client." He looked up. "She actually had an affair with this boy a few years back. Then he set her up in business. You might say he's been sort of her benefactor."

"I think there's another name for it."

Rita shook her head and looked at the candy rack in front of her. She reached up and emptied a box, depositing the candy bars on top of the box of Milky Ways. Then she pulled the empty box from the shelf and replaced it with the full box. Only then did she see that she had topped off the Milky Ways with Hershey Bars. "Shit!" She pulled the Hersheys out, then looked around in frustration for a place to put them. "Damn it!"

"I think shit is a better word for him than dammit," Dave said.

"You want my help or not?" Rita demanded. "I've got plenty of things at the salon that need doing. I didn't have to come over to help you!"

"Yes you did," Dave said. "How else could you bitch and moan about Darlene if you didn't come over here?"

She shook her head, deposited the Hershey Bars a little further down the aisle, on top of the boxed doughnuts, which at least offered a flat surface. Then she scrabbled around for the old box of Milky Ways and worked them into the new box.

"How much money is she getting?"

Rita shook her head, pulled out one of the two new boxes of Hershey Bars and united them with their older siblings from atop the doughnuts. "Beats me." She set down the candy. "That's probably the most depressing part: Darlene would do this for a new Camaro . . . hell, Darlene would do this for the down payment."

"She's just young, Rita."

"I know that, Dave. That's why I'm so worried. I was young too. Young and stupid."

"I don't remember the stupid part." He grinned at her from the bargain bread.

"Remember the part when I left you for Wendell?"

"Oh yeah." He shook his head. "That."

"But I never, in my stupidest moment, never would have agreed to have a baby for money."

"How about sex?"

Rita frowned. "Does jewelry count?"

"I'll be in the back," Dave said. He took hold of the dolly. "Looking for jewelry."

He was taking it all right, Rita thought, but she figured that was just because she herself was still so upset. She concentrated on the candy for a while. Two cars pulled up to the pumps and got gas, but no one even looked in to see if they were open.

At ten, Dave came out to the front and flipped off the lights at the island, leaving just the perimeter lights on outside. He triggered the electric lock. "I've got about another hour in the back," he told her. "You want me to run you home?"

Rita had walked over, but she knew it was much colder out now. "I'll stick around," she said. She smiled. "Count the cash for you."

"I'll bet."

When she finished what she knew to do on the shelves, she wandered to the back, but he had moved over to the garage. He was dragging equipment around and muttering to himself. She seated herself on the stool next to the pegboard where they hung work orders and customer keys. "So what do you think I should do?" she asked.

"Rita, what can you do? She's pregnant. She wants the money. They'd probably sue her if she got an abortion, anyway. So she's going to have that baby. 'My way of thinking, what you can do is look after Tiffany and try not to upset Darlene too much."

"You're awfully calm about this. My daughter's taking money to have a baby—"

"Well at least—"

"—and it makes my skin crawl."

"—it's something she already knows how to do."

Darlene had done enough of these tests to skip the directions, but she reviewed them anyway. She wanted to make sure she knew how long the stick stayed in her urine stream and what direction to turn it. "A thousand and one," she counted. "A thousand and two." She counted all the way up to ten, just to make sure, and then pulled the indicator. She slipped the cap over the wet end, then turned the thing face up so she'd be able to see the little plastic window. The directions said to wait at least a minute, but Darlene had worn her watch to make sure she waited at least three.

Then she looked. And then she looked again.

This had never happened before. Maybe she just needed to wait a little longer. Maybe it was different because of the shots, and that's why they told you not to bother with home tests. Maybe it was too early. She set down the indicator and reread the instructions.

Invalid. If there is no line visible in Control Window the test did not work properly. Darlene felt like a fool, recalling the tests in the store, and how easy it would have been to buy a double pack. She stared again at the indicator, at the round window and the rectangular one, marked *control* and *test*. How could the thing be blank? And why did it have to happen now? She was so sure!

Outside, she heard Earl's car in the driveway. She checked the mirror, plucked at her hair with her fingers to spike it up a little. She had meant to be wearing something—her short silk robe, maybe, or that little white nightie 'Keesha had given her last birthday—but here she stood in cotton tank and panties.

Maybe, thought Darlene, my hand moved when I was holding it and I didn't get it wet enough. Maybe I could just pee on the thing a little more and it would work. She studied her face in the mirror to calm herself. Maybe she should pierce her left eyebrow, put a little gold ring there. She didn't really like things that were uneven, though, and piercing both eyebrows wasn't cool. Maybe a little sparkler on the side of her nose . . .

Darlene heard the car door slam. Get a grip! she ordered herself. Earl would be inside in a minute. Unless she wanted to wait till after breakfast, she had to decide now. Why did this have to happen to her? Why didn't this happen to some girl who was married and it didn't matter if she found out today or next week?

Darlene's eyes filled with tears. I must be pregnant, she thought, I never cry like this. She waved her hand in front of her eyes to help dry the tears and turned to take the cap off the test stick. I'll just try again, she thought. Then she looked at the stick.

Both lines, bright as day!

Darlene clutched the stick to her and shook her head. All you had to do was wait!

She heard the front door open and close. "Dar?" Earl called. "You up?"

Darlene checked her hair one more time, straightened the straps of her tank, then opened the bathroom door and stepped out. "Guess what?" she said to him. "Good news!"

She surprised him. One second she was waving that little stick and the next second she tossed the stick over her shoulder and stood there in the doorway holding her arms out to him.

"That's great!" he said, stepping forward, then stopping.

She frowned, stretched her arms out farther.

He moved into striking distance and she took his hands and pulled him to her. "Hey," she laughed. "I'm one step closer to forty grand. I get five as soon as the lab confirms!"

Her arms tightened around his waist. Earl's hands stayed at his side, but then she moved hers a little lower.

"That's great," he repeated, feeling the warmth rising through his body.

She pulled back a little so he could see her face. "Great? I figured you'd be overjoyed." Her hands pressed a little tighter. "You know what this means? Huh?"

"That you're pregnant," Earl mumbled, concentrating on his breathing.

Now she bumped against him with her hips, rubbing with her lower body. He felt her little giggle. "It means we don't have to worry about getting pregnant because I am pregnant! Get it?"

"I—" He hadn't expected this so soon. He had figured he'd have to wait till she had the baby. She'd know him better by then, she'd be used to him, and it would just happen naturally. "Do you—"

"Yes! I do!" She backed away and took his hand. "C'mon, I know you've been waiting for this!"

Only a fool would waste this. Earl stumbled after her into her room, which had been his room as a boy. "What's the matter?" she whispered. "Afraid of what Aunt Gladys and Uncle Ray would say?"

"I'm not afraid," he said, barely choking out the words. Her hands were already undoing his belt. "Um," he started, "we need—"

"Right there on the night table," she whispered. Her hands didn't stop. "And you'd better put one on pretty quick!" She laughed as she helped him out of his pants.

He found himself perched on the edge of his narrow boyhood bed, his shirt open and his pants gone, tearing the top off the variety pack. She bounced onto the bed behind him, threw her arms around him. When had she removed her top? The open box bounced from his hands and he grabbed a foil packet off the bed as he swept the others onto the floor. She slid around so that he could see her breasts. There was no way to get the packet open now!

"Here," she whispered, "let me help you with that." The foil was gone in an instant, and her fingers generated explosive heat as she took over the business of unrolling the sheath onto him. "There," she said, and she ran her fingers up and down as if admiring her work.

Not until she straddled him and he was inside her did he realize that this was their very first kiss. Then she put both hands on his shoulders and moved herself up and down. He forgot about whose room they were in and he forgot his plans—how he always imagined they'd start with a bath in Gladys and Ray's oversize tub, how he'd fill the place with candles, and pour champagne for her while they luxuriated in the bubbles.

She bounced up and down with such fury he could barely balance. *We've got to slow down.* He tried to say it, but he produced only a pitiful combination of grunt and whimper. He knew that sound, knew that in a few seconds it would be replaced by the roaring of his own blood in his ears. Now he prayed that he wouldn't slip off the edge of the bed.

In another second, he was falling backward with her on top of him. Damn! he thought as she gave one more jiggly bounce. Damn! The roaring subsided. When he opened his eyes, she sat astride him and, from a great distance, smiled gently, then laid her head back on his chest.

Her friendly nuzzling didn't fool Earl one bit: he knew it was over too fast.

Here he was in his boyhood bed, naked except for his socks, with the girl he had wanted his whole life, wishing with all his heart that he'd done it differently. He stroked her back as he adjusted her body on top of him. She didn't weigh anything.

Darlene snuggled against him, but he was lost in bitter review of his bath plans. After they were both slick and bubbly, he had planned to wrap her in a big towel and carry her into the bedroom. *His* bedroom, with the king-size bed.

He ran his hand up her leg and over her bottom, and kissed the side of her face. Her skin was so smooth.

She had been way ahead of him. That business with the condoms had caught him by surprise. He should have stopped and gotten one out of the night table in the other room; he was used to those and had a bunch of them. Instead, he had panicked, grabbed the extra-sensitive. Even now, he winced at what she must have thought of his fumbling. And he couldn't bear to ask what she was thinking now.

Her body felt good, though. Those little panties and that top . . . did she know what that looked like, when all he had ever seen before was three inches of butt waiting for a shot? That top was like an undershirt, but with lacy little straps, and hugging her body so her nipples showed. Just thinking about it, and how quickly it had disappeared, excited him.

He kept one hand on her bottom and moved his right hand up her back and into her hair. It surprised him how soft it was; it looked so stiff.

"Unhh," she said as he stroked her head. From where he lay, he could see her closed eyes, the curve of her back, that round butt, their intertwined feet and the spill of foil-wrapped rubbers all over the floor. Earl grasped her soft bottom, stroked it a little. Then he slid his other hand down her back and around to her nipple. He rubbed it a little, just to see.

She wriggled against him, fitting herself to his hand a little better. He wanted to press against her, but he held back. Go slow, he told himself. Real slow.

He rubbed her butt a little more. "I'll tell you what," Earl whispered to her, stroking her back as he eased her off of him and onto the bed. He leaned over her, kissed her bare neck. "I'm going to fill that tub up with bubbles and you and I can take a bath." He stroked her butt one more time. "You stay right here."

Chapter Fourteen

"Chemo. Radiation. Baldness. Diarrhea. Internal bleeding." Harry Ballangee listed all the possibilities in his kindly, professorial tone, making Jill feel that her father's trusted friend and colleague was bandaging her knee after a spill on the tennis court. "All that to destroy Taylor's marrow, before he's even ready to accept new cells. And then the protocol itself. Josh has drafted guidelines, but no one's ever done this kind of transplant for hemoporosis. We've refined guidelines for leukemia, but this is a new procedure . . . an experimental one."

"But if it works—" Jill said.

"Then the new cells will go right to his marrow and start producing healthy cells. Hopefully, his body will accept it without requiring massive antirejection therapy." Harry leaned forward in his chair, put his hand over hers. "But Jill, this is very, very dicey." He seemed to forget Ryan and concentrate on her alone. "This is a last-chance procedure, an experiment, based on what we know about leukemia treatment. Your best hope, always, is still spontaneous remission. He's holding his own right now. There's a real chance that if we care for him and keep up his strength, his body will right itself."

"But with remission," said Ryan, "there's the chance that it would recur."

"True," conceded Harry, turning slightly to include Ryan in his response. "But that chance is less than ten percent. And you know, if he stays in remission awhile, with genome mapping . . ." His voice trailed off with the possibilities.

Jill knew better. She didn't fear recurrence after remission; she feared the year or more it might take to coax Taylor's body into producing normal blood cells. There was nothing spontaneous about remission. It could take an eternity. In the interim, every cell in his body would suffer from lack of oxygen. His muscles would atrophy. His breathing would grow labored. And his brain . . . Jill couldn't bear to think of Taylor growing listless, duller and duller as the hemoporosis suffocated him. She knew that was what terrified Ryan: that his bright, agile child would no longer be the quickest, the smartest, the one who outshone all the others.

"We're pregnant, you know. With a gestational carrier and a perfect match."

"Ryan told me. But you know, Jill," Harry's voice was gentle, "A lot could happen between now and the birth of that baby."

"Babies," Ryan corrected. "There are two. But you're right: we're jumping the gun. If Taylor stays in remission, we'll be fine." He grinned at Jill. "There'll just be a few more of us."

Jill smiled back at her husband, warming to his cheer. Other parents had to put their faith in strangers, specialists with long titles and advanced degrees who might know something that could save their child. But she had Ryan and Harry Ballangee, guiding her through the maze of possibilities and decisions, recommending in ways she knew they would never risk for patients they didn't know and families they didn't love.

While Harry talked, trying to convince them that Taylor could stay in remission, she thought about the genetic diagnosis on the embryos. Would she even have known to ask if they could determine the match before they implanted? Her son's life depended on this match, and she would have rolled the dice!

Instead, every day of Darlene's pregnancy brought them a day closer to two perfect donors! She shook her head as Harry droned on about the dangers of transplants. Thank God Ryan had thought everything through, had known how much better it would be to hire a gestational carrier. Jill understood: Ryan couldn't bear to see her risk miscarrying the baby who might save Taylor. He wanted to spare her the heartbreak. And the heartbreak could double, she thought, blinking to focus on Harry's discussion and failing: making a baby with such a disease and then failing to deliver the one who could cure him.

Jill took a breath. Harry was still talking, but she interrupted him. "We want to go forward. What's the next step?"

He exchanged looks with Ryan. "My office has put together the paperwork; Carol, our specialist, will go through everything with you."

Jill nodded. "And we'll continue transfusions?"

"We'll continue as needed," Harry said. "But it's a balancing act, Jill." Harry and Ryan exchanged quick looks. "We may want to look at a more selective component therapy. Transfuse platelets, granulocytes, a smaller volume of red cells. Crowd out the cells Taylor's making."

"It's just a refinement, Jill." Ryan looked to Ballangee for a nod of confirmation. "Like an adjustment to his medication."

"So should we still go ahead with the blood drive?" She turned from Ryan to Harry. "Our church."

"Oh, by all means, we always need the blood. It wouldn't have gone to Taylor necessarily anyway."

"I know. I just meant, will we need to be asking these people later to give the specific components?"

Harry shook his head. "Let the blood bank worry about that one. You all go ahead." He smiled gently. "It's a good thing to do."

"And Jill's a crack organizer," Ryan chimed in now. "She and her church brigade are rounding 'em up!"

"Here," Jill said, pulling a flyer from her portfolio and handing it to Harry. "Why don't you post this in your waiting room."

Harry smiled at the picture of Taylor in his Superman costume.

"Jill thought of the 'Be a hero' theme," Ryan said. He shot a quick look at her. "You might want to give him one of the generic posters. His patients probably won't track down the church for that one drive."

Jill nodded, pulled out a poster with the blood center information. "Try this," she said, passing it over to Harry.

Harry smiled again, then cleared his throat.

"So you understand," he said, "we've got to do what we can to build Taylor up now. See how far we can get him into remission."

She could tell that building Taylor up was a project to keep her occupied. Keep her focused on rest, nutrition, vitamins, blood drives while enough time passed to see if the remission held. But Jill was a doctor's wife and a doctor's daughter. She knew that their chances were slim and that it had nothing to do with hugs and vitamins.

Instead of building Taylor up, she needed to build her own strength. A stem cell transplant wouldn't work unless Taylor's stem cells were destroyed. She would have to maintain her resolve to drip poison into her son's veins, to watch him weaken and almost die before he was ready to receive the transplanted cells. Jill knew that the real hardship would be Taylor's, and that she, his mother, would have to insist that the torture continue until they could be sure it would work.

When she and Ryan returned to the car, she let out a long, deep breath. "Why do we have to drag Harry Ballangee along each step of the way? Does he ever get excited? Enthusiastic?"

He glanced over at her as he backed the car out of the parking space. "He's just cautious," Ryan assured her. "It's his job." He waved his card at the reader on the gate, and they exited into the sunlight.

Jill squinted and settled back against the car seat. "He doesn't think it's right, does he? The carrier?"

"What do you care? Taylor's not his son."

"Do you think he's told Daddy?"

Ryan shook his head. "I doubt it. But we'll have to soon enough, anyway. Your dad won't object. Especially when he learns he's the grandfather of twins."

Jill rested her head against the passenger window, stretching the shoulder belt so that it edged up against her neck. She closed her eyes and tried to remember why she would care what her mom and dad would think, but she couldn't even remember why she had asked if they knew. Instead, she thought about the babies and how exciting it had been to hear Lantinatta confirm the progesterone level. Not only was Darlene pregnant, they were sure it was multiples. They were going to have twins.

There would be a sonogram at six weeks. In her fantasies, Jill pictured taking the video home to show Taylor, miraculously healthy. She could hear him giggle as Ryan pointed to the pulsing blobs on the screen and told him those would be his siblings. That was her best dream: that they would have the babies and not need them. Then Harry Ballangee would stop frowning and know that they brought these twins into the world because they wanted them in their family.

"You want lunch?" Ryan's voice jerked her back to the car.

"It's up to you," she said. "The sitter's there till three, but I thought you'd want to get back to the office."

"I do, but there's something else—"

"About Taylor?" If there was more bad news, why hadn't Ballangee told her directly?

"No, no, nothing like that. Old news: I got another letter from Kim's lawyer."

"Did Elliott see it?"

"They actually sent it to him, he faxed it over to me. And he says they're right, at least in theory. It's five years since the divorce, the kids are older, she's entitled to ask for a little more."

"And what are we supposed to do?" Jill asked, wishing she could see his eyes behind his sunglasses.

"Elliott's drafting a reply, explaining everything, but he still thinks we'll end up paying something."

Jill always knew when he was holding back, but it didn't usually bother her. Most of the time, Ryan came out with the whole story; he just had his own timetable. This time, though, he seemed uncertain. "Does he know how much?" she asked.

Ryan shook his head. "You know Elliott. He doesn't commit unless he has to. They're asking for a lot, but we're not obligated to support them in the lifestyle Kim's become accustomed to."

Jill suppressed a smile. Kim's remarriage rankled Ryan. After he dumped Kim for Jill in a divorce requiring liberal application of money, Kim had had the nerve to go out and marry a urologist with a practice far more lucrative than Ryan's. Jill was glad. Kim would never divorce her new husband, which meant that Jill rarely worried about Ryan harboring regrets about divorcing Kim to marry her.

"Internal medicine can't hold a candle to what that pisser's bringing in," Ryan said now.

Jill shook her head. "We do pretty well. We live well. And you do support four children."

"Yeah, well, he supports three." It was true: Marshall Capstein had two children from *his* former marriage, as well as the one with Kim. "Anyway, I'm telling you because Elliott's letter . . . we've got to tell her about Taylor."

"That makes sense," Jill said, but she bit her lip just the same. She barely knew Kim, but she shuddered to bare her son's illness to that woman. "I'm sure the kids have told her some of it anyway. And they're bound to talk about the blood drive." Jill planned to have the kids help with the refreshments.

"Oh, before I forget—"

"Now for the bad news?"

"Not that bad. I just think, while we're talking about the blood drive—you know, the church is one thing—maybe we shouldn't be so free with the posters. I mean, it's a drive in Taylor's honor, his name's all over the poster. We don't need to plaster them around the hospital or some place Darlene might show up."

"I didn't think about that."

"The church, the neighborhood . . . not too much to worry about. But she's all over the hospital, and in a lot of doctors' offices."

"Oh, God! Ryan, you don't think she'll find out?"

He glanced over at her. "Sooner or later—after the birth, I mean—she probably will find out."

"But not now," Jill said. "That kind of girl sees people like us and she thinks we're made of money."

"That'd be Darlene." He chuckled. "Anyway, let's just confine the blood drive stuff to the church."

"Amen."

"Uh—"

"Yes?"

"There really is something else I have to tell you," he said.

Her heart lurched. "What's that?"

"There's a reason Kim wants more money now."

"What do you mean?"

"Kim's pregnant again."

"Really?" It was all she could think to say. "What do the kids think?" Ryan Jr., Blake, and Jennifer lived with Kim and Marshall.

"I'm not sure they know," Ryan said. "I'm calling Kim to ask. Have they said anything to you?"

"Not a word." Jill grinned. "And you know Jennifer: she tells me everything!"

He chuckled.

"You didn't want to tell me, did you?" she asked.

He shook his head. "I just feel like . . . no matter what I do . . . it won't be enough for you. Because what if Taylor doesn't get better? What if Josh is just blowing smoke with this? Or Darlene fucks up and loses the babies? It's like, I'm pedaling as fast as I can, Jill, and this is so unfair. This is her fourth child, and they're all healthy."

She nodded and bit her lip. "I think that same thing every time I see a woman with a baby. Especially those stupid teenagers. You go into McDonalds and there they are, guzzling Cokes and bouncing babies on one arm while one or two cheery, robust toddlers pig out on fries and cheeseburgers, and you just want to rip those dirty-faced, neglected babies out of their arms." She hurried on. "But that's something I've learned: no new baby will fix this for us. Babies are all the same—all joy and potential—before they're born, even twins, but once they're people, it's different. No new baby will make this right, because what we want now is Taylor."

Kat thought it was unusual to see this many specialists at a local meeting, but they no longer had the time that they used to have to pursue their continuing-ed requirements. At least that was what they told her when they stopped by her booth. She had almost skipped exhibiting, but Nick had convinced her that since he was lecturing on fertility treatments, they could share dinner and stay the night in Dallas.

Kat smiled at an ear-nose-and-throat doc she knew from Arlington and inquired about her office manager, whose hostility to Kat had prevented a system sale. When the doctor replied that she had a new manager, Kat offered to call on her the following week. "I'd appreciate it," the doctor said. "I'll be with patients, but Ellen can talk with you."

"I'll call her," Kat promised as the doctor moved toward the beverages located at the center of the exhibits hall.

Kat's feet hurt and her legs ached, even though she was wearing flats. She always enjoyed the first two hours of any trade show, and then she hated it. By the time Ryan Plummer showed up, she was seated on one of the two folding chairs furnished by the exhibition company, sorting through the cards that had been dropped into the fishbowl stationed next to her candy dish.

"How's it going?" Kat asked. "Find yourself a new associate?"

"Two, actually," Ryan replied. "We've expanded a little. Still in the same place, though." He frowned, remembering. "I think Joan was supposed to call you about—"

"—about the partnering module. She did," Kat assured him. "We installed six months ago. Glad you noticed."

He grinned and Kat could see why Darlene had fallen so easily. "Sorry about that," he said. "But if I didn't notice, that's a good sign, isn't it? Everything must be running right along."

"Right along," Kat confirmed. "How about you? How's Jill? And your kids?"

Ryan waved a hand in the air, dismissing it all. "Fine. Fine. And . . . expensive."

Kat smiled indulgently, then took a chance. "You know," she said, "I'm a partner at the Ladies Farm, I work with Rita Eleston . . .

Darlene Kindalia's mother." His eyes grew stony. "We're all—Della, the other partner, and Rita and I—all pretty fond of Darlene."

He pressed his lips together, and stayed silent a moment. Around them, men and women in suits and hard shoes spoke in groups of two and three, or reached over them to take a wrapped candy and drop a business card into her fishbowl. "I don't think Darlene cares much for that place: Sydonia. She seems pretty anxious to get out."

Kat chuckled. "That's true. She'd do almost anything to get out. But that's only because she's never been anywhere else."

"Well, I'll do my part." He regarded Kat a moment, started to speak, then stopped. Finally he said, "She's an adult, you know. Getting paid for something she does well."

Kat shrugged. "So she tells us."

They were about to leave it that way when a tall, thin, scholarly type detached himself from another group. "Ryan?"

"Hey, Harry."

It was Harry Ballangee, the pediatric hematologist. Ryan introduced him to Kat, who held out her hand. "You have quite a reputation," Kat said. "I'll bet half my clients have taken classes with you."

He had a warm, shy smile, and his hand was so cold she wondered how he ever touched a child. But he was the best. Now that he had a fuller practice in Fort Worth, maybe she should call on him. He turned toward Ryan before she could ask about his office. "Speaking of students, how are you doing?"

"Well, the pregnancy's going great," Ryan replied. "Our carrier's the daughter of Kat's friend; we were just talking about her."

Ballangee's nod was grave, as befit a doctor who dealt with the most seriously ill children. If Kat's knowledge of the gestational carrier surprised him, he did not reveal it. Neither did he indicate why he—a pediatric hematologist—knew about Ryan and Jill Plummer's gestational carrier. He merely waited, and Ryan continued as if anticipating his unasked questions.

"Still twins," Ryan said.

"That's good," replied Harry Ballangee.

"But why would he know about it?" she quizzed Nick, who was delivering on his promise of dinner in magnificent fashion. They were seated in the Nana Grill, the restaurant that topped the tower at the Anatole Hotel.

Kat had always dismissed Nana as an expense-account restaurant, but the serene atmosphere and generously spaced tables encouraged deep conversation in extraordinary comfort. She glanced down at the amber liquid in her small glass, then back to Nick.

"It's just the Dallas physicians' network," Nick observed. "I don't think I'm revealing patient confidences here: you know Jill's father set Ryan up, and not just financially. I'll bet Ryan's referrals doubled when he married Jill. And Harry Ballangee probably bounced Jill on his knees when she was growing up. I'm sure Ryan's played more than one round of golf with Harry, particularly now that they've both ended up in Fort Worth."

Kat shook her head. "I just don't trust Ryan."

"But Darlene does. Isn't that what matters?"

Now Kat sipped a little of her scotch. It had a mellow taste, with just a hint of smoke. "This really is good," she told Nick, who raised his own glass and tilted it toward her.

"To good tastes, then."

Kat tilted her glass, then sipped again. But her meeting with Ryan—or maybe simply Darlene's situation—troubled her. "I guess I feel responsible," she said. "After all, I'm the one who told Ryan I knew just who could help him with his transcription problems."

"Well, my guess is that you and your friends ought to let this little girl grow up. I mean, she's got—what?—two kids?"

"One."

"One. And two on the way."

"Two on the way."

"For what I bet is a pretty sum."

"Twenty-five thousand. Which bolsters my argument: Darlene's a child who needs looking after. Who would agree to be pregnant with someone else's twins for twenty-five thousand dollars?"

Nick started to respond, then paused as the waiter set down their appetizer, a plate of spring rolls accompanied by a sesame-peanut sauce. They each helped themselves before Nick resumed the conversation. "You'd be surprised at how many women become carriers for free. Mostly for sisters and sister-in-laws, or for friends. It might surprise you."

"Probably. I wish I thought Ryan and—what's her name?—Jill

were friends of Darlene." She speared one of the tiny spring rolls and dipped it in the sauce. "Try this," she told him. "This is exquisite."

Nick complied, then frowned.

"Don't you like it?"

"What?" He shook his head. "It's fine, good, really." He shook his head again. "I was thinking about Ryan and your friend: Darlene. I wonder if . . . you should ask Darlene if they did PGD: preimplantation genetic diagnosis."

"Genetics on the embryo?"

"Yeah. Usually it's to determine the sex of the child. Don't look so shocked; I'd rather implant the embryo of choice than know that they're testing after implantation. And most of our patients are so desperate for children, all they want is a healthy baby."

"So why would they—"

He shrugged. "Don't know. Wes—the embryologist—handles all that."

"Would you tell me if you did know?"

He smiled, shook his head in the negative. "But I don't. Wes just sends it all back to the OB-GYN, they pick which embryos they want. Sometimes when there's family history, you'd want to check first. I'm sort of the general contractor," he grinned, "or maybe the plumber, in all this. You know, artificial insemination, implantation . . . these are very expensive, and fraught with difficulties. So you do what you can to rule out any problems."

"Oh, I'm the one person who actually appreciates the ability to rule out problems. Which probably appalls you."

He speared another spring roll, dipped it in the brown sauce, and held it across the table to her, with his left hand cupped beneath to catch the drippings. Kat leaned forward and took the morsel into her mouth, crunching down to release the taste of savory and spice, sweet and hot. "Good?" he asked.

She nodded.

He smiled. "Do me a favor: Don't tell me what does and does not appall me."

"Mama?"

"What is it, Tiff?"

"Will you come sleep with me?"

Darlene peered toward the bedroom door, thought she could discern Tiffany's silhouette. "Come here, honey. It's all right."

A shadow detached itself from the doorpost and moved toward her. Darlene held out her arms. "What's the matter, baby?" Darlene whispered. "Did you wet your bed?"

"No."

"Did you get scared?"

Tiffany nodded. "Can you come sleep with me?"

"Here, honey," Darlene said, moving over a little and pulling Tiffany up. "Umph." She kissed her daughter's head and stroked her hair as Tiffany settled in. "You just stay here with Mommy."

Behind her, Earl stirred a little, and Darlene could tell he was awake, but he lay still and said nothing. She draped an arm over Tiffany and pulled her close, then scooted backward to fit herself up against Earl. As she settled her head down onto the pillow, Earl curled himself around her, squeezing her with his arm around her middle.

She awoke to whispers and giggles. Darlene kept her eyes closed against the light, but there was no denying Tiffany, who stood beside the bed and brought her face close to her mother's before asking, "Are you awake?"

"No!" Darlene said, rolling away. But Tiffany hoisted herself onto the bed and clambered over to get nose-to-nose again.

"Yes, you are," Tiffany insisted. "I saw you. If you're awake, you can have this surprise! Open your eyes!"

Earl stood in the doorway, tray in hand. There was coffee—decaf—and buttered toast and two sunnyside-up eggs. Tiffany related all this as she bounced on the bed. By the time Earl drew close enough for the coffee aroma to hit her, Darlene was headed for the bathroom. "Just toast!" she hissed as she dove past Earl. "Dry toast!"

Chapter Fifteen

"To confirmation," Ryan said, holding his glass aloft.

"To confirmation," Jill responded, touching her glass to his. She let the bubbles tickle her nose a little as she tilted the glass to drink. "It's fun to be expecting and still be able to drink," she said.

"There are advantages to technology."

She nodded. Life felt very full today. Taylor was doing better. Since the playground incident, he had grown sturdier, enough so that she felt comfortable leaving him with her parents and borrowing their lake house for this belated celebration. They had stopped to pick up barbecue and now they sat on the dock, feet over the water, with the smoked brisket sandwiches and fries and her father's good champagne. It was still warm enough that their jackets lay on the dock, and early enough in the year that there were no mosquitoes.

"What's that smile for?" he asked.

"I forgot how nice it is, just the two of us."

"We haven't had much of that lately, have we?"

"And we won't again, for a while," Jill said. "The babies. And Taylor. Even if we start as soon as they're born, we've still got to get him through the next nine months. He could come out of remission any second."

"He seems to be doing better," Ryan said. "We just have to keep adjusting the components."

Jill nodded. "And Monday, we've got to make more blood drive calls." Her friends had signed up thirty donors, but their goal was a hundred.

"So it's just right now," Ryan said, pushing himself up from the dock. He held a hand out to her. "Come on," he said. He took the glass from her and set it on a piling, then helped her up. "Remember those blankets in the boat?" he whispered.

She giggled. "Ryan! That was a long time—"

"I'll bet there's something in the boat," he said. "Come on. Let's see."

Kat supposed they'd make an interesting study on the effects of technology on small business: three owners of a rustic bed and breakfast discussing how to accommodate a group of Orthodox Jewish women from New York on a road trip/retreat through Texas. Della had just explained that kosher food would present no challenges, since Alana and her group would order everything over the Net and have it delivered to Tony's shop in Fort Worth. Voila! Fresh kosher food. Alana had mapped out a route, via Yahoo maps, of course, putting them in major cities by Friday noon so that they could celebrate the Sabbath with an Orthodox congregation . . . at least until they got to the Big Bend.

And, in a burst of enterprise that could have been engineered only by Earl, Rita had tracked down a line of beauty supplies from Israel. Mud facials and bath salts from the Dead Sea. Israeli music and aromatic cedar incense to set the stage for restorative massage. "They have this kind of ritual bath," said Rita. "It's called a *mikva*. It has to be fresh water. They strip off everything, even their nail polish, and then they get in and say their prayers." Rita glowed with new knowledge. "I'm sure that if we rigged up some kind of tank under the spillway—"

"We're not building any outdoor baths!" Della said. "It'll be years before anyone wants to use the thing again."

"You don't know that," Rita countered. "What if we become a hot spot for Jewish women? What if bunches of them show up here and we end up making that whole Hutto place a kosher Mecca!"

Kat forced herself not to crack a smile. "Maybe Della could ask Alana about it in her next e-mail. Sort of by-the-way." She shrugged at Della. "We ought not to pass up a chance at a new market. The healing powers of the Nolan River have yet to be explored."

"I'm glad someone's got an open mind," Rita said.

Kat nodded her thanks, then took a breath. "What we need to do now is get the Hutto house ready."

Della glanced at Rita, then raised her eyebrow at Kat.

"We've got to talk to Earl and Darlene," Kat told Rita, who glared back at her.

"I know that," she said. "I'll talk to them."

"Why don't you let Kat?" Della said. They both stared at her. "Look, Rita, right now, Darlene's barely talking to you. We've settled on the property, and we've got to get the place ready: painting, cleaning. They can move in here, if they need to. But we don't owe Earl and Darlene perpetual access to that house."

Kat winced. Then she glanced at Rita's stunned expression. "Look," Kat said, "Darlene's going to come 'round."

"I said I'll talk to her."

"That's what I mean. If you wait and do it when she comes 'round, then you can talk about what's important: about the two of you, and this pregnancy. If you start by evicting her and tell her she's got to move in here with you—and all of us—she's never going to come 'round. Not to mention that you'll never get Earl on your side."

"I don't need Earl on my side; he needs me on his. That's why he's so helpful with the computer!"

"Why don't you let us do this for you?" Della asked.

Kat fought not to break the silence as Rita looked from one to the other. "Oh, yeah, this really is for me."

At least she spoke, thought Kat. She could have stormed out. "It's not just for you," she said. "It's for us, too, because we've got to get the place ready. But it's up to you: I'll talk to her when I drive her into Fort Worth tomorrow. Or you can go over and talk to her. She's your daughter, Rita."

Kat supposed now that Rita would tell them that she had to talk to Dave. Or Earl. Everything with Rita revolved around men. It irritated Kat with the intensity of tormenting a toothache with her tongue. It's your daughter! she wanted to scream.

"Well, wait a minute," Della said. "What are we telling her?"

That she can move in and stay with us forever, Kat thought. "That she can stay here—she and Earl," Kat replied. "And Tiffany." And be the daughter we wish we had. She looked at Rita. "Right?"

Rita nodded.

"And she can have the Janis Joplin," Della prompted.

Kat shook her head. "Well, maybe we put Earl and Darlene in the Janis Joplin, and move Tiffany down the hall to one of the singles," Kat said, "the Sarah Weddington, say, or the Cynthia Parker." She looked at Rita. "You think that'd work? Or should we try the suite? If they took the Governor Ann, they'd have the big room for themselves, the small one for Tiff, and the bath in-between."

Rita's chin came up and she shook her head. "Not the suite," she said emphatically and Kat breathed out again. "That's our biggest moneymaker. These kids just need a place to roost till they find their own place; this might be the push they need."

Kat and Della exchanged glances, but neither spoke.

"Anyway," Rita continued, "you go ahead, Kat. You talk to Darlene. Let me know what she says." Rita rose and stretched, her knit top rising high on her bony midriff in a gesture reminiscent of her daughter. "I appreciate the help."

"So it's confirmed?" Carla asked. They had dragged two chairs onto the deck and propped their feet up on the railing. Carla glanced back over her shoulder, into the house. "Does Earl know?"

"Well, if he didn't know when I waved the stick in his face, he caught on when I started puking twice a day. Besides," Darlene smiled, remembering Ryan's glower, "he drove me to the doctor's for the confirmation."

"*You're* puking?" None of Carla's pregnancies had been as easy as her younger sister's.

"Twice a day. First thing in the morning and then before dinner. About the moment the Spaghetti-Os hit the pan. Hard to believe, isn't it?"

"Well, each pregnancy's different. Maybe because it's twins. Or not your genes or something. Even so, you're lucky," Carla informed her sister with a wave of her hand. "When I was pregnant with Maria, I never knew when it would happen: full stomach, empty stomach, crackers, club soda. Carlos had to sleep with Little C, he was afraid to touch me."

Darlene grinned. "We're not having that problem."

Carla grunted. "Enjoy it while you can."

"Oh, I am," Darlene said. Despite her intentions, her grin widened.

"We are still talking about Earl?" Carla asked.

"He . . . uh." In a rush, she capitulated to her compulsion to share. "Earl's not like the boys we used to run around with. He really . . . it's not like he knows everything, it's like he doesn't know anything, so he's . . . he goes—" Darlene glanced at her sister, then plunged ahead, "he goes real slow . . . I mean, he—"

"I know what you mean," Carla said. "I just don't know how this can be Earl Westerman. He was such a dork!"

Darlene didn't even get mad. "Well, he's no dork in bed! I mean, he does everything . . . everything so I . . . and I mean everything . . . I don't mean just once, either. He's so thorough you know, with his mouth and—"

"Whoa!" Carla held up a hand. "Too much information!"

Darlene ignored Carla. Instead, she smiled and wiggled back down in her chair. "That's why my morning sickness is so easy: Earl's got the right treatment!"

"Yeah, right." Carla shook her head and produced a mock shudder. "Well, just be careful."

Images of Jimmy and the stolen Camaro mediated Darlene's irritation at Carla's big sister act. "Earl's already got a car," Darlene said. "And I haven't got anything left worth stealing."

"That's not what I meant, stupid." Carla raised an eyebrow and held her sister's gaze until Darlene caught on.

"Oh, I forgot: the rubber queen. In case you didn't notice, I'm already pregnant. And, besides—"

"He learned all those skills somewhere, Darlene."

"And besides," Darlene said, "Earl's a blood donor." She sat back and closed her eyes against the sun. "He gets tested every fifty-six days." She wasn't about to admit to Miss Know-It-All that they used condoms almost every time.

"They don't test for everything."

"I'll take my chances."

"Earl Westerman! God!" Carla said. "I don't believe this!"

"Neither do I," Darlene said. She opened her eyes and grinned at her sister. "You want to know the best part?"

"I think I already do."

Darlene grinned. "Well, yeah. But the second-best part? I've never faked anything with Earl."

"Give it time," Carla counseled.

"No, I mean *anything*. He knows everything, Carla. Because I never have to worry about what he's thinking. I mean, he knows about Rita, he knows about Tiffany wetting the bed, he knows about my bounced checks, he even knows—"

"God! You're falling for Earl Westerman!"

Darlene shook her head. "That's the thing: it's *because* he's Earl Westerman. That's why I don't have to worry. A year from now I'll be set up and meanwhile, he thinks whatever I do is wonderful!"

But Carla had stopped listening. "You do seem different," Carla mused. "It's like you're, you know: happy."

"All I'm telling you," Kat said, "is that the group has reserved the Hutto house. We promised them a place of their own."

"Well, why don't you give them your house?" Darlene snapped. They were in the Suburban on their way to Fort Worth, and Darlene shifted her weight in jerky motions as they rounded the curves on the two-lane farm-to-market road. "You could sterilize your kitchen, or whatever it is you have to do, throw Dave out for the week, and those ladies could run around there without their head covers."

Kat sighed. The idea of covering her head in the presence of men struck her as bizarre, and she resented having to defend it to Darlene, but it was, after all, the mission she had undertaken. "They want their privacy," she repeated one more time. "We promised them a house of their own. And you," she slowed, picking her way, "you'll be more comfortable at the Ladies Farm anyway." She pressed her lips together, proceeding even more slowly. "You know, Darlene, you'll still have your privacy. You just won't have to be cooking or cleaning. And we'll all be around to help with Tiffany." They rolled to a stop at the intersection with the highway. It took both hands to sail the Suburban to the right and Kat gunned the engine to make the behemoth accelerate onto the wider road.

"Yeah, right." Darlene all but flounced on the seat. "It'll be so private."

This thing's sputtering, Kat thought. Dave always assured them that the Suburban would run longer than anything else they owned, but not necessarily more smoothly, or with less attention. She peered out through the windshield at the dark sky. It had rained early that morning and now new clouds were rolling in. That's all I need, she thought, to get stuck on the road in a storm.

"Turn on the radio," Kat instructed. "Let's see if there's

weather." Since the tornado that had torn through downtown Fort Worth a few years back, they'd all grown more vigilant, especially in the spring. Sweeping winds, dramatic temperature shifts, flooding, and drought plagued the Texas prairie, no matter how settled and developed. Kat knew she was overcautious, but it gave her a moment to think.

It took only a minute for Darlene to locate a weather report. While they were under a thunderstorm warning, there was no talk of flooding or siting of funnels. Which left Kat free to discuss Darlene and Earl's move to the Ladies Farm.

"Darlene," Kat said as softly as she could, "Rita wanted to talk to you about this, but I—Della and I—thought it was better for me to do it. We thought that you and Rita are still fighting over things that happened when you were growing up, things Della and I don't know anything about."

"You're right about that."

"So," Kat continued in her softest voice, heartened by Darlene's listening stillness, "we know there's nothing we can do about that. That's between you and your mom. But, you and I, we're both businesswomen, and we can talk directly about business. We need the house. So it's only a question of where you and Earl want to live. And I know that's not the Ladies Farm. But it makes sense, Darlene, at least until you've delivered this new baby."

Now it was Darlene who studied the sky above Fort Worth. She peered through the windshield, squinting and turning her head to the southwest, from which most of their violent weather arose. Kat wondered if Darlene even knew she was looking southwest, if it was just something you learned early in Central Texas.

"Whenever it got like this when we were growing up . . . ?" Darlene began.

Kat nodded.

"Carla'd call Rita at work and Rita would send someone—a lot of times it was Dave—to drive us out of the trailer park. We used to wait out storms at the gas station. He didn't have a store then. We'd make this obstacle course out of tires on the cement floor if there was a service bay open. Sometimes Rita had to wait on the Nolan to go down a little—that was when they had that old wooden bridge."

Seement, Kat thought. *Lottatimes. Wait on the Nolan.* "Sounds like stories to tell your grandchildren."

"Yeah." Then, "Let me talk to Earl. Whatever we do, we'll be out of your way."

"Thanks, Darlene."

They were headed for the hospital; Kat was going to call on two of the doctors who had been at the trade show; Darlene was checking in with the transcription supervisor for overflow. Then Darlene was meeting up with Earl, and Kat was going to have lunch with Nick and afterward fill the Suburban with groceries before she returned to Sydonia.

"Della's gotten so bossy about the groceries," Kat grumbled now.

"Why don't you just order on the Net?" Darlene asked.

"We do. But it's extra to deliver to Sydonia, and she wants someone to actually look at the produce. And there are some things we can't get from the wholesaler—we don't use enough—so I have to stop at the store."

"It's tough duty," Darlene said. "I guess she's missing Pauline. Plus that Richard guy."

"I suppose," said Kat, whose own relationship with Pauline had not been as close. She didn't want to dwell on Pauline, and she especially didn't want to think about Richard. It didn't even bother her that she wanted to forget her romantic attachment; after all, that had been brief, and over for many years before his death. But she continued to miss his mentoring, his referral of new clients, and his strategic advice. Change the subject, she ordered herself.

"You're looking pretty good, Darlene."

"Thanks. Just mornings and before dinner, I'm getting sick. And I'm a little sleepy, but not much."

"Did they give you vitamins?"

"Oh yes. And they drew all this blood for tests."

Kat smiled. "They're going to clone you: the world's healthiest pregnant woman. Did they do PGD?"

Darlene shrugged. "I guess. They did everything else."

"Preimplantation Genetic Diagnosis?" Kat pressed. "Before they implanted?"

"Oh. Yeah. That's not on me. That was the embryos. Lantinatta asked Ryan about it."

"He did?" It jumped out before she could stop it. "Did they say why? Were they trying to determine the sex of the child?"

"Children," Darlene corrected. "Don't know. Don't care, really. What difference does it make?"

"I don't know, actually." Now Kat made herself toss her head a little, making her hair rise and then fall back into place. "It's one of those semi-creepy things, selecting what kind of child you want, screening for diseases, that kind of thing. I understand why they would, but, I don't know, I always wonder—"

"Well I don't," Darlene said. "I don't wonder at all. That's the thing: it's their baby, I'm just sitting on the nest for a while."

Chapter Sixteen

"I thought Miriam was going to print out the membership list," Val said as she slid her organizer and car keys onto the Plummers' kitchen countertop and took a seat at the kitchen table.

"Oh, Miriam! Bless her heart," Jill said, laughing a little to show that she knew they understood about the church secretary. "I thought: she's got so much to do, in that office. We'll end up calling the people we know anyway, why don't we just use the church directories."

"I rounded up extras," Sally said, passing out the spiral-bound books their church updated yearly.

Jill smiled at her friends, who had come straight from Pilates, hair still damp, redolent of conditioner and moisturizers. Becky, who had a phone in one hand and a bottle of water in the other, gestured at Jill. "Why don't we just call out the ones we know best, then divide the alphabet into four parts?" Becky grinned. "We can stop when we get a hundred pledges."

"Hundred and ten," Val overrode her. "Overbook."

Jill felt her eyes filling and she struggled to join their laughter. She thought of all the projects on which the four of them had worked together. She thought of how they had traded pregnancy stories and baby clothes, how they had addressed invitations and designed posters, all around this same table. We are so lucky, she thought. So lucky.

"Rita! I told you," Kat said. "She said she'll get back to us after she talks to Earl."

"Well, I mean, what did she sound like?" Rita persisted. "Did she sound like she was really thinking about it or that she just needed to convince Earl to back her up?"

Kat shook her head and collapsed back into a peach-colored dryer station, shoving the bonnet up out of the way as she groaned with exasperation. Rita continued restocking her supplies, pouring lotions and gels from gallon bottles into smaller, pump-top containers.

"What does she need to talk to Earl about, anyway? She's Tiffany's mother. She ought to know what's best for her daughter!" Rita grabbed a cloth and wiped off the tops of the bottles one by one.

Kat stared at her. "Wouldn't you consult Dave about where to live?"

Rita stared back. "Honey, Dave would live with me on Mars; the only thing he cares about is where we sleep." She grinned. "Besides, Dave's already trained. He knows to answer 'Yes, dear.' She's taking a chance with Earl." Rita stopped, considered. "Or, maybe not. You think she's going to stay with him?"

"Who knows. What do you hope will happen?"

Rita waved a cloth in the air, slumped into another dryer station. "That she drops those twins, and she and Earl buy a house here in town and make me another grandkid or two. That Tiffany chucks beauty-queen training for astrophysics. That Darlene grows her hair out and wears one pair of earrings at a time. Oh, fuck!" She leaned her head back and let tears stream down her face. "What I really hope is that she forgets what a crappy mother I was and sees what a good mother I am now."

Kat leaned over and put a hand atop Rita's. "Now that you've grown up?" she teased.

Rita shrugged. "You know what? I'm going to go back to blonde. I'm going to grow my hair out. Sort of soft and loopy, framing my face."

"Loopy," Kat repeated, studying Rita. "You know you can't go back and change it. At least you were there for her—Darlene—and Carla, too."

"Except they wished I wasn't there."

"Rita! No girl wants her mother around most of the time. Except when she wants her mommy. You were there then."

Rita said nothing, picked up a color wheel and started dialing in on the blondes.

Kat looked at her, thought again about how tiring it must be to stand up and style hair all day. "You kept them fed and clothed," she pointed out. "And you were there."

Rita dropped the wheel into her lap. "There's not that much to being there, at least most of the time. I mean, unless you die or something."

Kat took a second to assure herself that confession to boost a friend's ego surely ranked higher on the moral scale than confession to console yourself. Then she said to Rita, "I have a daughter and I was never there for her."

Darlene thought Rita looked smaller through the wavy glass in the front door of the Hutto house. She could still recognize her, though. Through the frosted panes, Rita's spiky hair resembled a wooly cap and her dangling earrings seemed to bounce on her shoulders. The rest of her made a blurry smear of denim and rhinestones.

Darlene considered not answering, but there was no point to delaying the inevitable. "I'm not moving to the Ladies Farm," she told Rita as she opened the door.

"I didn't come to tell you what to do," Rita said. Darlene stepped to one side and let her mother enter.

Rita stood awkwardly just inside the doorway, her expression impassive as she surveyed the open living area with the wall of windows and the compact kitchen tucked into the near corner. Darlene was glad they had moved Tiffany into Earl's old room; it looked much neater now that the toys and clothes weren't spilling out from behind the screen divider. There were just the two folding tables, side by side, with the two computers—hers and Earl's—facing inward with their screen savers flashing. Earl had even found her a reclining office chair that matched his; to Darlene, the setup looked like the bridge of a spaceship. Her mother probably just wondered who had paid for the bewildering array.

"You don't have to stand there," Darlene said. "There's a sofa." She led the way and backed herself down onto the dark leather, air hissing out of the cushion as Rita joined her. They each took a corner, leaning awkwardly against the ornate wood arms.

Rita nodded at their surroundings. "This is nice," she said. "I hadn't seen it since the Huttos moved out."

"Did you think we trashed the place?"

Rita shook her head. "You never trashed anything," she said mildly. "You know, Darlene, I didn't come here to fight with you."

"No, you just came here to tell me where to live."

Rita chewed her bottom lip a second before she spoke. "No," she said finally, studying her hands and smoothing the manicured nails on her left hand with her right forefinger. "I just came here to make you a promise."

"What's that?"

"If you come stay at the Ladies Farm, I promise I won't interfere with you and Earl. Or Tiffany."

Darlene snorted. "You not interfering would be like . . . like . . . I don't know, like Dave not tinkering with cars, or Earl not fiddling with computers, or . . . Wendell not trying to cop a feel!"

"Now, Darlene, why do you have to go spoiling this with Wendell? Here we are having an adult conversation about us, today, and your future, and you have to drag that up."

"I'm just saying," Darlene started, then stopped. "Oh, forget it!" She thought a second. "What do you care, anyway?"

Rita looked astonished. "Why, I care about you, baby! You and Tiffany."

Darlene started to tell her mother that she wished she had cared more when Wendell had chased them around the trailer, but her mother was right. That was in the past, and it wasn't nearly as bad as it might have been. It's not as if Wendell had ever really cornered her, or Carla either. In the end, it had just been a lot of grabbing, something to laugh at if she hadn't been so scared. Even so, Rita had failed to protect her from that terror.

Rita, with her usual obtuseness, forged ahead as if Darlene's silence were enthusiastic acceptance of her maternal concern. "You know, when you start getting big, Darlene, you're going to want someone to help you with Tiffany, getting her in and out of the tub, ready for school, taking her shopping and to the doctor's. Plus, at the Ladies Farm, you don't have to cook, all that's taken care of. And even if you don't like talking to me, I know you like Kat and Della. And they're thinking—at least Della is—they might could pay you for helping some in the office if you're interested."

"I've got all the work I can handle," Darlene informed Rita, not bothering to correct the *might could*. "I'm thinking about taking on extra help."

Rita raised her eyebrows, nodded approvingly.

Darlene thought for a second about not saying more, but only for a second.

"I'm thinking now's the time to find some nice little duplex for Tiff and me, and Earl, of course."

"Well, I'm glad to hear Earl's sailing on this ship!"

"I'm not the one who runs out on men!"

Rita shook her head, ignored the comment and focused on the money. "It's only twenty-five thousand, Darlene. Can you afford it?"

Well, thought Darlene, no one ever called Rita slow about money. "Actually, Earl talked him up to forty."

"Forty thousand!" Rita was full of false enthusiasm. "That's great Darlene."

"Yeah." Darlene smiled in spite of herself. "And it's not like Earl doesn't bring anything to the party."

Now Rita laughed. "Oh, I know what Earl's bringing to this party." She grew serious. "I am glad he's helping you though. I mean, as your financial adviser and all that."

Darlene frowned. "He is a good adviser. Earl's real smart." She thought of something else. "You know," she said, "Earl was really good, but Ryan didn't really fight that much. It was almost like, once he saw we wanted more, he was offering money. I mean," she recalled, "he negotiated, but we closed pretty fast."

"Really?"

Darlene nodded. "Why do you think . . ." She looked at Rita, but Rita was studying her for answers. "I mean, now that I think about it, Earl was good, but Ryan wasn't that tough. I swear!"

She could hear Rita struggling to keep her voice mild. "Why would he do that?" she asked. "Give you more money?"

"Well," Darlene said, "he does need to keep on my good side. You know, because of Jill."

"Jill . . . oh!" Rita give a short chuckle. "You're not the kiss and tell type."

"No," Darlene agreed. It was a point of pride with her. "Not that he'd know that, though. Just because I didn't tell before, he might think now . . . that asshole!"

"Well, you've got to admit—"

"Admit what? That he's paying me to keep quiet?"

"I didn't say that," Rita replied. "Only, that the last thing he needs is for you to tell Jill about your little fling."

"Oh, yeah," Darlene said. "We can't do anything to upset poor Jill." She tossed her head a little, ran her hand through her shorn hair. "It's not like it means anything to him. He's got tons of money, he can afford to throw a little at me."

"Especially if he thinks it'll keep you from running off with those babies," Rita said.

"Why would I run off?"

"Well, girls do," Rita retorted. "You hear about it all the time: these poor couples pay all this money, then these girls get gooey over the baby and want to keep it."

Darlene rolled her eyes. "Believe me, I'm not keeping Ryan's baby! Besides, I signed about a thousand papers promising I'd give it to them."

Rita inclined her head and arched one plucked, blackened brow. "He's probably nervous, Darlene. Right now, you're—you and those babies—are their future."

"Well, maybe that's it," Darlene said slowly, shaking her head.

"Honey, don't you think, with all this, you'd be better off staying with us? I mean, it's mighty complicated."

"You mean, like, how could I possibly take care of myself and Tiff, you're my only friend—"

"Oh, Darlene! Honey, I just want you to understand, if you're thinking you don't want to stay with us because of me, well . . . well, then . . . I just want you to know I'm not going to interfere, I'm not going to run your life, or try to."

Darlene couldn't remember Rita this contrite. "I don't think I can stay there," Darlene mumbled.

"Just think about it," Rita urged. "Just until those girls leave, and then you can move back in here. Talk to Earl about it."

Earl knew why Kat asked him to help her with Nick Lantinatta's metal sculpture, but he didn't see any harm in it. The ladies were hot to have him convince Darlene to stay at the Ladies Farm. Unfortunately, as he assured Kat on their way to Dallas, he had already tried and it was no use. "Darlene's set on moving to Fort Worth," he said.

Kat had leaned way back in the big passenger seat and had her eyes closed, but he could tell she wasn't sleeping by the way her brow furrowed just a little. "You know, if she were really enchanted by city lights, she'd head for a real city: New York or Chicago, or Houston, at least."

"Fort Worth's a city," Earl protested. He hoped Kat didn't issue this challenge to Darlene. He wasn't nuts about moving to Fort Worth, even with Darlene. He couldn't handle New York or Chicago. "How much does this statue weigh?" he asked in an effort to change the subject.

Kat frowned. "I have no idea. Nick moved it around in his Suburban. This thing'll hold the same weight as a Suburban, won't it?"

"Of course it will." Actually, Earl had no idea what weight it would hold, but he hated it when people slighted the Expedition. "If Dr. Lantinatta moved that statue by himself, this thing'll haul it."

Kat smiled. "Earl, you can call him *Nick*."

"Oh, well, especially if *Nick* moved it by himself." He grinned over at her.

"So you're sticking with the girl?" She shielded her eyes from the bright spring sun through the windshield. "Pretty slick."

They had reached the interstate and he studied the on-ramp as he accelerated. "Yeah," he said, but he kept his eyes on the road.

"Not as exciting as it used to be, huh?"

"Oh, it's exciting," he said. The Expedition glided into the center lane. Earl debated setting the cruise control because he thought Kat would approve, but he really didn't like the sensation of the beast driving itself.

"But?"

"Huh?"

"It's exciting, but . . . ?" Her voice had a teasing lilt, which was the reason he liked the ladies so much. He always felt like he could tell any one of them anything. Even Della, who didn't always say what she was thinking, would never betray one of his confidences or laugh at his confessions. They might tease, but they weren't mean. And Kat was smart. She might know something he didn't about Darlene.

"Well, it's always different, isn't it?" Earl observed. "You dream about a person night and day, and you do everything you can, twist this way or that just to get a smile out of them, and then, finally, they start to see you, and like you. It's not till then, you know, not till you really spend time together, not just dating, I mean, but living time, that you see what they're like."

"And Darlene's not like what you thought?" Kat had opened her eyes and she studied him from her half-reclining position in the passenger seat.

"Well, who ever is?" Earl countered. "I mean, that was the whole point from my side, wasn't it? To get Darlene to see I wasn't just some bumbling ex-tackle run to fat. So she's seeing me like I am, and I'm seeing her."

"And she's not the angel you imagined, huh?" Her tone remained sympathetic.

"I never said she was an angel," he muttered. "It's just, you know, this gestational carrier stuff, it's not exactly . . . I just thought once she got pregnant she'd be . . . actually, I don't know what I thought."

"Oh, sure you do," Kat chided. "You thought Darlene as gestational carrier would be just the same as Darlene not pregnant, except that she'd be fatter . . . and totally dependent on you."

"Well, she is plumping out a little."

"She's carrying twins, Earl. She's going to plump out a lot."

"I know that," Earl said. "My wife—ex-wife—had a baby, you know, we went through the whole thing."

"But that's not what you mean, is it? You mean you didn't know how greedy Darlene was. Greedy and self-centered."

"She's not greedy! That's not fair! She's just . . . Darlene's had a tough time. She's had to be tough for herself, and for Tiffany. She's just looking out for them because, until now, she didn't have anyone to look out for her."

"And now she has you."

"Well, yeah."

"Only now," Kat smiled gently, "you're not sure what you've taken on."

He nodded. Then he sighed. "I like taking care of her."

Kat didn't say anything, and he didn't risk a glance over. He didn't want to see her expression: he could stand cynicism, but pity for poor, dumb Earl would be too much.

"And she appreciates me, too," Earl said. "She tells me all the time how much she appreciates the shots, and living there, and taking Tiffany to school." He thought about the time they spent in bed and how he loved just to stroke her skin. Darlene appreciated that, too, but he ordered himself to move on before he started blushing. "It's just, I guess I don't like this baby business much. I didn't like it at first, anyway, having a baby for money. And now, knowing that it's confirmed, it's really underway, it's kind of . . . I don't know . . . it's kind of creepy."

"It's more than creepy, Earl, it's science fiction meets the whims of the rich and spoiled."

"Not that part."

"What, then?"

Earl concentrated on the road. They were in Arlington, now, between Fort Worth and Dallas. The highway would be crowded the rest of the way, bordered by the large-scale amusements that had found homes between the two cities: The Ballpark, Six Flags, Hurricane Harbor, the Wax Museum, Lone Star Park horse track.

"Are you warm?" he asked. "You want the air conditioner?" The sun was fierce through the window, even though the temperature wasn't much above seventy.

"I'm fine," Kat assured him.

"It's the money," he said.

"The money? She told me you were the one who helped her negotiate."

"I did. But it's like she . . . she really thinks she has to do this. Like she can't make a living."

"Well, it's going to take a long time for Darlene ever to feel comfortable about money," Kat told him. "For now, it's like you said: you're in it. No turning around."

"I suppose not." But it made him glum.

They rode the rest of the way in silence, punctuated by Kat's directions into North Dallas and the inevitable comments about snarled traffic and bad drivers. Kat seemed especially annoyed that drivers were rude on the Tollway, as if paying for the privilege of driving on the road would make them more considerate. Earl figured it made them feel entitled to rudeness, like the bumper sticker that said "As a matter of fact, I do own the road," but he didn't share that thought with Kat.

Nick's office occupied the second floor of a five-story building just off of Northwest Highway. There was a loading dock where Earl parked along the side of the ramp. Hopefully, this artwork would balance on the dolly and they could wheel it right to the back of the Expedition.

They had timed their visit for early afternoon, when Nick was done with patients. So the waiting room was empty and one of the women behind the glass partition waved them back to Nick's office. Earl followed Kat through the back halls and parked the dolly at the doorway of Nick's plushly carpeted domain.

"Looks like something Dave would do," Earl said when he spied the conglomeration of metal parts fashioned into a life-size couple who were kissing. He headed for the artwork.

"No engine," Kat responded, walking up to Nick and giving him a quick kiss.

The statue was cute, but Earl still wasn't sure why Kat wanted it so much, except that it was something of Nick's for her to keep at the Ladies Farm. That was the kind of thing women liked to do. Even his Aunt Gladys had kept a little desk compass of Uncle Ray's on the windowsill in the kitchen. She'd been careful to take it with her when they moved out to the Big Bend. Even with both of them retired, she'd remarked, there were times she just liked looking at something of her husband's.

Earl stooped down and lifted the base a little, to test the weight. It wasn't that heavy. He guessed that was due to the intertwined bodies being made of car mufflers, which were hollow. Most of the weight was in the base, and Earl figured if he could lift it enough to get it over to the dolly he'd be home free.

He started to explain that to Nick and Kat, preparing himself to fend off offers to help, but when he glanced back at the two of them grinning at each other like fools, he said nothing and stooped back down, lifted the thing and carried it out to the dolly. I'll get it into the truck, Earl thought, and then I'll come back up for Kat.

He rolled it back down the hall, pushing the dolly with his right hand, steadying his cargo with his left, his eyes fixed on the floor ahead, careful not to smudge the molding along the pale walls. So when he turned the oblique angle that opened into the second, interior waiting room—the one where family waited for women undergoing procedures, the one with the banks of pamphlets and the bulletin board of posters, the one with the water cooler and the coffeepot—Earl raised his eyes and looked right at the flyer with the picture of Taylor Plummer. It wasn't one of those papers tacked onto the crowded bulletin board; it was taped to the otherwise immaculate wall, the only spot of color against the muted surface. The boy's name appeared in eighteen point type, not as big as the type that announced the blood drive, but big enough. *Taylor Plummer,* it read, *son of Ryan and Jill Plummer.*

Earl stopped, rested the dolly in a standing position and glanced over his shoulder. Then he tugged gently at the edge of the paper, separating it from the wall. He folded the page in half once, twice and three times, and tucked it into his pocket.

"Hemoporosis." He whispered it to himself in the elevator. As soon as I get the statue unloaded, I'll look it up on the Net, he thought.

In Rita's dream, she could never tell whether the force that swept through the trailer was an impending tornado, or just Wendell. The floor tilted at crazy angles, and precious items—papers, perfume bottles, bracelets, and rings—swirled through the air amid a deafening roar. Carla clutched at her skirt, her face contorted, her wailing lost in the thunder.

Rita screamed at Carla to hold on, but it was mostly for her own comfort. Carla always held on, Carla would stumble after her and never loosen her grip. It was Darlene they sought, dodging the tables and chairs that slid toward them, grabbing at the papers to clutch the paid-off loan receipt for the trailer, a card for food stamps, Wendell's discharge papers, a sheaf of divorce decrees. Rita screamed and screamed, but her voice had no sound, or maybe it, too, was lost in the thunder.

By the time they reached the door, which was thrown open and shut, open and shut, in the force of the wind, they were on their hands and knees. Rita peered over the edge of the doorsill and realized that they were airborne. There was only a second or two to jump to safety.

She squeezed her eyes shut and in an instant repeated all the things she knew about Darlene: that she was a survivor, that she had found a safe hiding place a million times before, that even now she was curled up tight in some hollow, or picking her way to a haven at the library, or some neighbors. With her eyes shut tight to hold the picture of her little girl safe outside the trailer and the door about to slam shut again in the wind, Rita reached back for Carla's hand and jumped with her into the night.

The roaring ceased, allowing Rita to hear the ringing of the phone. Why, it's Darlene! *she thought.* Calling to let me know she's safe. *That had never happened before.*

This was where she normally awoke anyway, trembling with relief that it was only a dream, knowing that Carla and Darlene were grown women with their own children now, safely away from the trailer and Wendell and bad storms. Rita blinked in the darkness, feeling her heartbeat slow. Only then did she realize that the phone *was* ringing, that Dave was turning over, mumbling.

"You gonna get that?"

The phone was on her side of the bed, and she fumbled over her alarm clock and a paperback novel before touching the receiver and lifting it from the cradle.

It *was* Darlene, in a fierce whisper not to disturb Tiffany and Earl, Rita guessed. Or maybe, she thought, because she couldn't speak louder.

"Mama! Mama?" Darlene hissed through the phone. "Mama, when you were pregnant, did you ever bleed? I mean really bleed?"

Chapter Seventeen

The funny thing was, it didn't hurt. She'd had periods that hurt more than this; lying behind the partition in the emergency room, Darlene thought that it was a pretty sad joke that delivering a healthy, breathing baby brought screaming pain, but expelling a dead one didn't feel like anything except very wet. And messy.

"Don't you worry about a thing," Earl had babbled on the way over. "This is all gonna clean right up, even that sofa'll be just spotless."

Rita had looked ready to strangle him, but Darlene thought it was sweet. He was just babbling because he was so worried about her, she thought as the doctor studied the ultrasound.

"You were carrying twins?" the doctor asked.

"Yes."

He shook his head. "This is so rare." He turned the monitor so she could see it, and pointed to a small, dark circle. "I think you must have aborted one of them." He tapped the screen. "The other one's right here."

"I lost one?" she asked. She could barely see the dot on the screen, but she was sure she saw it moving. Pulsing.

Darlene let out a breath and closed her eyes, then opened them again as the doctor spoke.

"It probably got flushed away in that first flow," the doctor assured her now. "I don't want you," he glanced at Earl, "either one of you, worrying yourselves about this, as if you could have done something different. In cases like these, it's over very quickly, with that first set of cramps. If you had been right here in this hospital, we couldn't have done a thing for you."

Darlene figured this was mostly for Earl, who looked stricken. She had always heard stuff like this happened in early pregnancy; it was part of the beauty shop credo. She was glad they'd gone to Sydon Memorial; if they'd gone to one of the ERs in Fort Worth, no one would have paid them even this much attention. The doctor, a guy not much older than Earl, was just getting to the part that concerned her.

"I've put a call in to Dr. Kaplan. I'm sure she'll want to see you tomorrow. But the ultrasound looks okay, and I think the other baby is all right for now. I wouldn't even keep you overnight except I think you'll be more comfortable here. And I want to hear from your doctor before I let you go."

"Don't you think we should call Nick . . . Dr. Lantinatta?" Earl said.

"Dr. Lantinatta?" The attending physician looked at Darlene.

"He's a fertility specialist," Darlene explained. "In Dallas." Then she shook her head no. "My OB is Marta Kaplan. She's the one we should call."

Darlene shot a warning glance at Earl, then rattled on about their immediate arrangements.

"We'll send Tiff to school with Rita," Darlene instructed, "then she can bring her back here this afternoon. Then you can take her home and feed her dinner."

Earl nodded, his brow furrowed.

"I don't want her to worry. I want her to see I'm okay before you feed her dinner."

Earl nodded, then mumbled, "I'll go talk to Rita." He entangled himself in the cloth partition for a moment as he backed up, then untwirled himself, nodding to the doctor as he disappeared.

"What are the chances," Darlene asked the doctor, "that I'll keep the other one?"

"Let's let Dr. Kaplan help with that," the doctor suggested.

"I'm asking what you think."

"There may be . . . most of the time, when this happens—losing one twin—the pregnancy goes forward without a hitch. But it's too early to say that right now. We want to make sure it's a true spontaneous abortion, rule out some underlying conditions. For right now, the most important thing is for you to take it easy. Let us take care of you tonight, let your husband and your mother hold down the home front for a few days."

Darlene returned the doctor's smile and closed her eyes a second, then opened them and tried to sit up.

"What is it?" the doctor asked. "Here," he put his arm around her shoulder. "Lie back down."

"I'll be able to have other ones, right? I'll be okay?" She let him lower her back down flat.

He nodded. "Ms. Kindalia, Darlene, you're still pregnant, of course you'll have other ones. You're going to have another one."

"I mean, after this," she said insistently. "Could I get pregnant?"

"There's nothing that's happened here that would prevent that." He took her hand. "I can't promise, of course. There are a lot of things that can prevent pregnancy, but this—losing one fetus in a multiple pregnancy—this will have no effect on your ability to conceive."

She looked up at him. He was young and pleasant and she doubted that anything bad had ever happened to him. She squeezed his hand and he held on tight.

"Do you have children?" she asked.

He shook his head. "Not yet." He stood waiting to see if she had any other questions, but she let her hand slip free and tucked it under the sheet.

In a moment the doctor was replaced by a nurse who explained the logistics of getting her up to a room. Darlene closed her eyes again as the nurse murmured on, and then the nurse, or maybe someone else, changed the pad beneath her. Nothing hurt, everything felt blood-soaked, and Darlene didn't think she had the strength to raise her head again. It didn't matter.

She wanted to feel sad, but she just felt tired. I'll feel sad later, she thought. When I'm stronger and have a chance to think about it. For a second, she imagined herself holding the new baby, the one still safe inside her. I guess when I look at that one, thought Darlene, I'll remember this one I lost, and I'll miss it then. She struggled to remember if any of the papers she'd signed would prevent her from seeing the baby, but it was too hard to remember all that.

She'd rest before Tiffany saw her, and she'd get Earl to bring her robe so Tiffany didn't get spooked by the hospital gown. As she nodded off, she thought that even if she lost the second one, Ryan and Jill would pay her. The worst-case possibility, as far as she could see, was that they would insist on trying again. And she was willing.

* * *

"Well, miscarrying like that," Rita told Kat, "that's not near as bad as getting close to term and then losing it. Or giving birth and then . . . oh shit," she said. "I'm sorry."

They were sitting in a waiting area which, even at eight in the morning, was littered with half-filled plastic cups. Across the room, Tiffany amused herself with an oversize Lego assembly, constructing shelters of brightly colored, interlocking blocks that fit onto the Lego-style tabletop.

Kat shook her head. "It's okay. I know what you mean. I even agree." She gave a short laugh, and Rita thought Kat's entire personality would be different if her baby had been normal. Or even if Kat and Hal had kept the child and raised her themselves.

"Then why didn't you ever have another one?" Rita asked.

Kat looked thoughtful. "That sounds so reasonable, now. I don't know though. Back then . . . first we were getting over the loss of the first one. Then Hal and I busied ourselves being mad at each other. Then I just filled the space with work, so I wouldn't have to think about it." She frowned. "You know, they told us it was just a freak occurrence—an anomaly—but I guess you're always afraid, after that happens. I mean, what if it happened again? Would I have to give away two babies? I couldn't have done it!"

Maybe you shouldn't have, Rita thought, but that's not what she said. "So what do you want to do now?"

"Now?"

"About Laurie . . . your daughter. Don't you want to see her again? Maybe have her visit?"

"Visit?" Kat shook her head. "She's severely disabled, Rita. I don't think I could handle her. You should see all the modifications they have in their house."

"Don't you think Dave and Tony could rig up what we needed? And Nick, of course," she added.

Kat frowned, squinted at Rita. "Nick?"

"Don't you think he'd like to help?"

"He's just not—" Kat put her hands up in exasperation "Mr. Do-It-Yourself. Anyway, you're sweet to think of all this, but I can't really imagine Laurie here. It's not like I'm really her mother anymore, you know." She shook her head. "They adopted her, Rita. They're her real parents."

"They're probably such real parents," Rita observed, "they

haven't had a vacation in all this time. And they probably won't till their other kids are old enough to take care of her."

"Well, I don't think . . . those younger ones might not ever be able . . . they're obviously delayed—"

Rita raised an eyebrow.

"Well, they've got two grown children, biological children; they're not without support, and a lot of social service organizations in that area—"

She stopped, silenced, Rita suspected, by her lack of real argument.

"Well, we've got our hands full," Rita said, motioning toward the waiting room. "But we pretty much turned the place into a hospice for Barbara last year. You think about it, once we get Darlene settled, and those women—Alana's bunch—come and go. You don't have to turn it down right this minute." Rita grinned, feeling like herself for a second. "Give it a few weeks before you say no."

" 'Scuse me. Mrs. Eleston?" Earl stepped forward tentatively.

Her heart lurched. "I was Rita yesterday," Rita said faintly. "What'd they say?"

Earl filled them in, told them he thought it would be better to wait until Darlene was moved to her room before Rita saw her. "She just needs a little while," he said.

"A decade or two?" Rita asked.

Even that made Earl flush, and she hurried to show him she still liked him. "What else can we do, darling?"

"She says—Darlene—she wants to know if you can take Tiffany to preschool, then pick her up later and bring her over here." He thought for a second. "But you could come back in between, you know. Visit."

"Well, sure. We can do that. Can't we, Kat?" Rita's mouth felt almost too tired to smile. She focused on Tiffany, who was instructing a little boy on how to build a skyscraper, handing him blocks and directing their placement.

Kat nodded.

"I'll be back in a while. That okay?"

"I guess." He looked around, looked longingly at the seat next to Rita, then remained standing. "Do you think—" he looked down at his clothes, which were stained red, "I've just never seen so much blood. How can she be all right after that?"

Rita stood up and took his hands in hers. "Now, don't you

worry about Darlene, she's going to be fine," she promised. "That girl's strong as an ox. That blood's a little scary, but she's got plenty of it and she'll be back to fighting strength in no time. I know my girl. You just watch!"

"So it's okay?" Darlene asked, her eyes fixed on the monitor over the examining table.

Dr. Kaplan's expression did not change and she did not hurry to respond. She studied the screen, blinking a little, the fluorescent light glinting off her dark hair. "Position looks good, internal is clean. Strong pulse. We'll send your blood sample to the lab, but your pressure's good, and you're looking fine." She straightened up, smiled at Darlene. "I think we'll be okay. Why don't you get dressed," she suggested, "and we can talk in my office."

When Darlene seated herself in the straight-backed chair before Dr. Kaplan's cluttered desk, she knew she was being called on the carpet. But she had to know the baby was healthy before anyone told Ryan.

"Technically," Dr. Kaplan explained, "you are still Dr. Lantinatta's patient. Since I'm so much closer, here in Fort Worth, I thought it best to examine you myself, but Dr. Lantinatta should examine you before he releases you to my care. And he needs to notify the Plummers."

"I thought I'd call Ryan—Jill and Ryan—myself," Darlene said, wondering how long it would take for Ryan's most recent check to clear. "After all, they should know. And Ryan calls me every few days to see how I'm feeling, so I'll have to talk to him anyway."

"My office will call Dr. Lantinatta's office and set an appointment for this afternoon or tomorrow," Dr. Kaplan told her. "Right now, I'm seeing a good pregnancy, mother and child both healthy. But Dr. Lantinatta should check you out."

"Shouldn't I rest for a few days?" Darlene asked. "At the hospital, they said I should take it easy."

Dr. Kaplan smiled. "I agree."

"There was a lot of blood, too," Darlene said. She recalled that cold feeling, seeing the violent crimson all over her clothing.

"It's shocking, I know, to see that much blood. But it's deceptive, the volume is not nearly what it seems, which is why they didn't transfuse you at the hospital." Dr. Kaplan seemed anxious to reassure her. "Your body will make plenty of blood for you and the baby." She smile. "But it's important for you to do your part, eat a good, varied diet and take your vitamins and iron. Plenty of fluids. And rest, of course."

"Do you think . . . what caused this . . . could this happen to the other one, too?"

Dr. Kaplan shook her head. "It's impossible to know at this point, Darlene. Everything looks fine."

"Will . . . I have to ask you something."

"What's that?"

"In confidence."

"All right."

"I mean, really in confidence, you can't tell Lantinatta and you can't tell the Plummers."

"I don't know if I can do that, Darlene. What if it's something the Plummers are entitled to know? Is this something that affects your health, or is it about the baby?"

"Well, both, really." Darlene was ready to say forget it. After all, she knew plenty of doctors, she'd just find one she'd worked for and call that one.

"Why don't we do this?" Dr. Kaplan proposed. "Why don't you ask your question as a general, *what if,* question, not about you specifically, but about pregnancy generally, such as, *what if a woman drinks alcohol during her pregnancy? Could that cause a spontaneous abortion?*"

"Oh, I haven't touched alcohol," Darlene hastened to assure her.

"Of course not. I was just using that as an example of the kind of thing you might want to ask, a way of phrasing a question without indicating anything about this particular pregnancy that would need to be conveyed to the designated parents."

"Oh." Darlene reddened. "I see." She thought for a second. "Say a woman was just pregnant and then she had sex, could that cause a miscarriage?"

Dr. Kaplan nodded her understanding. "A spontaneous abortion, which is what occurred with you, for instance, is usually caused by something intrinsic to the embryo—the baby itself. I doubt that sexual relations would cause that. Though, of course, I believe that gestational carriers do pledge to abstain from intercourse until the pregnancy is confirmed and matured enough that the implantation is complete."

"Oh, of course," Darlene said. "Otherwise, how could you tell whose baby it was, anyway?"

"And, of course," Dr. Kaplan continued as if Darlene had never spoken, "it's wise to use condoms, to reduce any chance of infection."

"Oh, of course," Darlene said again.

"Sometimes," the doctor continued, "couples think that if they use condoms most of the time, they're safe. Some couples will even initiate intercourse, and then put the condom on midway, because they think that as long as it's on before ejaculation, that's all they need. You have to use condoms every time. Properly, every time."

Darlene sighed. Now Dr. Kaplan was going to whip out a sample condom and unroll it over a banana or a bottle, or—since she was a doctor—maybe even a life-size model. Darlene had seen this a dozen times; she knew how to use them. So did Earl. *How* was never a problem. *Wanting to* was something else. Even so, Darlene thought it was smarter to let Dr. Kaplan proceed.

While she smiled appreciatively at the doctor, Darlene thought about what she'd tell Ryan. Maybe it would be better to call Jill, Darlene thought. Except that Jill would be upset, and call Ryan immediately. Then he'd call Lantinatta, or maybe Dr. Kaplan. So Darlene might as well call Ryan first, and let him handle Jill. She frowned, feigning concentration.

She guessed Dr. Kaplan didn't think it was funny to unroll a condom onto the three fingers of her left hand, but Darlene struggled to stifle her giggles. She'd have to tell Earl about this. Maybe they could make puppet faces.

"Puppet faces!" 'Keesha rocked back in her chair and shook her head. They were sorting through invoices on 'Keesha's dining room table, reviewing monthly statements before they sent them out.

Darlene laughed. "Well, that's all I could think of. I guess I was just so upset when I lost the baby, and then I was so relieved when she told me the other one is okay, I got a little over the top."

"I guess so." 'Keesha frowned at the small stack of invoices in front of her. Even though they generated their bills automatically, they had learned to double-check each client before they sent statements. "You know, our turnaround time's gone to hell."

"Well, I'm sorry," Darlene said. "I've been a little busy, miscarrying and all that."

"I just mean, we ought to look at getting some backup."

'Keesha stayed so calm, Darlene felt silly. "I know. I tried talking with Cindy Haslett, but she's not interested. She's looking to place overflow. Maybe we could try the voc ed at the high school, get some student in the afternoons."

"I'll call," 'Keesha said. "But she'll have to come here, I don't want that stuff walking off with some teenager. Besides, she'll probably need a computer. She can use Eddie's."

"If we can find someone," Darlene warned.

"I'll call around the other hospitals, too. Maybe someone's left, on maternity leave or something." She picked up a few of the invoices and studied them for a moment. "So," she said, still studying the invoices, "you told that doctor you use condoms a hundred percent?"

"Of course I did," Darlene said. "What would you say?"

"I would say I'm married to the same man two babies worth, I better not need any condoms." 'Keesha smiled her sly smile and looked up from the paperwork. "But if I were you, then I might think to say the truth, which is probably that I use them whenever I think about them and we're not out in the car or on the deck or sitting up in one of those leather office chairs and I don't have to stop any serious action to go get them."

"I use them," Darlene said, wishing she hadn't told 'Keesha so much. "Besides, Earl's—"

"A blood donor. I know." 'Keesha reached for the statements and started matching them to the stacks of invoices. "And, to tell the truth, I doubt old Earl's ever going to pass much along."

"Then what's the big deal?" Darlene leaned over and motioned for 'Keesha to hand her some of the statements. When 'Keesha complied, she too began placing statements atop the appropriate invoices.

"That's what I'm wondering," 'Keesha replied. "Earl's pretty safe, you're already pregnant, why not be straight with that doctor? Lie about the stuff you have to."

Darlene shrugged. "Why get them all excited? I mean, I'm already pregnant, I'm not getting any disease, what's the big deal? Why should I tell them any more than they need to know? What I do with Earl's my own business."

Chapter Eighteen

Darlene didn't know which was stranger: that two doctors stood over her debating the advisability of amniocentesis while she lay on a table with her feet in the stirrups or that she was getting paid to be ignored this way.

"Of course we need to do it," Ryan said. "There could be intrinsic irregularities."

"The sonogram looks fine," Nick countered.

"You said yourself it's small. This is a waste of time, Nick. You know I've got the right to ask, contractually."

"There's no medical—"

"There is. You want to wait, but I don't," Ryan said evenly. "It's not fair to Jill and me, and it's cruel to Darlene. We should do it now, while she's here."

She grinned as the two of them looked at her for the first time in this debate. "Oh, don't mind me," Darlene said. She motioned toward her draped lower body. "I love hanging out like this."

"Darlene—" Nick said.

"Nick," she mimicked. She propped herself on her elbows, included the nurse in her glance. "Ryan's right; if we're going to do this, we might as well do it now."

Ryan looked at Lantinatta.

"Darlene," Lantinatta started again, "amniocentesis will yield genetic information about the fetus, including the possibility of genetic defects. I think," he stopped, fumbling the words, "I think you need to think through—talk with Jill and Ryan—what you'll do, what the response—"

"We talked about that," she said. "With the counselor. Before I signed anything. It's Ryan's call." Anyway, she thought, I'm healthy as a horse and this baby's fine now that it's got the whole place to itself.

"Nick, I don't mean to push you on this." Ryan sounded contrite. "I can get someone else. I just have to tell you we're going to do this."

Dr. Lantinatta nodded and looked once more at Darlene.

"Could you get Earl?" she asked. "He could at least hold my hand."

After the long needle and the effort to stay still, Darlene lay on the table and let the thin sheen of sweat cool while Ryan and Lantinatta slipped out just ahead of the nurse.

"Are you all right?" Earl asked.

Darlene felt sure it was less than thirty seconds since the last time he asked. "I'm fine. I'm just shaky, that's all. It hurts real bad for a second and then it's over." She managed a smile.

"Why'd you say okay?" Earl whispered.

Darlene looked up at the ceiling. "That was the deal." She pushed herself up, let him support her as she sat. "Besides, what difference does it make? Now or later? This baby's healthy, I can feel it." Her eyes narrowed. "What's the matter?"

"You get dressed," Earl muttered. "I'll get straightened out with Lantinatta, see if there's any medicine or anything for you. Let's get out of Dallas."

But Darlene couldn't wait until they were out of Dallas. It could take forever on those choked freeways, and she needed to know why Earl was alarmed. She made him pull off at the Galleria, and she dragged him through Saks and down to the skating rink itself, to an empty bench. "What is it?"

He sat with his forearms resting on his legs and his shoulders slumped forward, and she could barely see him shaking his head. "I should have told you." He lifted his head. "I was just waiting for you to get better, after losing the baby."

"I'm better now," she said, trying to encourage his confidence.

He looked grateful. "Taylor—their son—is really sick. I found this blood drive poster at Lantinatta's office, with his picture, and I looked up the disease and all, but I couldn't figure it out until you were in the hospital. I thought we should hear if the baby was okay and you were okay before we talked about it. I didn't know about the amnio."

"What's he—"

"Hemoporosis. It's a blood disease. See, your red cells get these holes in them, can't carry oxygen." Pride in his research animated him. "It's fatal if it doesn't reverse on it's own, all they can do is give the kid blood. I guess that's why they had the blood drive."

"So Ryan and Jill . . . their son could die?" There was a rushing sound in her ears and her face felt hot.

"I don't know. I take it from the poster and the church Web site—it's the church that's having the blood drive—I take it he's a pretty sick little boy."

"Oh my God," she whispered. She closed her eyes. "Oh, I'm so glad this baby's all right." The whooshing in her ears subsided and she heard the regular mall noises, two girls who must have cut school fooling around on the ice, some sort of tinny music, laughing echoes from the balconies that towered one above the other over the rink.

"It's not just that."

She opened her eyes.

"I kept looking on the Net, I looked at all these sites. They have an association, they have sites, different research groups, at hospitals. I found this one place they were looking for patients for experiments, two or three different ones really."

"What do you mean: experiments?"

He didn't know. Not for sure. We can't be sure, Darlene thought, listening to him enumerate the different possibilities, drugs, transfusions, marrow transplants.

"Well, there's hope for them," Darlene said. "Taylor could get better on his own, or there could be some new treatment—"

Earl shook his head. "That's why they did that diag—PGD—preimplantation diagnosis. That's what I asked Lantinatta, while you got dressed. I mean, he wouldn't talk about you, or Ryan, but he told me enough to figure it out: they could do a marrow transplant, if they had a baby who was the right match. It doesn't take a doctor to see that."

Another time, she might have flattered him about how smart he was. He deserved it. And you could tell he wanted something, some little thank you for looking out for her. But right now, with the whooshing returned to her ears and the heat in her face, she just wanted to feel steady enough to stand.

"I should have told you when I found the flyer," he said. "But I wanted to look up hemoporosis first, and then you—"

She shook her head, which brought a wave of nausea. "We have to go," she whispered, but she remained seated.

"We have to stop at the bank."

"ATM's right here," he replied.

"I need to withdraw cash," Darlene told him.

"Well the ATM—"

"All the cash. I think we'd be better off doing it in Fort Worth, where they won't question it."

"Why would they question . . . what are you going to do with cash?" Earl asked. She could hear the condemnation in his voice; the very nature of cash offended him.

"Start a new bank account. Somewhere else."

"Darlene, you can't—"

"Don't tell me what I can't . . . don't you get it?"

"I guess not," said Earl.

"Well, you weren't there for the sonogram. That's why they . . . why Ryan wanted the amnio. He doesn't need to check the marrow match, they did that before they implanted. Unless it's not his baby."

"Why wouldn't it be his? Theirs?"

"Small. Lantinatta said the baby's small. Ryan said it when they got into it about the amnio." She breathed out hard, but it didn't slow her racing heart. "I didn't miscarry one, I miscarried two: both of their babies. That's why there was so much blood!"

"Well, not necessarily," Earl said. He fixed his eyes on the rink, where the two girls were practicing spins. "It might not be that way at all. One could have been a lot smaller than the other, it's two separate embryos, after all. Or," he brightened, "remember when Nick told us how sometimes the embryos actually split, just like real twins, so the first embryo could have split, which made the twins we saw, and the one that's left is the second embryo. It was just hiding, that's all." He smiled without turning toward her.

Did he not get it? Or did he not want to get it? Darlene shook her head, tried to stay calm, but the need to plot her escape jolted her forward. "Honey," she said sweetly, "do you remember that time we were riding back from Fort Worth in the rain? When you wanted to explain those different kinds of clouds to me. Remember how we pulled over in that park? I had on that nice, loose dress, and you just sat right here in the passenger seat. Remember?"

He reddened and looked around to make sure no one had overheard.

"And there was that time, a week or two later, when you coaxed me into a nice, bubbly tub to calm me down when I was mad at Rita. And we did it right on the bathroom floor."

He shook his head. "We used one then," he whispered. "I remember getting up to get it!"

"I know. I remember too. And then we fell asleep, remember? And when we woke up, you just rolled me over on top of you. Remember that one?"

"Oh, God!" He forgot to whisper. "That's just two times, Darlene! And you were already pregnant."

"I know, Earl. But you're packing some Olympic-grade swimmers in there. That's the only thing it could be."

He regained his calm. "Well, no, you heard what Nick said in the very beginning. There are these other possibilities, maybe one of the two embryos split, or maybe this is one of the original two."

"Who said that?" she asked.

"Dr. Lantinatta, I just told you."

"Who?" she insisted again.

"Darlene, what—"

"You notice Ryan Plummer, M.D., never spun any of those fairy tales. And now he's going straight for the amnio. He's thinking I've fucked this up, I've killed his only son's last chance! This isn't the right baby, Earl! We've fucked the whole thing up, and now his son, his boy's going to die!" She burst into tears.

Earl shook his head, but he had no response.

"And you know what that means?" she asked between sobs. "I'm responsible. Me! I'm the one who signed all those papers saying we wouldn't do it till the six-week checkup! I've sentenced that boy and now Ryan's coming after me!"

Earl had learned not to challenge Darlene when she got manic. Instead, he took her to the bank, where she withdrew almost all of the cash Ryan had paid her to date, minus a large chunk that she put into Earl's account.

"What do I say if they ask me about it?" he queried, but she blew him off with a wave of the hand. "They won't get to that until much later, until lawsuits and subpoenas and all that, and by then, I'll have found a safe place for it."

Her bravado didn't fool him, though. She was no more experienced in secreting money than he was. And he didn't know why she got so many large bills. He knew that made everything traceable. Not to mention setting off alarms in the minds of folks who took in that kind of bill. Drug money, for sure, they would think.

Earl kept wishing he had someplace safe for Darlene, someplace where no one would bother them for awhile. He kept thinking that he had started out trying to care for Darlene, and now she was getting away from him because he had failed; he couldn't care for her in the way she needed. But a woman with a baby on the way (maybe his baby, but he would think about that part later, he wasn't sure his swimmers were that great) needed a safe, calm place to think things out. Even if they did have to give the money back, Ryan would never sue. And Earl could support her . . . them. Darlene and Tiffany and even the new baby.

Where would she go, anyway? What if she found her way back to Jimmy, in Shreveport? Or disappeared in one of the big cities, like Kat had said? Darlene could make her way in Los Angeles or New York; she was smart enough and pretty enough. Earl shuddered.

He half-listened to Darlene chatting up the bank officer, which was what you had to do when you withdrew a lot of money without warning, and he conjured up some haven, peopled by folks who could look after Darlene while Earl did battle with the forces of Ryan and Jill. He heard Darlene chirping her responses in a way the bank officer would never challenge and he struggled to firm up the picture in his mind. There was a place, he was sure. It was right near . . . right . . .

Del Rio perched on the Rio Grande, right across from Acuña, Mexico. The trip there took forever, since their driver was Mama A, Carla's mother-in-law, who insisted on meandering down via Fredericksburg so she could get in some antique shopping. Carla had sent her two younger kids, Johnny and Maria; the oldest, Little C, was in kindergarten and Carla didn't want to take him out of school.

Tiffany so enjoyed the company, plus Mama A's extravagance, that she barely noticed the hours in the big Lincoln, cruising through the hill country down toward the border. After Fredericksburg, where Mama A loaded up on refrigerator magnets and picture frames adorned with bluebonnets, they headed west. In the back, the kids traded the handheld games Mama A had bought them, haggling a little but calm enough that Darlene actually napped.

She woke up in Junction, where Mama A checked them into a new motel. "You want to drive tomorrow?" the older woman asked, and Darlene nodded sleepily, then helped drag the bags up to their second-floor room.

"Tomorrow," Mama A promised the kids, "we'll be at Aunt Cee Cee's, and your cousins will be so happy to see you."

Darlene doubted that Cee Cee's two girls, thirteen and eleven, would be that excited, but sometimes girls that age liked to babysit. And she worried that Cee Cee herself would not be thrilled about boarding Darlene and Tiffany for a few days, but she supposed they would all survive.

"Mom, I want to sleep with you," Tiffany said to her as they stepped into the room with the two queen-size beds.

Darlene glanced at Mama A, who shrugged. "Sure, honey," Darlene said.

They found burgers and fries across the highway from the motel, then administered perfunctory baths and got the kids down. Darlene had lost track of the special action figures and game pieces they had acquired since taking off from Carla's house, but she could make only a superficial attempt to impose order on the trail of debris before tumbling down next to Tiffany.

"C'mere," she whispered. She pulled her daughter close to her and buried her face in Tiffany's damp curls.

"Mama," Tiffany whispered, squirming away, "we didn't do the talent show."

"We did one last night."

"But we had a new one!" Tiffany insisted. "We made it up in the car."

"We'll do it tomorrow, for Regina and Emily. And Aunt Cee Cee and Uncle Joe."

Tiffany turned back to her. "Mama, are Regina and Emily my cousins too?"

"Well, sure they are!" Darlene replied. "They're Maria and Johnny's cousins, and Maria and Johnny are your cousins, so Regina and Emily can be your cousins too!"

"And Earl Junior?"

"Earl Junior?" It took Darlene a second to recall that Earl had a little boy whose picture adorned a variety of spots in the Hutto house. "Well, he's not exactly a cousin."

"Is he my brother?"

The longing in her voice brought tears to Darlene's eyes and she steeled herself. "I can't say that right now, honey." She wrapped her arms around her daughter. "Do you want a brother?"

She felt the child nod.

"And a sister," Tiffany said. "So we could do shows whenever we want." Darlene could almost hear her thinking in the dark. "And I would help," Tiffany promised. "I would take care of them, so we wouldn't be any trouble."

"You're never trouble," Darlene assured her. "I love you, Tiffany Jewel."

"I love you too," Tiffany answered back, a little too mechanically.

Darlene could feel her still awake, but Darlene kept silent for awhile, and eventually she felt the child relax and her breathing slow. Darlene had thought that she herself would drop right off, but now found herself staring into the dark.

She hadn't thought much about Earl in the past three days. The only time he had crossed her mind was in those little shops that lined the main drag in Fredericksburg. Then, making her way through the wind chimes and candles, she had imagined him instructing all those women shopkeepers to put their inventory online, to establish links with travel and lifestyle sites.

Darlene smiled. I'm starting to think like him, she thought. She rested her hand on her belly and sighed. It didn't feel that big, but she'd have to get new clothes soon. Mama A, who had spent a lifetime handling clothing at the family cleaners, assured her that Cee Cee had a trunk full of various-sized clothing that she wouldn't need for at least a while.

Lying in a motel bed, in a place where no one knew her, felt so safe. It was an illusion, Darlene knew, but she let it calm her, even if she couldn't sleep. She and Earl had agreed that they wouldn't phone each other at all: no mobiles, no pay phones, nothing. Her only news would come through Carla to Mama A, but even then, she wouldn't hear anything until tomorrow. And she didn't know how Earl could get the amnio results on her behalf, especially if Ryan realized that she had left town.

Tiffany shifted, kicking Darlene as she twisted the blanket around her. From the other bed, Darlene heard a stifled giggle under the light snores of Mama A. Darlene envied Carla her mother-in-law, who, with her husband, had built a family business without ever seeming to skip a grandchild's desires, overwhelming them all with hugs and sweets and useless, mind-wasting entertainments denied by sensible parents. Darlene drifted off wondering how many little ones had snuggled up against this ubiquitous grandmother.

Earl barely had time to get Darlene on the road before he vacated the Hutto house. With Darlene away, it seemed silly to move anywhere but the Ladies Farm. So he negotiated a refund of the deposit he and Darlene had made on a duplex in Fort Worth, exchanging a load of bathroom fixtures for their thousand dollars. The ladies assigned him the Janis Joplin room that had been Darlene and Tiffany's. Then Kat and Della surprised him by rearranging the furniture in the first-floor office formerly occupied by Kat and Pauline, the partner who had died.

"It was time," Kat assured him, motioning toward the space where Pauline's rolltop had sat. He moved Darlene's table and computer over to Lakeesha's, who installed the equipment without comment. His own system fit easily into the space that had been Pauline's. "It'll be nice to have company," Kat added. "Della's a bear when she's working." Earl guessed that was why Della occupied the next room by herself.

He did what he could at the Hutto house to move furniture and even clear the kitchen under the ladies' direction, but he doubted his contributions offset their generosity. He knew they wanted to keep him close, and he tried to respond warmly, but he spent hours upstairs in his room or huddled in his office to avoid Rita. He wanted to scream that it wasn't his fault, that Darlene had pursued this course on her own. Inside, though, he knew he had helped and, even worse, in ways he couldn't identify, had failed to provide the care that could have altered her course.

Earl had scheduled his first online auction of the odd bits he had collected in warehouses in the past two years, and he gave it all his time. He was sitting at his workstation when the minivan full of women pulled up, and Della invited him outside to meet Alana and her friends.

The four women all looked alike to him, their heads covered with floppy hats, their arms and legs draped with fabric. Even the flowery prints seemed East Coast to Earl, their muted colors and voluminous skirts looking oddly formal next to the faded denim sported by Della, Kat, and Rita. Standing out by the minivan, he felt surrounded by hugging, murmuring females, but he was greeted only by nods and averted eyes.

Alana, though, knew something. As he followed the group into the main house for a brief tour, he saw her glance back at him with curiosity. Della told her something, he thought. Warming her up for the pitch.

Sitting in his office, holding the faxed amnio results in his hand, Ryan called Nick Lantinatta.

"Did you explain all this to Darlene?" Ryan asked when Lantinatta answered.

There was a pause. "I haven't checked today, but we haven't heard from her. If she calls, of course, I'll tell her."

Ryan inclined his head, smiled a half-smile. "I doubt she'll call. Don't you?"

"I never know what patients are going to do," said Lantinatta.

"And Jethro? If he calls?"

"Jethro?"

"Her boyfriend," Ryan said. "Earl."

"He's not a party."

"Anyone else?" Ryan asked. "Her mother? A family friend?"

Again a no. "I've sent a copy on to Marta Kaplan."

Ryan smiled at the phone. "I'd like to show this to Ballangee."

"I understand."

Chapter Nineteen

Plans for the eight-day visit of the "Kosher Krew" to the Ladies Farm seemed evenly divided between beauty treatments and exploring the territory around Sydonia. Earl barely noticed when Della led the group along the river path into Sydonia so that they could visit the antique and artisan shops that surrounded the courthouse square, or when they drove over to Dinosaur Valley State Park to hike along the ridge over the Paluxy River and stare at the dinosaur tracks embedded beneath the clear water.

At dinner, Della regaled Earl and the other ladies with the Krew's amusement at the creationism museum that sat just outside the park; Rita, on the days the women gave themselves over to her ministrations, sang the praises of their skin, always shielded from the sun, and fretted about the long-term effects of covering their hair. "I just don't see how it can grow right," she said, shaking her head, "always covered like that."

Earl considered it his duty to better hair days to stay out of the way, since the women could leave their heads uncovered unless there were strange men around. He felt some satisfaction when he gazed out his window one morning and saw the bunch of them bareheaded in canoes on the river. He had moved the bed over so that the sun would wake him and he could lie in bed and look out at the slender Nolan River and the hill on the opposite bank where he had lived with Darlene.

He closed his eyes and thought guiltily that, with Darlene away and the ladies providing a home, he had attained a peace he merely wanted to savor, without planning a next step. The lilting voices of the Orthodox women drifted in with the spring air; without Darlene, he had indulged his preference for leaving the windows open all night. Too soon, he thought, they'd seal everything against the heat. Already he could feel his own sweat as the sun poured in from between the hills across the river.

Sitting up in bed, he reached over and pulled the shade down to shield the women from inadvertent immodesty. Then he stood and gazed for a second at the photos of Darlene and Tiffany that Rita had shared with him. The pictures were wedged in the frame of the bureau mirror: one of Darlene, in jeans and tee, with her back to the photographer as if she were just stepping into the Camaro when Rita called to her and she whirled around to face the camera; the other a glamor shot of Darlene in evening clothes and Tiffany in a glittery Little Miss Bayou Queen costume.

" 'Morning, girls," Earl said to the photos, trying to make eye contact with Darlene as she turned from the car. "I'm missing you," he told them, "and with all these ladies keeping an eye on me, I'm behaving myself."

It surprised him, when he came down to breakfast, to find the Krew seated in the dining room, sipping coffee from their own thermos and munching muffins they had baked at the Hutto house and brought over to share with their hosts. "Sorry to interrupt," Earl mumbled, starting for the kitchen. Until now, these women had eaten only at the Hutto house.

"We won't bite," the one named Jessica advised with a laugh. "Please sit. We've brought you breakfast," she said, gesturing to the bountiful table. "To thank you for giving up your house."

"Oh, well, it's not really mine, not even my aunt and uncle's anymore." He noticed as he seated himself that they had all donned their headgear, but other than that they looked perfectly at home. Kat and Rita were also at the table, and he could see Della moving around in the kitchen. "Give him some of that quiche," she instructed, and Alana motioned to him to pass his plate.

"This is salmon quiche," Alana said. "All fish and dairy," she instructed. "We don't mix dairy and meat."

"Some spread," Earl pronounced as he surveyed the plate they had filled for him: crusty bagel, grapefruit salad, a wedge of gouda along with the quiche.

"Now, tell us all about this girlfriend of yours," Alana requested after he had taken a few bites.

The others laughed. "Alana!" said Marti, "let him eat first!"

"He can eat and talk," Rita assured them. She turned to Alana. "You know, Darlene's my daughter."

"Yes, of course. And you met in high school?" Alana directed this question at Earl, who supposed the ladies had filled them in.

Earl nodded. "She didn't notice me much, back then."

"Darlene just noticed those flashy boys," Rita said. "You know, the ones with tattoos and fast cars. She liked 'em wild, back then, but of course, she was wild then, too."

Their guests nodded as if this jibed with their own experience.

"So she runs off with this boy who gets her pregnant. They get married, then he runs off," Rita continued. "Barely sent a penny for Tiffany, hasn't seen her in years."

Earl wondered what they thought now, and he hastened to resurrect Darlene in their eyes. "But Darlene's smart as a whip," he assured his audience. "She starts out doing medical transcription at the hospital, but, you know, that's slave wages, so she starts talking to these doctors, in Fort Worth, and she gets herself a computer and sets herself up in business—with a partner, a black gal named Lakeesha—and they start freelancing for doctors and pretty soon, she's left the hospital. Hell—" he stumbled a second as Della, who now leaned in the doorway to the kitchen, glowered at him, "excuse me—anyway, she's got so many clients now, they've had to take on another girl!"

"But why isn't she here?" one of them asked.

"Uh, well—"

"Oh, she's off visiting," Rita said.

"That's why," Kat took it up, casting a glance at Earl, "we thought, since you are covering so much territory, you could pick her up—them, actually: Darlene and Tiffany—and move them along on their next leg."

There was a startled silence, the others looking to Alana as their speaker. "Well, of course," she said, laughing a little. "We'd love to have her hitch a ride with us."

Earl studied Alana. Della had told him about Alana's help the previous year in New York, when Della had gone to the Jacoby family to liquidate diamonds. He had expected someone like Kat, albeit in long sleeves and with some sort of foreign accent; instead, Alana was closer to Darlene's age, and her accent, while vaguely Northeastern, was hardly foreign. She was pretty, too. Not like Darlene, of course, but in a dark, exotic way, with luminous eyes and bronze, polished skin.

He passed his coffee cup down to Marti, the woman handling the thermos, and he watched the shimmer of jewelry as they passed the mug one to the other. The married ones, Della had confided, were the beneficiaries of husbandly devotion and the tradition of marking the new moon with gifts to their brides. He wrestled with his desire to tell them the whole story, to be honest and, at the same time, convince them of Darlene's value. These women, who obviously could not imagine turning down a request to give a stranger a lift across Texas, would appreciate the truth, he was sure.

He smiled at Rita. "And did you tell everyone Darlene's about to make you a grandmother again?"

Rita looked alarmed. "I didn't know we were announcing—" She turned to Alana. "She's just a few weeks along, still real early."

"You must be very excited," Alana said, puzzle in her eyes. "And do you have other grandchildren?" she continued smoothly.

"Oh, you bet!" Rita responded. She launched into descriptions of Carla's kids, while the women passed the coffee back to Earl and he sipped cautiously. Were they like nuns? he wondered about the Kosher Krew? Was it impossible to separate one from the herd and get her alone for a little talk?

Ryan shook his head and looked down into his drink. "No matter how well he does, I guess we'll always worry."

"No getting around it," Tommy told him, shaking his head.

They were sitting in the bar at the club, huddled away from their fellow golfers. With what he hoped had been appropriate finesse, Ryan had let Jill's old man take him for fifty dollars on the golf course. Now the old fox was consoling him with whiskey. "I know what you mean," Tommy said. "Last week, when we took him over to that arcade at the mall, he got to running back and forth between the space capsule and the motorcross, then as soon as we got home, he dropped and Hallie had a fit, just because he dropped for a nap."

Ryan set his drink atop the small pedestal table, rested his hands on the arms of the plaid barrel chair, and considered how to proceed. "That's the way it happens. The worry never stops. Even though he's doing great."

"That's what Jill said."

"Ballangee tried cell stimulation, differentiated cell stimulation:

leukos, platelets, the whole spectrum minus the red cells. Maybe it's the kick he needed."

Tommy sipped, nodded. "Let's hope."

"The thing is, a crisis can come on in an instant. One second he's fine, the next he's in crisis. They don't even know why; maybe that the faulty cells are stored and released en masse, via some trigger." He shook his head. "We're in the dark about this. Look, you know how this works. Maybe he'll stay in remission, maybe he won't. We could ride this roller coaster till he's grown, and that's if we're lucky. I can't take this, and I know Jill can't."

"You have a choice, son?"

Men stomped in in groups of two and four, nodding at Ryan and Tommy but gathering away from their corner.

"I talked with Josh Wittstein, my pal at NIH. He might have something for us."

Now Tommy set his drink down. "You're not planning on experimenting with my grandson?" His eyes, set deep and wide in his bronzed face, appraised his son-in-law.

Ryan knew he was being tested. "If that's our best hope, I am."

The old man waited.

Ryan took a breath and moved forward. "Harry Ballangee's agreed to be a protocol site." Was that a flicker in the man's eyes? Quickly, Ryan outlined the procedure, then moved on to the donor problem. This was tricky—Tommy and Hallie knew nothing about Jill's tubal ligation—but Ryan danced successfully around the issue of whether the embryos were fresh or frozen, emphasizing instead the efficacy of preimplantation gestational diagnosis.

"So," Ryan wound it up, "we're pregnant."

"And it's a match?" Tommy reached for his drink.

"Yes sir," Ryan said, lifting his glass to accept his father-in-law's silent toast.

Tommy settled back against his chair and Ryan took another breath. "Of course, nothing goes smoothly. Even with a gestational carrier."

"It's smart," Tommy said carefully, "not to put Jill through a pregnancy right now."

Ryan nodded. "I'm glad we did it this way. But—" he broke off, shaking his head. He shrugged. "I guess I just want everything to go perfectly . . . you know, for Jill and Taylor."

Tommy nodded, waited.

"But even a gestational carrier's no simple thing."

"I suppose not. How's she carrying?"

"Well, we started out with twins, but she lost one right out."

"That's pretty common, I hear." Tommy waved it off.

"Everything else is great, so far. Other than," he looked his father-in-law in the eye, "I haven't told Jill she lost the one twin. It may take me a while, you know?"

"I wouldn't let that go too long," Tommy advised.

"I'm just waiting for the right moment. You know."

"Any other holdups?"

"Well, it's all part of the same thing. When I talk with Jill, I want to be able to tell her it'll all work out. But the carrier . . . you get them to sign every document under the sun, but if they change their minds, you're still at their mercy."

"She can't keep this baby, can she?"

"Oh, no," Ryan said. "Nothing like that. At least I don't think so. It's just, after agreeing to everything, she may be thinking she wants a little sweetener. Since she's learned about the donor match."

"What does it cost: something like that?"

"Well, she agreed to forty, but—"

"Forty thousand?" Tommy's voice was low, but Ryan could hear the shock.

"That's just the tip of the iceberg," Ryan said. "Then there's the *in vitro*, the implantation, the drugs. Nick Lantinatta, you know?" He stared down into his whiskey glass, then looked up at his father-in-law. "I just tell myself we'll work it out somehow, that it's for Taylor . . . and Jill."

Around them, the lounge buzzed with the exchange of greetings and incidental information. Men in sweaters and knit shirts shook hands, pushed on each other's shoulders, asked about bets and golf swings, joked about mutual acquaintances still out on the course. Ryan and his father-in-law sat silently for a moment as the old man absorbed the shock. Finally, Ryan spoke again. "The way I figure it, Jill and I are blessed. We're both healthy, we've been lucky all our lives, we have a wonderful home," he motioned toward Tommy, "a great family, I've got a great practice, thanks to you . . . so maybe we were overdue. I mean," he leaned forward to share the biggest secret of all, "you and I know better than anyone else here, no one gets out of here without some kind of sorrow. So," he squared his shoulders, "I'll just do what I have to here. If our carrier wants more money, I'll just go to the bank." He met Tommy's gaze fully. "I'll do what I have to for my family."

For the first time in the conversation, Tommy chuckled. "I can see that bet's going to be the costliest thing I've ever won."

"Oh, no, Dad! I wouldn't think of asking you and Hallie to cover this! You've done more than enough, this is my responsibility!"

"Son," Tommy drawled, "you leave Hallie out of this. Jill too. And you tell that carrier to keep her mouth shut, no sense those women worrying over the money, they've got more than enough on their minds. You just call me Monday—or e-mail me, that's better—and let me know what you need and when you'll need it. I'll transfer it as it's needed."

"Really, Dad, Taylor and Jill are my responsibility!"

Tommy shook his head. "Don't you ever think you're in this alone, boy. Not when we're talking about Jill and Taylor."

There was no reason, Ryan told Jill, why she should miss her mother's installation as president of the North Dallas Medical Auxiliary. "Your mom's worked long and hard for this, you should be there for her crowning moment. Let me take Taylor to see Ballangee. I'll call as soon as we're done. I promise."

"It's just a bunch of pushy old women," Jill objected, but weakly. "They don't care about anything except how much you've given, or might give, to their pet projects."

"Your mom and dad'll be crushed if you don't show," he pointed out. "Do you want to reschedule the appointment? He could probably slip us in tomorrow, or Monday."

Alarm flickered in her eyes at the idea of delaying even a regularly scheduled appointment. Taylor was stable, but it was a precarious stability, one that allowed no risks, particularly after the last attack. "No." She shook her head. "You go. But call me," she instructed. "As soon as you're done."

Ryan smiled at his wife. "I'll have Taylor call," he promised. "He can congratulate his Nana!"

Jill returned his smile, then grew serious. "And call Nick Lantinatta. What's taking so long on the amnio?"

Later, when the nanny they had engaged after the last attack brought Taylor to his office, Ryan marveled at the boy's resiliency. "I even think he's gained weight," he remarked to Harry Ballangee later, when the hematologist examined Taylor.

Ballangee smiled at the boy who sat on the examining table

swinging his legs. "Let's put you on the scale," he invited, lifting Taylor down to his feet and motioning to the corner. "Here, stand still; that's it."

Ballangee glanced at the chart in his hand, then again at the digital readout. "Four pounds." He placed the chart on a table and made a note on the inside jacket. Then he turned back to Taylor. "I'll bet you're taller, too," he encouraged the boy, reaching for the pullout lever to measure height.

"He's thriving," Ballangee told Ryan after they had sent Taylor to the care of the assistant.

"It's alarming," Ryan confessed. "To have seen him so weak and now actually growing."

"He's quite alert," Ballangee said. "Absorbing everything. His eyes follow every move you make, you know."

They were standing side by side, leaning back against the examining table. Ballangee motioned with his hands. "If he continues this pattern, you should see a resumption of his exploring. He'll take on more physical challenges: climbing, lifting, et cetera. Just let him go with that, he can sustain the usual bumps and bruises."

Ryan nodded. He had set the folder down on the table behind them, and now he reached around to retrieve it. "Here," he said, slipping a page from the folder and handing it to Ballangee.

Ballangee studied the report as Ryan spoke. "Spontaneous abortion."

"She lost both fetuses?"

Ryan nodded, then motioned to the page in Ballangee's hand. "That's what's left."

"You know," said the older doctor, "Taylor may not need any sort of transplant at all. Or," he set the sheet of paper atop his own file on the table, "he may not need one for a very long time."

"I'm not trading on false promises, Harry. Taylor can go into crisis at any moment. He's doing well, but that's the transfusion therapy. Jill and I both know that."

Ballangee rested his hand on the papers that lay on the examining table. "The HLA: have you talked to Josh?"

"I faxed him a copy when I got it," Ryan replied. "It's not an ideal match, but he says he's seen plenty that had fewer that worked."

"He's talking about leukemia, I imagine," Harry cautioned.

"But there's nothing to suggest it would be any different."

"There's absolutely no purpose served in going forward if Taylor is doing well," Ballangee said.

"I'm not asking that," Ryan said. "I won't ask that." He sighed. "But we have a donor. And Taylor may be a patient. And there may be others, now that notice of the study's gone out. Don't back off, that's all I'm saying. Josh wants to go forward with you; just be ready."

Ballangee nodded. "One site in Los Angeles, one in Boston, and us. We'll have a wide area to draw from. There may be another case or two. We'll continue."

"I haven't told Jill yet."

Ballangee waited.

"I . . . there are other embryos, but they don't match. I'm not sure what else . . . she'll be so disappointed about the baby, I'm not sure what I—what we'll—want to do now."

"Well," said Harry Ballangee, "there wouldn't be any need for me to discuss it with you and Jill unless Taylor goes into crisis."

Earl placed the package of transcripts and tapes on Ryan's desk. "There's an invoice inside," Earl said.

Ryan leaned back in his chair and let his eyes flicker over Earl. He smiled and reached for the large envelope. "'You Darlene's delivery boy now?"

Earl helped himself to one of the chairs in front of Ryan's desk. "Darlene needs to take it easy right now," Earl said. "After all she's been through."

Ryan kept his eyes on Earl while he opened the envelope and pulled out transcripts and tapes, scattering them on his desk. "I'm glad Darlene's taking care of herself. And the baby."

Earl nodded slowly and smiled in a man-to-man way.

"She staying close to home, now?"

Earl nodded again, forcing himself to move his chin up and down slowly while he maintained eye contact.

"I guess y'all have seen the amnio."

"Not really," said Earl.

"No?"

Earl leaned back in his chair. "I think we were kind of counting on you," he said slowly. "I mean, Darlene always says you're really the patient, at least with Lantinatta. So I guess we were just waiting for you to get in touch."

"Is that right?" Ryan asked. "So, maybe we could get her on the phone now, have a little conference call." He reached across his desk and lifted a folder out of his *In* box.

"We know about Taylor."

Ryan's arm froze, his hand grasping the folder in midair. He turned his head to stare at Earl, who nodded at him.

"We saw the thing about the blood drive. Pretty stupid, you know. It was all over the Net, all anyone really has to do is run a search on your name, it takes you right to the church site."

Ryan let the folder slide back onto the stack and withdrew his hand.

"So how's your boy doing?"

"Just fine, actually." Earl couldn't read his expression. "Much better. Responding to therapy, grown a little, put on a few pounds."

"Glad to hear it. Darlene and I would do anything we could to help, you know. It's pretty painful you didn't feel you could tell us. I mean, you trusted us with the pregnancy, but you couldn't tell us about Taylor."

"Obviously, it was a mistake to trust you with the pregnancy." It started as a drawl, but Ryan nearly spat the words out at the end. "Congratulations. You're going to be a father." He glared at Earl. "You or someone else."

Earl struggled to see himself from Ryan's point of view: a lumbering impediment to a cure for his baby boy. Inclining his head toward Ryan, Earl shook his head, then looked up. "We held off, you know, all through those shots, and the procedure. Hard to believe, now, but we did. Just after we learned she was pregnant, and everything seemed okay—"

"Spare me."

"Well, I want you to know Darlene feels as bad . . . worse, really than I do. Especially that you didn't trust her. And that your son needed this baby—"

"We still need the baby. And it's still mine. Ours. Mine and Jill's."

Earl shifted in his chair.

"This baby's still a good match for Taylor." Ryan shrugged, looked out the window, then back at Earl. "Luck of the draw."

"So, you mean you could still use . . . still take—"

"The stem cells. Umbilical stem cells."

"So it's not really marrow?"

Ryan smiled, a generous, professional smile, before he explained that it was the stem cells in the marrow that could make new blood cells; that the stem cells in the umbilical cord, the cord blood, would be harvested and transplanted to Taylor.

"So Darlene—"

"Landed on her feet as usual," Ryan said.

Earl closed his eyes a second.

"Got a free pass," Ryan continued. "A walk. A second chance to make money doing what she does best. Or second best."

Earl opened his eyes.

"Darlene and I had a deal," Ryan said. "She made a promise to Jill and me, and I know she's doing her best to keep it. Because," Ryan leaned forward, "you know, if she failed to deliver what we wanted—Jill and I—then we could take some action. Make a claim on your baby. Even if Darlene won, in the end, it would still cost more than anything she'd get from us."

Earl guessed it was hard being Ryan, dependent on Darlene. It was a good idea to let Ryan think he had regained control.

So when Ryan passed him the big envelope and smiled, Earl smiled back.

"I want Darlene to take care of herself and the baby. I want her to have good prenatal care, and to arrange delivery in a place where her obstetrician can be joined by a specialist with a kit to harvest the stem cells."

Earl took the envelope.

"It will be difficult to explain to Jill what happened. I really feel that I'm the best person to do that, don't you?"

"I'm sure Darlene agrees," said Earl. "After all, Jill's your wife."

"And then, once everything's in order—once the stem cells are harvested—any baby could belong to the biological parents." Ryan smiled. "I'll even sign a release then. Jill and I will. If that's necessary."

"You know, Earl's pretty good on the Net," Kat said.

"Is he?" Nick asked.

They were getting dressed to go out, Kat running her hands over the "doctor's companion" wardrobe she had assembled in the "hers" side of the master closet. She glanced over at Nick, who was slipping into a shirt, to make sure he was listening. "It's easy to underestimate him."

Nick nodded as he buttoned.

"But," Kat continued, "Earl's not that good." She pulled a silk two-piece suit with a fitted paisley bodice from the rack.

"Now what do you mean by that?" he asked.

For a second, she considered putting a silk shell underneath the suit jacket, then remembered she was off-duty and could afford to look sexy and donned the top. "I mean, why was he tracking down Ryan Plummer on the Net?" She looked over at Nick. "Don't you think he'd already done that research, before he let Darlene go ahead?"

He smiled, walked over to her and put his hands under the unbuttoned top, kissing the side of her face. "What are you asking?" he said.

"What made Earl check out that blood drive?"

He stepped back, and tilted his head to one side as he buttoned the vee-necked jacket for her. He ran a finger along her collarbone and avoided her gaze. "I thought he told you: he saw that flyer on my office wall."

"I guess what I'm asking," she said, "is why it was there? On your wall? Did Ryan ask you to put it up?"

"Not exactly."

"So why was it there, all by itself, when Earl and I showed up to move the statue?"

"Well, maybe someone just saw it somewhere else, say in an art supply store near the church, and just took it with him." Nick grinned. "That person would be doing a good deed, wouldn't he? Putting up a flyer for a blood drive?"

"But why would someone do that particular good deed?" she persisted.

"Things that are public are public," Nick replied. "No harm in raising the awareness of others."

"Because you knew?" she whispered back, nuzzling the top of his hand as it rested on her shoulder.

"What I knew," he said, backing away and taking both her hands in his, "is that there was a flyer for a blood drive posted in a public place." He shrugged. "Who knew what Earl would make of it?"

Gently, Kat pulled her hands free and turned to search the shoe rack for her pumps. She leaned against the wall with one hand and slipped first one shoe, then the other, onto her feet. "The idea that they were doing that, growing their own donor inside Darlene without telling her, turns my stomach."

He had unzipped his pants to tuck in his shirt, then shrugged as he zipped and buckled.

She smiled despite the conversation. She had forgotten the satisfaction of watching a man dress.

Nick ignored the smile. "What you and I think doesn't matter," he said. "This is between Darlene and Ryan and Jill." He headed back into the bedroom from the closet, then stopped just outside the doorway. "And the ever-vigilant Earl."

Kat shook her head, but had nothing more to say.

Following him into the larger room, she stopped in front of the dresser mirror to check her hair.

"You look great," Nick assured her. "C'mon. This place has great hors d'oeuvres."

She nodded her thanks, then picked up her purse. It took getting used to: the way he switched gears, separating himself from a patient case, even a patient he knew. Or a patient I know, Kat thought.

Dear Darlene,

Alana said she'd take this letter to you, so we don't have to make any phone calls until you get to Aunt Gladys and Uncle Ray's.

Just like Della said, she and her friends are very religious and we can trust them all. I told Alana everything about us because I wanted her to know why we had to be so careful. So she knows everything and you can talk to her.

I know you're worried about the doctor's report, but when I called Nick's office they told me you had to contact them directly, but you probably don't want to call from where you are. I'm going to pick up transcripts from Lakeesha and deliver them to Ryan's office myself, so maybe we can talk on the phone after you reach Alpine.

Rita's sending some more vitamins. I hope that doesn't make you mad and that you take care of yourself. Aunt Gladys says there's only one OB in Alpine but that he's real nice.

I miss you and Tiffany and I want to tell you how much, but I'm not good at that stuff, and it makes me lonely just to think about it. I have your pictures on my dresser and I think about you every morning and every night . . . especially at night, if you know what I mean!

Alana is a jeweler and she helped me pick out something for you and Tiff so you can remember how much I care about you.

I know that after Alana leaves I'll think of a lot of things I should have said, but I'll be out to Alpine before you know it and then I can tell you myself.

I think everything will work out okay, and I don't think anyone's going to do anything right away to bother you, but it's still better if you're out in the Big Bend instead of hanging around here. It will let everyone cool off and then we can figure out what to do. I guess I'm saying that I'm sorry I said you shouldn't leave because now I'm glad you'll be with Aunt Gladys and Uncle Ray.

I feel funny telling you this in a letter, but I love you, and I'll be able to tell you in person soon.

Love,
Earl

P.S. I love Tiffany too.

Darlene sat on a stone bench near a desert willow in the cactus garden at the Judge Roy Bean Visitor Center in Langtry, Texas. It was the first week in April and it was ninety degrees out and the light was blinding. She could barely read the letter, and the air was so dry, she couldn't even cry. Her longing for Earl produced only an irritating moisture at the corner of her eyes. When she brushed at them with her hand, she felt as if she ground sand into her eyes.

She had been gone for two weeks, during which she must have gained a hundred pounds. Even Cee Cee's jeans cut her at the waist, and sweat poured into the skin folds that were enveloping her body. Poor Earl, she thought, in love with such a mess! She fingered the gold ankle bracelet he had sent her. It had two hearts, engraved with their names, and a delicate chain that she would barely notice until her ankles swelled to twice their normal size and the bracelet cut off circulation to her foot.

The desert willow rustled a little in the breeze, its silvery leaves barely casting shadows over the bleached landscape. Darlene swiveled around on the backless bench so that both legs were out straight in front of her. Then she leaned forward and fastened the bracelet around her left ankle.

He had sent one for Tiffany, too. It had three hearts, two large and one small. The small one bore Tiffany's name; the two larger said *Mom* and *Earl*. Darlene wasn't sure about the sense of giving real gold to such a little girl, particularly one who wore running shoes and socks most days, but she knew it would make Tiffany feel good. Standing, she slipped the bracelet into the watch pocket on her jeans and looked for a second down toward the canyon below Langtry.

When she and Cee Cee and the girls had tumbled out of the van and met Alana, Marti, Jessica, and Amy in front of the visitors' center, Marti had made a joke about schlepping their law west of the Pecos. Darlene hoped the deep canyon where the Pecos tumbled into the Rio Grande was a boundary. She hoped she was crossing into some new place where she wouldn't have to be accountable for all the things she had done to this point, that maybe this would be a place for her to start again. Of course, she was bringing a lot of problems with her, but for now she wouldn't think about that.

After all, if Judge Roy Bean had been the only law west of the Pecos, and he was dead, maybe they were all free to choose their own laws. Alana and her friends could choose theirs, and Darlene and Tiffany and Earl could choose for themselves, too.

Tiffany had stayed inside, spending her last hour with Regina and Emily in the air-conditioned comfort of the Judge Roy Bean theatre. By now, Alana and Cee Cee and the rest would have finished comparing minivans and were probably examining The Jersey Lilly, the bar where Judge Bean had meted out his frontier justice.

Earl's letter was over a week old. A lot of things could have happened since he wrote it. Who knew what would happen now? She admitted to herself that Earl had been right about the cloak and dagger: no matter how much good it would do her to spend time in the Big Bend, she probably could have driven straight there herself if she had had a car.

But Darlene, standing and stretching in the sun, knew that Ryan was only waiting. He couldn't hurry the baby, and it didn't matter where she spent the months of pregnancy. It only mattered later, when the baby came. And then, the less he knew about her whereabouts the better. She was glad she had headed to this rough place. No matter whose baby it turned out to be.

Chapter Twenty

"Your mother is so talented," Alana told her once they were on the highway. The women had insisted that Darlene take the front passenger seat, though none mentioned her pregnancy.

"That's my mamaw," Tiffany piped up from behind Darlene. "Isn't it, Mom?"

"Yes, honey. You're not putting sticky fingers on the car upholstery, are you?" Darlene heard the light scrape of Tiffany releasing the back of the passenger seat.

"No."

On the map this highway stretched straight out to El Paso. The van lumbered along, weighted with passengers and luggage, and Darlene nodded sleepily, then forced herself to make conversation. "Did she do your hair?"

"She did mine!" Marti exclaimed from the back. "She layered it and shaped it, and I love the way it fluffs back up when I take my shaidl off."

Darlene guessed that was the kerchief she wore, that she tied back behind her ears. The women had all removed their head coverings when they hit the van.

"Mine too," Alana said, tossing her head a little to let her lustrous black locks move over her shoulders.

"I like your earrings," Darlene said. They were the long, dangly kind, which Darlene considered old-fashioned, but their ornate filigree fit Alana's style. "I didn't expect—" she turned her head to encompass them all—"I guess I didn't expect y'all to be so, I don't know, so—"

Alana laughed. "Modern? American? Or just ordinary?"

Darlene was glad she laughed. "I think it's the ordinary part. I thought you'd be more like nuns or something, all covered up."

"Well, we do cover up. But we also make ourselves attractive for our husbands . . . or in my case, future husband."

"Are you engaged?"

Now they all laughed, while Alana shook her head. "No. I'm just the only single one. Which means I'm the only one without children."

"That's what makes this such an escape," Jessica informed her from the back. "We've left the kids behind for a change."

"How many do you have?"

Evidently, this signaled the women to produce pictures and hand them all up to Darlene. She was stupefied. Jessica had four children, Amy three, and Marti two. "Well, my sister has three," Darlene said to them. "But I've just got one."

"Just me, Mama. Right?"

"So far," Darlene said.

"And," Tiffany continued for the benefit of these new friends, "maybe Earl Junior. He's Earl's son, and maybe he could come live with us too, so Earl will be my daddy and Earl Junior will be my brother."

"Tiffany!" Darlene protested. "We don't know, right now—"

"And," Tiffany said, raising her voice to drown out her mother, "AND, my mom had another baby right in her tummy, but it fell out and she had to go to the hospital, so we didn't get that one. Didn't you, Mommy?"

Darlene shook her head. "Tiffany," she said, "we don't have to tell that to everyone. Remember when we talked about that?"

"I had that happen, too," Amy said. "Just a few months ago. It's really scary when that happens, isn't it?" she addressed Tiffany.

Darlene couldn't see, but she knew Tiffany's silence meant that she was nodding.

"But I'm hoping I'll have a baby in my tummy soon again," Amy went on. "And maybe your mommy will, too."

It was, Kat realized, the first time they had ever sat down to dinner at the Ladies Farm with more men than women. The fact that it was only Earl tipping the balance didn't matter. It was the shock of coincidence, that each of them—Della, Rita, and herself—had a man in her life . . . at the same time!

The catalyst was Earl's plunder, via a series of trades that had included a load of pig iron and a cache of Appalachian Mountain quilts, leaving him with a warehouse of power tools and, as a sweetener, ten briskets ready for smoking. Quickly, he had unloaded the power tools, saving only a few exotic drills for his inner circle, and presented the briskets to the ladies for their hospitality.

Thus began the smoke-a-thon, for which Tony, Nick, and Dave all brought their personal smokers to the Ladies Farm to join Earl in smoking the briskets, starting very early Sunday morning. It gratified Kat that they had selected Nick's brisket, smoked over brandy-apple wood chips and basted with whiskey, for their own feast. The other briskets, save one Earl was taking to his aunt and uncle, would be sliced and frozen for the gustatory pleasure of Ladies Farm guests.

"More beer!" Rita sang out, setting a dripping six-pack on a tray atop the server in the dining room.

"What about margaritas?" Kat inquired.

"Tony's mixing them now," Rita said. "I don't know why you can't drink beer like the rest of us."

"It's not just me," Kat defended herself. "Della drinks them, too."

"Must be non-Texans," Rita grumbled.

"I'm a Texan."

"Naturalized Texan," Nick amended. He bore a cutting board crowned by the whole brisket, and his entrance was followed by Earl, bearing carving instruments, and Tony with the much awaited pitcher of margaritas.

"Della!" Kat called her partner. "Tony's got our poison!"

"She's fussing with those cobblers," Rita said. "She won't leave them till they're perfect and she can get them out of the oven."

Kat filled her blue-edged glass mug with ice and let Tony pour her drink and a fresh one for Della. She doubted her eye-hand coordination, and attributed a sudden surge of sentimentality to the potency of Tony's creation.

Preserving peaches had been Della's first kitchen project following Pauline's death. For what seemed like weeks they had put up with the crunching of sugar underfoot and a convention of flies around the compost heap as it filled with peach pits and discarded peelings. Della had been maniacal in her quest for perfectly preserved fruit, and serving peach cobbler had become her determined memorial to her accomplished friend.

"Here," Kat said to Della. She held up the drink as she crossed the kitchen threshold. "Fortification!"

Della set a large pan of cobbler on the kitchen counter and stood back proudly before she looked at Kat and the proffered drink. As Kat stepped forward, Della reached across the counter and took the margarita. "To Pauline's peach cobbler," she toasted.

"To Pauline, Pauline's peach cobbler, and us," Kat amended. Then, after they sipped, she inclined her head toward the dining room. "Nick's carving."

"Why not Dave?" Della asked, motioning them both into the next room. "Didn't Earl give him some souped-up power saw to divvy up that thing?"

"This calls for more of an artiste," Kat said, leading the way.

Nick stood at the head of the table, the brisket on the board before him. Kat smiled to see that he wore latex gloves for the operation and that Earl, nurse-style, was holding the platter onto which Nick placed the sliced beef.

"We could try a blind taste testing," Tony proposed. "Maybe when there's a full house. My mesquite. Dave's special sauce. Your apple wood."

"I'm game," Nick said.

"Up to the girls," Dave said. He glanced at Rita. "Put the guests on the spot."

"Up to the *women*," Della corrected. Then she laughed. "Meat-lovers special! Carnivore competition!"

"Well," Rita opined, "it's been a long time since we had a house full of women who would all eat red meat. What's happened, anyway?"

"Uh, have you missed the last decade?" Della asked.

"I know all that," Rita defended herself. "But this is Texas, you know. Where people raise cattle. Chisholm Trail and all that."

"Well," Kat considered, "brandied apple wood is not exactly traditional Texas barbecue."

Earl cleared his throat. "Uh, actually, this meat's out of Omaha. Though it came to me via a broker in Korea."

"You know, that's a little scary when you think about it," Dave ventured. "You take a little one, like Tiffany, she'll never know a time when the meat on her table came from the place down the road."

"Or her buzz saw was made in America," Rita said. "Not to mention her Honda."

"Actually," said Tony, "I think most Hondas are made in America. It's Fords and Chryslers that are suspect." He nodded toward Earl. "Are y'all ready to pass that?"

The barbecue was sublime, spicy and faintly fruity, overlaid by a rich, smoky taste. Kat, who had ended up at the foot of the table, looked up at Nick as she swallowed her first bite. "Perfect," she pronounced, and the others agreed.

"Speaking of Tiffany," Tony resumed the earlier conversation, "what have y'all heard from them?"

He addressed the question to Dave, who had become his buddy over the past year, but it was Rita who rushed to answer.

"Well, Tiffany's just fine," she gushed, "she and Darlene are both just doing fine, aren't they, Earl?"

Kat could see Della glaring at Tony while Rita rolled her eyes toward Nick in warning.

"Everything's fine," Earl confirmed, nodding, before the entire table settled into silence broken only by the scrape of flatware against crockery.

"Well," pressed Tony, "is Darlene—"

"Tony!" commanded Della.

At the same time, Nick said, "I think what we're trying to convey here is the sense that whatever I, as the doctor who implanted an embryo into Darlene, don't hear about her is what I can't repeat to others who might be interested in Darlene's activities. So, why don't you tell me about the quick-print business while someone passes another beer down my way."

"Gotcha," said Tony, nodding.

"I'm serious about quick-printing," Nick said. "We do a ton of patient handouts, and it seems like we're always shelling out for new copiers and printers and binders."

"But you'll never catch up with us," Tony told him. "Your volume will never justify the kind of equipment we have. For most of that stuff, training materials especially, you'd be better off e-mailing us the file, and letting us print, collate, bind, and deliver. I've got customers who've saved a whole staff position by working with us."

"Tony's real popular with laid-off employees," Della cracked.

It wasn't until later, when the dishes were done and Della, Rita, and Kat had reviewed reservations for the coming week, that they realized that they were all spending the night at the Ladies Farm. "I guess I'm the chaperone here," Earl said as they stood awkwardly at the bottom of the staircase. He started up the stairs, then turned to address them in a deep voice. "And I expect you youngsters to behave yourselves."

"It's like a dorm room," Nick said when he stood with Kat in front of her four-poster. "Dorm rooms with queen-size beds."

"Della's got a king," Kat informed him. "I'm more modest."

"Or I am," he murmured, stepping over to the window.

Her room was in the older part of the house and overlooked the street and downtown Sydonia. At night, the tiles of the courthouse gleamed under the combination of moonlight and street lamps. The new foliage on the giant magnolias and post oaks obscured every hard edge, parting now and then to reveal the network of paved streets that formed the town's center.

"It's far away from Dallas, isn't it?" she whispered.

"Unless you count the type-A trading maniac procuring briskets and power tools from the Far East. And a hairdresser who's the beta test site for nouveau chic."

"I meant the way it looks."

"Oh, the way it looks." He put his arm around her. "Looks like another world," he agreed. "Everybody's hometown. Where single moms become gestational carriers to raise hard cash and middle-age innkeepers shack up with their paramours."

"We are a beehive of licentiousness." She nudged him with her hip. "Of course, Rita and Dave are married. And Tony and Della were married. So at least in the eyes of the church they're probably still husband and wife." She stared out the window without seeing much. "Of course, not *their* church."

"You ever think about that?"

"Church?"

"Church is one way of thinking about it."

His voice was mild, neutral. *We'll schedule the procedure for next week. We're just going to run a few tests. This protocol has produced positive outcomes in many cases like yours.*

Kat tried to match his tone. "Are we talking about marriage?"

"Just a little. I mean, Kat, this is fun, but we can't keep this up, can we?"

"Well, I was hoping—"

"I meant the commuting. I think, in our youth, you'd be what we called GU: Geographically Undesirable."

"Oh. I guess Sydonia just doesn't measure up to Colleyville. No quick access to the airport, no gate to the community, no clubhouse."

"Whoa! Honey, I'm just saying I'd like a little less distance."

Kat looked out at Sydonia in the moonlight. She shrugged. "You're right."

Nick put his arm around her shoulder. "I wasn't proposing, Kat. I was just . . . discussing. Speculating."

She poked at his side. "Testing the water. Making sure you get a yes before you ask a question."

"In some way, yeah. I'm trying to figure out how you're feeling, Kat. If you're tired of this going back and forth. If you'd like to see me more."

"Affirmative." She took a breath. "I've never been this open with anyone, Nick. Not since Laurie's birth, maybe not since before that. It's an odd feeling."

"Good odd?"

Kat nodded. "But even if we know where we're going, we could go slow, couldn't we?"

"I guess." He looked out the window. "I'm not suggesting you uproot yourself. Just that if we're going to stay together, we make it easier to stay together. Does that make sense?"

Kat nodded and put both arms around his waist. "You know what else?" she whispered.

"What?"

"I'd like not to have to worry about who's listening in the next room."

"They're in the next room?"

Chapter Twenty-one

Gladys and Ray Hutto lived three miles off the highway to Alpine, down a rutted, unpaved road that wound up into the hills north of the Big Bend. "I thought you had a double-wide," Darlene said as she climbed down from the van.

Gladys snorted as she enfolded Darlene in her warm, tobacco-scented arms. "That's what we started with, but this suits us better." She motioned toward the small stucco house. "We needed a front porch to set the couch on." Gladys peeked into the van. "Hello, ladies."

Tiffany was out of the van in a shot, followed by the Krew, who blinked for a moment in the sunlight, shaking the wrinkles out of their skirts and turning to look with wonder at the mountains beyond the house. Darlene made the introductions, though she herself barely knew Gladys, except as Earl's aunt. Then they went inside, where Gladys offered cheese and crackers and fresh fruit, along with appropriate explanations about the origins of the food.

Gladys shuffled around in hiking boots and knit pants and shirt, showing Darlene and Tiffany to a room down a short hallway. Darlene supposed that the room at the end of the hall was a larger bedroom occupied by Gladys and Ray. Darlene and Tiffany's room had a window that looked out onto a vegetable patch with rows of tomatoes and peppers, and a hose on the ground leading from the house.

"I . . . we really appreciate this," Darlene said as she stood awkwardly in the center of the room. She had dragged her duffel in with her and now she leaned down and hefted it onto one of the twin beds.

Gladys chucked Tiffany under the chin and smiled at the child. "We're going to have so much fun out here! 'You ever seen a red racer?"

Tiffany shook her head.

"Well," Gladys looked down at Tiffany's sneakers, "first we'll get you some boots and then we'll just go out and find ourselves a red racer."

Tiffany looked at Darlene.

"It's a snake, hon," Darlene told her daughter. "Not one that would hurt you, just one that's real pretty. Wouldn't you say so, Aunt Gladys?"

"Oh, you'll love the red racers. Little Earl Junior just can't get enough of them when he comes out here."

Tiffany brightened. "Earl Junior comes here?"

"Why, right here, sugar. His mama sends him out on the train. He loves it out here."

"Where is his room?"

"Well, usually he sleeps right in here. But you know, honey, we have lots of room out here. We have a sleep sofa out there in the living room. And we have the double-wide. Know what that is?"

"Trailer."

"Right out there, see?" Gladys took Tiffany to the window and directed her gaze to the edge of the window. "See there. That's where Uncle Ray and I lived for a few months, till we got this place refinished."

Tiffany nodded.

"I like those girls," Gladys said to Darlene.

"Alana's kosher," Tiffany said.

"I know, honey. Has she taught you how to get kosher?"

"*Keep* kosher," Tiffany corrected. "*Keep*."

"Keep kosher."

Tiffany nodded approval. "No milk and meat." She shook her head. "No ham."

"Well, you do know!" Gladys said. She turned back to Darlene. "Do you think they'd like to stay the night?"

"They've got a campsite in the park," Darlene said. "They—I really took them out of their way, but they made some kind of promise to Earl and Rita."

"Rita's my mamaw," Tiffany explained to Gladys.

"Yes, honey. I know your mamaw well. Don't you remember

when I lived right across the river from your mamaw? Up the hill?" Gladys winked. "I think that's when you still lived in Fort Worth."

Tiffany frowned but did not answer. Gladys smiled, touched her shoulder. "I wonder if those girls would like to stop here on their return trip out of the park?"

"They might," Darlene said. "They're pretty good company. They might like to walk up in those hills; they like to hike. We stopped at Seminole Canyon, and they're going up Emory Peak tomorrow." She looked down at Tiffany, who was trying to slide past her to the door. "Stay inside," she instructed as Tiffany made it to the door. "No running around until we get you some boots."

"I wish I had thought of boots in Del Rio." Darlene shook her head as she unzipped her bag and started pulling out blouses to hang in the closet. "You know," she returned to the Kosher Krew, "if they leave the park on Friday, they have to stop before sunset. They won't drive until Saturday night."

"Well, let's talk to them about it," Gladys resolved. "They might like to walk in to the springs." She stood still, looking at Darlene. "How's Earl?" she asked.

"Fine, I guess. You've probably talked to him more than I have; I haven't talked to him since I left. He sent me a letter; he said he'd come here."

"Oh, he will," Gladys said. "He called to say so. He wanted to know about the power and the phone lines, he's setting up a computer in the double-wide."

"He's running a phone line?"

"Actually, DSL," Gladys said proudly, though Darlene was sure she didn't know what it meant. "Our phone service is pretty up to date."

"I didn't think we were planning on staying that long," Darlene said. "That we'd run phone lines." She looked at the clothes in her hand. "I didn't mean to start doing this. I just wanted to get our bags out of the way."

"Sometimes," Gladys suggested, "we just do things without thinking."

"Not me!" Darlene laughed. "Couldn't you tell?"

Later, after more hugging and kissing, and a promise to return in a few days, Alana and her gang headed back to Big Bend. Tiffany fell asleep on the living room sofa, and Darlene began unpacking for real. "I'll help with dinner," she promised Gladys before returning to her room. She was contemplating the pile of laundry she and Tiffany had accumulated on the road when the phone rang. As precious as water is out here, thought Darlene, you'd better haul this pile to the laundromat.

Gladys stuck her head in the doorway. "For you," she said, motioning to the extension on the little night table.

"Hey!"

"Earl? Oh, God!" Darlene looked back over her shoulder, but Gladys had disappeared, and, in a second, she heard the soft click of Gladys hanging up the phone in the living room.

"You okay?" he asked her.

"Pretty good." After imagining his voice for so long, the actual sound of it jarred her, and she wanted him to keep talking long enough to grow familiar with it again.

"Tiff?"

"She's fine," Darlene said. "What's going on there? Did you get the thing from Ryan?"

"Yeah."

Had he always been this short-spoken? "Well?"

"What you thought."

"So it's ours," she said. Darlene sat on the bed and stared at the wall.

"That's not all. This one's still a match. We can still do the transplant. The stem cells. He's not even that mad."

"He's mad, Earl." She considered what he had just said. "So really, they just want the stem cells?"

"Right."

"The stem cells, not the baby?"

"Darl, that's what I said."

"You don't sound like you understand it, Earl. We—you and I—are going to have a baby."

"Well, Darl, we kind of knew that, didn't we? I mean, you're glad, aren't you?"

"Honey, of course I'm glad." But it was too simple. "Has he told Jill?"

"I don't think so. He said—uh, he sent along a little envelope—he said we should let him tell Jill. He's her husband, the twins were theirs, it's going to break her heart. Except they'll have that transplant for Taylor."

Darlene picked at the chenille bedspread. It was the white, wedding-ring style that had been popular the last time chenille had swept America, and there were spots where the nap had been washed away completely.

"You still there?"

"Yes." She roused herself. "Earl, I'm glad about the baby. We just . . . we need to talk . . . I mean together."

"I know. I'll be there soon."

It made no sense, she thought. Earl's physical presence couldn't do a thing for her fears about another baby. But still, she was tired of the phone. She laughed a little. "Hey! You know what?"

"What?" She wished he sounded happier.

"I'm wearing that bracelet . . . the ankle bracelet."

"Yeah?"

Definitely puzzled, she thought. "I haven't taken it off. Even in the tub."

There was a long silence, and she imagined him coloring as he stood looking at the phone and remembered times they had spent together in the tub.

"Does Tiff like hers?" he asked.

"I was waiting till we got here to give it to her. But she'll love it." She shifted back on the bed and lay on her back. "Gladys says you're running DSL out here."

"I just asked about it," Earl mumbled.

"But you're coming out, right?"

"I said I am."

"He'll probably figure out where you've gone," Darlene said. "Where we are."

"What difference does it make now? Anyway," Earl said, "I don't think anyone can stay hidden in Alpine very long. Especially a pregnant woman."

"It's too easy. Take the money. Hand over the stem cells. Keep the baby."

"We've just been handed a gift, Darlene. After all the bad breaks, something fell our way."

Darlene doubted he believed that, but she didn't want to argue; she felt sure they could figure it out once he got there.

"I miss you," he said, sounding, finally, like himself.

"I miss you too," she said.

"Did he say when he's coming?" Gladys asked her while Darlene started putting plates on the round table in the kitchen.

"He didn't say, really." *He said I'm pregnant with his baby. He said Ryan wants only the stem cells. He said he misses me.*

Gladys had fixed spaghetti, and now she emptied the pot into a colander in the stainless sink. As she turned around to look at Darlene, the steam rose behind her like a cloud. "I—we haven't seen him in almost a year. I didn't think I'd miss having him around so much."

"He kind of grows on you," Darlene said. *He's coming here to help me get ready for our new baby. And he asked about Tiff just like she was his.*

"Well, he's had to grow up, I guess. Maybe our moving away forced him to figure out what he wants. Here," Gladys directed, "reach up on that shelf, I can never reach that high, and get a jar of that tomato sauce." She looked out over the counter that separated the kitchen from the open living room. "Ray, take Tiffany to wash her hands."

"Let us just finish this game," he said. "C'mere, Tiff," he instructed. "Now you can jump all my men. Just pick up that blue marble and jump over all these guys." Ray, with his arms around Tiffany, took her hand and showed her how to jump in Chinese checkers. "You're going to put me right under!"

After dinner, Darlene got Tiffany bathed and into bed, then sat with her for a few minutes. "You like Aunt Gladys and Uncle Ray?"

Tiffany nodded. "They're Earl Junior's aunt and uncle."

"Yes." Darlene reached over and caught a strand of Tiffany's hair. For a second, she held it between two fingers, then pushed it back out of Tiffany's eyes. The hair was almost mocha colored; within a few years, Darlene knew, her blonde angel would be brunette.

That damn Jason and his black hair! she thought. Then she smiled. "Honey, what if you and Earl Junior got a new baby brother or sister?"

"Which one?"

"Well, I don't know yet."

Tiffany propped herself up on one elbow. "Where is it?"

"Here inside me."

"In your tummy?"

Darlene nodded.

"Can I touch it?" Tiffany stuck an open hand out from under the blanket and reached for Darlene's belly.

Darlene, leaning back to facilitate Tiffany's touch, breathed in her daughter's sweet, soapy scent. "You know what else?" Darlene said.

Tiffany leaned back against her pillow as Darlene first sat up, then stood to work her hand into the pocket of her jeans. "Earl sent you something special."

Tiffany's gaze remained steady.

Darlene sucked in at the waist to fish the small chain out of her watch pocket. "Look," she said. "It's an ankle bracelet. Just like mine."

Tiffany reached out a hand and took the bracelet, studying it in the dim light. "It's hearts."

"Here," said Darlene, pulling back the blanket and motioning to her daughter.

Tiffany stuck out her left foot, then pulled it back and stuck out her right. "That's my best one," Tiffany advised.

Darlene nodded, concentrated on fastening the tiny clasp.

"When is my brother or sister coming?"

"It'll be a while," Darlene said. "About six months."

"When's that?"

"November," Darlene informed her daughter. "My due date is November."

Rita and Dave liked to get their coffee together at Dave's store. On nice days, they walked over, then Rita would jog back on her own. It was only a few blocks, but it made her feel virtuous.

The coffee was pedestrian. Rita kept ceramic mugs at the shop so at least they weren't drinking out of Styrofoam, but the coffee itself was the sturdy type that kept for hours on the counter. Even fresh, it required a lot of cream and sugar.

Rita perched up on the chair behind the register while Dave leaned against the counter. "What I'm thinking," Rita told Dave, "is that she'll be due around November. Which means by the time school starts in late August, she'll be six and a half, seven months. We've got to have Tiffany back here by then."

Dave, as usual, didn't reply immediately. He stared down into his cup, then looked up. He raised his eyebrows. He grimaced. Then he sipped, cautiously, and pressed his lips together hard as he swallowed.

Rita bit back her impatience. "Don't you think so, honey? So she can get settled in before the first day of kindergarten?" She smiled, imagining it. "I figure, we can walk her over there most mornings, on our way here. Of course, we'll drive her in bad weather."

"Well, it's nice for a little girl to be able to walk to school," Dave acknowledged, then fell silent again.

"But?" she encouraged.

"But?" He looked puzzled.

"Listen, mister, there's a *but* as big as Texas hanging off that statement. *It's nice for a little girl to walk to school* but!"

Rita supposed with all the stuff he dumped in his coffee it had cooled enough to gulp it the way he did without scorching his esophagus, so she waited him out, not bothering to conceal that her patience had not lasted long.

"Well," he stepped forward and set the cup on the counter, "I'm thinking that maybe her mother wants to be walking Tiffany to school and all that." He looked thoughtful. "I mean, nowadays, I thought pregnant women are supposed to walk and work out and everything."

"You don't think Tiffany should live here . . . in Sydonia . . . with us?"

"Now, honey," he said.

"Don't *now honey* me," Rita said. It never failed to annoy her that the same even-toned, steady, level-headed demeanor for which she had married the man made him unbearable when he failed to take her side. "Tell me what you think."

"I think this conversation's heading into trouble," Dave said. "That's what I think."

"I can tell you don't agree with me. Why don't you just say it?"

He shook his head and grinned. "Not on your life. You're too ready to pounce."

"You don't think I'm a good mother," she accused.

"Honey, I think you're a wonderful mother." He looked relieved to be able to compliment her. "To Carla and Darlene. And you're the all-time best grandmother to Tiffany, and the other kids, too."

Rita shook her head. "I'm good to Tiffany, but Carla's kids get it a lot better from Mama A. I don't think she even raised her own kids, I think she went directly from teenager to grandmother." Rita grinned. "I wish she were *my* grandmother." Her smile faded. "What's the problem?"

He shifted his weight from one foot to another, but he held his ground. "You're Carla and Darlene's mother. Tiffany's mother is Darlene. That's who should be taking her to kindergarten."

"Shoulda, coulda, woulda," Rita said. "Darlene's got her hands full. She doesn't know where she's going to be when school starts."

"Did she say that? Have you talked to her?"

"Well, no. But I've talked to Earl. And I know Darlene. She's not giving that baby to Doctor Ryan and she's not giving back any money. So where does that leave Tiffany?" Rita pressed. "Who's looking out for her?"

"Honey, Darlene and Earl are looking after her. And Gladys and Ray, for now."

"Oh, great! Gladys and Ray, who never had any children of their own! They're looking out for my grandbaby!"

"They raised Earl," Dave said. "Honey, why can't you let this be?"

Rita shook her head. "I just hate to think of my little granddaughter, my sweet baby starting school in those mountains while Darlene tries to grow up and manage a new baby." She slid off the stool and walked around the counter to take his hands. "Dave, I just want to talk to Darlene, to offer my help." She saw his skepticism. "She's going to need help, Dave."

"How are you going to do that?" Dave asked. "Talk to Darlene?"

"I'll have to go there," Rita said. "You'll have to help get me there."

Chapter Twenty-two

Alana bowed out of the hike to the springs. So Darlene invited her to ride along to Alpine to the laundromat. "How'd you like the park?" Darlene asked as they rolled off the unpaved road and took the highway toward town.

"Loved it," Alana said. "I could have stayed forever, except, of course, for the bear warnings. We hiked up Emory Peak, and the Lost Mine Trail, and then yesterday we did the Window, which goes down this canyon until you're actually standing in a crevice in the face of this sheer cliff. So beautiful."

"I haven't been there yet," Darlene said. "But I want to take Tiff. Walk around a little bit. That's why Gladys and Ray are getting the hiking boots." Darlene shook her head. "I don't know why I didn't think of that in Del Rio."

"You've got a lot to think about right now," Alana observed.

"I guess Earl told you the whole story, huh?"

"Well, I don't know if I heard the whole story, but a good bit of it."

"I guess I didn't hear the whole story either," Darlene said. "I thought I knew everything, but it turns out Ryan and Jill had their own agenda."

"How did you meet Ryan?" Alana asked.

"Oh, I was working transcription at the hospital, and he had a lot of overflow at his office, asked my supervisor to recommend someone to do it freelance."

"Ah. The reward for good work."

"Yeah. And then one thing led to another. You know, I'd go there to pick up tapes and then maybe he'd tease me or something, and we'd sit around for a few minutes. It got so I left his stuff till the end of the day, maybe go home and change before I went over there so the office staff would be gone already. You know what I mean." As soon as she said it, Darlene realized that Alana probably had no idea what she meant. And that Earl had never told this part of her story.

"I mean, maybe you don't know what I mean, exactly, but just that he and I got to be friendly pretty quick and then, you know, one thing led to another and pretty soon we were doing it in his office." Despite her intentions, Darlene smiled at the memory. "Mostly in his office chair—oh, God! I didn't mean to, you know, offend you."

"Despite what you may have heard, Jews—even Jewish women—have sex, Darlene."

"Oh, I know that." She struggled to regain her composure. "I just meant, you know, with a—out of wedlock, you know: with someone else's husband."

"Well," Alana laughed. "I've never been intimate with someone else's husband, that's true. But you know, there's a reason it's so rare to find unmarried people—men or women—among the Orthodox. All of us have the desire to be close in that way. And some Orthodox Jews, believe it or not," Alana laughed, "have probably had sex sitting up in office chairs. Though probably home offices. With their spouses."

In that way. Intimate. Darlene figured she was going eighty-five miles an hour in a seventy-mile zone toward Alpine when she realized that she and Ryan had never been intimate. But Earl! Earl and I . . . She took her foot off the accelerator and the rhythm of the rattling in Ray's truck slowed, though the volume remained as a comforting white noise.

"So, is that why Ryan asked you? Because you had this relationship?"

On either side of the road, the brushy hills rose softly, capped by straight-angled bluffs of brownish stone. "What?" Darlene asked, focusing on the road. Maybe you should think about laundry, she thought. "You know," she said, "you'd better remind me to stop at the Allsups and see if I can get a roll of quarters from them."

Darlene took a breath. "I don't know, now, why Ryan chose me. I thought at first it was because he knew me. You know, it's not something you'd ask a stranger: have a baby for me. He knew I had a healthy baby. He knew I didn't smoke—I never did, except a little bit in high school—and I didn't drink much."

Darlene set her jaw and kept driving, gripping the oversized steering wheel on the old truck. "Of course, I don't drink at all now, not while I'm pregnant." She felt that she was rattling as much as the truck, and with as little chance of stopping. "But it didn't have anything to do with that. It had to do with money: that I needed it so much." She blinked hard. "And stupid . . . he thought I was stupid—so stupid—that I wouldn't ask, I'd swallow whatever story he gave me about him and Jill." Her jaw started to tremble, her whole mouth trembled, but she just clenched harder until she could talk again. "Broke and stupid."

Alana helped her carry the laundry, three Hefty bags' worth, into the laundromat. "Weekday morning," Alana said. "That's why it's empty. Though—umph!" she deposited one sack on the table, "you'd never find one this empty, or this clean, in New York."

Darlene pulled the sheets first; hers, Tiff's, and Gladys and Ray's all fit into one machine, which she supposed was the advantage of plain old double beds. "Earl's got a king," she remarked to Alana. "Those sheets take up a whole wash by themselves."

"I know," Alana said, opening the sack with the darks and brights. "Do you do these in cold?"

Darlene nodded.

"My mother still has a king; my dad died two years ago, and she hasn't remarried, so I live with her. You should see how much laundry two grown women produce!"

Darlene measured out detergent, closed the top of the washer, and pried quarters out of her fresh roll. "You live with your mother?" she asked, placing the coins and pushing the slide in to start the machine.

"I moved back home when my father got sick, she needed so much help."

Darlene nodded to show she was listening, attacked the rest of her first bag.

"And now," Alana confessed, "she's a pretty good roommate!"

"I guess I just thought—I don't know much about New York, except like *Sex and the City*, or *Will and Grace*, stuff like that—I thought everyone there just lived with their friends . . . I mean you'd live with your *girl*friends, of course, if you were going to do that. You wouldn't live with a gay guy, I guess, or someone not, you know, from your culture."

"Well, people do get pretty desperate for living space in New York," Alana said.

Darlene had to look at her to make sure Alana was teasing before she let herself laugh.

"Actually, though," Alana continued, "my mother's a pretty good roommate. And my friends," she made a wry face, "are all married. Everyone's married."

"Well, not everyone," Darlene countered. "I'm not. Kat's not. Your mother's not."

"But she is seeing someone. And I expect she will. Though, of course, I'm sure they'll still be happy to have me live with them, too. But I meant my contemporaries. That's what I meant before: In our community, everyone marries. Early." She grew sober. "No one knows what to do about a young single woman."

"Well," Darlene drawled, "in our community, we marry early too. And often!"

When they'd gotten all the washers churning, they walked back to the Allsups for sodas and drank them outside, sitting on a crumbling retaining wall. "What would happen," Darlene asked, "if you just married someone, you know, not Orthodox? I mean," she motioned with her hand, "there are plenty of men, single ones our age. You all, your community, are the only ones that marry so early and then stay married. You're really pretty, too! Couldn't you just marry someone who's divorced?"

"Divorced, yes," Alana said. "Or widowed, yes. There are some of those in New York, but not many, and mostly a little older." She paused, sipped. "But not Jewish, no. I used to think that was just old-fashioned, my parents' rule, you know? But now . . . now I think it's me . . . I've internalized it so much, the way I was raised, I couldn't love a man who isn't Jewish."

"That's so . . . so prejudiced!" Darlene said. "Like you don't think anyone else is good enough?"

"That's not what I meant," Alana said. "There are lots of good people, good men, who aren't Jewish. I just meant, to share a life with someone, a whole life, you have to have the same values, the same goals. I don't think that would happen—for me, I mean—unless that person was Jewish."

"Well, I think you're just not looking hard enough! Look at Earl and me. In high school, I couldn't have imagined ever—ever, ever,

ever!—hooking up with him. But now, after Jason and Jimmy and Ryan, Earl's just . . . you know, it's like I didn't see him before."

"So, are you and Earl going to get married?"

Darlene shrugged her shoulders. "Don't know. He hasn't asked me."

"But you are going to have this baby? And he is the father? At least, that's what he thought when he told me about it."

"Oh, he's the father, all right. But, you know, it's, like, the twenty-first century. I don't have to get married."

"Well, of course you don't have to," Alana said. "I meant, don't you want to? Don't you want Earl to be your husband?"

The mid-morning sun had crept over the summit crowned by Sul Ross University and poured down light on the tiny grid that comprised Alpine's downtown. With the sun in her eyes, Darlene couldn't read Alana's expression. All she could see was the fiery shimmer of hair blown loose from the wide-brimmed hat that shadowed Alana's face.

"I don't know."

Foiled by the wind, Alana pulled off her hat and wound her hair up in a knot. With one hand holding her hair on top of her head, the other hand grasping her cloth hat, and her oversize wooden hairpin still in her mouth, she gazed at Darlene and shook her head. "You don't know?" Alana asked as she retrieved the hairpin with the hat-hand and secured her hair for at least the moment.

"Aren't you cold?" Darlene said. They were almost a mile up, and even a sunny day stayed cool till afternoon. "Let's go back inside."

They walked back to the laundromat, where the six washers were still sloshing away and a backpacking couple were debating the merits of washing their sleeping bags along with the rest of their laundry. "We'll just stuff them in the bottom, then throw the rest of the stuff on top. It'll work," the leggy girl encouraged, stuffing the second of the bags into a second machine.

"I know it'll work," the guy said, shaking his head as he emptied laundry from a nylon drawstring bag. He had reddish-gold hair on his legs, and a nice, tight butt. "I just don't know that we can get them dry enough for tonight, without melting them."

The girl's hair was as short as Darlene's, but dark, and she wore no jewelry. Her clothes—hiking shorts, long-sleeved shirt, down vest—featured zippered pockets and a stunning selection of rings, clips, and grommets. Even her hiking boots had loops on their backs, and key pockets laced onto the uppers. "Trust me," the girl said, grinning. "I'll make it worth your while."

They barely glanced at Alana and Darlene as they got their two machines loaded and then chased outside to hunt down supplies while their laundry washed.

Alana grinned, shrugged her shoulders at Darlene. "You see, it's universal," she said.

Darlene grunted. She was thinking that that was one thing about Earl: no matter how much he worked out, he'd always have that broad linebacker's ass. These days, though, a guy like the camper didn't seem that appealing. A tight body like that didn't offer enough comfort.

"I hope I didn't offend you," Alana said. She stood awkwardly at the long, white-topped table where Darlene had thrown herself into one of the folding chairs. "Maybe you just haven't thought about it."

"Well, I haven't. No, that's a lie. I have thought about it, I just don't feel like I have to get married. What good is a husband, anyway?"

"Well, no good," Alana laughed, "if you don't want him." She slipped into the chair opposite Darlene. "But I thought you did want Earl."

"I do. Just not as a husband." She looked at Alana. "Trust me on this, I've had one and you haven't, and it can really suck. I mean, the husbands in your community may be faithful and kind, but the plain old Texas variety turns into a creep the second he says 'I do.' As in 'I do believe I'll treat my new wife like shit.' Or 'I do like beer better than I like married life.' Or 'I do think I'll screw around on my wife while she's knocked up.' Or—"

Alana held up her hand. "I get the picture. And it's up to you. But do you really think Earl will be that way?"

"Well, I didn't think Jason Kindalia, Tiffany's father would be that way. And I didn't think Jimmy would be that way. And Rita sure didn't think Wendell would be that way. But they were."

"Who's Wendell?"

"My father."

"And you think Earl's like that?"

"I think all guys are like that."

"So why did you have sex with him?"

"Because I wanted to!" Darlene spat out. "Because I . . . he . . .

shit! You think you're better than everyone else!" She jumped up. "The wash is done!"

Silently, they stood side by side, emptying the wash into wheeled baskets, then loading the two dryers. Silently, Darlene offered the roll of quarters. Silently, Alana pried the coins off the top; silently they started both dryers.

"Look," said Darlene. "Let's just drop it, okay? Maybe I will marry Earl and maybe I won't. And you can be the first to know."

"After Earl and Tiffany," Alana suggested.

"After Earl and Tiffany."

"I just want to say," Alana took a breath, "I just want to say, whatever you do, you know, because of Ryan and your circumstances, if you ever need help, if you want to come to New York, you can stay with me."

"With you and your mother?" Darlene studied her.

"With my mother and me, yes," Alana said. "We can always make room for you; for you and Tiffany and Earl, if you'd like."

"Well . . . um . . . thank you. I . . . there's not many people who would make that offer."

"Oh, but there are," Alana corrected. "There's Earl himself. And your own mother. And Mr. and Mrs. Hutto. You have a lot of friends."

She's right, thought Darlene. And she doesn't even know Lakeesha or Carla. Or Mama A. "I would like to visit New York sometime," Darlene said. "It'll be good, having someone to visit."

Alana looked down at the empty laundry cart and shook her head a second. "I'm not sure I should say this, but I have to make sure you understand. Because we've never talked about it. But Darlene, whatever you choose to do, even if . . . I'm saying you could come to New York if you . . . if you decide . . . if you change your mind, if you decide this isn't the best way." She motioned with her hands in exasperation and looked up at Darlene. "If you decide you want to end this pregnancy, if you decide to wait until later to have another child, with or without Earl, you could come to us. In New York. It might be easier in New York."

She heard them talking the night after Alana left: his vigilant questioning, her patient replies.

"Well, what *is* she going to do?"

"Have her baby. Wait here for Earl. Look after little Tiffany."

"How long is all that going to take?"

"What difference does it make? It's nice, having kids around. That baby's Earl's. That makes us great-aunt and uncle. And we've got the room."

"These are the wide open spaces."

"Don't be sarcastic. She—she and Tiffany and Earl—need our help, and we're able to give it."

"I'm just saying, maybe she should get a job in town. Part-time. She could ride into town with me when I teach."

"Just give her a little time."

"You mean, give you a little time to spoil that little girl."

"That won't hurt Tiffany or me. Or you, for that matter."

Darlene heard him sigh. "It just makes it that much harder when they leave."

Chapter Twenty-three

Darlene wasn't looking for a job, she was only looking for a sandwich. But even with the college, there wasn't a big labor force heading into tourist season. When Janine, the shop owner, realized that Darlene was free all day, she asked if Darlene knew how to make sandwiches. How to chop. How to shred. How to pour. How to heat. Then Janine whipped a stool over the counter and, with a quick glance at Darlene's ankles, patted the seat. "You can make 'em sitting down," Janine said. "All you've got to do is make them fast. And neat."

When Darlene explained it to Gladys and Ray, she thought she could ride in with Ray on Monday, Wednesday, and Friday, and perhaps borrow the truck Tuesday and Thursday. "You know," she said. "Until Earl gets here."

"You heard us arguing," Gladys stated. She took another puff on her cigarette and squinted accusingly at Darlene as she exhaled into the twilight.

"No I didn't," Darlene said, then dropped it. "Well, maybe I did, but that's not why." She reached for her Dr Pepper, which sat on the wooden arm of the upholstered couch. "The money'll cover Tiffany's preschool. She's excited about preschool. Aren't you, Tiff?"

Tiffany, ensconced in Ray's lap on the porch swing, nodded agreeably. "They do shows," she reported on their recent visit. "They sing farm songs. They read the words." Then, "Push!" she directed Ray, whom she had charged with keeping the swing in motion.

"Animal sounds," Darlene confirmed to Gladys. Darlene leaned back and rested her feet on an upturned milk crate. She had learned to savor these after-dinner porch sessions. They were the best time to talk with Gladys and Ray.

"When's that boy going to get here?" Ray asked.

"Just a few weeks, now," Darlene assured him. "He's got a couple of deals to clean up, and he needs to finish up some things he was doing for Kat and Della. Installing software and redoing their Web page. That kind of stuff. In exchange for room and board."

"They've been after me to teach at that preschool," Gladys remarked.

"I remember when you used to visit our school," Darlene recalled. She smiled. "I'd forgotten you did that. I guess I didn't even know Earl then."

"What grade were you in then?"

"I guess it was elementary school, fifth grade maybe. We called you Senora Cubana. You used to tell us about Havana, taught us Spanish words."

Gladys lifted an eyebrow. "That's why they're so hot for me now: Spanish. You remember any of the words I taught you?"

Darlene shook her head. "Not a one!"

Gladys looked stricken. "That's why I'm not in any hurry." She took another puff.

"But we loved you!" Darlene protested. "*Frijoles negros. Buenos Dias. Buenos Noches.* See, I remember something! Besides, you can't judge anything by me." She lowered her voice and turned away from Tiffany. "I was a slow student. I was way behind," she whispered.

"Well, you sure caught up," Gladys said. "Your mama's pretty smart," she said to Tiffany. "Isn't she?"

Tiffany nodded.

"Not like Tiffany," Darlene chimed. "Tiffany's really smart!"

Ryan began as soon as Elizabeth McCutcheon closed her office door.

"I understand it's pretty common for gestational carriers to bolt," Ryan explained. "Or at least think about it. And Jill and I want to give Darlene all the space she needs right now."

Dr. McCutcheon nodded.

"After all," he reasoned, "Darlene's young, and maybe it's just now hitting her what a tough job she's undertaken." He leaned forward a little. "We—Jill and I—believe she'll come 'round, but we're afraid . . . we can't be sure . . . we want to know what you think."

Dr. McCutcheon smiled sympathetically. "This must be an anxious time for you. After your call, I pulled Darlene's file, and I have to tell you, Darlene impressed me as a remarkably resilient young woman."

"Yes, yes," Ryan said. "That's why we picked her. But this," now he looked down at his clasped hands, "this is more—" he looked up in appeal "—we did a terrible thing, we . . . I guess you could say we tricked her." He held Dr. McCutcheon's gaze. "Not we, really. I. I tricked her."

"I imagine, from what you said on the phone, that Darlene is quite angry. There's quite an issue of trust here. Not to mention paternity."

"I don't really care," said Ryan. "I don't care about the paternity, I just want to make sure that if that baby can help Taylor, that she'll agree to it." His locked eyes with Dr. McCutcheon's. "We need Darlene's help."

"Yes, I understand." She peered at him. "Is there a reason your wife—Jill—isn't here with you?"

"She's with Taylor," Ryan said. Then he shook his head. "That's not the whole thing. It's that Jill doesn't know the details. She knows Darlene lost a baby and that she's still pregnant. I haven't . . . I can't tell her the rest until I'm at least sure we'll get the stem cells. You see my bind: I gave Darlene every reason to distrust me, but we're entirely dependent on her help. That's why I'm so interested in your advice."

"Any word on where she is?"

"For all I know," Ryan said, "she's safe at home in Sydonia, with her mother. But no one's heard a word. We don't want to start sending out search teams: you know, hiring detectives and the like. But we're—our whole future—is totally dependent on her. We're hoping Darlene will contact us eventually. Is that realistic?"

"You flatter me!" Dr. McCutcheon laughed. "I'm a psychologist, not a fortune teller!" She grew serious again. "I don't know. My inclination would be to wait at least a few months to see if she'll surface. After all, her family and friends are in this area. She's going to need medical care, including whatever records are with Dr. Kaplan and Dr. Lantinatta."

Ryan smiled. "That's exactly what I've been thinking."

"And you've got a little time. Darlene seems pretty level-headed. I doubt if she'd do anything harmful to herself, or the baby."

Ryan looked beseechingly at Dr. McCutcheon. "I . . . we want to give Darlene as much room and time as she needs. But Jill—Jill and I both—are sick with worry over this. What if Taylor . . . what if things take a bad turn, and we need to find her right away? What if we need the stem cells right away? Wouldn't we be better off, at least knowing where she is?"

Dr. McCutcheon pressed her lips together. "I don't know," she said finally. "Dr. Plummer, when you talk about needing the stem cells, what do you mean? Are you saying you want to abort the fetus?"

"Well, I . . . we hope not. But that was part of the deal. Anyway," he hurried on, "that's not our immediate concern." He smiled broadly. "Taylor's really doing fine right now. The most likely scenario is that Darlene will deliver at full term, we'll freeze the stem cells in case we need them in the future, and we can all go our separate ways."

She didn't return his smile. "Have you discussed this with your wife?"

"You're the expert in this field. You know what Darlene, Jill, and I signed down to the last word. So, yes, in broad terms she knows that we have the right. And she—Jill—is very knowledgeable about our son's illness. So she knows there's a possibility that we could need the stem cells before Darlene's ready to deliver. If you think about it, you knew that too, as soon as I told you about the stem cell transplant."

"But Jill doesn't know that this is actually Darlene and Earl's baby?"

"I just haven't told her yet."

"My advice is that you tell her immediately. Certainly before you make any decisions about terminating someone else's pregnancy."

Ryan gave himself a second and then bit his lip as he studied his hands. "It's so hard, telling Jill. She wanted that baby, those twins. If I—please understand me—if I made it sound as if I would act without Jill . . . I could never do that."

Dr. McCutcheon seemed to uncoil. "Good. But you have a lot of work to do." She paused. "Have you—the two of you—thought about counseling for yourselves? You have several issues here:

Darlene, of course. This baby. The possibility of an experimental treatment. And the very real chance that your son could die. Have the two of you discussed this?"

Ryan stared at the woman.

Again the gentle smile. "The issue I'm raising here has to do with how you—the two of you—will handle decisions about how to treat Taylor." She spoke carefully. "There may come a point when you have to decide whether or not to go forward with further treatment, or just let this disease run its course. Have you talked—I mean have the two of you talked—about that?"

Ryan shook his head hard. Was she trying to gauge his sincerity? His intentions? "We're a long way from that!" He breathed out hard. "I understand what you're saying, and I appreciate your thinking about us here. But, trust me, we have studied this disease, and our son's case, until we should have Ph.D.'s in it. We know everything there is to know about it and, yes, somewhere down the road, it's possible we'll have to think about what you've suggested. But we've got a lot of options, a long way to go here. Don't forget," he reminded her, "many of these kids right themselves and live good, healthy lives. Right now, Taylor could be well on his way to perfect health.

"Our plan here," he leaned forward, taking Dr. McCutcheon into his confidence, "is to focus on keeping Taylor in remission, doing everything to build up his strength, and to do whatever we can to make sure Darlene delivers a healthy baby."

Dr. McCutcheon nodded, but he knew she wasn't convinced.

"This is why I came to you. I wanted your assessment on how to proceed with Darlene. What's best for her. And for Taylor. And for Jill and myself. And," he paused for a second, "we need your help in preparing in case things don't go the way we all hope they will. A fallback position." He paused again, hoping she recalled without prodding her legal obligations to them as the actual clients, and the release of records Darlene had signed. "Because it's as you said: this is Taylor's life we're dealing with. We've got to consider every possibility."

Dr. McCutcheon waited.

"If we have to find Darlene," he started. "If we have to take measures to safeguard the baby—the baby and her—we have to be ready. Prepared. I've talked to our lawyer. If we need to get some kind of, you know, protective custody, we have to be ready. Everything has to be in place. Taylor's life could depend on it. So we need to think about affidavits. Witnesses. Petitioning the courts. To make Darlene . . . to make sure Darlene does . . . that we all do what's best for Darlene and the baby."

It didn't take much time to master the roll-ups and the bread-and-dressing combinations. She particularly liked the breakfast crowd, now that she could enjoy the aroma of coffee and muffins again. Darlene grew adept at slicing and spreading bagels, as well as wrapping eggs, cheese and sausage in tortillas—whole wheat, flour, corn, or sun-dried tomato.

Breakfast wasn't as rushed as lunch, and she got to like the regulars, the boys from the gym across the street, and the ones who worked for the post office. "It's a little like Sydonia," Darlene said. "Courthouse town."

"Quieter, I'll bet." Janine was artsy, with dangling earrings she had made herself, and clothes she ordered from Central America. The whitewashed walls of the small dining room were covered with hangings Janine had woven and now offered for sale.

"Not much is quieter than Sydonia," Darlene laughed. "More visitors here." She glanced up and smiled at the man whose coffee she had just poured. "Same courthouse crowd, though."

"Shifty clients and shiftier lawyers," said the customer. He handed her exact change for the coffee and bagel.

"Not to mention gossipy clerks!" Janine added.

"You can say that," said the customer. He winked at Darlene. "But we shifty types have to mind our p's and q's." Hands full, he nodded his thanks at Darlene, and turned to make his way to the counter.

Darlene looked at Janine.

"Ben Autalia," Janine said. *Lawyer*, she mouthed, shaking her head and waving her hand in dismissal.

"You're a good cook," he told her when he handed over his cup for a refill on the coffee. "Half caf," he instructed.

"Janine cooked, I just rolled it up."

He took the coffee from her. "Well you're a good roller, then."

Darlene smiled. "Thank you." It was nice to have a strange man compliment her, even an undeserved compliment. She wiggled her fingers at him. "Typist's fingers."

"Really?" He had started back for the counter and the outspread *San Antonio Express*, but he stopped. "Just typing or word processing?"

"Oh, word processing," said Darlene. "All kinds of transcription."

"Earl's convinced Tony we should bottle barbecue sauce and sell smoked briskets beside," Della announced.

Kat looked up from her spreadsheet. "Bottle barbecue sauce?"

Della dropped her portfolio on her desk in the adjoining room. "Peddle it on the Web!" she said over her shoulder. "Sell briskets, too. Muffins! Peach preserves!" She returned to the doorway between the two offices.

Kat grinned at Della. You could always tell when Della had had sex, even if she had driven all the way back from Fort Worth afterward. Bright patches of color reddened her cheeks, and creeped up the base of her neck from under her collar. "How is Tony?"

Della grinned back. "Better, now," she laughed. "I'm telling you, though, Tony's serious about this sauce business."

"I would have thought you'd distract him," Kat drawled.

Della shook her head and colored a little more. "He thinks we can smoke briskets out here, sell them to guests and on the Web site."

"Who does he think is going to mix up all this sauce?" Kat asked. "Not to mention gather firewood for all these smokers?" She frowned. "We just got the damn Web site up and running. Folks can barely make reservations. How're they going to order briskets?"

"Oh, to hear Tony, he and Earl have got it all figured out. They're going to form a consortium—and they're asking Nick, too, because of that whiskey sauce—and Earl's going to take care of all the warehousing and shipping."

"Well what about Dave?" Kat asked.

"Oh, you know they'll ask Dave. He's the only one of them who actually knows how to work anything mechanical."

"Nick can work a speculum," Kat protested. "And a blowtorch," she added. "He can reassemble all the metal pieces so they're more pleasing to the eye."

Della smiled her acknowledgement of Nick's artistic abilities, then invited herself into the office and sprawled onto the sofa. "The thing is, we've got to do something. You know: to make more money."

Kat nodded. Purchase of the Hutto place, plus legal fees to defend themselves against suits by Pauline's son, had left them short of cash. Eventually, it would all pay off, particularly now that they could accommodate small groups. But the short term wouldn't produce much income. This affected Rita and Kat less than Della, who had no outside income. "I know we need to make this place pay, but food?" Kat said. "Shouldn't we be doing something more . . . something related to what we know?"

"I know food. I mean, a year ago it might not have made sense. But now, after cooking for a year, it doesn't sound that far-fetched. We already pack picnics and boxes for the guests to take home with them. Our kitchen's up to code. What would it hurt if we have a few jars of peach preserves or a smoked brisket in inventory?"

Kat shook her head. "Della, you're talking about a whole new business."

Suddenly, Della squinted at Kat's desk. "Did you get a new picture?"

Kat reached over and handed her the metal frame.

"Is this Laurie?"

Kat nodded.

"Weren't you going to say anything? Are these the Kroszyks?"

"Pam and Tom."

"She has . . . I think her hair color is like yours."

"Like mine was," Kat said.

"Did they send any others?"

Silently, Kat swiveled to retrieve the envelope, then turned back to Della and handed them over. She watched Della sorting through the snapshots, knowing which ones were making her smile, which ones she studied to determine Laurie's specific disabilities from the way the girl's head tilted or how her hand rested atop the chair control.

"Weren't you going to say anything?"

Kat shook her head.

"Why not?"

"I think I liked it better when you used to leave things unsaid."

"That's funny. I was trying to be more like you." Della drew down a corner of her mouth. "I don't know, ever since Pauline died—and Barbara—I feel like I have to say everything right out. And do things right away, too. I even told Tony I'd work up the pro forma."

"On the food business?"

Della smiled. "On the food business." She placed the photos

back in the envelope, studied the handwritten address a second, then held the envelope out to Kat.

"I think you're right: we should look at it." Kat took the envelope. "Especially if it's something you want to do. Though, you have to admit, it is ironic: you, interested in cooking for a living."

"Not cooking: food processing. But yeah, you're right. Still, it's not ceramics. Or jewelry making."

Kat smiled back. "Can you imagine Laurie here?"

"Here?"

"Rita thought maybe she could come stay with us."

"Laurie? Staying with us?"

"For a vacation. Rita thought—and she's probably right—that Pam and Tom probably have never had a vacation on their own. So she thought—Rita—from what I told her, that the two little boys could stay with Pam and Tom's grown children and Laurie could come here. You know, on the first floor, in the Babe."

No one had stayed in the Babe Didrikson Zaharias room since Barbara died, and Kat thought Della flinched when she mentioned it. They had thought it would be inspiring to name a handicap-accessible room after a superlative athlete. Now it sounded cruel. But it was the only feasible place at the Ladies Farm.

"She rides," Kat said. "Special lessons. There's a place in Fort Worth that we could take her to."

Della nodded. "What about feeding her? Bathing her?"

"I'd do it," Kat whispered. "We'd have to hire someone—home health—to help. But I'd do most of it. I know how."

"And lifting her?" Della asked. "Don't we need special slings? And a bed?"

"All that," said Kat. "All that and more."

Della sat back on the sofa. "I'm going to work on my pro forma," she said, though she didn't move. "Maybe you should do the same. Work up some sort of plan. I'll do this—I'll do whatever I can. We all will. You know that."

Kat nodded. "And I'll do what I can about the food. Everything except cook, of course."

It was nearly the Fourth of July when Earl showed up. Flags had popped up in downtown Alpine and the Theatre of the Big Bend was readying its alternating productions of *I Hate Hamlet* and *The Music Man* at the Kokernot Amphitheater. Earl called Darlene early that morning to let her know he had spent the night in San Angelo, and would be there sometime in the afternoon, after he called on a few folks along the way. He called again at noon, but by then Darlene was at Ben Autalia's office, and Gladys relayed the message that Earl would call for her around four.

Tiffany, who was rehearsing for her role as a citizen of River City in *The Music Man*, could ride home with Ray when he returned from Van Horn, where he had addressed the Rotary about his adventures as a rock hound. Darlene, replacing the phone on the desk, leaned back in her chair, glanced around to see if anyone was watching, and then scratched at her stomach. She could feel her skin stretching and, looking down, saw her stomach poking straight out.

She had worked breakfast at Janine's, then walked over to Ben's to catch up his dictation. Pulling her cotton shirt down over her bare belly, Darlene sighed. Earl had taken his time about coming out west. What would he think when he saw her? She was going into her fifth month and even her face had puffed up.

When finally he stood in the doorway to Ben's office, she sat still for a second, looking at him. He had cut his hair close to his scalp, and his skin, particularly compared to the weather-beaten cowboys and bronzed backpackers she saw in Alpine, looked pasty. She didn't recognize the olive shirt over the cream-colored tee. But those were the same wide shoulders, that was the same tentative grin.

She rushed to him, closing her eyes as she pushed her face into his chest. "I'm fat," she whispered. "My skin's blotchy, my ankles are swollen."

She could feel him nuzzling her hair, inhaling its scent.

"C'mon," he said.

She shut down her computer, switched on the answering system, left a note for Ben, and locked the door behind her. As they hurried down the stairs, she pulled at her shirt, fluffed at her hair with her fingers.

"I knew you weren't fat!" he laughed, looking back at her over his shoulder. "You don't even look pregnant."

Clattering down the steps behind him, she reached a hand out to touch the top of his bristly head. "Did Rita do this?" she asked.

"Yeah!" he said, turning as he reached the small lobby. "You like it?"

"I guess," she said. "I'm just . . . I've been looking at your picture every night, and now you look different."

"Hey!" He held open the door, motioned her onto the street. "You too!"

She grimaced. She knew how she looked.

"You look beautiful, you know." They stood on the sidewalk on the One-Way, the eastbound side of Interstate 90, close to the blinking red light. "How're you feeling?" He put an arm around her shoulders, steered her across to the railroad station, where he had parked the Expedition and the U-Haul.

Darlene put her arm around his waist. She didn't want to talk about how she felt. She listened to the noise of the few cars passing behind them and walked with him to the car. The sun was still high, and the heat warmed the ache in her hip that developed every time she sat for too long. "Do you want to get something to eat?" she asked him.

"Nah. I have to stay hungry for Aunt Gladys's chicken and dumplings."

They stood next to the car and she looked up at him again. He had grown familiar in the time it had taken them to cross the street, and she reached a hand to the side of his face and pulled him to her for a kiss. He tasted warm and salty and, after his initial surprise, responded passionately, wrapping his arms around her and pressing hard. They stood there, locked against each other, until he pulled away enough to start kissing the side of her neck.

She pressed her little belly against him and stretched up on her toes so he could get down her neck. "Quick!" she whispered. "Come back upstairs. Ben'll be out till later. We can use the office."

Chapter Twenty-four

By August, Taylor could swim without his floaties, though Jill insisted he wear them unless she was standing in the water with him. At the checkup that followed his third birthday, in September, he had grown into the ninety-fifth percentile for height and ninety-third for weight. "Big boy," the pediatrician had said.

"Tall, like his parents," Jill's dad had opined, watching the boy cavort with Ryan. It pleased Jill that her father had stopped questioning Ryan about the details of his practice or his long hours. It was more the way it had been in the beginning, when he had brought Ryan and Kim, his then-wife, home for dinner because he liked to mentor bright doctors. Taylor's illness had brought them closer, Jill thought. Her father and her husband shared the frustration of having to watch and wait, their professional skills of little use to her boy.

"I keep telling myself," she told the Secret Sharers group, "that I should live right in this moment, in this sweet, sweet time with Taylor, and not think about the miscarriage."

"Well, how can you not think about it?" another woman asked. "I think about my sweet baby every night and every morning. She'll always be with me."

Jill nodded her thanks for the woman's support, but she knew that very few women who came to these meetings in the fellowship den understood what had happened to her. Most of them had lost children, or had children who were battling fatal diseases. She had noticed over the past few months that women tended to drop out once they learned they were pregnant, and that the ones who hung on were the ones who couldn't have more children. There weren't any whose children had survived. She detected a hint of disdain for her mourning the loss of one embryo in someone else's womb. They were more solicitous of Taylor.

"I think that last attack was the last hurrah for hemoporosis," Jill told the group. They all pictured disease as an invading army or sole marauder. "There's not enough research to know how the disease runs its course, the way you can tell with measles, say, or polio. But he has bounded back, ever since we started the new therapy." Her eyes darkened. "But I can't share that with Ryan." She shook her head to the rapt expressions around the circle. "He only goes by cell counts and growth indicators." She managed a brave smile. "Empirical measurements."

Then, hoping to brighten the mood, she said, "I have a new picture!" She passed around the birthday shot, a studied, casual pose of the three of them at home, sitting on the glider on the wood deck, with the pool sparkling in the background.

"He looks just like you!" one woman exclaimed, but Jill shook her head.

"He's got Ryan's build: broader through the chest. We're all long and lean in my family," she said. She watched the framed picture of her family passing from hand to hand around the circle. As it traveled, another woman began her sharing, and Jill thought about how much spare room there was on the glider.

The new baby could look like Taylor, Jill thought. Fair, blue-eyed. She wanted to speak again, but she had held the floor a long time and didn't want to interrupt again. *Ryan says we have to wait for her to contact us, that she'll call when she's ready*, Jill could imagine herself saying. *But in my heart*, she could hear herself as the photograph returned to her, *I know it would be better if Taylor and Ryan and I were close by, talking to the baby. Because Darlene's just the baby-sitter. We're the family.*

"I don't know, Darlene." Earl shook his head. "I'm not sure exactly, I just said something like, 'well, you write out the directions and I'll smoke the damn briskets!' I mean, I figured smoking the briskets was the easiest part of this!"

He watched as Darlene eyed the load of cartons and crates in the back of Ray's pickup and shook her head. The boxes contained parts for three commercial-size smokers, which Earl could hardly wait to assemble.

She sat on the steps of the double-wide and leaned back with elbows on the step behind her while Earl and Ray unl crates. They placed them onto the newly constructed pavilion, a hard-packed dirt square protected by a roo three openings to accommodate chimneys. Straining and grunting, they took care to set the crates directly under the openings while they bragged for Darlene's benefit about how much they had lifted and dragged in other projects.

"Didn't notice you around when it came time to lift the beams for this house," Ray accused as they stomped back over to the six-pack that sat next to Darlene.

"You should have called me!" Earl grinned at his uncle. "I woulda come a-running!"

He picked up a beer, nodded toward Darlene. "Isn't she pretty?"

"Pretty as a picture!" Ray replied, smiling at her. He nodded at a point above her head, where Tiffany had come to the door. "There's another one, too."

"Mama!" Tiffany said. "I want to come out." She pushed the screen door open to where it just touched the back of Darlene's head. "I can't get through."

"You know how to ask," Darlene replied.

"Please."

"Please what?"

"Please, I need to get out!" Tiffany's voice rose.

Earl knew he shouldn't have laughed so hard when he saw Darlene set her teeth.

"Come on, Darl," Earl said. He stepped forward, took her hand, and pulled her to a stand. "Say thank you," he told Tiffany, who skipped down the steps and headed toward the smokers.

"Thank you!" she called.

Earl, with a glance over his shoulder at his uncle, followed Darlene into the house, where she whirled around on him. "Don't do that ever!" she demanded.

"Do what?"

"Overrule me in front of Tiffany."

"Over—What are you talking about?" His voice came out so high it almost squeaked.

"You think I want her to be like that: no manners?"

He stared at her and tried to figure out how to calm her down.

"What is the matter with you?" Earl asked. "She's five. She said please."

She blinked at him and for a second he thought she was going to cry, but then it looked as if she was just staring at something that had taken her by surprise.

"Darl?" he asked. "You okay? Want to sit down?"

"I'm fine!" she snapped, but she jerked a chair out from the little table and sat anyway. Then she put her elbows on the table and let her head sink into her hands. "I am so sick of everything getting blamed on me being pregnant!" she moaned.

In an effort to see her face, Earl sat next to her at the table, and leaned over so he could look up at her. "I'm not blaming anything. Or anyone," he said softly. "I just don't want you to feel bad." He took a breath. "Look, I'm sorry I upset you about Tiffany. I guess I just think of her as . . . you know . . . as my own." He felt his face getting hot, but he hurried forward. "Hell, with the baby and everything, I just thought . . . you know . . . maybe I'd just adopt her."

She kept her head down. "Don't you think you're leaving out a few steps?"

"Well, yeah, I guess I am." He started to point out to her that Ben Autalia handled adoption cases. Then he thought about how they'd have to track down Jason Kindalia, whereabouts unknown, who hadn't sent child support in over a year. It was only when he opened his mouth that he remembered he couldn't adopt Tiffany unless he married Darlene. "But we're working on our future here, Darlene." He grinned. "We'll get through all the steps."

"Anyway," she said, "I want Tiffany to have manners."

"Well, I do, too, Darlene. I didn't think I was being rude. I already said I'm sorry."

"I know."

Their quarrels always ended this way. It didn't bother Earl to apologize; he was sorry he had upset Darlene and he knew she saw a lot of things he didn't, particularly about Tiffany. But he was losing daylight on the smokers, and he wanted to get those briskets marketed by October so they could pick up some Christmas traffic. He was toying with a barbecue-of-the-month program, but he suspected he'd need to wait till next year.

"Darl, honey, listen to me: I want to talk this all out with you. But I can't leave Ray out there alone and you probably want to lie down."

"I can't," she said, lifting her head at last. Her eyes were dry, but her face bore red marks where she had rubbed at it with her hands. "I told Janine I'd help her with supper. It's Friday, and that new girl called in sick." Darlene shook her head. "I don't think she'll last long."

"Darlene, why don't you quit all this work? He reached a hand out to stroke her arm. "Just do a little freelance, until the baby comes."

She glared at him. "We've got a few expenses coming up. I mean," she gave a short laugh, "I don't think my friend Ryan's advancing us any more cash."

"We're not spending his money anyway, Darlene. Honey, you should be taking it easy."

She gave a short laugh. Then she returned to the money. "We're going to need all that money and more," she said. "You don't know Ryan."

Earl looked down and studied his hands. Ben had advised them that Ryan had no claim to the baby, but could make a claim for return of the money.

"You're right, Darlene, I don't know Ryan. But, you know what? If you think I can't handle him, you don't know me. And if you think the two of us, together, as far as we've come," he gestured with his arm to indicate the double-wide, the smokers, Alpine, the Big Bend, "can't handle all this, including Tiffany, and the new baby, and smoking briskets, you haven't even started to know us together."

Darlene looked at him.

"What're you going to do with Ryan's money?" Earl asked.

"Buy a new computer. Get myself some wheels. Put a down payment on a house."

"We could do that anyway," Earl said. "Darlene, you know, we don't make bad money, the two of us. And this brisket thing—"

"Oh, fuck the brisket thing!" Darlene said. "By the time you and your five thousand partners get done paying for three smokers and divvying up what's left, it'll be about a buck-fifty apiece."

Earl stayed calm. It was the easiest thing in the world to stay calm when someone underestimated his business judgment. Even Darlene. "I make enough money to support both of us," he pointed out. "You make money, too. We don't need Ryan's money. It's just trouble for us."

"You want to give it back?" She jerked her head forward, as if jolted awake.

He hadn't meant to get things so out of order. The way he planned it, he would buy a ring, then he would propose, then they would plan the wedding and, some time in there, he would talk her into returning the money so they could start married life free of Ryan. Meanwhile, there she was, staring at him, waiting on an answer.

"I've been thinking about it," Earl admitted.

"After all this? You'd give it back?"

"Every penny," Earl said, thinking he was really into it. "Why not? What good has Ryan's money done us?"

"What good?" Darlene sputtered. "What good?"

"Darlene," he said as calmly as he could. "Honey. Listen just a second. I'm not mad."

"You're not mad?"

"I mean," he backtracked, "when . . . after you headed out here . . . when I was by myself, all I could think about was you."

"Well, all I could think about was you," she countered. "And how great it would be for us to have enough money for once in our lives!"

"What I'm saying," he continued patiently, "is that I had time to think—really think—about us, and about our life together."

"Did you think about how I was going to get around without a car? Did you think about where we would live? Did you figure out how much it would cost for Tiffany's clothes?"

"Yes. I thought about all that." He sighed. "I think we need to calm down a little, Darl. Talk about the long term. Think about this: what good is Ryan's money if all we use it for is to fight Ryan?"

"He lied to me," she said. "Used me. If he had told me—"

"If he had told you, we wouldn't have had sex so soon, and you would have delivered those twins and you'd have the money and we could go on our way."

"That's right."

"That is right, Darlene. So instead of waiting a year or two for us to have a baby, we're having it now. And instead of having Ryan's money free and clear, we have to fight about it. But you still have the chance to give the stem cells to their little boy. You've done that part."

Tears filled her eyes and she started to speak, but all she did was move her lips a little and stare at him.

"You're doing your part, Darlene. You'll help that little boy. Not exactly the way Ryan planned, but you're right: if he wanted your help, he should have been straight with you. Instead, we'll have our baby, give them those stem cells and go on. Just like we would have if we had never gotten into this."

"You think, if I hadn't gotten into this, we would be together?"

He couldn't tell what answer she wanted. Her eyes were still wet, but her voice was low and strong. "Yes," said Earl, believing it as he spoke. "Yes, one way or another. You wouldn't have needed shots, but maybe you would have needed a place to stay. Or a new computer. Or someone to find you a car on the Net. And I would have helped you. And there we'd be."

"There we'd be," she repeated.

"You know what?" he said suddenly. "We have a way to be free of Ryan, and free of Rita and free of Sydonia, and all we have to do is work our butts off and take care of Tiffany and this new baby and smoke briskets till we're sick of them. And that's what I'm going to do, Darlene."

Having said it, Earl felt himself coming 'round to his own articulated vision. "I'm going out," he said, slowly, evenly, and as kindly as possible so she understood he wasn't fighting. He was just stating facts now. Calmly and reasonably. "I'm going out to check on Tiffany and Uncle Ray, and then I'm going to start uncrating those smokers. I'm not going to make you return that money, Darl. But those smokers: that's the life I'm working on."

Chapter Twenty-five

Ryan smiled when he realized that this was the first time he had welcomed a call from Josh Wittstein. "You won't believe my patient!" Ryan said after they exchanged greetings.

"Glad to hear he's doing well," Josh said.

Ryan described the course of Taylor's progress, taking care to refer to Jill and himself in the third person.

"And his growth chart?" Josh asked.

"You know, I was going to fax it to you," Ryan said. "Let me do that, as well as Ballangee's report. Basically he's released him back to his pediatrician, with three-month checks back with Ballangee."

"Well, that's great," said Josh, but Ryan picked up on the disappointment.

"It's a big country," Ryan tried to console him. "Unfortunately, there will be other kids. You'll have test subjects."

"I feel like crap," Josh confessed. "Imagine how relieved those parents are. We're jerks to feel cheated."

"Ballangee's putting the word out to the medical association. Texas and the rest of the region."

"Yeah. Listen," Josh said. His tone grew optimistic again. "I was really calling about something else. Two things, actually."

"What's that?"

"One is moot for you, I guess, and that is that Ballangee's certified. He's ready to go, once he finds a subject."

"That's great," Ryan assured him. "Some family who needs it will be really glad. Believe me. And," he added with a chuckle, "maybe you guys would let me consult. I feel invested, you know."

"Well, funny you should mention that. Here's the second thing: are you still in touch with the family?"

"Sure. Why?"

"Did they ever mention the kid's urine . . . the color?"

"No. But you know, we always did samples, any time he was admitted, whenever we did CBCs. Why?"

"We found an enzyme. We're calling it HPR-1. Part of a protein that makes up the red cell wall."

"The normal wall?"

"Yeah," Josh said. "That's the quirky part. What we think is that the marrow—or maybe a virus when it attacks the marrow, or maybe something else entirely—when it's producing hemoporotic cells, produces more of this enzyme, and that somehow breaks down the protein in the cell wall."

"But it's an enzyme that occurs in the wall naturally?"

"Not in free form. It would be bound up in the protein."

"So it's in the urine?"

"We don't know," said Josh. "We're trying to collect data. That's why I'm wondering if the family would be willing to participate . . . say, maybe collect samples for us."

"You think it would be there, even if he's better?"

"I have no idea," said Josh. "I'm thinking not, but who knows? And we don't have any way of checking right now. There's no way to test for its presence, but now that we've got the enzyme, we can develop a test quickly."

Ryan looked at the newest family picture Jill had framed for his desk. She had made the frame herself in her ceramics class, adorning the white frame with red and gold hearts. Taylor was better. Why test him when he didn't have the disease?

"I'm not sure the family would go for it," he said. "They're kind of burnt out. But I can ask, maybe they'd be willing . . . you know . . . because it would help other families."

"I suspect your patient is just a control. But why don't you go ahead and mention it to them," Josh suggested. "Oh! And tell them, too, to keep an eye out for a greenish tint to the urine."

"Like asparagus?"

"Like . . . hell, I don't even know." Josh's voice was filled with frustration. "We just think, from the way it tagged after amplification, it would be greenish. We're guessing—our imaging guys are guessing—from the way similarly tagged enzymes turned out."

"Don't you think they would have noticed that before?"

"It may be very faint," Josh cautioned. "They'd have to be really looking."

"Anything else? Odor?"

"Odors don't image, Ryan."

"I was just asking," Ryan said. He guessed it made Josh feel better, resuming their med school roles.

"There's so little to go on. But this could be something. Maybe you could just ask them to keep an eye out for that change. Maybe it would alert them to a crisis."

"I'll talk to them," Ryan promised.

Jill knew it was juvenile, but it still made her feel special to have lunch with her dad on a Wednesday afternoon. If her mother guessed the true mission—assisting her father in selecting her mother's birthday gift—she gave no hint when Jill brought Taylor to her for the afternoon. Her mom opened both arms wide to her grandson and waved her daughter off with promises to spoil the child mercilessly.

Jill talked her father into Chinese food because it had been her favorite growing up, and they went to the restaurant near his office, where the owner knew them and caught them up on the achievements of his grown children. Then, arms linked, she and her dad strolled over to the jewelry store.

"She likes those little boxes," her dad said. "Limoges. But I don't know which ones."

"You could just buy her all of them, like you did the watches that time."

"No, I learned my lesson," he vowed. "I have to take the time to think about her, what she likes," he recited. "I have to show her that I care, not just that I'm willing to spend money. That," he deadpanned, "would be vulgar. Pain and suffering: now that's love!"

Jill laughed, and he put his arm around her shoulders and pulled her close. "It's good to hear my girl laugh again."

"Oh, Daddy, I never knew I'd be so glad to have things just be normal!" They had stopped on the sidewalk, and in the sharp sunlight she could see every line in her father's weathered face. She turned a little to hug him, inhaling the faint mingling of aftershave and sweat, feeling the sun on her own face and registering the hint of flesh around his middle and the mild shock that she was almost as tall as he was.

"Sometimes normal's the toughest thing in the world," her father whispered.

They resumed their stroll, her father facing away for a second to swipe a hand at his eyes. "We'll get ice cream after we get the gift," he promised as if she had clamored for a cone when they passed the ice-cream parlor.

The jeweler's name was Mrs. Schultz, and Jill had never noticed that the woman flirted unrelentingly with her father. "Personally, I'd love any man who gave me this one," Mrs. Schultz gushed as she placed a hinged ceramic box topped by intertwined cupids on the velvet cloth.

Jill and her father stared at the little box as Mrs. Schultz opened the top.

"Do you have any of the newer ones?" Jill asked. "With things inside?"

"Oh, honey, wait till you see these!"

They exchanged glances as Mrs. Schultz bustled off to the back and returned with two new boxes. Both were adorned with hand-painted flowers; one said *To my love* and the other *I love you*. "Let's see inside," Jill said, reaching toward the *I love you* box.

"Here, honey, let me," Mrs. Schultz insisted, opening the hinged top to reveal the flat porcelain letter that said *forever*.

"That's the one," Jill's father said.

"Don't you want to see the other one?" Jill asked.

Mrs. Schultz opened the *To my love* box, but he had already stood to pull out his wallet.

"Oh look!" Mrs. Schultz said. "Sealed with a kiss!"

"We'll take the other," said Jill's father. He smiled at Jill. "Want an ice-cream cone?"

"So why was I along?" Jill asked, when she was nibbling at a low-fat, mocha-fudge waffle cone.

He smiled, looked down at his sherbet cup.

"Dad?"

He shook his head, tasted the raspberry sherbet.

Suddenly, Jill stared at her father. "You wanted protection? From Mrs. Schultz?"

He nodded. "I should never have encouraged her," he confessed. "I mean, not that anything ever happened. But, you know, she would always tease, and then I'd tease back, and then we went to lunch and then, I don't know, I think she thought—"

He stopped, looked perplexed. "It never occurred to me there would be anything on her mind . . . short of the teasing, I mean!"

"Daddy!" Jill didn't know whether to laugh or be appalled. He looked so guilty! "Then why didn't you just go somewhere else?"

He shrugged. "I've been going there for years. It would just be cowardly. I pass by there every day or two. I wanted her to know we could just always be the way we were."

Now Jill did laugh. "I don't think so," she said. "I think you're going to have to buy a whole lot more jewelry."

He frowned. "I don't understand this . . . you women. You're going to . . . I think I'll just get your mother down here," he said, exhibiting satisfaction. "Let her pick out her own jewelry."

"Daddy! You led on Mrs. Schultz!"

"She started it!"

"Right." Jill licked at her cone. "If I ever catch Ryan at that—"

"Well, your mom's going to like that box. I'm going to take her to dinner, have them serve it with dessert."

"That'd be sweet."

"Listen," he leaned forward, "I've got another surprise. For Taylor. Now that he's better."

"What's that?"

"C'mon out to the car."

They strolled out, her father patting his chest pocket to make sure he had the gift. It was hard to see in the parking garage, but the trunk light came on when he opened the trunk and she saw it immediately. "It's light as a feather," he promised her, lifting it out and placing it in her hand.

He had placed her own racket in her hand years ago. He had stood behind her, dropping the ball over her shoulder on the sunlit court, guiding her forearm and instructing her to watch the ball. Keep watching the ball, he would say. Keep watching.

This racket was different, of course. Light enough for a three-year-old. Ridiculously expensive, Jill was sure. Silly, really. Despite herself, she dropped her hand, lifted the racket back.

"I'm saving it for this weekend," her father promised. "When he spends the night. But I wanted you to see it. I got a kick out of it."

She didn't trust herself to speak.

"Is it okay?" he asked finally, and she nodded, and hugged him.

"We're so predictable," she scolded him. "All we do is buy each other gifts and spend as much as we can."

"I've seen enough sick children in my life to appreciate a healthy one," her father told her. "I'm not apologizing for spoiling my grandson. Or my daughter."

"Oh, I am spoiled," she assured him. "And I know it." She looked down. "I'm so spoiled, I'm afraid to say Taylor's well, just in case. You know what I mean?"

"Of course I do. I—your mother and I—feel the same way. Lucky. And afraid. It's only natural."

Her eyes had adjusted to the dark of the garage and she studied his face. "So you think someday I'll take him for granted again?"

Her father shook his head. "I hope not. And," he placed the racket back in the trunk, motioned her around to the passenger side, "you've got kind of an insurance policy with that baby."

"Baby? You mean Darlene?"

He was opening the door for her, she was getting into the car to let him drive her to where she had parked.

"That's a lucky break, honey: losing both your embryos and then producing one of her own who's a match for Taylor. Now time's on your side. The older Taylor gets, the more time to build up his strength. The more time to perfect the technique, increase the chances for success. All you have to do is keep track of that girl and her child."

Rita had one head under the dryer and another one in the chair when the phone call came. "Ladies Farm Salon!" she chirped, rolling her eyes in the mirror to let her customer know she disliked the interruption.

"Mrs . . . is this Rita?"

"Yes. May I help you?"

"Um. My mother asked me to call."

"Did she want an appointment?"

"No, no. Nothing like that."

The voice was young, but adult. She couldn't identify the accent. Maybe California.

"Who is this, then?"

"Cindy . . . My mother's Sally Jamison, she—"

"Sally Jamison, Wendell's wife?" Rita spun around to face away from customer and mirror. "What is this about?"

"She doesn't want anything. She just wanted me to let you know Wendell died. In his sleep. Had a heart attack, they think."

"Wendell's dead?" Rita couldn't believe the roaring in her ears.

"Yes. The funeral's Wednesday, here, in Las Vegas."

"Could I . . . could I get your mama's phone number?" Rita asked. "I'd like to call her sometime later . . . when we can both talk. Would that be okay?"

"Mama was wondering if you were planning to come to the funeral."

"Come to Wendell's funeral? No, dear. No, tell your mom no."

Rita listened to the click on the other end of the line, then stared at the receiver in her hand before she placed it back in the cradle on the wall phone.

"Well, did you call her back?" Della asked when Rita related the call.

Rita nodded.

"And?" That was Kat, who looked very impatient.

"I talked to Sally." Rita turned to Della, who was seated next to her on the office sofa. "You remember her? She waited tables down at The Old Mill. In fact, that's how they renamed it Wendell's: she worked on the owner to rename it in that deadbeat's honor."

Della shook her head. "I remember The Old Mill, but I don't remember any of the waiters."

"Bleached blonde, big tits," Rita prompted, using her hands to demonstrate. "I mean out to here."

Again, Della shook her head.

"What did Sally say?" Kat asked. She had been working at her desk and still sat in her high-backed office chair.

"Sally said Wendell died. Just like that." Rita shook her head. "No warning, nothing."

"Were they married?" Della asked.

Rita nodded. "They got married a few years ago, after she followed him out to Vegas. Of course," she drawled, "he forgot to tell her he was still married to me. After my lawyer contacted him, I had to hide out here, with Pauline. Remember?"

Della nodded.

"We were afraid he'd come after me with a gun," Rita said for Kat's sake. "All I wanted was to be divorced from him."

"Did Wendell have kids with her?" Della asked.

"No. Not that I know of. That girl that called—Cindy—I think she had her here. I don't even remember who she was married to then. We'll have to ask Gladys Hutto; she'd remember."

Kat sighed. "Could we skip the Sydonia Historical Society minutes and cut to the good stuff? Have you told the girls?"

"Well, I'm telling you now," Rita said.

"I meant your daughters?"

Rita frowned. "I'm just now getting used to the idea. I told Dave."

"What'd he say?" Della asked.

"What should he say? Good riddance to bad rubbish. Don't forget, Dave's the one used to take me in when Wendell went on a rampage." She felt her face grow hot. "The first time, of course. When I married that bastard a second time, Dave wouldn't even talk to me. He did look after Carla and Darlene every now and then, though."

"Why did you— Oh! hell!" Kat said as the phone interrupted her. "Ladies Farm," she answered. "May I tell her who's calling?" Her eyes widened and she put her hand over the mouthpiece. Then she held the telephone out to Rita. "Your day for phone calls," said Kat. "It's Jill. Jill Plummer."

Chapter Twenty-six

For Jill, the biggest change was not confronting Ryan. When she recalled how she had stormed in to him after Darlene first contacted her, she felt that she was watching a stranger, a spoiled child demanding that Ryan right everything. Now, there was no way things could be right. Just different.

She called Lantinatta first, made him explain the amnio results; then Ballangee, her son's specialist, her father's friend. "Of course Ryan told me," she had said to them. "Of course." Just as she had assured her father. "Only," she pleaded, "don't let Ryan know I called. Don't let him know I asked. It would hurt him, make him think I was double-checking, as if I didn't trust him."

If Ryan noticed that she didn't enthuse anymore about the new baby, it was probably with relief. He assumed she had accepted his dictum that they would have to wait. That Darlene would take care of the baby and that she would resurface sooner or later. They talked about it now and then, but Jill told him everything was ready, so Ryan didn't question why she wasn't shopping. They had even picked out names, just a few months ago: Hallie and Thomas. Meanwhile, they agreed, Ryan should get ready to track down Darlene if that became necessary.

It was laughably easy, thought Jill, to call Rita. The woman had fallen all over herself apologizing for Darlene, exclaiming over Taylor, who had regaled her with stories of the dump truck combat he was conducting beneath the table at Starbucks.

"Now," Jill told the women in Secret Sharers, "now, after all the mourning for the first twin, now that I've lost the other, now I'm ready to love every second with Taylor. He's so perfect. So funny.

He's counting. He's swinging his tennis racket. He's using the potty like a big boy, no more diapers. He's learning his colors. Making up for all the lost time."

She took a breath, looked around the room, realizing how grateful she was to have people with whom she could speak freely. "After all that, I didn't really feel anything when I learned she'd lost that second one. It's—she's—so far removed from me. And from Taylor. I feel so blessed," Jill told them.

She gestured to the woman next to her to indicate she was yielding the floor, and the woman launched an update on her husband's Alzheimer's. Jill continued to smile, basking in the joy of her son's recovery. She hadn't told them about Ryan, of course. Too soon for that.

When she picked Taylor up from the baby-sitter down the hall, he ran to her to tell her how he had gone to the bathroom like a big boy. "I think we've mastered that one," she laughed, kissing his head and nodding at the baby-sitter.

"Gween!" he said, holding out his motorcycle rider. "Gween!"

"Neevil's red, honey. Red, white and blue!" she laughed. "Just like the flag."

Darlene was not surprised to see Rita in Alpine, but she was stunned to see Rita in the Camaro in Alpine. Rita, who never drove anything except big, four-door Continentals, and never drove at all if she could get someone else to drive for her, had driven straight from Sydonia, stopping only once to gas up and a few times to pee.

It wasn't Dave's usual make-do repair job, either. The thing had been finished inside and out, so when Rita pulled up next to the Expedition, Darlene noticed the Camaro for its deep, metallic blue. That's exactly what my car would look like if we got it painted, she thought.

She and Earl had just dropped Tiffany at kindergarten, and now Earl was taking her to Ben's office. He'd pick her up again at one. In between, he'd be smoking briskets and mixing sauce. He set the smokers in the morning and let the briskets smoke overnight. Except for the never-ending aroma of meat, sugar and apple-scented wood, she barely noticed the briskets.

Outside Ben's building, Earl leaned over and kissed her, and then she opened the door and slid onto her feet. Earl waited until she turned around and closed the door and pursed her lips and blew a little kiss through the window before he pulled away. That's when Rita pulled the Camaro up beside her and rolled down the passenger side window. "Hey, babe," she called out. "Want a lift?"

Rita gave Darlene the wheel and motioned to her to drive.

"Can't you use a telephone?" Darlene asked her. She grunted a little as she pushed the seat back to accommodate her belly.

Rita worked on her seat belt, then lowered the seat back to recline as she grinned at her daughter. "I wanted to bring you the car. Like it?"

"How'd you know what color?" Darlene asked.

"Because you told us, remember? Whenever we talked about it and you complained about the crappy job Dave would probably do?" Rita grinned some more. "Remember that?"

"It's cool," Darlene said. "Thank you."

Well, score one for me, Rita thought. Then she said, "I came because we have to talk. I didn't want to tell you on the phone."

"What is it?"

Rita studied her daughter a second, noted the color in her cheeks, the fluffy curve to her hair. "You look good, honey," she said.

"I look like a whale," Darlene replied tiredly. "What is it we need to talk about?"

"Wendell."

"Oh, God!" They had driven straight out of town, and Darlene pulled the car over to the shoulder. "You're not . . . you're not seeing him again?"

"No honey! Not at all!" She would have laughed, but she could see Darlene's terror. "No, no, honey. It's just that, you know, he's your father and, well, I just didn't want to tell you over the phone, but his new wife called, and he died. Heart attack. In his sleep." Already, Rita could see that this part could have been conveyed by phone. Even e-mail.

Darlene stared at her. "That's why you came?"

Rita shook her head. "I came because I wanted to see you. And I thought the car was a good reason." She ducked her head and looked up at Darlene. "Don't you like it?"

"I love it. Honest!" She ran her hands around the steering wheel. "Tiffany's going to go crazy!"

Her little laugh pierced Rita to the heart. "Let's drive some more," Rita said. "Where does this go?"

"Marfa," Darlene said, shifting gears. She tilted her head as she accelerated. "He worked on the engine. Listen to it!"

"I made him," Rita said. "I told him if he had time for those damn briskets, he had time for your car. And damn if he didn't listen!"

"What's he doing with the briskets?"

"Storing them. He's got that walk-in fridge for the store." She chuckled. "Tony's working on a catalog for all this, so guess who he's spending late nights with?"

"Tony and Della were already spending late nights together," Darlene retorted. "What else did you want to talk about?"

"Jill Plummer."

"Jill? What about her?"

"Maybe driving wasn't such a good idea," Rita said. She looked out at the landscape, which had flattened and browned. "Is there a place to stop?"

"We can stop anywhere," Darlene said. She glanced over at her mother. "Or we can head back to town."

They ended up at the amphitheater. "This is the old one," Darlene offered as they picked their way among the overgrown terraces. "The new one's back there." She motioned with her hand to a small complex behind them.

Rita let Darlene find a place for them on one of the dark stone ledges. The university rose on the hill to their right, and the modest municipal park spread out to the left, its pool and ball fields just visible through the trees along the creek. "This is where we used to wait for Tiff to finish rehearsals. Earl and I."

"I'll bet she loved being in that show," Rita said.

Darlene nodded as she turned herself to prop her feet up.

Rita smiled at her daughter's effort to make herself comfortable. It was a good sign, Rita thought, that Darlene hadn't pressured her to talk about Jill until they settled down.

"Jill called me," Rita said, watching Darlene's face. "She asked if we could meet, and I met her at that Starbucks in Fort Worth . . . the one in that bookstore. Downtown."

Darlene waited.

"She . . . she asked me where you were. She said they knew you weren't in Sydonia, but she didn't say how they knew. Not that it's any secret of course. You could just ask at the fountain in the drugstore."

"We weren't trying to keep it secret," Darlene said.

"No. Well, you didn't. But if she knows where you are, she's not saying."

"They'll figure it out," Darlene assured her. "I just don't want to see them before the baby's born."

"So you're figuring on having the baby here?" Then, as Darlene studied her, "Darlene, I swear, I didn't tell her a thing. And I won't."

"There's a hospital right here," Darlene said. "We've made all the arrangements."

"And you're sure . . . you know, sure you're going to have it? The baby?"

"Yeah."

Rita nodded, trying to stay neutral.

"This baby's healthy, too," Darlene said. "I had an ultrasound, but we told the doctor not to tell us what it is."

"Well, I'm glad it's healthy. What're you and Earl going to do?"

"Who wants to know?" Darlene asked. "You or Jill?"

"Honey, I told you—" Rita shook her head and gave a small laugh. "Honey, we all want to know. Della, Kat, Dave, Tony, Nick . . . all of us!"

"I don't know about Earl and me," Darlene said. "I'll tell you when I know."

Rita started to ask what the problem was, but Darlene held up her hand. "Tell me what Jill wants," she said. "You drove five hundred miles to tell me, so tell me."

"First of all, Jill said to tell you the boy's much better. They think he's over it."

"Really?" Darlene said. "You believe her?"

"I saw him. Adorable! And she brought a copy of his last physical. 'No sign of hemoporotic cells' it said. 'Normal growth.' "

Darlene's shoulders rose and fell with her heavy breath. "So what does she want?"

"She wants the stem cells," Rita said. "And she wants to see you. I promised her I'd tell you, and I told her that the way Earl had explained it, you're going to give them the stem cells. That they could be collected when you had the baby. Wherever."

Rita took a breath. "Did she . . . did they—Ryan—explain about the transplant, the marrow, or the stem cells?"

"Well Ryan finally explained it to Earl, after he knew. But still, no one's ever tried it for this disease, hemoporosis."

"It's research," Rita said. "Turns out Ryan's got this friend at

NIH, they were going to do some experiment on the boy. But now they don't have to."

"Well, I don't blame her for wanting the stem cells. They can freeze them, in case they need them later." Darlene thought a second. "What was she like?"

Rita shook her head. "Sad. I mean, glad that Taylor's doing better, really enjoying that, you know?" She waited for Darlene to nod. "But, I don't know, sad. I think she's decided she can't have any more kids. Losing those twins seemed to just take it all out of her. I mean," she gestured at Darlene, "for us it's all ages ago. But for her, it's like it happened just yesterday."

Darlene looked down and her face drooped. It occurred to Rita that no one had ever given Darlene any time to get over losing those babies. It had to have hurt her, no matter how early in the pregnancy.

"Earl found all this stuff on the Net for me," Darlene said without lifting her head. "He thinks that our baby kind of pushed theirs out. That some kind of hormone change occurred."

"Is that what you think?"

Darlene looked up. "Yeah. I think so. I mean, Earl's usually right about things, you know."

Rita could not conceal her amusement.

"I guess you think it's funny: Earl and me."

"What I think is funny," Rita drawled, "is you thinking any boy's smart enough for you to listen to. Mostly you've just led them around by their dicks."

"Well I had a good teacher!"

"And it says something that you learned to appreciate Earl so much younger than I did Dave."

"Well," Darlene threw out, "I like to think I'd have known better than to go back to Wendell after leaving him once."

"That's because you're still young." Rita said.

Darlene jerked herself to a standing position. "I have to walk around," she said curtly. "I can't sit like that for a long time. My hip just kills me." Gingerly she followed the steps up to the stone clubhouse, then started along a path to the park.

Rita trailed along behind, Jill's sadness still weighing her down. But Darlene didn't want to talk about Jill.

"I don't know why you ever went back to him. And married him!" Darlene fumed. "After Dave, too."

Rita stopped. Darlene walked several more steps before she realized she had gone on alone and wheeled around.

"What?" Darlene demanded.

Rita shook her head. "I was bored," she mumbled.

"What?" Darlene stepped toward her. "What did you say?"

Rita looked up. "I didn't say it was a good reason. But it is the reason."

"What is?" Darlene looked ready to slap her. "I couldn't hear you. What is the reason?"

"I was bored. That's all. Bored with Dave. With living such a good life. So quiet."

"What?" Darlene was practically screeching now, but Rita knew that this time she had heard perfectly.

"Dave just seemed too ordinary. Wendell and I . . . there was just a kind of spark, Darl. Once I felt safe again, with Dave, then I started to miss—"

"Felt safe? Did you ever think about how we felt, Carla and I? A thousand years with Mr. Ordinary couldn't have made us feel safe!"

"No?" Rita said. "Is that how come you ran off with Jason Kindalia? And then moved in with Jimmy? At least Wendell never stole my car!"

"You never had a car, back then! You never had shit!"

"No," Rita agreed. "I never did. And I never did say I did the right thing, going back with Wendell. But you asked why. And I told you. That's all the reason I have, Darlene. I was young and foolish. More foolish than you are now."

Darlene spun around and resumed her walk. More of a hike, thought Rita as the path dipped through some brush. As much as a pregnant girl could hike.

"Oh, come on, Darlene! There's plenty that had it worse than you. At least I've stood by you now," Rita called ahead, hurrying to close the gap between them. "At least I didn't give you girls away."

"I wish you had!" Darlene threw back over her shoulder. "It would have been way better for us!"

"Maybe it would have," Rita huffed, catching up enough to put a hand on her daughter's shoulder. "Maybe my faith was misplaced."

Darlene spun around, and gave a bitter laugh.

"Faith that there was a future for us, Darlene." She looked down at Darlene's belly. "Takes faith to raise a baby, Darlene. Having them's an act of God. Raising them . . . that's an act of faith, babe."

Darlene turned away and started walking again.

"I had enough faith to keep you," Rita called after her. "That's more than your idol, Kat. She gave up her daughter. But I kept mine, when I went back to Wendell. That's what I chose!"

"You chose a drunk!" Darlene yelled back. "A wife beater! A mean, nasty—"

"I chose your father," Rita said. "I was wrong, but that's what I was thinking. I was your mother, he was your father."

Darlene stopped and turned once more. "What'd you mean about Kat?" she asked. "Kat had a baby?"

"Yeah. She kept it secret a long time. The baby has a lot of handicaps, poor thing. Kat and her husband didn't think they could take care of her, so they placed her. Guess who helped?"

"Who?"

"Dr. Nicholas Lantinatta."

"He placed Kat's baby?"

"Evidently he specialized in that kind of thing. Genetics, placement, fertility."

"Where's the baby now?"

Right there, in the mid-morning sun, Rita filled Darlene in on Kat's maternal history. Somewhere in the middle, they made their way to a bench, where they sat again, and Darlene eventually slipped out of her sandals and rested her feet in her mother's lap. "So Kat saw her?" Darlene asked.

Rita nodded.

"Now what?"

Rita shrugged. "Hard to know. You know Kat: she plays it close to the vest. Maybe she'll have the girl—Laurie—visit us at the Ladies Farm. She'll tell us when she's ready."

"So," Darlene said as if she were just continuing the conversation, "you think I should meet with Jill?"

"Only if you want to," Rita hedged. "I told her you wouldn't. Of course, she said you could keep the money. Actually," Rita smiled brightly, "it turns out it's her daddy's money. Or at least some of it is. So she says she can handle Ryan, if you'll just give them the stem cells. And you're home free and clear with the money."

"Well, that's a little more tempting."

"A lot more," corrected Rita, reluctantly. "Because it's not just the money you got already, it's the whole amount."

"Forty thousand?" Darlene asked offhandedly.

Rita frowned at her.

"Okay, sixty."

Rita tugged at Darlene's toes. "Of which you've got forty." She laughed. "I know what Ryan gave Earl!"

Darlene grimaced. "Well, yeah. So she'll give me the other twenty if I turn over the stem cells?"

"Yes."

"Stem cells they may never need?"

"I guess."

"And you believe her?"

"Honey, I only met the woman once. I don't know why she'd lie, though."

"So I get the money and Ryan will never bother me again?"

Rita nodded.

Darlene chewed her lip a little. "Of course, if Ryan came after me, I could tell his wife about us. Or I'll tell the medical society about his transplant plan. I'm sure there's about a dozen ethics violations there."

"It'd be pretty messy," Rita said.

"It wouldn't be that bad. We could stay out here till it all died down."

"What about Earl?" Rita asked.

"He wants to give it all back."

"All the cash?"

"Yeah." Darlene wiggled her toes a little to get Rita to resume her rubbing.

"Your ankles look pretty good," Rita said. "You look good all over, baby." The minute she said *baby* she was sorry, but Darlene didn't pick up on it.

Slowly, Darlene bent her knees and pulled back her feet, then sat up. She stretched, her arms reaching to the sky, and then stood, yawning, and slipping her feet back into her sandals. "I think we should keep it," Darlene said. "I have to walk again."

They started back for the car.

"They tried something new," Rita said. "On the boy . . . Taylor . . . something to make him produce more white cells, so he wouldn't make so many red ones. They think that's what turned him around."

"But it could still happen, couldn't it? He could have another attack."

"I guess," Rita said. "I guess that's why she wants the stem cells. It's like insurance."

"Not enough insurance," Darlene replied. "You could never have enough insurance for that. Earl says—"

"I don't know why you don't marry that boy and just put him out of his misery," Rita told her. "As good as he is to you."

"He hasn't really asked," Darlene countered.

"No, but he would if you'd give him the least bit of encouragement. Besides," Rita tried not to sound as sly as she felt, "don't you want to be married by the time that baby gets here?"

"I'm in no hurry," Darlene said.

"You're just worried something better'll come along," Rita accused. "And believe me, something will . . . better looking, better talking, better dancing. There's always something better till things head south."

"You would know," Darlene retorted. She moved across the parking lot with determined speed.

Ship under full sail, Rita thought as a wind made Darlene's blouse billow out from her body. "That's what the money's for," Rita yelled into the wind as she hurried to catch up with her daughter.

Darlene's hand froze on the Camaro's door latch.

"It's your escape, if Earl doesn't work out."

The money made a surprisingly small package. Even though she had replaced most of what she had spent, it all fit into a gift tote she had received with a cosmetics purchase. The tote lay inside a suitcase which she had slid under the bed when she and Earl moved into the double-wide. The thing she liked about the tote was that it could be thrown into suitcases or car trunks anytime without anyone ever noticing.

She was standing in the bedroom, looking at the bed, when Earl came up behind her. He'd grown fond of holding onto her belly and standing still until he felt the baby move. It didn't take sixty seconds this evening. "That is so cool," he said, rubbing lightly through the big shirt she wore to bed. He kissed the side of her face and pushed her forward a little in order to enter the room.

"You coming to bed?" he asked.

"I don't know. That whole dinner's just sitting right on top of the baby like a lump of cement."

"Gladys did kind of go overboard," Earl conceded. He sat on the bed and started pulling at his boots. "She's just showing off for Rita."

"It wasn't Gladys," Darlene said, placing her hands where his had just been. "It's that I can't eat anything past six or it won't go down." She frowned. "You think the kid would be tired enough to sleep, now. Rita and I must have walked five miles."

He paused and looked at her.

"Well, two at least."

"You're still thinking about it, aren't you?"

She walked over and sat next to him on the bed. "I guess."

She leaned against him, wishing there was some way to prop her feet up without getting up to move a chair over to the bed. "Twins. I feel like I'll always owe that woman twins."

"I know." He squeezed her shoulder.

"I'm giving the stem cells to them," Darlene said.

"Is that what you want to do?"

"Oh sure. Yeah. You think Ben could draw up something for us? Some kind of contract about donating the stem cells"

"I guess," Earl said. "You know I love you, Darlene?"

She turned toward him. "I do know, Earl. I love you too." She leaned toward him and he put his arms full around her. She waited for the rest. Ask me, she thought. Ask me now.

But he just kissed the side of her face again. Then he stood up and carried his boots over to the closet. "You talk to Ben," he encouraged her.

Darlene smiled at him. "You're pretty focused on this."

"I'm focusing on our future, Darl. When that baby gets here, I want to be free and clear: of Ryan, of Jill. And guilty consciences, too."

"I know."

"Do you?"

She nodded. "Here's what I think: I think we should get all this done and call her. Jill. Tell Jill to come here."

"Here?"

"Here. Herself. Away from Ryan. I just want to sit down with her," Darlene said. "Just Jill and me."

Chapter Twenty-seven

"It turned greenish," Ryan confirmed to Josh. "I took him to Ballangee, we did counts every thirty minutes. Boom! Crisis in three hours."

"And you're taking samples?"

"You betcha."

"How're you treating him?"

"Right back to cell stimulation. Plus red cells, of course. He's coming around. But Josh, we—the family—can't do this again."

"How long are you going to do the stimulation?"

"As long as it takes."

"Fever?"

"Moderate."

"He could convulse. He could stroke out."

"I know all that. We've got to transplant."

"We can't. Can't, Ryan. He's got to stabilize, we've got to radiate. This is a controlled procedure, Ryan."

"Tell that to his mother."

"You think he's coming here?"

"I don't know, Darlene." Kat sounded tired of repeating herself, but Darlene wanted her to stay on the phone. "I'm just telling you, someone called Lakeesha asking for you and wouldn't leave a name. And Nick's been subpoenaed."

"I thought you said his records—"

"I mean, his records. Your records."

"I'll talk to Ben. Even if he comes here, he can't do anything,

Kat." Darlene, sitting way back from her desk, looked down at her belly, then looked up at the door to Ben's office.

"I wish you were here," Kat said.

"I'm better off in Alpine," Darlene assured her. "Even if Ryan drags an army of lawyers out here, it's still better here. Where they know me. I'll talk to Ben," she said again. "And call 'Keesha."

"How's Rita?"

"Ready to go home," Darlene said. "She can't stay away from work too long. She's done Gladys's hair twice, and can't stop braiding Tiffany."

"She came a long way for you," Kat said.

"Yeah, she did." Darlene smiled at the image of Rita in the Camaro. "And she's heading back next week," Darlene retorted. "We got her a ride with Janine's mother. Janine was my boss before Ben." She glanced again at the closed door, wishing he would finish with his current appointment.

"So we'll see Rita next week."

"Yeah. Late. And Janine's mom. Linda. For one night."

"We'll put a light in the window."

"I'll tell Rita. Hey! Speaking of telling . . . or not telling—"

"This isn't about barbecue, is it?"

"Actually, it's about your daughter."

"I still can't believe I've told anyone," Kat said. "Let alone that I've spent time with Laurie, that I've fed her and cleaned her. That I've put her to bed and kissed her good night."

"It must have been hard, going through all that."

"It was. When I—when Hal and I—handed her over, we thought she'd be raised in an institution. And she was until she was four."

"I meant, it must have been hard on her."

"Inhaling is hard on her. Chewing is a chore. Being abandoned by your parents—by your mother and father—is incomprehensible. Do you want me to say I did a terrible thing, Darlene? I did a terrible thing!"

"I didn't say that." Automatically, Darlene lowered her voice to a whisper as she glanced nervously at Ben's door.

"You want it both ways, Darlene: you want me to feel bad for placing my child and your mother to feel bad for holding onto you. And trying to hold onto Tiffany."

She's losing it, Darlene thought with horror. At least, before, you could always count on Kat staying cool. "Look," Darlene said, "I didn't mean to make you feel bad. But, Ben's going to be out of that meeting in a second, and I need to call 'Keesha. 'You okay?"

"Oh, I'm peachy," Kat assured her. Darlene heard a sigh before Kat's voice resumed its normal tone. "I just wanted you to know about Ryan."

Jill didn't know what to put in the note. She sat at her pull-down writing table and fumbled to pick a pen from the porcelain cup. The pen tipped the edge of the cup, knocking the remaining pens and pencils onto the desktop. Ignoring the mess, she managed to uncap the pen and pull out a loose sheet of paper, but then she just stared.

I'll dress, she told herself. I'll dress and then I'll scribble something. She slipped the pen into her bathrobe pocket, then remembered the cap and jerked the pen out and capped it before she slammed it back on the desk.

Her perfect closet yielded no clue about what to wear and she found herself blinking at the three walls of clothing. Finally she yanked a pair of jeans and a tee shirt from their hangers. Today, when everything depended on the impression she made, she could not fathom how to give herself an advantage.

The daytime LVN was named Kay Lee. She had dressed Taylor, and he was sitting up in bed, watching as she prepared to inject his main line. "Now we're going to wake up your blood cells. Wanna do that?"

Taylor nodded, and Jill, leaning in the doorway to his room, drew a quick breath at her child's trust. Fight harder! she exhorted him. Make us do more!

She waited until Kay Lee had emptied the syringe into the tube in his chest and had buttoned his shirt. "You want to go for a ride?" Jill asked Taylor. He nodded, smiling, and began to climb off the bed.

"We need to fly out to West Texas for a few hours," Jill explained to Kay Lee. "I think we'll be okay for that time, but it'd be better if you can come."

"Shoot, yes," Kay Lee said. "I love to fly." She considered. "I'll just call Dr. Plummer."

"No need," Jill said. "We just talked. I told him." She smiled. "It's pressurized. Twin engine. We'll be real comfortable."

She turned to Taylor. "C'mon, honey, let's saddle up. Get Neevil. Tell him we're going to fly!"

* * *

Earl knew what was in the tote bag, but he ignored it. The more pregnant Darlene had grown, the more stuff she carted around. A mountain of stuff—bags of sandwiches, oversize envelopes of proofreading for Ben, sacks of jackets and spare socks, changes of clothes for Tiffany—lived in the backseat of the Camaro. The tote bag looked at home in the heap. Earl didn't ask about it.

"Fort Stockton. Midland-Odessa. Even Alpine. All those places have better airports than Iraan," he grumbled, settling into the passenger seat.

"We've been through this," she reminded him. "I told her to pick the place, Iraan is what she picked." Darlene drove quietly for a few minutes, her arms high on the steering wheel to clear her belly.

"You've got your briskets smoking," she said, smiling. "Why don't you relax and enjoy this ride."

"Hey! I'm just your support team," he told her. "Just here to facilitate."

She nodded down toward her belly. "I think you've done enough facilitating."

Earl reached over and patted her. Then, "Know what you're going to say?"

"Sure. Just like we talked about: Hi, how are you, I'm sorry I lost your babies, I'll give you the stem cells."

He leaned back. It had been simple, really. Just a few clicks to arrange for a kit to be sent to their obstetrician, so the cells could be harvested from the cord right after delivery. They could be frozen and stored for years.

"It's a piss-poor trade," she added.

Of course, no one knew if any transplant would work for hemoporosis patients because no one knew if it was the red cells themselves or something else that affected their ability to hold oxygen. But that's not our problem, Earl thought. We can make the treatment possible. We can't make it work.

Jill said a quick prayer of thanks that her father had such accommodating friends. And that, somehow, she had convinced them that her critically ill child could have his spirits restored only by a visit to the municipal park near their family ranch. "He's well enough for a short day trip," she had reported. "We're grateful for that." And, of course, they had respected her request that no one advise her father. He would just insist on canceling his appointments to join them, and it wasn't necessary. Jill smiled a little.

She looked over at Kay Lee as Taylor slid off her lap and ran over to the windows on the opposite side of the aisle. "Just a short hop," Jill promised Kay Lee, but Kay Lee seemed delighted to be in the air.

"I had this one patient—terminal—his family used to fly him down to the Hill Country every weekend. Every Friday afternoon: down there; every Monday morning: the whole troop of them back up." She tilted her head, recalling. "And you know, the funny thing? They never needed me on the plane and almost never while they were down there. Even though I made every trip. Up till the very end. And he died on a Monday night, like he just wanted to get back home first, so he didn't disrupt anyone's weekend."

"I think Taylor's doing much better," Jill said. "Don't you?"

"He's a little feverish." Kay Lee looked at the boy, who had settled into his own seat and was showing the green-brown landscape to his motorcycle doll. "There's a price for all that cell stimulation." She checked her watch. "We can try some more Tylenol in another hour."

"But he's way better than he was when he went into crisis," Jill pressed.

"Oh, sure," said the practical nurse.

"When we get there," Jill instructed, "we'll go to the park. There're these big comic strip characters . . . huge . . . a dinosaur and a guy with a cigar . . . Alley Oop and Dinny . . . from *Alley Oop*. Darlene—my friend—will want to see him. Then he can play. He might need a jacket."

"Is it in the mountains?"

"Part of the Pecos valley," Jill said. "Sort of plains backed up against the hills. Oil town. They named it for a couple: Ira and Ann. We used to go out there sometimes to ride." She smiled, remembering. "I think if my mom had let him, Daddy would have packed it all in and moved out here. Been a country doctor."

"Pretty remote, for a city girl," Kay Lee said.

"Rough country," Jill agreed.

The note said, *Had to get out of the house. Back late this afternoon. Love, J.* He didn't know why she thought he'd buy into it, any more than he knew why she thought her meeting with Darlene's mother had been a secret. But he did know that Darlene probably trusted

Jill a lot more than him. So he wasn't too concerned that Jill had a head start.

But, as he explained to his friend with the two-seater, he had been trying to spare Jill the most gruesome details of Taylor's illness. "Even with the nurse," Ryan explained. "She shouldn't have him out like that. And it's my fault."

Thankfully, his friend flew out of Meacham in Fort Worth, whereas Jill, Ryan was sure, would have driven to somewhere around Dallas. Maybe Addison, in the North Dallas suburbs. He knew, probably, five family friends who might have flown her to Alpine. But who, exactly, and to what destination, took a little phone time. Relax, he kept telling himself. You want her to have a head start.

Seven months, he thought. Even if he convinced Ballangee they had to go ahead on their own and they started radiation tomorrow, it would be a good two weeks before Taylor was ready. Seven and a half months. That would be fine, thought Ryan. Seven and a half months would give them an umbilical cord full of stem cells. Healthy stem cells to make new blood for Taylor.

In a way, it was better that Jill had reached out on her own. It made her more credible. She'd dangle Taylor in front of Darlene, trying to turn her heart. Then Ryan could offer more cash. He didn't mind being the bad guy. Once Jill realized what their options were, she'd be glad for his strength.

"I'll just get out at the park," Darlene requested. "Then you pick her up at the airport and bring her to the park. That way, no one has to sit in the backseat."

"We should have taken the Expedition."

"I know, Earl. But Gladys and her bird-watching friends were going into Big Bend, and they needed it."

Earl just grunted.

"Oh, you're just worried you'll be bored in Iraan."

"Nah, I'll hang out at the airstrip. Maybe trade for a plane."

She flashed him a smile. When she told him she wanted to meet with Jill by herself, he had not argued, and she was grateful.

Most of Iraan lay along a one-mile stretch of US 190. She bypassed the park to hit the ladies room at the convenience store. She stocked up on bottled water, then doubled back to the park. "Here," she told Earl, "I'll just get this stuff out of the back." She took a pile of manila envelopes, plus the six-pack of bottled water and the little tote bag. "Can you hand me that jacket?" she asked, nodding at his old red zip-up. He reached over and held it out to her, then got out of the car to take the wheel.

It was clear and a little windy, blowing her hair around on her forehead. "You okay?" he asked her, one hand on her arm, the other pushing the stray hair back behind her ear.

She nodded.

"Okay. I'll bring her back as soon as she gets here. Got your phone?" She nodded. He kissed the side of her face. "See you in a few minutes."

She kissed back.

He lowered himself back into the Camaro, reminding her of what a sacrifice it was to ride around in a girlie car. "Hey!" she said, motioning him to roll down the window. She leaned her head inside and kissed him again. "Thanks."

The park was called Fantasyland. It was a large, flat expanse interrupted by a few trees, and dominated by two colossal cartoon characters: Dinny the dinosaur and a cigar-smoking Alley Oop. They were brightly painted, and Darlene resisted the urge to climb the stepladder onto Dinny's back. After the baby, she promised herself. We'll bring Tiff and we'll all climb up there.

She sat at a canopied picnic table, placing the envelopes next to her on the bench and setting the tote on top of the table. Then, from the top envelope, she withdrew the stem cell harvest agreement that Ben had prepared. She smoothed the papers, weighted them with a water bottle, and considered what they would mean to Jill. The wind whipped steadily, rattling the table and the fiberglass canopy at a low hum.

She was proofing a transcript for Ben when she saw the Camaro. Darlene thought she caught a shrug from Earl, and he waited next to the car as Jill and another woman advanced. She supposed he was looking for some sign from her about whether she needed him to stay. After a moment, he got back into the car and drove away.

Jill approached, her little boy in her arms.

"I wanted you to see Taylor. Honey, this is Mommy's friend, Darlene."

Darlene, cornered, took Taylor into her arms. "Hi there," she said, trying to sound unsurprised at his presence. His pale hair glistened in the sun, and she inhaled hard, searching for that sweet baby scent she missed now in Tiffany.

He offered up a chewed-on stuffed toy and a metallic, medicinal smell. "Oh, what's that?" she laughed, trying not to panic at the boy's fevered gaze. She looked at the drool-dripping motorcyclist. "Is that your friend? Hmm? Here," she said, "want to go back to Mommy?"

"He looks great!" Darlene lied, handing the weightless child back to Jill.

"He's doing much better," Jill said. "Uh, this is Kay Lee, our nurse."

"I'll just wait over there," the nurse said, motioning toward Dinny as Jill and Darlene headed toward the table.

Taylor pointed toward the nurse and started to fuss, but Jill shushed him in a practiced way and settled him on her lap. Darlene sat opposite mother and child, simultaneously pushing the stem cell agreement toward Jill as she swept the tote bag off the table.

"That's for the stem cells," Darlene said. "Before you say anything else, I want you to know that the stem cells will be taken—harvested—at birth and delivered to whatever hospital you want. And," Darlene took a breath, "I have to tell you something."

Jill took the papers and looked at them for a moment, then set them down. "What?" she asked, kissing the top of Taylor's head.

"I'm sorry." Darlene felt her lips trembling, but she remained dry-eyed. "I wish I hadn't . . . that Earl and I hadn't . . . that I had been able to stay pregnant with those twins."

"Yeah."

"I mean—"

"I understand what you mean." Then Jill whispered in Taylor's ear. "You want to go play with Kay Lee?"

Taylor nodded, pushed off. Jill called to the nurse, who looked up and started toward the boy. Taylor wobbled forward, and she hurried in and scooped him up.

"He's living on cell stimulators," Jill said. Her face sagged. "They make all the other blood cells, so they kind of crowd out his own red cell production. Then we transfuse healthy red cells."

"Well that's great!" Darlene enthused. "You've got a way to treat—"

"It's temporary," Jill said. "Look at him!" She shook her head and her tone turned bitter. "Ryan thinks I don't know anything, how dangerous this is, these drugs, the fever, the transfusions." She held Darlene's gaze. "It's no way to live."

Despite her resolution, Darlene's eye's filled with tears.

"I wanted you to see him."

"That's rotten," Darlene said, but without force. "Making me feel so bad seeing him."

"It doesn't matter," Jill said. She managed a weak smile. "About the twins. I mean, even if you were pregnant with the twins now, what good would that do us? No more than your stem cells when you deliver."

"But you'd have—"

"Don't you dare finish that! Don't you dare! I don't need any substitute child. Don't you ever say that."

"I'm sorry."

"Sorry. Sorry. Sorry. God!" Jill shook her head. "I am so sick of hearing sorry. Everyone who hears about Taylor is sorry. Just don't. Okay?"

"I guess," Darlene said slowly, "I don't really understand why you came. I mean, Rita, my mother, told you I'd give you the stem cells, right?"

Jill took a quick glance over at Taylor who was climbing over Alley Oop with Kay Lee's help. Then, as quickly as Darlene could follow her glance and the sweep of her hands, Jill took the agreement and tore it into pieces. She whipped another agreement from her bag and handed it over to Darlene. "Sign that!"

"What?"

"It's the same agreement. Except that it's with me alone."

"You mean without Ryan?"

"Is that so surprising?" There was a glitter to Jill's eyes. "Wouldn't you rather do business with me?"

"I never thought of it as business," Darlene said.

"Darlene." Jill sounded very patient and very tired. "You signed an agreement to be implanted and then you accepted a lot of money and then you broke the terms of your contract. And then you accepted more money from my husband. Of course it was business. So now," she smiled in a kind way, "I'm giving you a way to get out of a bind. Darlene," Jill's gaze was unwavering, "you know how Ryan can be."

Darlene did not disagree.

"All I want is control of the stem cells."

"But you and Ryan—"

"Are probably splitting up." Jill smiled.

"But why?"

Jill kept smiling. "Ryan just can't be honest, Darlene." Her face started to crumple. "Darlene, what difference does this make to you? You can keep the money."

Darlene shrugged, took the pen Jill held out to her. "None, really." She scribbled her name on a blank line on the last page. "Shouldn't there be witnesses? A notary?"

"Not really. Easy, isn't it?" Jill reached for the papers.

Darlene nodded. She just wanted this to be over. The baby picked that moment to execute a roll, and she felt the ripple across her belly. "Here," she said. She reached down and pulled up the tote. "Take this." She passed the bag across to Jill.

Jill peeked in the bag.

"It's all there," Darlene said. "I was saving it because I figured you might try to sue me."

Jill shook her head. "I would never have done that. I just wanted to make Taylor well."

"So did Ryan," Darlene said.

Jill gazed down at the table.

"So what did he lie about?"

"What difference does it make?" Jill asked.

You have no idea, thought Darlene, but she didn't share that idea. Instead she gestured to the tote bag. "You ought to take that before I change my mind." Jill just stared at it. She's still stuck on Ryan's lies, Darlene thought. "You know," she said, "you could always have the other embryos implanted in you, if you wanted. You could even have eggs extracted the same way I did. Just because you had the tubal doesn't mean you can't be pregnant again."

"You knew I had the tubal ligation?"

"Ryan told me," Darlene said. "You know, when he first asked me."

Jill clutched at the tote bag and drew it to her. Then she looked again toward her son.

"I . . . oh!" Jill shook her head and stood up, tears flowing freely. She stumbled away from the table. Darlene watched her rushing toward Alley Oop, where Kay Lee helped Taylor balance on the end of the cigar.

"Damn it!" Darlene jumped up and headed after Jill.

When Ryan's plane landed, Earl realized he had half-expected it. He sat atop the hood of the Camaro, his back against the windshield, recalling the poster he had seen in Marfa of James Dean, in jeans and boots, sitting in a convertible and pining for Elizabeth Taylor. As Ryan approached, Earl studied his own boot tips and pursed his lips. Take it easy, he told himself for the thousandth time. Darlene's okay.

"Where are they?" Ryan demanded.

"Good afternoon," Earl drawled. He held up his phone. "Darl said they'd call when they're done."

"Dammit, my son needs medical attention!" Ryan cast a quick look back at the pilot, then shook his head. "Look, I just need to get to Taylor. And," he glanced at Earl, "you and I need to talk."

Earl swung his legs onto the ground and stood up. He missed high school, where at least he could have stuffed Ryan into a locker and repented by running laps. "Talk," he invited.

"My boy is sick," Ryan said. "Darlene—you and Darlene—can save his life. But we have to act quickly. Right now."

"You want the stem cells," Earl said.

Ryan nodded.

"No change there. That's what she's telling Jill now: we'll have them collected when the baby's born and they can be frozen and shipped to you."

Ryan looked at the ground, nodding sagely as if he were agreeing with wise advice. Then he released a long sigh. "If only it were that simple," Ryan said.

"What do you mean?"

"We need the stem cells now."

"But it's another two months till—"

Ryan had only to hold his gaze to complete the thought.

"Let's go see Darlene and Jill," Earl invited.

"It'd be the same as completing the deal," Ryan promised, getting into the car. "We'll see that you get the whole sixty thousand."

Chapter Twenty-eight

Darlene stopped halfway to Alley Oop to call Earl on the cell.
"We're on the way," he answered.
"We?"
"Doc Plummer and I."
By that time she could see the Camaro and she resumed her walk toward Alley Oop, where Jill had crawled out on the cigar to join her son. The nurse, who still held Taylor from below, was laughing a little.
"Are you up high?" Kay Lee cooed. "Are you and Mommy up high?"
Jill seated herself and pulled Taylor onto her lap, the tote bag full of money slung over her arm and dangling at an angle.
"Jill?" Darlene said, but Jill just looked at her. "That cigar doesn't look too sturdy."
"I just want to sit here with my son," Jill said to no one in particular.
"Oh, come on," Darlene urged, still startled by how quickly Jill had clambered onto the metal figure and crawled out to the cigar. "That thing's going to break off, and then where will you be?"
"Now, Mrs. Plummer, she may be right," said Kay Lee. "Let's get Taylor down from there." She reached up from below, but Jill didn't respond.
"Come on, Jill, this is stupid," Darlene said. "Look what you're doing to Taylor!"
"What I'm doing?" She laughed a little, then nodded at a spot behind Darlene. "I'm keeping him out of Ryan's hands."

"Honey, no one's putting that child in Ryan's hands. But how about coming back to earth," Darlene said.

"Here," said the nurse. "C'mere, Taylor."

Taylor looked down at her, then clung a little tighter to his mother.

Darlene turned toward Earl and Ryan.

"Honey?" Ryan asked, hurrying toward them. "What's going on?"

"Ryan's got a new offer," Earl said, ambling up behind Ryan.

"Too late," Darlene said. "I signed with Jill."

"Jill?" Ryan said.

Jill looked down and smiled regally. "Hello, sweetheart."

Ryan wheeled toward Darlene. "We need to talk."

"Talk," she said.

"Let's go sit down," he suggested, glancing nervously toward Jill. "Honey, you want to hand Taylor down to Kay Lee?"

"Not really," Jill sang out.

"We can talk here," Darlene said. "Jill and I don't have any secrets."

"Darlene," Ryan said, "Taylor's really sick. We have a new therapy—"

"An experimental therapy, isn't it Ryan?" Darlene said.

"Yes. Our one hope. And we need the stem cells now."

Darlene stared at Ryan. "No!" she said.

"You have to listen!" Ryan said to Darlene. "You don't understand—"

"I don't have to listen anymore, I gave the money back. Talk to your wife."

Ryan gave a bitter laugh and motioned toward Jill. "Does my wife look as if she's listening to me? Jill, honey," he tried again, "let's talk about all this."

Jill closed her eyes as she clutched Taylor to her. Ryan motioned to the nurse to stay close, then turned back to Darlene and Earl.

"It will take two weeks to prepare Taylor for a stem cell transplant." Ryan spoke rapidly. "You'll be seven and a half months pregnant. We can deliver safely, strip the stem cells and transplant."

"I was thinking you wanted Darlene to abort," Earl said.

"I would never ask that," Ryan said.

Jill let out a laugh. "You told that shrink you wanted to abort."

"That's enough," Ryan said, advancing toward Alley Oop. He

scrambled up the side of Alley Oop's bearded face and crept out toward his wife. "Honey, I talked about all kinds of things with Dr. McCutcheon." His voice softened. "Including how to talk to you. How to tell you something that would break your heart."

Jill stared at Ryan and Darlene drew a little closer to Earl. "Oh God," whispered Darlene.

Earl put his arm around her and they watched in silence as Ryan edged over to Jill. Ryan was whispering to her, stroking her arm. They heard snippets: *family, Taylor, working together, so hard. So sorry.*

Darlene shook her head. "She'll go right back to him," she whispered to Earl.

"I don't care," Earl whispered back. "I just wish she'd get down from there."

It's not really that high, thought Darlene. Even if that baby slipped away from her, he'd fall right into the nurse's arms.

Ryan was murmuring steadily now, his arm around Jill and his other hand stabilizing Taylor. Darlene and Earl stepped closer.

"I just couldn't tell you," Ryan was saying to Jill. "I'm the one who had to tell you about Taylor. I'm the one who had to explain the chances, and how the disease would progress. Then we had that one hope. And you were so happy. Did you know," he pleaded, "did you know you were whistling in the bathtub?"

"I don't whistle."

Darlene swore she heard Jill giggle. She studied the way the two of them were leaning into each other. "Come on," she heard Ryan coaxing.

Darlene stared. This was all to get his attention, Darlene thought. She'll do whatever he wants, now that he's apologized.

"I just need a few minutes," Jill replied. "Just sit here." She smiled down at the nurse. "I think we're okay, Kay Lee."

Kay Lee took a step back.

"So what do you guys say?" Ryan offered to Earl and Darlene.

They looked at each other.

"Look," Ryan said. "Let me explain. Maybe you don't understand what we're asking."

Darlene and Earl just stared at the man perched on the cigar with his wife and child.

"We want you to induce labor. In about two weeks. You'll be seven and a half months." He paused, watching them. "You understand? Just deliver a little early."

Ryan ran a hand through Taylor's hair. "It won't hurt things. Chances are the baby will be just fine."

"Chances are?" Darlene asked. "What does that mean?"

"Look, Darlene, babies are born every day at seven, seven and a half months. We can do so much: we can protect them from infection, we can help them breathe, help their hearts. We'll do whatever it takes. Your baby will be fine.

"Come back with us to Fort Worth," he urged. "We can take better care of newborns there," Ryan said. "Better equipment. Specialists."

"Would there be surgery?" Earl asked.

"Well, no," Ryan said. "I don't . . . I mean, unless there was something that required immediate—"

"Because I've always heard there are a lot of heart and lung problems in premature babies," Earl said. "That they can have, you know: problems."

Darlene frowned. She started to think about Kat.

"Well, things can happen," Ryan conceded. "Maybe a little more often when babies come early."

Kat's daughter couldn't even visit the Ladies Farm. They had thought about it, but they couldn't figure out how to care for someone so severely disabled. Instead, Kat and Nick were going to spend a month in Virginia, taking care of the girl while her parents took a long vacation.

Ryan was still talking. ". . . and I promise you we'll do whatever your baby needs."

Darlene looked up at Ryan and Jill. "Tell me something: did you ever plan for me to give birth?"

It took Ryan a second to notice that she had spoken and then to make his own mouth quit and force himself to understand what she said.

"Did you think," Darlene demanded over his garbled mutter, "that if you paid me enough money, I'd end it when you said and you could just strip out the stem cells? That you could make up some story for Jill, and never have that baby you didn't want?"

"Darlene, I . . . that's ridi—"

"Oh, spare me!" she said. "Do you really think I'd let you arrange delivery now?" She took another step toward Ryan. "Knowing how many little things could go wrong while I'm drugged and you've sent Earl out of the room? How many tiny mistakes . . . the kind no one would question!" Even Earl was staring at her now. "You and your specialists!"

Suddenly she realized how long she had been standing and how dry her mouth was.

"Darlene?" Earl said.

"I need to sit," she told him.

"Well here," he said, stripping off his jacket.

Darlene started to explain that she wanted to head back to the picnic table, but then it made more sense to sit right there. She lowered herself to the ground, thrust her legs straight out and leaned back on her outstretched arms.

She smiled at Earl, who hovered anxiously. "Would you explain to him that he can have the stem cells when I give birth," she said.

Earl stood straight. "Ryan, I'm sorry, we can't do what you're asking. Can't you continue therapy till the baby's born? Isn't the cell stimulation working? Do you really want to put him through the preparation for a transplant now?"

"Earl, pretty soon you're going to be a father. Ask me that then."

"We're not risking it, Ryan. End of discussion."

From where she sat, Earl looked huge. Ryan, Jill, and Taylor seemed to float above her.

"Come here a second," she croaked to Earl.

"What is it?" he asked.

"I—" she started to cry. "I don't know about this. What if he dies?"

He knelt next to her, hugging her. "I know. But he'll probably be fine. Ryan's not exactly logical right now."

"Really?" She glanced back up at Ryan and Jill.

"Think about it," said Earl. "The cell stimulation has been working. He just had this setback, and they caught it really fast because they know what to look for now."

"Then why—"

"He's afraid, Darl. We all are. But I'm not risking our baby."

"I'm afraid too. I've been afraid this whole time."

"So have I, Darl. Afraid you'd leave, afraid you'd keep the money, afraid to ask you to marry me because you might say no. We're all afraid. It doesn't matter."

"I wouldn't say no."

"Well, that makes me braver, but if you'll wait a bit, I'll ask you right." He glanced up.

Ryan persisted. "What're you going to tell your baby when it's time to go to college and you don't have the money?" Ryan said. "Do you know how much you can make if you invest thousands of dollars at one time, Darlene?"

She sighed. "Ryan, you and Jill should climb down from there. Jill," she addressed Ryan's wife, "whatever you and Ryan decide, you need to get Taylor back on the ground."

Darlene tried to remember why sixty thousand dollars had sounded like so much just a few weeks ago. It had been the price for producing a stem cell match, she thought. And not talking to Jill about sleeping with Ryan.

She saw Ryan slipping forward, landing easily on his feet with a small "oof." He turned back to Jill and held his hands out for his son, who, unnoticed, had fallen asleep on Jill's lap. Jill leaned forward and the child slid into his father's arms. Jill landed lightly in front of her husband.

With a groan, Darlene pushed herself to standing. "I was going to do this for twenty-five," she recalled.

"Right!" said Ryan. "And now you can make lots more."

"Just so I could move out of the Ladies Farm." She blinked, shook her head a little.

"How can you say no?" Ryan asked. "How can you tell me you won't help?"

"We're giving you the stem cells."

"Taylor could die by then."

"Don't say that!" Jill commanded. She pressed a hand on the sleeping child's forehead. "Ryan, he's burning up." They both looked to the nurse, who had moved off to the picnic table.

"Let's get him some more Tylenol," Ryan said.

Darlene followed, aware now of how much she had to pee. Earl took her elbow and steadied her as they walked. She shivered a little, despite the sun.

Ryan and the nurse tended to Taylor while Jill stood by. "You look wobbly," Jill said, as if it were her task to keep conversation flowing.

"I feel wobbly," said Darlene.

"What could happen," Jill said brightly, "is that Taylor will stabilize, but he'll have convulsions from the fever caused by all the transfusions. Or his brain cells could be dying by the millions because they're not getting enough oxygen. Or he could just stop growing."

"Don't do this," said Earl. "Go home. Take your son home. I'll drive you back to the airport."

Those things could happen, thought Darlene, watching Earl shepherd them all back to the Camaro. She sat on the bench and watched them walking away. Those things could have happened anyway, she thought.

She closed her eyes, but still pictured the pale, limp child.

I did the right thing, she told herself, opening her eyes to watch Ryan place Taylor in the car. And it will be years before we know for sure. Years and years. It wasn't really about whose child lived, she thought. It was about which child got the better chance.

She stood and took a few stiff steps toward the park entrance as the Camaro pulled away. When she glanced back at the bench, she saw the tote bag. Earl will take me home, she thought, resting a hand on her belly and staring at the tote: hot pink and chartreuse, a retro sixties thing she got for buying twenty-five dollars' worth of cosmetics. Now it was stuffed with money and sitting forgotten on the bench.

She toyed with the idea of leaving it, or donating it to the Hemoporosis Society, but when she picked it up, she knew they'd return it to Jill. Jill and not Ryan, she thought. Though she doubted that Jill would hide anything from him. But then we'll be done, she thought, amazed that she hadn't noticed the weight of the bag before. She wished Earl would hurry.

It'll just be us. Earl and me. Tiffany and the baby. Gladys and Ray. And Mama, thought Darlene. Which would never erase the sight of Taylor slack in his mother's arms. The terror of her own choices.

Hurry! she thought to Earl, closing her eyes and willing the image to fade. Hurry back and take me home.